Truxton King
A Story Of Graustark

by
George Barr Mccutcheon

Truxton King
A Story Of Graustark
by George Barr Mccutcheon

Copyright © 2024

All Rights reserved.

No part of this publication may be reproduced, stored in a retrieval system, or transmitted in any form or by any means, electronic, mechanical, photocopying or Otherwise, without the written permission of the publisher.
The author/editor asserts the moral right to be identified as the author/editor of this work.

ISBN: 978-93-68096-43-6

Published by

DOUBLE 9 BOOKS

2/13-B, Ansari Road
Daryaganj, New Delhi – 110002
info@double9books.com
www.double9books.com
Tel. 011-40042856

This book is under public domain

ABOUT THE AUTHOR

American playwright and novelist George Barr McCutcheon (1866–1928) was well-known for his contributions to early 20th-century literature. McCutcheon, who was born in South Raub, Indiana, on July 26, 1866, first attended Purdue University to study mechanical engineering. But his love of writing propelled him into a career in journalism, where he was employed by publications including the Chicago Record and the Lafayette Daily Courier. With the release of "Graustark" in 1901, McCutcheon became well-known in literature. Readers were enthralled by the romantic adventure set in a made-up European realm. With this achievement, McCutcheon launched a successful literary career that produced a large number of novels with recurring themes of humour, romance, and adventure. George Barr McCutcheon was a well-liked and esteemed character in American literature because of his skill at storytelling and capacity to draw readers in with gripping tales. He wrote continuously until his passing on October 23, 1928, leaving a body of enjoyable and significant works.

CONTENTS

CHAPTER I
TRUXTON KING 7

CHAPTER II
A MEETING OF THE CABINET 22

CHAPTER III
MANY PERSONS IN REVIEW 34

CHAPTER IV
TRUXTON TRESPASSES 48

CHAPTER V
THE COMMITTEE OF TEN 63

CHAPTER VI
INGOMEDE THE BEAUTIFUL 72

CHAPTER VII
AT THE WITCH'S HUT 86

CHAPTER VIII
LOOKING FOR AN EYE 97

CHAPTER IX
STRANGE DISAPPEARANCES 108

CHAPTER X
THE IRON COUNT 118

CHAPTER XI
UNDER THE GROUND 129

CHAPTER XII
A NEW PRISONER ARRIVES 138

CHAPTER XIII
A DIVINITY SHAPES 148

CHAPTER XIV
   ON THE RIVER 158
CHAPTER XV
   THE GIRL IN THE RED CLOAK 167
CHAPTER XVI
   THE MERRY VAGABOND 177
CHAPTER XVII
   THE THROWING OF THE BOMB 189
CHAPTER XVIII
   TRUXTON ON PARADE 199
CHAPTER XIX
   TRUXTON EXACTS A PROMISE 211
CHAPTER XX
   BY THE WATER-GATE 223
CHAPTER XXI
   THE RETURN 235
CHAPTER XXII
   THE LAST STAND 246
CHAPTER XXIII
   "YOU WILL BE MRS. KING" 255

CHAPTER I
TRUXTON KING

He was a tall, rawboned, rangy young fellow with a face so tanned by wind and sun you had the impression that his skin would feel like leather if you could affect the impertinence to test it by the sense of touch. Not that you would like to encourage this bit of impudence after a look into his devil-may-care eyes; but you might easily imagine something much stronger than brown wrapping paper and not quite so passive as burnt clay. His clothes fit him loosely and yet were graciously devoid of the bagginess which characterises the appearance of extremely young men whose frames are not fully set and whose joints are still parading through the last stages of college development. This fellow, you could tell by looking at him, had been out of college from two to five years; you could also tell, beyond doubt or contradiction, that he had been in college for his full allotted time and had not escaped the usual number of "conditions" that dismay but do not discourage the happy-go-lucky undergraduate who makes two or three teams with comparative ease, but who has a great deal of difficulty with physics or whatever else he actually is supposed to acquire between the close of the football season and the opening of baseball practice.

This tall young man in the panama hat and grey flannels was Truxton King, embryo globe-trotter and searcher after the treasures of Romance. Somewhere up near Central Park, in one of the fashionable cross streets, was the home of his father and his father's father before him: a home which Truxton had not seen in two years or more. It is worthy of passing notice, and that is all, that his father was a manufacturer; more than that, he was something of a power in the financial world. His mother was not strictly a social queen in the great metropolis, but she was what we might safely call one of the first "ladies in waiting." Which is quite good enough for the wife of a manufacturer; especially when one records that her husband was a manufacturer of steel. It is also a matter of no little consequence that Truxton's mother was more or less averse to the steel business as a heritage for her son. Be it understood, here and now, that she intended Truxton for the diplomatic service: as far removed from sordid steel as the New York post office is from the Court of St. James.

But neither Truxton's father, who wanted him to be a manufacturing Croesus, or Truxton's mother, who expected him to become a social Solomon, appears to have taken the young man's private inclinations into consideration. Truxton preferred a life of adventure distinctly separated from steel and velvet; nor was he slow to set his esteemed parents straight in this respect. He had made up his mind to travel, to see the world, to be a part of the big round globe on which we, as ordinary individuals with no personality beyond the next block, are content to sit and encourage the single ambition to go to Europe at least once, so that we may not be left out of the general conversation.

Young Mr. King believed in Romance. He had believed in Santa Claus and the fairies, and he grew up with an ever increasing bump of imagination, contiguous to which, strange to relate, there was a properly developed bump of industry and application. Hence, it is not surprising that he was willing to go far afield in search of the things that seemed more or less worth while to a young gentleman who had suffered the ill-fortune to be born in the nineteenth century instead of the seventeenth. Romance and adventure, politely amorous but vigorously attractive, came up to him from the seventeenth century, perhaps through the blood of some swash-buckling ancestor, and he was held enthralled by the possibilities that lay hidden in some far off or even nearby corner of this hopelessly unromantic world of the twentieth century.

To be sure there was war, but war isn't Romance. Besides, he was too young to fight against Spain; and, later on, he happened to be more interested in football than he was in the Japs or the Russians. The only thing left for him to do was to set forth in quest of adventure; adventure was not likely to apply to him in Fifth Avenue or at the factory or—still, there was a certain kind of adventure analogous to Broadway, after all. He thought it over and, after trying it for a year or two, decided that Broadway and the Tenderloin did not produce the sort of Romance he could cherish for long as a self-respecting hero, so he put certain small temptations aside, chastened himself as well as he could, and set out for less amiable but more productive by-ways in other sections of the globe.

We come upon him at last—luckily for us we were not actually following him—after two years of wonderful but rather disillusioning adventure in mid-Asia and all Africa. He had seen the Congo and the Euphrates, the Ganges and the Nile, the Yang-tse-kiang and the Yenisei; he had climbed mountains in Abyssinia, in Siam, in Thibet and Afghanistan; he had shot big game in more than one jungle, and had been shot at by small brown men in more than one forest, to say nothing of the little encounters he had had in most un-Occidental towns and cities. He had seen women in Morocco and

Egypt and Persia and—But it is a waste of time to enumerate. Strange to say, he was now drifting back toward the civilisation which we are pleased to call our own, with a sense of genuine disappointment in his heart. He had found no sign of Romance.

Adventure in plenty, but Romance—ah, the fairy princesses were in the story books, after all.

Here he was, twenty-six years old, strong and full of the fire of life, convincing himself that there was nothing for him to do but to drift back to dear old New York and talk to his father about going into the offices; to let his mother tell him over and over again of the nice girls she knew who did not have to be rescued from ogres and all that sort of thing in order to settle down to domestic obsolescence; to tell his sister and all of their mutual friends the whole truth and nothing but the truth concerning his adventures in the wilds, and to feel that the friends, at least, were predestined to look upon him as a fearless liar, nothing more.

For twenty days he had travelled by caravan across the Persian uplands, through Herat, and Meshed and Bokhara, striking off with his guide alone toward the Sea of Aral and the eastern shores of the Caspian, thence through the Ural foothills to the old Roman highway that led down into the sweet green valleys of a land he had thought of as nothing more than the creation of a hairbrained fictionist.

Somewhere out in the shimmering east he had learned, to his honest amazement, that there was such a land as Graustark. At first he would not believe. But the English bank in Meshed assured him that he would come to it if he travelled long enough and far enough into the north and west and if he were not afraid of the hardships that most men abhor. The dying spirit of Romance flamed up in his heart; his blood grew quick again and eager. He would not go home until he had sought out this land of fair women and sweet tradition. And so he traversed the wild and dangerous Tartar roads for days and days, like the knights of Scheherazade in the times of old, and came at last to the gates of Edelweiss.

Not until he sat down to a rare dinner in the historic Hotel Regengetz was he able to realise that he was truly in that fabled, mythical land of Graustark, quaint, grim little principality in the most secret pocket of the earth's great mantle. This was the land of his dreams, the land of his fancy; he had not even dared to hope that it actually existed.

And now, here he was, pinching himself to prove that he was awake, stretching his world-worn bones under a dainty table to which real food was being brought by—well, he was obliged to pinch himself again. From the broad terrace after dinner he looked out into the streets of the quaint, picture-book town with its mediæval simplicity and ruggedness combined; his eyes tried to keep pace with the things that his fertile brain was seeing beyond the glimmering lights and dancing window panes—for the whole scene danced before him with a persistent unreality that made him feel his own pulse in the fear that some sudden, insidious fever had seized upon him.

If any one had told him, six months before, that there was such a land as Graustark and that if he could but keep on travelling in a certain direction he would come to it in time, he would have laughed that person to scorn, no matter how precise a geographer he might have been.

Young Mr. King, notwithstanding his naturally reckless devotion to first impressions, was a much wiser person than when he left his New York home two years before. Roughing it in the wildest parts of the world had taught him that eagerness is the enemy of common sense. Therefore he curbed the thrilling impulse to fare forth in search of diversion on this first night; he conquered himself and went to bed early—and to sleep at once, if that may serve to assist you in getting an idea of what time and circumstances had done for his character.

A certain hard-earned philosophy had convinced him long ago that adventure is quite content to wait over from day to day, but that when a man is tired and worn it isn't quite sensible to expect sleep to be put off regardless. With a fine sense of sacrifice, therefore, he went to bed, forsaking the desire to tread the dim streets of a city by night in advance of a more cautious survey by daylight. He had come to know that it is best to make sure of your ground, in a measure, at least, before taking too much for granted—to look before you leap, so to speak. And so, his mind tingling with visions of fair ladies and goodly opportunities, he went to sleep—and did not get up to breakfast until noon the next day.

And now it becomes my deplorable duty to divulge the fact that Truxton King, after two full days and nights in the city of Edelweiss, was quite ready to pass on to other fields, completely disillusionised in his own mind, and not a little disgusted with himself for having gone to the trouble to visit the place. To his intense chagrin, he had found the quaint old city very tiresome. True, it was a wonderful old town, rich in tradition, picturesque in character, hoary with age, bulging with the secrets of an active past; but at present, according to the well travelled Truxton, it was a poky old place about which historians either had lied gloriously or had been taken in shamelessly. In either case, Edelweiss was not what he had come to believe it would be. He had travelled overland for nearly a month, out of the heart of Asia, to find himself, after all, in a graveyard of great expectations!

He had explored Edelweiss, the capital. He had ridden about the ramparts; he had taken snapshots of the fortress down the river and had not been molested; he had gone mule-back up the mountain to the snowcapped monastery of St. Valentine, overtopping and overlooking the green valleys below; he had seen the tower in which illustrious prisoners were reported to have been held; he had ridden over the King's Road to Ganlook and had stood on American bridges at midnight—all the while wondering why he was there. Moreover, he had traversed the narrow, winding streets of the city by day and night; never, in all his travels, had he encountered a more peaceful, less spirit-stirring place or populace.

Everybody was busy, and thrifty, and law abiding. He might just as well have gone to Prague or Nuremburg; either was as old and as quaint and as stupid as this lukewarm city in the hills.

Where were the beautiful women he had read about and dreamed of ever since he left Teheran? On his soul, he had not seen half a dozen women in Edelweiss who were more than passably fair to look upon. True, he had to admit, the people he had seen were of the lower and middle classes—the shopkeepers and the shopgirls, the hucksters and the fruit vendors. What he wanted to know was this: What had become of the royalty and the nobility of Graustark? Where were the princes, the dukes and the barons, to say nothing of the feminine concomitants to these excellent gentlemen?

What irritated him most of all was the amazing discovery that there was a Cook's tourist office in town and that no end of parties arrived and departed under his very nose, all mildly exhilarated over the fact that they had seen Graustark! The interpreter, with "Cook's" on his cap, was quite the most important, if quite the least impressive personage in town. It is no wonder that this experienced globe-trotter was disgusted!

There was a train to Vienna three times a week. He made up his mind that he would not let the Saturday express go down without him. He had done some emphatic sputtering because he had neglected to take the one on Thursday.

Shunning the newly discovered American club in Castle Avenue as if it were a pest house, he lugubriously wandered the streets alone, painfully conscious that the citizens, instead of staring at him with admiring eyes, were taking but little notice of him. Tall young Americans were quite common in Edelweiss in these days.

One dingy little shop in the square interested him. It was directly opposite the Royal Café (with American bar attached), and the contents of its grimy little windows presented a peculiarly fascinating interest to him. Time and again, he crossed over from the Café garden to look into these windows. They were packed with weapons and firearms of such ancient design that he wondered what they could have been used for, even in the Middle Ages. Once he ventured inside the little shop. Finding no attendant, he put aside his suddenly formed impulse to purchase a mighty broadsword. From somewhere in the rear of the building came the clanging of steel hammers, the ringing of highly tempered metals; but, although he pounded vigorously with his cane, no one came forth to attend him.

On several occasions he had seen a grim, sharp-featured old man in the doorway of the shop, but it was not until after he had missed the Thursday train that he made up his mind to accost him and to have the broadsword at any price. With this object in view, he quickly crossed the square and inserted his tall frame into the narrow doorway, calling out lustily for attention. So loudly did he shout that the multitude of ancient swords and guns along the walls seemed to rattle in terror at this sudden encroachment of the present.

"What is it?" demanded a sharp, angry voice at his elbow. He wheeled and found himself looking into the wizened, parchment-like face of the little old man, whose black eyes snapped viciously. "Do you think I am deaf?"

"I didn't know you were here," gasped Truxton, forgetting to be surprised by the other's English. "The place looked empty. Excuse me for yelling."

"What do you want?"

"That broad—Say, you speak English, don't you?"

"Certainly," snapped the old man. "Why shouldn't I? I can't afford an interpreter. You'll find plenty of English used here in Edelweiss since the Americans and British came. They won't learn our language, so we must learn theirs."

"You speak it quite as well as I do."

"Better, young man. You are an American." The sarcasm was not lost on Truxton King, but he was not inclined to resent it. A twinkle had come into the eyes of the ancient; the deep lines about his lips seemed almost ready to crack into a smile.

"What's the price of that old sword you have in the window?"

"Do you wish to purchase it?"

"Certainly."

"Three hundred gavvos."

"What's that in dollars?"

"Four hundred and twenty."

"Whew!"

"It is genuine, sir, and three hundred years old. Old Prince Boris carried it. It's most rare. Ten years ago you might have had it for fifty gavvos. But," with a shrug of his thin shoulders, "the price of antiquities has gone up materially since the Americans began to come. They don't want a thing if it is cheap."

"I'll give you a hundred dollars for it, Mr.—er—" he looked at the sign on the open door—"Mr. Spantz."

"Good day, sir." The old man was bowing him out of the shop. King was amused.

"Let's talk it over. What's the least you'll take in real money?"

"I don't want your money. Good day."

Truxton King felt his chin in perplexity. In all his travels he had found no other merchant whom he could not "beat down" two or three hundred per cent. on an article.

"It's too much. I can't afford it," he said, disappointment in his eyes.

"I have modern blades of my own make, sir, much cheaper and quite as good," ventured the excellent Mr. Spantz.

"You make 'em?" in surprise.

The old man straightened his bent figure with sudden pride. "I am armourer to the crown, sir. My blades are used by the nobility—not by the army, I am happy to say. Spantz repairs the swords and guns for the army, but he welds only for the gentlemen at court."

"I see. Tradition, I suppose."

"My great-grandfather wrought blades for the princes a hundred years ago. My son will make them after I am gone, and his son after him. I, sir, have made the wonderful blade with the golden hilt and scabbard which the little Prince carries on days of state. It was two years in the making. There is no other blade so fine. It is so short that you would laugh at it as a weapon, and yet you could bend it double. Ah, there was a splendid piece of work, sir. You should see the little toy to appreciate it. There are diamonds and rubies worth 50,000 gavvos set in the handle. Ah, it is—"

Truxton's eyes were sparkling once more. Somehow he was amused by the sudden garrulousness of the old armourer. He held up his hand to check the flow of words.

"I say, Herr Spantz, or Monsieur, perhaps, you are the first man I've met who has volunteered to go into rhapsodies for my benefit. I'd like to have a good long chat with you. What do you say to a mug of that excellent beer over in the Café garden? Business seems to be a little dull. Can't you—er—lock up?"

Spantz looked at him keenly under his bushy brows, his little black eyes fairly boring holes into King's brain, so to speak.

"May I ask what brings you to Edelweiss?" he asked abruptly.

"I don't mind telling you, Mr. Spantz, that I'm here because I'm somewhat of a fool. False hopes led me astray. I thought Graustark was the home, the genesis of Romance, and I'm more or less like that chap we've read about, who was always in search of adventure. Somehow, Graustark hasn't come up to expectations. Up to date, this is the slowest burg I've ever seen. I'm leaving next Saturday for Vienna."

"I see," cackled Spantz, his eyes twinkling with mirth. "You thought you could capture wild and beautiful princesses here just as you pleased, eh? Let me tell you, young man, only one American—only one foreigner, in fact—has accomplished that miracle. Mr. Lorry came here ten years ago and won the fairest flower Graustark ever produced-the beautiful Yetive—but he was the only one. I suppose you are surprised to find Graustark a solid, prosperous, God-fearing little country, whose people are wise and happy and loyal. You have learned, by this time, that we have no princesses for you to protect. It isn't as it was when Mr. Lorry came and found Her Serene Highness in mediæval difficulties. There is a prince on the throne to-day—you've seen him?"

"No. I'm not looking for princes. I've seen hundreds of 'em in all parts of the world."

"Well, you should see Prince Robin before you scoff. He's the most wonderful little man in all the world."

"I've heard of nothing but him, my good Mr. Spantz. He's seven years old and he looks like his mother and he's got a jewelled sword and all that sort of thing. I daresay he's a nice little chap. Got American blood in him, you see."

"Do not let any one hear you laugh about him, sir. The people worship him. If you laugh too publicly, you may have your hands full of adventures in a very few minutes—and your body full of fine steel blades. We are very proud of our Prince."

"I beg your pardon, Mr. Spantz. I didn't mean *lesé majesté*. I'm bored, that's all. You wouldn't blame me for being sore if you'd come as far as I have and got as little for your pains. Why, hang it all, this morning that confounded man from Cook's had a party of twenty-two American schoolteachers and Bible students in the Castle grounds and I had to stand on my toes outside the walls for two hours before I could get a permit to enter. American engineers are building the new railroad; American capital controls the telephone and electric light companies; there are two American moving picture shows in Regengetz Circus and an American rush hand laundry two blocks up. And you can get Bourbon whisky anywhere. It's sickening."

"The Americans have done much for Edelweiss, sir. We don't resent their progressiveness. They have given us modern improvements without overthrowing ancient customs. My dear young sir, we are very old here—and very honest. That reminds me that I should accept your kind invitation to the Café garden. If you will bear with me for just one moment, sir." With this polite request, the old man retired to the rear of the shop and called out to some one upstairs. A woman's voice answered. The brief conversation which followed was in a tongue unknown to King.

"My niece will keep shop, sir, while I am out," Spantz explained, taking his hat from a peg behind the door. Truxton could scarcely restrain a smile as he glanced over his queer little old guest. He looked eighty but was as sprightly as a man of forty. A fine companion for a youth of twenty-six in search of adventure!

They paused near the door until the old man's niece appeared at the back of the shop. King's first glance at the girl was merely a casual one. His second was more or less in the nature of a stare of amazement.

A young woman of the most astounding beauty, attired in the black and red of the Graustark middle classes, was slowly approaching from the shadowy recesses at the end of the shop. She gave him but a cursory glance, in which no interest was apparent, and glided quietly into the little nook behind the counter, almost at his elbow. His heart enjoyed a lively thump. Here was the first noticeably good-looking woman he had seen in Edelweiss, and, by the powers, she was a sword-maker's niece!

The old man looked sharply at him for an instant, and a quick little smile writhed in and out among the mass of wrinkles. Instead of passing directly out of the shop, Spantz stopped a moment to give the girl some suddenly recalled instruction. Truxton King, you may be sure, did not precede the old man into the street. He deliberately removed his hat and waited most politely for age to go before youth, in the meantime blandly gazing upon the face of this amazing niece.

Across the square, at one of the tables, he awaited his chance and a plausible excuse for questioning the old man without giving offence. Somewhere back in his impressionable brain there was growing a distinct hope that this beautiful young creature with the dreamy eyes was something more than a mere shopgirl. It had occurred to him in that one brief moment of contact that she had the air, the poise of a true aristocrat.

The old man, over his huge mug of beer, was properly grateful. He was willing to repay King for his little attention by giving him a careful history of Graustark, past, present and future, from the time of Tartar rule to the time of the so-called "American invasion." ills glowing description of the little Prince might have interested Truxton in his Lord Fauntleroy days, but just at present he was more happily engaged in speculating on the true identify of the girl in the gun-shop. He recalled the fact that a former royal princess of Graustark had gone sight-seeing over the world, incognita, as a Miss Guggenslocker, and had been romantically snatched up by a lucky American named Lorry. What if this girl in the gun-shop should turn out to be a—well, he could hardly hope for a princess; but she might be a countess.

The old mart was rambling on. "The young Prince has lived most of his life in Washington and London and Paris, sir. He's only seven, sir. Of course, you remember the dreadful accident that made him an orphan and put him on the throne with the three 'wise men of the East' as regents or governors. The train wreck near Brussels, sir? His mother, the glorious Princess Yetive, was killed and his father, Mr. Lorry, died the next day from his injuries. That, sir, was a most appalling blow to the people of Graustark. We loved the Princess and we admired her fine American husband. There never will be another pair like them, sir. And to think of them being destroyed as they were—in the most dreadful way, sir. Their coach was demolished, you remember. I—I will not go into the details. You know them, of course. God alone preserved the little Prince. He was travelling with them, on the way from London to Edelweiss. By some strange intervention of Providence he had gone with his governess and other members of the party to the luggage van in the fore part of the train, which had stopped on a side track below the station. The collision was from the rear, a broken rail throwing a locomotive into the Princess's coach. This providential escape of the young Prince preserved the unbroken line of the present royal family. If he had been killed, the dynasty would have come to an end, and, I am telling no secret, sir, when I say that a new form of government would have followed."

"What sort of government?"

"A more modern system, sir. Perhaps socialistic. I can't say. At all events, a new dynasty could not have been formed. The people would have rejected it. But Prince Robin was spared and, if I do say it, sir, he is the manliest little prince in all the world. You should see him ride and fence and shoot—and he is but seven!"

"I say, Mr. Spantz, I don't believe I've told you that your niece is a most remarkably beau—"

"As I was saying, sir," interrupted Spantz, so pointedly that Truxton flushed, "the little Prince is the idol of all the people. Under the present regency he is obliged to reside in the principality until his fifteenth year, after which he may be permitted to travel abroad. Graustark intends to preserve him to herself if it is in her power to do so. Woe betide the man who thinks or does ill toward little Prince Robin."

King was suddenly conscious of a strange intentness of gaze on the old man's part. A peculiar, indescribable chill swept over him; he had a distinct, vivid impression that some subtle power was exercising itself upon him—a power that, for the briefest instant, held him in a grip of iron. What it was, he could not have told; it passed almost immediately. Something in the old man's eyes, perhaps—or was it something in the queer smile that flickered about his lips?

"My dear Mr. Spantz," he hastened to say, as if a defence were necessary, "please don't get it into your head that I'm thinking ill of the Prince. I daresay he's a fine little chap and I'm sorry he's—er—lost his parents."

Spantz laughed, a soft, mirthless gurgle that caused Truxton to wonder why he had made the effort at all. "I imagine His Serene Highness has little to fear from any American," he said quietly. "He has been taught to love and respect the men of his father's land. He loves America quite as dearly as he loves Graustark." Despite the seeming sincerity of the remark, Truxton was vaguely conscious that a peculiar harshness had crept into the other's voice. He glanced sharply at the old man's face. For the first time he noticed something sinister—yes, evil—in the leathery countenance; a stealthiness in the hard smile that seemed to transform it at once into a pronounced leer. Like a flash there darted into the American's active brain a conviction that there could be no common relationship between this flinty old man and the delicate, refined girl he had seen in the shop. Now he recalled the fact that her dark eyes had a look of sadness and dejection in their depths, and that her face was peculiarly white and unsmiling.

Spantz was eyeing him narrowly. "You do not appear interested in our royal family," he ventured coldly.

Truxton hastened to assure him that he was keenly interested. "Especially so, now that I appreciate that the little Prince is the last of his race."

"There are three regents, sir, in charge of the affairs of state—Count Halfont, the Duke of Perse and Baron Jasto Dangloss, who is minister of police. Count Halfont is a granduncle of the Prince, by marriage. The Duke of Perse is the father of the unhappy Countess Ingomede, the young and beautiful wife of the exiled "Iron Count" Marlanx. No doubt you've heard of him."

"I've read something about him. Sort of a gay old bounder, wasn't he? Seems to me I recall the stories that were printed about him a few years ago. I remember that he was banished from the principality and his estates seized by the Crown."

"Quite true, sir. He was banished in 1901 and now resides on his estates in Austria. Three years ago, in Buda Pesth, he was married to Ingomede, the daughter of the Duke. Count Marlanx has great influence at the Austrian court. Despite the fact that he is a despised and discredited man in his own country, he still is a power among people high in the government of more than one empire. The Duke of Perse realised this when he compelled his daughter to accept him as her husband. The fair Ingomede is less than twenty-five years of age; the Iron Count is fully sixty-five."

"She ought to be rescued," was King's only comment, but there was no mistaking the gleam of interest in his steady grey eyes.

"Rescued?" repeated the old man, with a broad grin. "And why? She is mistress of one of the finest old castles in Austria, Schloss Marlanx, and she is quite beautiful enough to have lovers by the score when the Count grows a little blinder and less jealous. She is in Edelweiss at present, visiting her father. The Count never comes here."

"I'd like to see her if she's really beautiful. I've seen but one pretty woman in this whole blamed town—your niece, Herr Spantz. I've looked 'em over pretty carefully, too. She is exceedingly attract—"

"Pardon me, sir, but it is not the custom in Graustark to discuss our women in the public drinking places." King felt as if he had received a slap in the face. He turned a fiery red under his tan and mumbled some sort of an apology. "The Countess is a public personage, however, and we may speak of her," went on the old man quickly, as the American, in his confusion, called a waiter to replenish the tankards. The steely glitter that leaped into the armourer's eyes at this second reference to his niece disappeared as quickly as it came; somehow it left behind the impression that he knew how to wield the deadly blades he wrought.

"I'd like to hear more about her," murmured Mr. King. "Anything to pass the time away, Mr. Spantz. As I said before, I journeyed far to reach this land of fair women and if there's one to be seen, I'm properly eager to jump at the chance. I've been here two days and I've seen nothing that could start up the faintest flutter around my heart. I'm sorry to say, my good friend, that the women I've seen in the streets of Edelweiss are not beauties. I won't say that they'd stop a clock, but they'd cause it to lose two or three hours a day, all right enough."

"You will not find the beautiful women of Edelweiss in the streets, sir."

"Don't they ever go out shopping?"

"Hardly. The merchants, if you will but notice, carry their wares to the houses of the noble and the rich. Graustark ladies of quality would no more think of setting foot in a shop or bazaar than they would think of entering a third class carriage. Believe me, there are many beautiful women in the homes along Castle Avenue. Noblemen come hundreds of miles to pay court to them."

"Just the same, I'm disgusted with the place. It's not what it's cracked up to be. Saturday will see me on my way."

"To-morrow the garrison at the fortress marches in review before the Prince. If you should happen to be on the avenue near the Castle gate at twelve o'clock, you will see the beauty and chivalry of Graustark. The soldiers are not the only ones who are on parade." There was an unmistakable sneer in his tone.

"You don't care much for society, I'd say," observed Truxton, with a smile.

Spantz's eyes flamed for an instant and then subtly resumed their most ingratiating twinkle. "We cannot all be peacocks," he said quietly. "You will see the Prince, his court and all the distinguished men of the city and the army. You will also see that the man who rides beside the Prince's carriage wheel is an American, while Graustark nobles take less exalted places."

"An American, eh?"

"Yes. Have you not heard of John Tullis, the Prince's friend?"

"Another seven-year-old?"

"Not at all. A grown man, sir. He, your countryman, is the real power behind our throne. On his deathbed, the Prince's father placed his son in this American's charge and begged him to stand by him through thick and thin until the lad is able to take care of himself. As if there were not loyal men in Graustark who might have done as much for their Prince!"

King looked interested. "I see. The people, no doubt, resent this espionage. Is that it?"

Spantz gave him a withering look, as much as to say that he was a fool to ask such a question in a place so public. Without replying, he got to his feet and made ready to leave the little garden.

"I must return. I have been away too long. Thank you, sir, for your kindness to an old man. Good day, sir, and—"

"Hold on! I think I'll walk over with you and have another look at that broadsword. I'm—"

"To-morrow, sir. It is past time to close the shop for to-day. Come to-morrow. Good day."

He was crossing the sidewalk nimbly before King could offer a word of remonstrance. With a disappointed sigh, the American sank back in his chair, and watched his odd companion scurry across the square. Suddenly he became conscious of a disquieting feeling that some one was looking at him intently from behind. He turned in his chair and found himself meeting the gaze of a ferocious looking, military appearing little man at a table near by. To his surprise, the little man's fierce stare maintained its peculiarly personal intentness until he, himself, was compelled to withdraw his own gaze in some little confusion and displeasure. His waiter appeared at his elbow with the change.

"Who the devil is that old man at the table there?" demanded young Mr. King loudly.

The waiter assumed a look of extreme insolence. "That is Baron Dangloss, Minister of Police. Anything more, sir?"

"Yes. What's he looking so hard at me for? Does he think I'm a pickpocket?"

"You know as much as I, sir," was all that the waiter said in reply. King pocketed the coin he had intended for the fellow, and deliberately left the place. He could not put off the feeling, however, that the intense stare of Baron Dangloss, the watch-dog of the land, followed him until the corner of the wall intervened. The now incensed American glanced involuntarily across the square in the direction of Spantz's shop. He saw three mounted soldiers ride up to the curb and hail the armourer as he started to close his doors. As he sauntered across the little square his gaze suddenly shifted to a second-story window above the gun-shop.

The interesting young woman had cautiously pushed open one of the shutters and was peering down upon the trio of red-coated guardsmen.

Almost at the same instant her quick, eager gaze fell upon the tall American, now quite close to the horsemen. He saw her dark eyes expand as if with surprise. The next instant he caught his breath and almost stopped in his tracks.

A shy, impulsive smile played about her red lips for a second, lighting up the delicate face with a radiance that amazed him. Then the shutter was closed gently, quickly. His first feeling of elation was followed instantly by the disquieting impression that it was a mocking smile of amusement and not one of inviting friendliness. He felt his ears burn as he abruptly turned off to the right, for, somehow, he knew that she was peeping at him through the blinds and that something about his tall, rangy figure was appealing to her sense of the ridiculous.

You will see at once that Truxton King, imaginative chap that he was, had pounced upon this slim, attractive young woman as the only plausible heroine for his prospective romance, and, as such, she could not be guilty of forwardness or lack or dignity. Besides, first impressions are always good ones: she had struck him at the outset as being a girl of rare delicacy and refinement.

In the meantime, Baron Dangloss was watching him covertly from the edge of the Café garden across the square.

CHAPTER II
A MEETING OF THE CABINET

At this time, the principality of Graustark was in a most prosperous condition. Its affairs were under the control of an able ministry, headed by the venerable Count Halfont. The Duke of Perse, for years a resident of St. Petersburg, and a financier of high standing, had returned to Edelweiss soon after the distressing death of the late Princess Yetive and her American husband, and to him was entrusted the treasury portfolio. He at once proceeded to endear himself to the common people by the advocacy of a lower rate of taxation; this meant the reduction of the standing army. He secured new and advantageous treaties with old and historic foes, putting Graustark's financial credit upon a high footing in the European capitals. The people smugly regarded themselves as safe in the hands of the miserly but honest old financier. If he accomplished many things by way of office to enhance his own particular fortune, no one looked askance, for he made no effort to blind or deceive his people. Of his honesty there could be no question; of his financial operations, it is enough to say that the people were satisfied to have their affairs linked with his.

The financing of the great railroad project by which Edelweiss was to be connected with the Siberian line in the north, fell to his lot at a time when no one else could have saved the little government from heavy losses or even bankruptcy. The new line traversed the country from Serros, capital of Dawsbergen, through the mountains and canyons of Graustark, across Axphain's broad steppes and lowlands, to a point at which Russia stood ready to begin a connecting branch for junction with her great line to the Pacific. All told, it was a stupendous undertaking for a small government to finance; it is well known that Graustark owns and controls her public utility institutions. The road, now about half completed, was to be nearly two hundred miles in length, fully two-thirds of which was on Graustark territory. The preponderance of cost of construction fell upon that principality, Dawsbergen and Axphain escaping with comparatively small obligations owing to the fact that they had few mountains to contend with. As a matter of fact, the Dawsbergen and Axphain ends of the railroad were now virtually built and waiting for the completion of the extensive work in the Graustark highlands.

The opening of this narrative finds the ministry preparing to float a new five million gavvo issue of bonds for construction and equipment purposes. Agents of the government were ready to depart for London and Paris to take up the matter with the great banking houses. St. Petersburg and Berlin were not to be given the opportunity to gobble up these extremely fine securities. This seemingly extraordinary exclusion of Russian and German bidders was the result of vigorous objections raised by an utter outsider, the American, John Tullis, long time friend and companion of Grenfall Lorry, consort to the late Princess.

Tullis was a strange man in many particulars. He was under forty years of age, but even at that rather immature time of life he had come to be recognised as a shrewd, successful financial power in his home city, New York. At the very zenith of his power he suddenly and with Quixotic disregard for consequences gave up his own business and came to Graustark for residence, following a promise made to Grenfall Lorry when the latter lay dying in a little inn near Brussels.

They had been lifelong friends. Tullis jestingly called himself the little Prince's "morganatic godfather." For two years he had been a constant resident of Graustark, living contentedly, even indolently, in the picturesque old Castle, his rooms just across the corridor from those occupied by the little Prince. To this small but important bit of royalty he was "Uncle Jack"; in that capacity he was the most beloved and at the same time the most abused gentleman in all Graustark. As many as ten times a week he was signally banished from the domain by the loving, headstrong little ruler, only to be recalled with grave dignity and a few tears when he went so far as to talk of packing his "duds" in obedience to the edict.

John Tullis, strong character though he was, found this lazy, *dolce far niente* life much to his liking. He was devoted to the boy; he was interested in the life at this tiny court. The days of public and court mourning for the lamented Princess and her husband wearing away after an established period, he found himself eagerly delving into the gaieties that followed. Life at the Castle and in the homes of the nobility provided a new and sharp contrast to the busy, sordid existence he had known at home. It was like a fine, wholesome, endless dream to him. He drifted on the joyous, smiling tide of pleasure that swept Edelweiss with its careless waves night and day. Clever, handsome, sincere in his attitude of loyalty toward these people of the topmost east, he was not long in becoming a popular idol.

His wide-awake, resourceful brain, attuned by nature to the difficulties of administration, lent itself capably to the solving of many knotty financial puzzles; the ministry was never loth to call on him for advice and seldom disposed to disregard it. An outsider, he never offered a suggestion or plan unasked; to this single qualification he owed much of the popularity and esteem in which he was held by the classes and the masses. Socially, he was a great favourite. He enjoyed the freedom of the most exclusive homes in Edelweiss. He had enjoyed the distinction of more than one informal visit to old Princess Volga of Axphain, just across the border, to say nothing of shooting expeditions with young Prince Dantan of Dawsbergen, whose American wife, formerly Miss Calhoun of Washington, was a friend of long standing.

John Tullis was, beyond question, the most conspicuous and the most admired man in Edelweiss in these serene days of mentorship to the adored Prince Robin.

There was but one man connected with the government to whom his popularity and his influence proved distasteful. That man was the Duke of Perse. On more than one occasion the cabinet had chosen to be guided by the sagacity of John Tullis in preference to following the lines laid down by the astute minister of finance. The decision to offer the new bond issue in London and Paris was due to the earnest, forceful argument of John Tullis—outside the cabinet chamber, to be sure. This was but one instance in which the plan of the treasurer was overridden. He resented the plain though delicate influence of the former Wall Street man. Tullis had made it plain to the ministry that Graustark could not afford to place itself in debt to the Russians, into whose hands, sooner or later, the destinies of the railroad might be expected to fall. The wise men of Graustark saw his point without force of argument, and voted down, in the parliament, the Duke's proposition to place the loan in St. Petersburg and Berlin. For this particular act of trespass upon the Duke's official preserves he won the hatred of the worthy treasurer and his no inconsiderable following among the deputies.

But John Tullis was not in Edelweiss for the purpose of meddling with state affairs. He was there because he elected to stand mentor to the son of his life-long friend, even though that son was a prince of the blood and controlled by the will of three regents chosen by his own subjects. He was there to watch over the doughty little chap, who one day would be ruler unrestrained, but who now was a boy to be loved and coddled and reprimanded in the general process of man-making.

To say that the tiny Prince loved his big, adoring mentor would be putting it too gently: he idolised him. Tullis was father, mother and big brother to the little fellow in knickers.

The American was a big, broad shouldered man, reddish haired and ruddy cheeked, with cool grey eyes; his sandy mustache was closely cropped and turned up ever so slightly at the corners of his mouth. Despite his colouring, his face was somewhat sombre—even stern—when in repose. It was his fine, enveloping smile that made friends for him wherever he listed, with men and with women. More frequently than otherwise it made more than friends of the latter.

One woman in Graustark was the source of never-ending and constantly increasing interest to this stalwart companion to the Prince. That woman was, alas! the wife of another man. Moreover, she was the daughter of the Duke of Perse.

The young and witty Countess of Marlanx came often to Edelweiss. She was a favourite at the Castle, notwithstanding the unhealthy record of her ancient and discredited husband, the Iron Count. Tullis had not seen the Count, but he had heard such tales of him that he could not but pity this glorious young creature who called him husband. There is an old saying about the kinship of pity. Not that John Tullis was actually in love with the charming Countess. He was, to be perfectly candid, very much interested in her and very much distressed by the fact that she was bound to a venerable reprobate who dared not put his foot on Graustark soil because once he had defiled it atrociously.

But of the Countess and her visits to Edelweiss, more anon—with the indulgence of the reader.

At present we are permitted to attend a meeting of the cabinet, which sits occasionally in solemn collectiveness just off the throne room within the tapestried walls of a dark little antechamber, known to the outside world as the "Room of Wrangles." It is ten o'clock of the morning on which the Prince is to review the troops from the fortress. The question under discussion relates to the loan of 5,000,000 gavvos, before mentioned. At the head of the long table, perched upon an augmentary pile of law books surmounted by a little red cushion, sits the Prince, almost lost in the hugh old walnut chair of his forefathers. Down the table sit the ten ministers of the departments of state, all of them loving the handsome little fellow on the necessary pile of statutes, but all of them more or less indifferent to his significant yawns and perplexed frowns.

The Prince was a sturdy, curly-haired lad, with big brown eyes and a lamentably noticeable scratch on his nose—acquired in less stately but more profitable pursuits. (It seems that he had peeled his nose while sliding to second base in a certain American game that he was teaching the juvenile aristocracy how to play.) His wavy hair was brown and rebellious. No end of royal nursing could keep it looking sleek and proper. He had the merit of being a very bad little boy at times; that is why he was loved by every one. Although it was considered next to high treason to strike a prince of the royal blood, I could, if I had the space, recount the details of numerous fisticuffs behind the state stables in which, sad to relate, the Prince just as often as not came off with a battered dignity and a chastened opinion of certain small fry who could not have been more than dukes or barons at best. But he took his defeats manfully: he did not whimper *lesé majesté*. John Tullis, his "Uncle Jack," had proclaimed his scorn for a boy who could not "take his medicine." And so Prince Robin took it gracefully because he was prince.

To-day he was—for him—rather oppressively dignified and imperial. He may have blinked his weary eyes a time or two, but in the main he was very attentive, very circumspect and very much puzzled. Custom required that the ruling prince or princess should preside over the meetings of the cabinet. It is needless to observe that the present ruler's duty ended when he repeated (after Count Halfont): "My lords, we are now in session." The school-room, he confessed, was a "picnic" compared to the "Room of Wrangles": a fellow got a recess once in a while there, but here—well, the only recess he got was when he fell asleep. To-day he was determined to maintain a very dignified mien. It appears that at the last meeting he had created considerable havoc by upsetting the ink well while trying to fill his fountain pen without an injector. Moreover, nearly half a pint of the fluid had splashed upon the Duke of Perse's trousers—and they were grey, at that. Whereupon the Duke announced in open conclave that His Highness needed a rattling good spanking—a remark which distinctly hurt the young ruler's pride and made him wish that there had been enough ink to drown the Duke instead of merely wetting him.

About the table sat the three regents and the other men high in the administration of affairs, among them General Braze of the Army, Baron Pultz of the Mines, Roslon of Agriculture. The Duke of Perse was discussing the great loan question. The Prince was watching his gaunt, saturnine face with more than usual interest.

"Of course, it is not too late to rescind the order promulgated at our last sitting. There are five bankers in St. Petersburg who will finance the loan without delay. We need not delay the interminable length of time necessary to secure the attention and co-operation of bankers in France and England. It is all nonsense to say that Russia has sinister motives in the matter. It is a business proposition—not an affair of state. We need the money before the winter opens. The railroad is now within fifteen miles of Edelweiss. The bridges and tunnels are well along toward completion. Our funds are diminishing, simply because we have delayed so long in preparing for this loan. There has been too much bickering and too much inane politics. I still maintain that we have made a mistake in refusing to take up the matter with St. Petersburg or Berlin. Why should we prefer England? Why France?"

For some unaccountable reason he struck the table violently with his fist and directed his glare upon the astonished Prince. The explosive demand caught the ruler by surprise. He gasped and his lips fell apart. Then it must have occurred to him that the question could be answered by no one save the person to whom it was so plainly addressed. He lifted his chin and piped up shrilly, and with a fervour that startled even the intense Perse:

"Because Uncle Jack said we should, that's why."

We have no record of what immediately followed this abrupt declaration; there are some things that never leak out, no matter how prying the chronicler may be. When one stops to consider that this was the first time a question had been put directly to the Prince—and one that he could understand, at that—we may be inclined to overlook his reply, but we cannot answer for certain members of the cabinet. Unconsciously, the boy in knickers had uttered a truth that no one else had dared to voice. John Tullis *was* the joint stepping-stone and stumbling-block in the deliberations of the cabinet.

It goes without saying that the innocent rejoinder opened the way to an acrid discussion of John Tullis. If that gentleman's ears burned in response to the sarcastic comments of the Duke of Perse and Baron Pultz, they probably tingled pleasantly as the result of the stout defence put up by Halfont, Dangloss and others. Moreover, his most devoted friend, the Prince, whose lips were sullenly closed after his unlucky maiden effort, was finding it exceedingly difficult to hold his tongue and his tears at the same time. The lad's lip trembled but his brown eyes glowered; he sat abashed and heard the no uncertain arraignment of his dearest friend, feeling all the while that the manly thing for him to do would be to go over and kick the Duke of Perse, miserably conscious that such an act was impossible. His little body trembled with childish rage; he never took his gaze from the face of the gaunt traducer. How he hated the Duke of Perse!

The Duke's impassioned plea was of no avail. His *confrères* saw the wisdom of keeping Russia's greedy hand out of the country's affairs—at least for the present—and reiterated their decision to seek the loans in England and France. The question, therefore, would not be taken to Parliament for reconsideration. The Duke sat down, pale in defeat; his heart was more bitter than ever against the shrewd American who had induced all these men to see through his eyes.

"I suppose there is no use in kicking against the pricks," he said sourly as he resumed his seat. "I shall send our representatives to London and Paris next month. I trust, my lords, that we may have no trouble in placing the loans there." There was a deep significance the dry tone which he assumed.

"I do not apprehend trouble," said Count Halfont. "Our credit is still good, your Grace. Russia is not the only country that is ready to trust us for a few millions. Have no fear, your Grace."

"It is the delay that I am apprehensive of, your Excellency."

At this juncture the Prince, gathering from the manner of his ministers that the question was settled to his liking, leaned forward and announced to his uncle, the premier:

"I'm tired, Uncle Caspar. How much longer is it?"

Count Halfont coughed. "Ahem! Just a few minutes, your Highness. Pray be patient—er—my little man."

Prince Bobby flushed. He always knew that he was being patronised when any one addressed him as "my little man."

"I have an engagement," he said, with a stiffening of his back.

"Indeed?" said the Duke dryly.

"Yes, your Grace—a very important one. Of course, I'll stay if I have to, but—what time is it, Uncle Caspar?"

"It is half past eleven, your Highness."

"Goodness, I had a date for eleven. I mean a engagement—an engagement." He glanced helplessly, appealingly from Count Halfont to Baron Dangloss, his known allies.

The Duke of Perse smiled grimly. In his most polite manner he arose to address the now harassed Princeling, who shifted uneasily on the pile of law books.

"May your most humble subject presume to inquire into the nature of your Highness's engagement?"

"You may, your Grace," said the Prince.

The Duke waited. A smile crept into the eyes of the others. "Well, what is the engagement?"

"I had a date to ride with Uncle Jack at eleven."

"And you imagine that 'Uncle Jack' will be annoyed if he is kept waiting by such a trivial matter as a cabinet meeting, unfortunately prolonged?"

"I don't know just what that means," murmured the Prince. Then his face brightened. "But I don't think he'll be sore after I tell him how busy we've been."

The Duke put his hand over his mouth. "I don't think he'll mind half an hour's wait, do you?"

"He likes me to be very prompt."

Count Halfont interposed, good-humouredly. "There is nothing more to come before us to-day, your Grace, so I fancy we may as well close the meeting. To my mind, it is rather a silly custom which compels us to keep the Prince with us—er—after the opening of the session. Of course, your Highness, we don't mean to say that you are not interested in our grave deliberations."

Prince Bobby broke in eagerly: "Uncle Jack says I've just *got* to be interested in 'em, whether I want to or not. He says it's the only way to catch onto things and become a regular prince. You see, Uncle Caspar, I've got a lot to learn."

"Yes, your Highness, you have," solemnly admitted the premier. "But I am sure you *will* learn."

"Under such an able instructor as Uncle Jack you may soon know more than the wisest man in the realm," added the Duke of Perse.

"Thank you, your Grace," said the Prince, so politely that the Duke was confounded; "I know Uncle Jack will be glad to hear that. He's—he's afraid people may think he's butting in too much."

"Butting in?" gasped the premier.

At this the Duke of Perse came to his feet again, an angry gleam in his eyes. "My lords," he began hastily, "it must certainly have occurred to you before this that our beloved Prince's English, which seems after all to be his mother tongue, is not what it should be. Butting in! Yesterday I overheard him advising your son, Pultz, to 'go chase' himself. And when your boy tried to chase himself—'pon my word, he did—what did our Prince say? What *did* you say, Prince Robin?"

"I—I forget," stammered Prince Bobby.

"You said 'Mice!' Or was it—er—"

"No, your Grace. Rats. I remember. That's what I said. That's what all of us boys used to say in Washington."

"God deliver us! Has it come to this, that a Prince of Graustark should grow up with such language on his lips? I fancy, my lords, you will all agree that something should be done about it. It is too serious a matter. We are all more or less responsible to the people he is to govern. We cannot, in justice to them, allow him to continue under the—er—influences that now seem to surround him. He'll—he'll grow up to be a barbarian. For Heaven's sake, my lords, let us consider the Prince's future—let us deal promptly with the situation."

"What's he saying, Uncle Caspar?" whispered the Prince fiercely.

"Sh!" cautioned Count Halfont.

"I won't sh! I am the Prince. And I'll say 'chase yourself' whenever I please. It's good English. I'll pronounce it for you in our own language, so's you can see how it works that way. It goes like—"

"You need not illustrate, your Highness," the Premier hastened to say. Turning to the Duke, he said coldly: "I acknowledge the wisdom in your remarks, your Grace, but—you will pardon me, I am sure—would it not be better to discuss the conditions privately among ourselves before taking them up officially?"

"That confounded American has every one hypnotised," exploded the Duke. "His influence over this boy is a menace to our country. He is making on oaf of him—a slangy, impudent little—"

"Your Grace!" interrupted Baron Dangloss sharply.

"Uncle Jack's all right," declared the Prince, vaguely realising that a defence should be forthcoming.

"He is, eh?" rasped the exasperated Duke, mopping his brow.

"He sure is," pronounced the Prince with a finality that left no room for doubt. They say that fierce little Baron Dangloss, in striving to suppress a guffaw, choked so impressively that there was a momentary doubt as to his ever getting over it alive.

"He is a mountebank—a meddler, that's what he is. The sooner we come to realise it, the better," exclaimed the over-heated Duke. "He has greater influence over our beloved Prince than any one else in the royal household. He has no business here—none whatsoever. His presence and his meddling is an affront to the intelligence of—"

But the Prince had slid down from his pile of books and planted himself beside him so suddenly that the bitter words died away on the old man's lips. Robin's face was white with rage, his little fists were clenched in desperate anger, his voice was half choked with the tears of indignation.

"You awful old man!" he cried, trembling all over, his eyes blazing. "Don't you say anything against Uncle Jack. I'll—I'll banish you—yes, sir—banish you like my mother fired Count Marlanx out of the country. I won't let you come back here ever—never. And before you go I'll have Uncle Jack give you a good licking. Oh, he can do it all right. I—I hate you!"

The Duke looked down in amazement into the flushed, writhing face of his little master. For a moment he was stunned by the vigorous outburst. Then the hard lines in his face relaxed and a softer expression came into his eyes—there was something like pride in them, too. The Duke, be it said, was an honest fighter and a loyal Graustarkian; he loved his Prince and, therefore, he gloried in his courage. His own smile of amusement, which broke in spite of his inordinate vanity, was the sign that brought relief to the hearts of his scandalised *confrères*.

"Your Highness does well in defending a friend and counsellor," he said gently. "I am sorry to have forgotten myself in your presence. It shall not occur again. Pray forgive me."

Prince Bobby was still unappeased. "I *could* have you beheaded," he said stubbornly. "Couldn't I, Uncle Caspar?"

Count Halfont gravely informed him that it was not customary to behead gentlemen except for the most heinous offences against the Crown.

The Duke of Perse suddenly bent forward and placed his bony hand upon the unshrinking shoulder of the Prince, his eyes gleaming kindly, his voice strangely free from its usual harshness. "You are a splendid little man, Prince Robin," he said. "I glory in you. I shall not forget the lesson in loyalty that you have taught me."

Bobby's eyes filled with tears. The genuine humility of the hard old man touched his tempestuous little heart.

"It's—it's all right, Du—your Grace. I'm sorry I spoke that way, too."

Baron Dangloss twisted his imperial vigorously. "My lords, I suggest that we adjourn. The Prince must have his ride and return in time for the review at one o'clock."

As the Prince strode soberly from the Room of Wrangles, every eye was upon his sturdy little back and there was a kindly light in each of them, bar none. The Duke, following close behind with Halfont, said quietly:

"I love him, Caspar. But I have no love for the man he loves so much better than he loves any of us. Tullis is a meddler—but, for Heaven's sake, my friend, don't let; Bobby know that I have repeated myself."

Later on, the Prince in his khaki riding suit loped gaily down the broad mountain road toward Ganlook, beside the black mare which carried John Tullis. Behind them rode three picked troopers from the House Guard. He had told Tullis of his vainglorious defence in the antechamber.

"And I told him, Uncle Jack, that you could lick him. You can, can't you?"

The American's face was clouded for a second; then, to please the boy, a warm smile succeeded the frown.

"Why, Bobby, you dear little beggar, he could thresh me with one hand."

"What?" almost shrieked Prince Bobby, utterly dismayed.

"He's a better swordsman than I, don't you see. Gentlemen over here fight with swords. I know nothing about duelling. He'd get at me in two thrusts."

"I—I think you'd better take some lessons from Colonel Quinnox. It won't do to be caught napping."

"I daresay you're right."

"Say, Uncle Jack, when are you going to take me to the witch's hovel?" The new thought abruptly banished all else from his eager little brain.

"Some day, soon," said Tullis. "You see, I'm not sure that she's receiving visitors these days. A witch is a very arbitrary person. Even princes have to send up their cards."

"Let's telegraph her," in an inspired tone.

"I'll arrange to go up with you very soon, Bobby. It's a hard ride through the pass and—and there may be a lot of goblins up there where the old woman keeps herself."

The witch's hovel was in the mountain across the most rugged of the canyons, and was to be reached only after the most hazardous of rides. The old woman of the hills was an ancient character about whom clung a thousand spookish traditions, but who, in the opinion of John Tuilis, was nothing more than a wise fortune-teller and necromancer who knew every trick in the trade of hoodwinking the superstitious. He had seen her and he had been properly impressed. Somehow, he did not like the thought of taking the Prince to the cabin among the mists and crags.

"They say she eats boys, now and then," he added, as if suddenly remembering it.

"Gee! Do you suppose we could get there some day when she's eating one?"

As they rode back to the Castle after an hour, coming down through Castle Avenue from the monastery road, they passed a tall, bronzed young man whom Tullis at once knew to be an American. He was seated on a big boulder at the roadside, enjoying the shade, and was evidently on his way by foot to the Castle gates to watch the *beau monde* assembling for the review. At his side was the fussy, well-known figure of Cook's interpreter, eagerly pointing out certain important personages to bun as they passed. Of course, the approach of the Prince was the excuse for considerable agitation and fervour on the part of the man from Cook's. He mounted the boulder and took off his cap to wave it frantically.

"It's the Prince!" he called out to Truxton King. "Stand up! Hurray! Long live the Prince!"

Tullis had already lifted his hand in salute to his countryman, and both had smiled the free, easy smile of men who know each other by instinct.

The man from Cook's came to grief. He slipped from his perch on the rock and came floundering to the ground below, considerably crushed in dignity, but quite intact in other respects.

The spirited pony that the Prince was riding shied and reared in quick affright. The boy dropped his crop and clung valiantly to the reins. A guardsman was at the pony's head in an instant, and there was no possible chance for disaster.

Truxton King unbent his long frame, picked up the riding crop with a deliberateness that astonished the man from Cook's, strode out into the roadway and handed it up to the boy in the saddle.

"Thank you," said Prince Bobby.

"Don't mention it," said Truxton King with his most engaging smile. "No trouble at all."

CHAPTER III
MANY PERSONS IN REVIEW

Truxton King witnessed the review of the garrison. That in itself was rather a tame exhibition for a man who had seen the finest troops in all the world. A thousand earnest looking soldiers, proud of the opportunity to march before the little Prince—and that was all, so far as the review was concerned.

But, alluringly provident to the welfare of this narrative, the red and black uniformed soldiers were not the only persons on review that balmy day in July. Truxton King had his first glimpse of the nobility of Graustark. He changed his mind about going to Vienna on the Saturday express. A goodly number of men before him had altered their humble plans for the same reason, I am reliably informed.

Mr. King saw the court in all its glory, scattered along the shady Castle Avenue—in carriages, in traps, in motors and in the saddle. His brain whirled and his heart leaped under the pressure of a new-found interest in life. The unexpected oasis loomed up before his eyes just as he was abandoning all hope in the unprofitable desert of Romance. He saw green trees and sparkling rivulets, and he sighed with a new, strange content. No, on second thoughts, he would not go to Vienna. He would stay in Edelweiss. He was a disciple of Micawber; and he was so much younger and fresher than that distinguished gentleman, that perhaps he was justified in believing that, in his case, something was bound to "turn up."

If Truxton King had given up in disgust and fled to Vienna, this tale would never have come to light. Instead of being the lively narrative of a young gentleman's adventures in far-away Graustark, it might have become a tale of the smart set in New York—for, as you know, we are bound by tradition to follow the trail laid down by our hero, no matter which way he elects to fare. Somewhat dismayed by his narrow escape, he confided to his friend from Cook's that he could never have forgiven himself if he had adhered to his resolution to leave on the following day.

"I didn't know you'd changed your mind, sir," remarked Mr. Hobbs in surprise.

"Of course you didn't know it," said Truxton. "How could you? I've just changed it, this instant. I didn't know it myself two minutes ago. No, sir, Hobbs—or is it Dobbs? Thanks—no, sir, I'm going to stop here for a—well, a week or two. Where the dickens do these people keep themselves? I haven't seen 'em before."

"Oh, they are the nobility—the swells. They don't hang around the streets like tourists and rubbernecks, sir," in plain disgust.

"I thought you were an Englishman," observed King, with a quizzical smile.

"I am, sir. I can't help saying rubbernecks, sir, though it's a shocking word. It's the only name for them, sir. That's what the little Prince calls them, too. You see, it's one form of amusement they provide for him, and I am supposed to help it along as much as possible. Mr. Tullis takes him out in the avenue whenever I've got a party in hand. I telephone up to the Castle that I've got a crowd and then I drive 'em out to the Park here. The Prince says he just loves to watch the rubbernecks go by. It's great fun, sir, for the little lad. He never misses a party, and you can believe it or not, he has told me so himself. Yes, sir, the Prince has had more than one word with me—from time to time." King looked at the little man's reddish face and saw therein the signs of exaltation indigenous to a land imperial.

He hesitated for an instant and then remarked, with a mean impulse to spoil Hobbs's glorification: "I have dined with the President of the United States."

Hobbs was politely unimpressed. "I've no doubt, sir," he said. "I daresay it was an excellent dinner."

King blinked his eyes and then turned them upon the passing show. He was coming to understand the real difference between men.

"I say, who is that just passing—the lady in the victoria?" he asked abruptly.

"That is the Countess Marlanx."

"Whew! I thought she was the queen!"

Hobbs went into details concerning the beautiful Countess. During the hour and a half of display he pointed out to King all of the great personages, giving a Baedeker-like account of their doings from childhood up, quite satisfying that gentleman's curiosity and involving his cupidity at the same time.

When, at last, the show was over, Truxton and the voluble little interpreter, whom he had employed for the occasion, strolled leisurely back to the heart of the town. Something had come over King, changing the quaint old city from a prosaic collection of shops and thoroughfares into a veritable playground for Cinderellas and Prince Charmings. The women, to his startled imagination, had been suddenly transformed from lackadaisical drudges into radiant personages at whose feet it would be a pleasure to fall, in whose defence it would be divine to serve; the men were the cavaliers that had called to him from the pages of chivalrous tales, ever since the days of his childhood. Here were knights and ladies such as he had dreamed of and despaired of ever seeing outside his dreams.

Hobbs was telling him how every one struggled to provide amusement for the little Prince at whose court these almost mythological beings bent the knee. "Every few days they have a royal troupe of acrobats in the Castle grounds. Next week Tantora's big circus is to give a private performance for him. There are Marionettes and Punch and Judy shows, and all the doings of the Grand Grignol are beautifully imitated. The royal band plays every afternoon, and at night some one tells him stories of the valorous men who occupied the throne before him. He rides, plays baseball and cricket, swims, goes shooting—and, you may take it from me, sir, he is already enjoying fencing lessons with Colonel Quinnox, chief of the Castle guard. Mr. Tullis, the American, has charge of his—you might say, his education and entertainment. They want to make of him a very wonderful Prince. So they are starting at the bottom. He's quite a wonderful little chap. What say, sir?"

"I was just going to ask if you know anything about a young woman who occasionally tends shop for William Spantz, the armourer."

Hobbs looked interested. "She's quite a beauty, sir, I give you my word."

"I know that, Hobbs. But who is she?"

"I really can't say, sir. She's his niece, I've heard. Been here a little over a month. I think she's from Warsaw."

"Well, I'll say good-bye here. If you've nothing on for to-morrow we'll visit the Castle grounds and—ahem!—take a look about the place. Come to the hotel early. I'm going over to the gun-shop. So long!" As he crossed the square, his mind full of the beautiful women he had seen, he was saying to himself in a wild strain of exhilaration: "I'll bet my head that girl isn't the nobody she's setting herself up to be. She looks like these I've just seen. She's got the marks of a lady. You can't fool me. I'm going to find out who she is and—well, maybe it won't be so dull here, after all. It looks better every minute."

He was whistling gaily as he entered the little shop, ready to give a cheery greeting to old Spantz and to make him a temporising offer for the broadsword. But it was not Spantz who stood behind the little counter. Truxton flushed hotly and jerked off his hat. The girl smiled.

"I beg pardon," he exclaimed. "I—I'm looking for Mr. Spantz—I—"

"He is out. Will you wait? He will return in a very few minutes." Her voice was clear and low, her accent charming. The smile in her eyes somehow struck him as sad, even fleeting in its attempt at mirth. As she spoke, it disappeared altogether and an almost sombre expression came into her face.

"Thanks. I'll—wait," he said, suddenly embarrassed. She turned to the window, resuming the wistful, preoccupied gaze down the avenue. He made pretence of inspecting the wares on the opposite wall, but covertly watched her out of the corner of his eye. Perhaps, calculated he, if she were attired in the gown of one of those fashionables she might rank with the noblest of them in beauty and delicacy. Her dark little head was carried with all the serene pride of a lady of quality; her features were clear cut, mobile, and absolutely flawless. He was sure of that: his sly analysis was not as casual as one might suppose under the circumstances. As a matter of fact, he found himself having what he afterward called "a very good look at her." She seemed to have forgotten his presence. The longer he looked at the delicate profile, the more fully was he convinced that she was not all that she pretended. He experienced a thrill of hope. If she wasn't what she pretended to be, then surely she must be what he wanted her to be—a lady of quality. In that case there was a mystery. The thought restored his temerity.

"Beg pardon," he said, politely sauntering up to the little counter. He noted that she was taller than he had thought, and slender. She started and turned toward him with a quick, diffident smile, her dark eyes filling with an unspoken apology. "I wanted to have another look at the broadsword there. May I get it out of the window, or will you?"

Very quickly—he noticed that she went about it clumsily despite her supple gracefulness—she withdrew the heavy weapon from the window and laid it upon the counter. He was looking at her with a peculiar smile upon his lips. She flushed painfully.

"I am not—not what you would call an expert," she said frankly.

"You mean in handling broadswords," he said in his most suave manner. "It's a cunning little thing, isn't it?" He picked up the ponderous blade. "I don't wonder you nearly dropped it on your toes."

"There must have been giants in those days," she said, a slight shudder passing over her.

"Whoppers," he agreed eagerly. "I've thought somewhat of buying the old thing. Not to use, of course. I'm not a giant."

"You're not a pigmy," she supplemented, her eyes sweeping his long figure comprehensively.

"What's the price?" he asked, his courage faltering under the cool, impersonal gaze.

"I do not know. My uncle has told you?"

"I—I think he did. But I've got a wretched memory when it comes to broadswords."

She laughed. "This is such a very old broadsword, too," she said. "It goes back beyond the memory of man."

"How does it come that you don't know the price?" he asked, watching her narrowly. She met his inquiring look with perfect composure.

"I am quite new at the trade. I hope you will excuse my ignorance. My uncle will be here in a moment." She was turning away with an air that convinced King of one thing: she was a person who, in no sense, had ever been called upon to serve others.

"So I've heard," he observed. The bait took effect. She looked up quickly; he was confident that a startled expression flitted across her face.

"You have heard? What have you heard of me?" she demanded.

"That you are new at the business," he replied coolly.

"You are a stranger in a strange land, so they say."

"You have been making inquiries?" she asked, disdain succeeding dismay.

"Tentatively, that's all. Ever since you peeked out of the window up there and laughed at me. I'm curious, you see."

She stared at him in silent intensity for a moment. "That's why I laughed at you. You were *very* curious."

"Am I so bad as all that?" he lamented.

She ignored the question. "Why should you be interested in me, sir?"

Mr. King was inspired to fabricate in the interest of psychical research. "Because I have heard that you are not the niece of old man Spantz." He watched intently to catch the effect of the declaration.

She merely stared at him; there was not so much as the flutter of an eyelid. "You have heard nothing of the kind," she said coldly.

"Well, I'll confess I haven't," he admitted cheerfully. "I was experimenting. I'm an amateur Sherlock Holmes. It pleases me to deduce that you are not related to the armourer. You don't look the part."

Now she smiled divinely. "And why not, pray? His sister was my mother."

"In order to establish a line on which to base my calculations, would you mind telling me who your father is?" He asked the question with his most appealing smile—a smile so frankly impudent that she could not resent it.

"My mother's husband," she replied in the same spirit.

"Well, that is *quite* a clue!" he exclaimed. "'Pon my soul, I believe I'm on the right track. Excuse me for continuing, but is he a count or a duke or just a—"

"My father is dead," she interrupted, without taking her now serious gaze from his face.

"I beg your pardon," he said at once. "I'm sorry if I've hurt you."

"My mother is dead. Now can you understand why I am living here with my uncle? Even an amateur may rise to that. Now, sir, do you expect to purchase the sword? If not, I shall replace it in the window."

"That's what I came here for," said he, resenting her tone and the icy look she gave him.

"I gathered that you came in the capacity of Sherlock Holmes—or something else." She added the last three words with unmistakable meaning.

"You mean as a—" he hesitated, flushing.

"You knew I was alone, sir."

"By Jove, you're wrong there. I give you my word, I didn't. If I'd known it, I'd surely have come in sooner. There, forgive me. I'm particularly light-headed and futile to-day, and I hope—Beg pardon?"

She was leaning toward him, her hands on the counter, a peculiar gleam in her dark eyes—which now, for the first time, struck him as rather more keen and penetrating than he had suspected before.

"I simply want to tell you, Mr. King, that unless you really expect to buy this sword it is not wise in you to make it an excuse for coming here."

"My dear young lady, I—"

"My uncle has a queer conception of the proprieties. He may think that you come to see me." A radiant smile leaped into her face, transforming its strange sombreness into absolutely impish mirth.

"Well, hang it all, he can't object to that, can he? Besides, I never buy without haggling," he expostulated, suddenly exhilarated, he knew not why.

"Don't come in here unless you expect to buy," she said, serious in an instant. "It isn't the custom in Edelweiss. Young men may chat with shopgirls all the world over—but in Edelweiss, no—unless they come to pay most honourable court to them. My uncle would not understand."

"I take it, however, that you would understand," he said boldly.

"I have lived in Vienna, in Paris and in London. But now I am living in Edelweiss. I have not been a shopgirl always."

"I can believe that. My deductions are justified."

"Pray forgive me for offering this bit of advice. A word to the wise. My uncle would close the door in your face if—if he thought—"

"I see. Well, I'll buy the blooming sword. Anyhow, that's what I came in for."

"No. You came in because I smiled at you from the window upstairs. It is my sitting-room."

"Why did you smile? Tell me?" eagerly.

"It was nature asserting itself."

"You mean you just couldn't help it?"

"That's precisely what I mean."

"Not very complimentary, I'd say."

"A smile is ever a compliment, sir."

"I say, do you know you interest me?" he began warmly, but she put her finger to her lips.

"My uncle is returning. I must not talk to you any longer." She glanced uneasily out upon the square, and then hurriedly added, a certain wistfulness in her voice and eyes. "I couldn't help it to-day. I forgot my place. But you are the first gentleman I've spoken to since I came here."

"I—I was afraid you might think I am not a gentleman. I've been rather fresh."

"I happen to have known many gentlemen. Before I went into—service, of course." She turned away abruptly, a sudden shadow crossing her face. Truxton King exulted. At last he was touching the long-sought trail of the Golden Girl! Here was Romance! Here was mystery!

Spantz was crossing the sidewalk. The American leaned forward and half-whispered: "Just watch me buy that broadsword. I may, in time, buy out the shop, piece by piece."

She smiled swiftly. "Let me warn you: don't pay his price."

"Thanks."

When Spantz entered the door, a moment later, the girl was gazing listlessly from the window and Truxton King was leaning against the counter with his back toward her, his arms folded and a most impatient frown on his face.

"Hello!" he said gruffly. "I've been waiting ten minutes for you."

Spantz's black eyes shot from one to the other. "What do you want?" he demanded sharply. As he dropped his hat upon a stool near, the door, his glance again darted from the man to the girl and back again.

"The broadsword. And, say, Mr. Spantz, you might assume a different tone in addressing me. I'm a customer, not a beggar."

The girl left the window and walked slowly to the rear of the shop, passing through the narrow door, without so much as a glance at King or the old man. Spantz was silent until she was gone.

"You want the broadsword, eh?" he asked, moderating his tone considerably. "It's a rare old—"

"I'll give you a hundred dollars-not another cent," interrupted King, riot yet over his resentment. There followed a long and irritating argument, at the conclusion of which Mr. King became the possessor of the weapon at his own price. Remembering himself in time, he fell to admiring some old rings and bracelets in a cabinet near by, thus paving the way for future visits.

"I'll come in again," he said indifferently.

"But you are leaving to-morrow, sir."

"I've changed my mind."

"You are not going?"

"Not for a few days."

"Then you have discovered something in Edelweiss to attract you?" grinned the old armourer. "I thought you might."

"I've had a glimpse of the swells, my good friend."

"It's all the good you'll get of it," said Spantz gruffly.

"I daresay you're right. Clean that sword up a bit for me, and I'll drop in to-morrow and get it. Here's sixty gavvos to bind the bargain. The rest on delivery. Good day, Mr. Spantz."

"Good day, Mr. King."

"How do you happen to know my name?"

Spantz put his hand over his heart and delivered himself of a most impressive bow. "When so distinguished a visitor comes to our little city," he said, "we lose no time in discovering his name. It is a part of our trade, sir, believe me."

"I'm not so sure that I do believe you," said Truxton King to himself as he sauntered up the street toward the Hotel. "The girl knew me, too, now that I come to think of it. Heigho! By Jove, I *do* hope I can work up a little something to interest—Hello!"

Mr. Hobbs, from Cook's, was at his elbow, his eyes glistening with eagerness.

"I say, old Dangloss is waiting for you at the Regengetz, sir. Wot's up? Wot you been up to, sir?"

"Up to? Up to, Hobbs?"

"My word, sir, you must have been or he wouldn't be there to see you."

"Who is Dangloss?"

"Minister of Police—haven't I told you? He's a keen one, too, take my word for it. He's got Sherlock beat a mile."

"So have I, Hobbs. I'm not slow at Sherlocking, let me tell you that. How do you know he's waiting to see me?"

"I heard him ask for you. And I was there just now when one of his men came in and told him you were on your way up from the gunshop down there."

"So they're watching me, eh? 'Gad, this is fine!"

He lost no time in getting to the hotel. A well-remembered, fierce-looking little man in a white linen suit was waiting for him on the great piazza.

Baron Jasto Dangloss was a polite man but not to the point of procrastination. He advanced to meet the puzzled American, smiling amiably and twirling his imposing mustachios with neatly gloved fingers.

"I have called, Mr. King, to have a little chat with you about your father," he said abruptly. He enjoyed the look of surprise on the young man's face.

"My father?" murmured Truxton, catching his breath. He was shaking hands with the Baron, all the while staring blankly into his twinkling, snapping eyes.

"Won't you join me at this table? A julep will not be bad, eh?" King sat down opposite to him at one of the piazza tables, in the shade of the great trailing vines.

"Fine," was his only comment.

A waiter took the order and departed. The Baron produced his cigarette case. King carefully selected one and tapped its tip on the back of his hand.

"Is—has anything happened to my father?" he asked quietly. "Bad news?"

"On the contrary, sir, he is quite well. I had a cablegram from him to-day."

"A cablegram?"

"Yes. I cabled day before yesterday to ask if he could tell me the whereabouts of his son."

"The deuce you say!"

"He replies that you are in Teheran."

"What is the meaning of this, Baron?"

"It is a habit I have. I make it a practice to keep in touch with the movements of our guests."

"I see. You want to know all about me; why I'm here, where I came from, and all that. Well, I'm ready for the 'sweat box.'"

"Pray do not take offence. It is my rule. It would not be altered if the King of England came. Ah, here are the juleps. Quick service, eh?"

"Remarkably so, due to your powers of persuasion, I fancy."

"I really ordered them a few minutes before you arrived. You see, I was quite certain you'd have one. You take one about this hour every day."

"By Jove, you have been watching me!" cried Truxton delightedly.

"What are you doing in Edelweiss, Mr. King?" asked the Baron abruptly but not peremptorily.

"Sight-seeing and in search of adventure," was the prompt response.

"I fancied as much. You've seen quite a bit of the world since you left home two years ago, on the twenty-seventh of September."

"By Jove!"

"Been to South Africa, Asia and—South America—to say nothing of Europe. That must have been an exciting little episode in South America."

"You don't mean to say—"

"Oh, I know all about your participation in the revolution down there. You were a captain, I understand, during the three weeks of disturbance. Splendid! For the fun of the thing, I suppose. Well, I like it in you. I should have done it myself. And you got out of the country just in time, if I remember rightly. There was a price placed on your head by the distressed government. I imagine they would have shot you if they could have caught you—as they did the others." The old man chuckled. "You don't expect to return to South America, do you? The price is still offered, you know."

King was glaring at him in sheer wonder. Here was an episode in his life that he fondly hoped might never come to light; he knew how it would disturb his mother. And this foxy old fellow away off here in Graustark knew all about it.

"Well, you're a wonder!" in pure admiration.

"An appreciated compliment, I assure you. This is all in the way of letting you know that we have found out something concerning your movements. Now, to come down to the present. You expected to leave to-morrow. Why are you staying over?"

"Baron, I leave that to your own distinguished powers of deduction," said Truxton gently. He took a long pull at the straw, watching the other's face as he did so. The Baron smiled.

"You have found the young lady to be very attractive," observed the Baron. "Where have you known her before?"

"I beg pardon?"

"It is not unusual for a young man in search of adventure to follow the lady of his choice from place to place. She came but recently, I recall."

"You think I knew her before and followed her to Edelweiss?"

"I am not quite sure whether you have been in Warsaw lately. There is a gap in your movements that I can't account for."

King became serious at once. He saw that it was best to be frank with this keen old man.

"Baron Dangloss, I don't know just what you are driving at, but I'll set you straight so far as I'm concerned. I never saw that girl until the day before yesterday. I never spoke to her until to-day."

"She smiled on you quite familiarly from her window casement *yesterday*," said Dangloss coolly.

"She laughed at me, to be perfectly candid. But what's all this about? Who is she? What's the game? I don't mind confessing that I have a feeling she is not what she claims to be, but that's as far as I've got."

Dangloss studied the young man's face for a moment and then came to a sudden decision. He leaned forward and smiled sourly.

"Take my advice: do not play with fire," he said enigmatically.

"You—you mean she's a dangerous person? I can't believe that, Baron."

"She has dangerous friends out in the world. I don't mean to say she will cause you any trouble here—but there is a hereafter. Mind you, I'm not saying she isn't a good girl, or even an adventuress. On the contrary, she comes of an excellent family—in fact, there were noblemen among them a generation or two ago. You know her name?"

"No. I say, this is getting interesting!" He was beaming.

"She is Olga Platanova. Her mother was married in this city twenty-five years ago to Professor Platanova of Warsaw. The Professor was executed last year for conspiracy. He was one of the leaders of a great revolutionary movement in Poland. They were virtually anarchists, as you have come to place them in America. This girl, Olga, was his secretary. His death almost killed her. But that is not all. She had a sweetheart up to fifteen months ago. He was a prince of the royal blood. He would have married her in spite of the difference in their stations had it not been for the intervention of the Crown that she and her kind hate so well. The young man's powerful relatives took a hand in the affair. He was compelled to marry a scrawny little duchess, and Olga was warned that if she attempted to entice him away from his wife she would be punished. She did not attempt it, because she is a virtuous girl—of that I am sure. But she hates them all—oh, how she hates them! Her uncle, Spantz, offered her a home. She came here a month ago, broken-spirited and sick. So far, she has been exceedingly respectful to our laws. It is not that we fear anything from her; but that we are obliged to watch her for the benefit of our big brothers across the border. Now you know why I advised you to let the fire alone."

King was silent for a moment, turning something over in his head.

"Baron, are you sure that she is a Red?"

"Quite. She attended their councils."

"She doesn't look it, 'pon my word. I thought they were the scum of the earth."

"The kind you have in America are. But over here—oh, well, we never can tell."

"I don't mind saying she interests me. She's pretty—and I have an idea she's clever. Baron, let me understand you. Do you mean that this is a polite way of commanding me to have nothing to do with her?"

"You put it broadly. In the first place, I am quite sure she will have nothing to do with you. She loved the husband of the scrawny duchess. *You*, my good friend, handsome as you are, cannot interest her, believe me."

"I daresay you're right," glumly.

"I am merely warning you. Young men of your age and temperament sometimes let their fancies lead them into desperate predicaments. I've no doubt you can take care of yourself, but—" he paused, as if very much in doubt.

"I'm much obliged. And I'll keep my eyes well opened. I suppose there's no harm in my going to the shop to look at a lot of rings and knick-knacks he has for sale?"

"Not in the least. Confine yourself to knick-knacks, that's all."

"Isn't Spantz above suspicion?"

"No one is in my little world. By the way, I am very fond of your father. He is a most excellent gentleman and a splendid shot."

Truxton stared harder than ever. "What's that?"

"I know him quite well. Hunted wild boars with him five years ago in Germany. And your sister! She was a beautiful young girl. They were at Carlsbad at the time. Was she quite well when you last heard?"

"She was," was all that the wondering brother could say.

"Well, come in and see me at the tower. I am there in the mornings. Come as a caller, not as a prisoner, that's all." The Baron cackled at his little jest. "*Au revoir!* Till we meet again." They were shaking hands in the friendliest manner. "Oh, by the way, you were good enough to change your mind to-day about the personal attractiveness of our ladies. Permit me to observe, in return, that not a few of our most distinguished beauties were good enough to make inquiries as to your identity."

He left the American standing at the head of the steps, gazing after his retreating figure with a look of admiration in his eyes.

Truxton fared forth into the streets that night with a greater zest in life than he had ever known before. Some thing whispered insistently to his fancy that dreariness was a thing of the past; he did not have to whistle to keep up his spirits. They were soaring of their own accord.

He did not know, however, that a person from the secret service was watching his every movement. Nor, on the other hand, is it at all likely that the secret service operative was aware that he was not the only shadower of the blithe young stranger.

A man with a limp cigarette between his lips was never far from the side of the American—a man who had stopped to pass the time of day with William Spantz, and who, from that hour was not to let the young man out of his sight until another relieved him of the task.

CHAPTER IV
TRUXTON TRESPASSES

He went to bed that night, tired and happy. To his revived spirits and his new attitude toward life in its present state, the city had suddenly turned gay and vivacious. Twice during the evening he passed Spantz's shop. It was dark, upstairs and down. He wondered if the unhappy Olga was looking at him from behind the darkened shutters. But even if she were not—la, la! He was having a good time! He was gay! He was seeing pretty women in the cafés and the gardens! Well, well, he would see her to-morrow—after that he would give proper heed to the Baron's warning! An anarchist's daughter!

He slept well, too, with never a thought of the Saturday express which he had lain awake on other nights to lament and anathematise. Bright and early in the morning he was astir. Somehow he felt he had been sleeping too much of late.

There was a sparkle in his eyes as he struck out across town after breakfast. He burst in upon Mr. Hobbs at Cook's.

"Say, Hobbs, how about the Castle to-day—in an hour, say? Can you take a party of one rubbernecking this A.M.? I like you, Hobbs. You are the best interpreter of English I've ever seen. I can't help understanding you, no matter how hard I try not to. I want you to get me into the Castle grounds to-day and show me where the duchesses dawdle and the countesses cavort. I'm ashamed to say it, Hobbs, but since yesterday I've quite lost interest in the middle classes and the component parts thereof. I have suddenly acquired a thirst for champagne—in other words, I have a hankering for the nobility. Catch the idea? Good! Then you'll guide me into the land of the fairies? At ten?"

"I'll take you to the Castle grounds, Mr. King, all right enough, sir, and I'll tell you all the things of interest, but I'll be 'anged, sir, if I've got the blooming nerve to introduce you to the first ladies of the land. That's more than I can ever 'ope to do, sir, and—"

"Lord bless you, Hobbs, don't look so depressed. I don't ask you to present me at court. I just want to look at the lilacs and the gargoyles. That's as far as I expect to carry my invasion of the dream world."

"Of course, sir, you understand there are certain parts of the Park not open to the public. The grotto and the playgrounds and the Basin of Venus—"

"I'll not trespass, so don't fidget, Hobbs. I'll be here for you at ten."

Mr. Hobbs looked after the vigorous, happy figure as it swung down the street, and shook his head mournfully. Turning to the solitary clerk who dawdled behind the cashier's desk he remarked with more feeling than was his wont:

"He's just the kind of chap to get me into no end of trouble if I give 'im rope enough. Take it from me, Stokes, I'll have my hands full of 'im up there this morning. He's charged like a soda bottle; and you never know wot's going to happen unless you handle a soda bottle very careful-like."

Truxton hurried to the square and across it to the shop of the armourer, not forgetting, however, to look about in some anxiety for the excellent Dangloss, who might, for all he knew, be snooping in the neighbourhood. Spantz was at the rear of the shop, talking to a customer. The girl was behind the counter, dressed for the street.

She came quickly out to him, a disturbed expression in her face. As he doffed his hat, the smile left his lips; he saw that she had been weeping.

"You must not come here, Mr. King," she said hurriedly, in low tones. "Take your broadsword this morning and—please, for my sake, do not come again. I—I may not explain why I am asking you to do this, but I mean it for your good, more than for my own. My uncle will be out in a moment. He knows you are here. He is listening now to catch what I am saying to you. Smile, please, or he will suspect—"

"See here," demanded King, smiling, but very much in earnest, "what's up? You've been crying. What's he been doing or saying to you? I'll give him a—"

"No, no! Be sensible! It is nothing in which you could possibly take a hand. I don't know you, Mr. King, but I am in earnest when I say that it is not safe for you to come here, ostensibly to buy. It is too easily seen through—it is—"

"Just a minute, please," he interrupted. "I've heard your story from Baron Dangloss. It has appealed to me. You are not happy. Are you in trouble? Do you need friends, Miss Platanova?"

"It is because you would be a friend that I ask you to stay away. You cannot be my friend. Pray do not consider me bold for assuming so much. But I know—I know *men*, Mr. King. The Baron has told you all about me?" She smiled sadly. "Alas, he has only told you what he knows. But it should be sufficient. There is no place in my life for you or any one else. There never can be. So, you see, you may not develop your romance with me as the foundation. Oh, I've heard of your quest of adventure. I like you for it. I had an imagination myself, once on a time. I loved the fairy books and the love tales. But not now-not now. There is no romance for me. Nothing but grave reality. Do not question me! I can say no more. Now I must be gone. I—I have warned you. Do not come again!"

"Thanks, for the warning," he said quietly. "But I expect to come in occasionally, just the same. You've taken the wrong tack by trying to frighten me off. You see, Miss Platanova, I'm actually looking for something dangerous—if that's what you mean."

"That isn't all, believe me," she pleaded. "You can gain nothing by coming. You know who I am. I cannot be a friend—not even an acquaintance to you, Mr. King. Good-bye! Please do not come again!"

She slipped into the street and was gone. King stood in the doorway, looking after her, a puzzled gleam in his eyes. Old Spantz was coming up from the rear, followed by his customer.

"Queer," thought the American. "She's changed her tactics rather suddenly. Smiled at me in the beginning and now cries a bit because I'm trying to return the compliment. Well, by the Lord Harry, she shan't scare me off like—Hello, Mr. Spantz! Good morning! I'm here for the sword."

The old man glared at him in unmistakable displeasure. Truxton began counting out his money. The customer, a swarthy fellow, passed out of the door, turning to glance intently at the young man. A meaning look and a sly nod passed between him and Spantz. The man halted at the corner below and, later on, followed King to Cook's office, afterward to the Castle gates, outside of which he waited until his quarry reappeared. Until King went to bed late that night this swarthy fellow was close at his heels, always keeping well out of sight himself.

"I'll come in soon to look at those rings," said King, placing the notes on the counter. Spantz merely nodded, raked in the bills without counting them, and passed the sword over to the purchaser.

"Very good, sir," he growled after a moment.

"I hate to carry this awful thing through the streets," said King, looking at the huge weapon with despairing eye. Inwardly, he was cursing himself for his extravagance and cupidity.

"It belongs to you, my friend. Take it or leave it."

"I'll take it," said Truxton, smiling indulgently. With that he picked up the weapon and stalked away.

A few minutes later he was on his way to the Castle grounds, accompanied by the short-legged Mr. Hobbs, who, from time to time, was forced to remove his tight-fitting cap to mop a hot, exasperated brow, so swift was the pace set by long-legs. The broadsword reposed calmly on a desk under the nose of a properly impressed young person named Stokes, cashier.

Hobbs led him through the great Park gates and up to the lodge of Jacob Fraasch, the venerable high steward of the grounds. Here, to King's utter disgust, he was booked as a plain Cook's tourist and mechanically advised to pay strict attention to the rules which would be explained to him by the guide.

"Cook's tourist, eh?" muttered King wrathfully as they ambled down the shady path together. He looked with disparaging eye upon the plain little chap beside him.

"It's no disgrace," growled Hobbs, redder than ever. "You're inside the grounds and you've got to obey the rules, same as any tourist. Right this way, sir; we'll take a turn just inside the wall. Now, on your left, ladies and—ahem!—I should say—ahem!—sir, you may see the first turret ever built on the wall. It is over four hundred years old. On the right, we have—"

"See here, Hobbs," said King, stopping short, "I'm damned if I'll let you lecture me as if I were a gang of hayseeds from Oklahoma."

"Very good, sir. No offence. I quite forgot, sir."

"Just *tell* me—don't lecture."

For three-quarters of an hour they wandered through the spacious grounds, never drawing closer to the Castle than permitted by the restrictions; always coming up to the broad driveway which marked the border line, never passing it. The gorgeous beauty of this historic old park, so full of traditions and the lore of centuries, wrought strange fancies and bold inclinations in the head of the audacious visitor. He felt the bonds of restraint; he resented the irksome chains of convention; he murmured against the laws that said he should not step across the granite road into the cool forbidden world beyond—the world of kings. Hobbs knew he was doomed to have rebellion on his hands before long; he could see it coming.

"When we've seen the royal stables, we'll have seen everything of any consequence," he hastened to say. "Then we'll leave by the upper gates and—"

"Hobbs, this is all very beautiful and very grand and very slow," said King, stopping to lean against the moss-covered wall that encircled the park within a park: the grounds adjoining the grotto. "Can't I hop over this wall and take a peep into the grotto?"

"By no means," cried Hobbs, horrified. "That, sir, is the most proscribed spot, next to the Castle itself. You *can't* go in there."

King looked over the low wall. The prospect was alluring. The pool, the trickling rivulets, the mossy banks, the dense shadows: it was maddening to think he could not enter!

"I wouldn't be in there a minute," he argued. "And I might catch a glimpse of a dream-lady. Now, I say, Hobbs, here's a low place. I could jump—"

"Mr. King, if you do that I am ruined forever. I am trusted by the steward. He would cut off all my privileges—" Hobbs could go no further. He was prematurely aghast. Something told him that Mr. King would hop over the wall.

"Just this once, Hobbs," pleaded his charge. "No one will know."

"For the love of Moses, sir, I—" Hobbs began to wail. Then he groaned in dismal horror. King had lightly vaulted the wall and was grinning back at him from the sacred precincts—from the playground of princesses.

"Go and report me, Hobbs, there's a good fellow. Tell the guards I wouldn't obey. That will let you out, my boy, and I'll do the rest. For Heaven's sake, Hobbs, don't burst! You'll explode sure if you hold in like that much longer. I'll be back in a minute."

He strode off across the bright green turf toward the source of all this enchantment, leaving poor Mr. Hobbs braced against the wall, weak-kneed and helpless. If he heard the frantic, though subdued, whistles and the agonized "hi!" of the man from Cook's a minute or two later, he gave no heed to the warning. A glimpse behind might have shown him the error of his ways, reflected in the disappearance of Hobbs's head below the top of the wall. But he was looking ahead, drinking in the forbidden beauties of this fascinating little nook of nature.

Never in all his wanderings had he looked upon a more inviting spot than this. He came to the edge of the deep blue pool, above which could be seen the entrance to the Grotto. Little rivulets danced down through the crannies in the rocks and leaped joyously into the tree-shaded pool. Below and to the right were the famed Basins of Venus, shimmering in the sunlight, flanked by trees and banks of the softest green. On their surface swam the great black swans he had heard so much about. Through a wide rift in the trees he could see the great, grey Castle, half a mile away, towering against the dense greens of the nearby mountain. The picture took his breath away. He forgot Hobbs. He forgot that he was; trespassing. Here, at last, was the Graustark he had seen in his dreams, had come to feel in his imagination.

Regardless of surroundings or consequences, he sat down upon the nearest stone bench, and removed his hat. He was hot and tired and the air was cool. He would drink it in as if it were an ambrosial nectar in— and, moreover, he would also enjoy a cigarette. Carefully he refrained from throwing the burnt-out match into the pool below: even such as he could feel that it might be desecration. As he leaned back with a sigh of exquisite ease and a splendid exhalation of Turkish smoke, a small, imperious voice from somewhere behind broke in upon his primary reflections.

"What are you doing in here?" demanded the voice.

Truxton, conscious of guilt, whirled with as much consternation as if he had been accosted by a voice of thunder. He beheld a very small boy standing at the top of the knoll above him, not thirty feet away. His face was quite as dirty as any small boy's should be at that time of day, and his curly brown hair looked as if it had not been combed since the day before. His firm little legs, in half hose and presumably white knickers, were spread apart and his hands were in his pockets.

King recognised him at once, and looked about uneasily for the attendants whom he knew should be near. It is safe to say that he came to his feet and bowed deeply, even in humility.

"I am resting, your Highness," he said meekly.

"Don't you know any better than to come in here?" demanded the Prince. Truxton turned very red.

"I am sorry. I'll go at once."

"Oh, I'm not going to put you out," hastily exclaimed the Prince, coming down the slope. "But you are old enough to know better. The guards might shoot you if they caught you here." He came quite close to the trespasser. King saw the scratch on his nose. "Oh, I know you now. You are the gentleman who picked up my crop yesterday. You are an American." A friendly smile illumined his face.

"Yes, a lonely American," with an attempt at the pathetic.

"Where's your home at?"

"New York. Quite a distance from here."

"You ever been in Central Park?"

"A thousand times. It isn't as nice as this one."

"It's got amilies—no, I don't mean that," supplemented the Prince, flushing painfully. "I mean—an-i-muls," very deliberately. "Our park has no elephunts or taggers. When I get big I'm going to set out a few in the park. They'll grow, all right."

"I've shot elephants and tigers in the jungle," said Truxton. "I tell you they're no fun when they get after you, wild. If I were you I'd set 'em out in cages."

"P'raps I will." The Prince seemed very thoughtful.

"Won't you sit down, your Highness?"

The youngster looked cautiously about. "Say, do you ever go fishing?" he demanded eagerly.

"Occasionally."

"You won't give me away, will you?" with a warning frown. "Don't you tell Jacob Fraasch. He's the steward. I—I know a fine place to fish. Would you mind coming along? Look out, please! You're awful big and they'll see you. I don't know what they'd do to us if they ketched us. It would be dreadful. Would you mind sneaking, mister? Make yourself little. Right up this way."

The Prince led the way up the bank, followed by the amused American, who stooped so admirably that the boy, looking back, whispered that it was "just fine." At the top of the knoll, the Prince turned into a little shrub-lined path leading down to the banks of the pool almost directly below the rocky face of the grotto.

"Don't be afraid," he whispered to his new friend. "It ain't very deep, if you should slip in. But you'd scare the fish away. Gee, it's a great place to catch 'em. They're all red, too. D'you ever see red fish?"

Truxton started. This was no place for him! The Prince had a right to poach on his own preserves, but a grown man to be caught in the act of landing the royal goldfish was not to be thought of. He hung back.

"I'm afraid I won't have time, your Highness. A friend is waiting for me back there. He—"

"It's right here," pleaded the Prince. "Please stop a moment. I—I don't know how to put the bait on the pin. I just want to catch a couple. They won't bite unless there's worms on the hook. I tried 'em. Look at 'em! Goodness, there's lots of 'em. Nobody can see us here. Please, mister, fix a worm for me."

The man sat down behind a bush and laughed joyously. The eager, appealing look in the lad's eyes went to his heart. What was a goldfish or two? A fish has no feeling—not even a goldfish. There was no resisting the boyish eagerness.

"Why, you're a real boy, after all. I thought being a prince might have spoiled you," he said.

"Uncle Jack says I can always be a prince, but I'll soon get over being a boy," said Prince Bobby sagely. "You *will* fix it, won't you?"

King nodded, conscienceless now. The Prince scurried behind a big rock and reappeared at once with a willow branch from the end of which dangled a piece of thread. A bent pin occupied the chief end in view. He unceremoniously shoved the branch into the hands of his confederate, and then produced from one of his pockets a silver cigarette box, which he gingerly opened to reveal to the gaze a conglomerate mass of angle worms and grubs.

"A fellow gets awful dirty digging for worms, doesn't he?" he pronounced.

"I should say so," agreed the big boy. "Whose cigarette case is this?"

"Uncle Caspar's—I mean Count Halfont's. He's got another, so he won't miss this one. I'm going to leave some worms in it when I put it back in his desk. He'll think the fairies did it. Do you believe in fairies?"

"Certainly, Peter," said Truxton, engaged in impaling a stubborn worm.

"My name isn't Peter," said the Prince coldly.

"I was thinking of Peter Pan. Ever hear of him?"

"No. Say, you mustn't talk or you'll scare 'em away. Is it fixed?" He took the branch and gingerly dropped the hook into the dancing pool. In less time than it requires to tell it he had a nibble, a bite and a catch. There never was a boy so excited as he when the scarlet nibbler flew into the shrubbery above; he gasped with glee. Truxton recovered the catch from the bushes and coolly detached the truculent pin.

"I'll have 'em for dinner," announced the Prince.

"Are you going to catch a mess?" queried the man, appalled.

"Sure," said Bobby, casting again with a resolute splash.

"Are you not afraid they'll get onto you if you take them to the Castle?" asked the other diplomatically. "Goldfish are a dead give-away."

"Nobody will scold 'cept Uncle Jack, and he won't know about it. He's prob'ly gone away by this time." King noticed that his lip trembled suddenly.

"Gone away?"

"Yes. He was banished this morning right after breakfast." The announcement began with a tremor but ended with imperial firmness.

"Great Scott!" gasped the other, genuinely shocked.

"I banished him," said the Prince ruefully. "But," with a fine smile, "I don't think he'll go. He never does. See my sign up there?" He pointed to the rocks near the grotto. "I did it with Hugo's shoe blacking."

A placard containing the important announcement, "NO FISHING ALOUD" stared down at the poachers from a tree trunk above. There was nothing very peremptory in its appearance, but its designer was sufficiently impressed by the craftiness it contained.

"I put it up so's people wouldn't think anybody—not even me—would dare to fish here. Oh, look!" The second of his ruddy mess was flopping in the grass. Again Truxton thought of Mr. Hobbs, this time with anxious glances in all directions.

"Where do they think you are, your Highness?"

"Out walking with my aunt. Only she met Count Vos Engo, and while they were talking I made a sneak—I mean, I stole away."

"Then they'll be searching for you in all parts of the—" began Truxton, coming to his feet. "I really must be going. Please excuse me, your—"

"Oh, don't go! I'll not let 'em do anything to you," said the Prince staunchly. "I like Americans better than anybody else," he went on with deft persuasiveness. "They ain't—aren't afraid of anything. They're not cowards."

Truxton sat down at once. He could not turn tail in the face of such an exalted opinion.

"I'm not supposed to ever go out alone," went on the Prince confidentially. "You see, they're going to blow me up if they get a chance."

"Blow you up?"

"Haven't you heard about it? With dynamite bums—bombs. Yes, sir! That's the way they do to all princes." He was quite unconcerned. Truxton's look of horror diminished. No doubt it was a subterfuge employed to secure princely obedience, very much as the common little boy is brought to time by mention of the ubiquitous bogie man.

"That's too bad," commiserated Truxton, baiting the pin once more.

"It's old Count Marlanx. He's going to blow me up. He hated my mother and my father, so I guess he hates me. He's turrible, Uncle Caspar says."

King was very thoughtful for a moment. Something vivid yet fleeting had shot through his brain—something that he tried to catch and analyse, but it was gone before he could grasp its significance. He looked with new interest upon this serene, lovable little chap, who was growing up, like all princes, in the shadow of disaster.

Suddenly the fisherman's quick little ears caught a sound that caused him to reveal a no-uncertain agitation. He dropped his rod incontinently and crawled to the opening in the shrubbery, peering with alarmed eyes down the path along the bank.

"What is it? A dynamiter?" demanded Truxton uneasily.

"Worse'n that," whispered his royal Highness. "It's Aunt Loraine. Gee!" To King's utter dismay, the Prince scuttled for the underbrush.

"Here!" he called in consternation. The Prince stopped, shamefaced on the instant. "I thought you were going to protect me."

"I shall," affirmed Bobby, manfully resuming his ground. "She's coming up the path. Don't run," he exclaimed scornfully, as Truxton started for the rocks. "She can't hurt you. She's only a girl."

"All right. I won't run," said the big culprit, who wished he had the power to fly.

"And there's Saffo and Cors over there watching us, too. We're caught. I'm sorry, mister."

On the opposite bank of the pool stood two rigid members of the Royal Guard, intently watching the fishers. King was somewhat disturbed by the fact that their rifles were in a position to be used at an instant's notice. He felt himself turning pale as he thought of what might have happened if he had taken to flight.

A young lady in a rajah silk gown, a flimsy panama hat tilted well over her nose, with a red feather that stood erect as if always in a state of surprise, turned the bushes and came to a stop almost at King's elbow. He had time to note, in his confusion, that she was about shoulder-high alongside him, and that she was staring up into his face with amazed grey eyes. Afterward he was to realise that she was amazingly pretty, that her teeth were very white and even, that her eyes were the most beautiful and expressive he had ever seen, that she was slender and imperious, and that there were dimples in her checks so fascinating that he could not gather sufficient strength of purpose to withdraw his gaze from them. Of course, he did not see them at the outset: she was not smiling, so how could he?

The Prince came to the rescue. "This is my Aunt Loraine, Mr.—Mr.—" he swallowed hard and looked helpless.

"King," supplied Truxton, "Truxton King, your Highness." Then with all the courage he could produce, he said to the beautiful lady: "I'm as guilty as he. See!" He pointed ruefully to the four goldfish, which he had strung upon wire grass and dropped into the edge of the pool.

She did not smile. Indeed, she gave him a very severe look. "How cruel!" she murmured. "Bobby, you deserve a sound spanking. You are a very naughty little boy." She spoke rapidly in French.

"He put the bait on," said Bobby, also in French. Here was treachery!

Truxton delivered himself of some French. "Oh, I say, your Highness, you said you'd pardon me if I were caught."

"I can't pardon you until you are found guilty," said the Prince in English.

"Please put those poor little things back in the pool, Mr. King," said the lady in perfect English.

"Gladly—with the Prince's permission," said King, also in English. The Prince looked glum, but interposed no imperial objection. Instead he suddenly shoved the cigarette box under the nose of his dainty relative, who at that unpropitious instant stooped over to watch King's awkward attempt to release the fishes.

"Look at the worms," said the Prince engagingly, opening the box with a snap.

"Oh!" cried the young lady, starting back. "Throw them away! the horned things!"

"Oh, they can't bite," scoffed the Prince. "See! I'm not afraid of 'em. Look at this one." He held up a wriggler and she fled to the rock. She happened to glance at Truxton's averted face and was conscious of a broad grin; whereupon she laughed in the quick staccato of embarrassment.

It must be confessed that King's composure was sorely disturbed. In the first place, he had been caught in a most reprehensible act, and in the second place, he was not quite sure that the Prince could save him from ignominious expulsion under the very eyes—and perhaps direction—of this trim and attractive member of the royal household. He found himself blundering foolishly with the fishes and wondering whether she was a duchess or just a plain countess. Even a regal personage might jump at the sight of angle worms, he reflected.

He glanced up, to find her studying him, plainly perplexed.

"I just wondered in here," he began guiltily. "The Prince captured me down there by the big tree."

"Did you say your name is Truxton King?" she asked somewhat sceptically.

"Yes, your—yes, ma'am," he replied. "Of New York."

"Your father is Mr. Emerson King? Are you the brother of Adele King?"

Truxton stared. "Have you been interviewing the police?" he asked before he thought.

"The police? What have you been doing?" she cried, her eyes narrowing.

"Most everything. The police know all about me. I'm a spotted character. I thought perhaps they had told you about me."

"I asked if you were Adele's brother."

"I am."

"I've heard her speak of her brother Truxton. She said you were in South America."

He stared the harder. Could he believe his ears?

She was regarding him with cool, speculative interest. "I wonder if you are he?"

"I think I am," he said, but doubtfully. "Please pardon my amazement. Perhaps I'm dreaming. At any rate, I'm dazed."

"We were in the convent together for two years. Now that I observe you closely, you *do* resemble her. We were very good friends, she and I."

"Then you'll intercede for me?" he urged, with a fervent glance in the direction of the wall.

She smiled joyously. He realised then and there that he had never seen such beautiful teeth, nor any creature so radiantly beautiful, for that matter.

"More than that," she said, "I shall assist you to escape. Come!"

He followed her through the shrubbery, his heart pounding violently. The Prince, who trotted on ahead, had mentioned a Count. Was she married? Was she of the royal blood? What extraordinary fate had made her the friend of his sister? He looked back and saw the two guardsmen crossing the bridge below, their eyes still upon him.

"It's very good of you," he said. She glanced back at him, a quaint smile in her eyes.

"For Adele's sake, if you please. Trespassing is a very serious offence here. How did you get in?"

"I hopped in, over the wall."

"I'd suggest that you do not hop out again. Hopping over the walls is not looked upon with favour by the guards."

He recalled the distressed Mr. Hobbs. "The man from Cook's tried to restrain me," he said in proper spirit. "He was very much upset."

"I dare say. You are a Cook's tourist, I see. How very interesting! Bobby, Uncle Jack is waiting to take you to see the trained dogs at the eastern gate."

The Prince gave a whoop of joy, but instantly regained his dignity.

"I can't go, auntie, until I've seen him safe outside the walls," he said firmly. "I said I would."

They came to the little gate and passed through, into a winding path that soon brought them to a wide, main-travelled avenue. A light broke in upon Truxton's mind. He had it! This was the wonderful Countess Marlanx! No sooner had he come to that decision than he was forced to abandon it. The Countess's name was Ingomede and she already had been pointed out to him.

"I suppose I shall have to recall Uncle Jack from exile," he heard the Prince saying to the beautiful lady. Truxton decided that she was not more than twenty-two. But they married very young in these queer old countries—especially if they happened to be princes or princesses. He wanted to talk, to ask questions, to proclaim his wonder, but discreetly resolved that it was best to hold his tongue. He was by no means sure of himself.

Be that as it may, he was filled with a strange rejoicing. Here was a woman with whom he was as sure to fall in love as he was sure that the sun shone. He liked the thought of it. Now he appreciated the distinction between the Olga Platanova type and that which represented the blood of kings. There *was* a difference! Here was the true Patrician!

The Castle suddenly loomed up before them—grey and frowning, not more than three hundred yards away. He was possessed of a wild desire to walk straight into the grim old place and proclaim himself the feudal owner, seizing everything as his own—particularly the young woman in the rajah silk. People were strolling in the shady grounds. He felt the instant infection of happy indolence, the call to luxury. Men in gay uniforms and men in cool flannels; women in the prettiest and daintiest of frocks—all basking in the playtime of life, unmindful of the toil that fell to the Sons of Martha out in the sordid world.

"Do you think you can find your man from Cook's?" she asked.

"Unless he has gone and jumped into the river, your—madam. In any event, I think I may safely find my way out. I shall not trouble you to go any farther. Thank you for overlooking my indiscretion. Thank you, my dear little Prince, for the happiest experience of my life. I shall never forget this hour." He looked boldly into her eyes, and not at the Prince. "Have you ever been in New York?" he asked abruptly.

He was not at all sure whether the look she gave him was one of astonishment or resentment. At any rate, it was a quick glance, followed by the palpable suppression of words that first came to her lips, and the substitution of a very polite:

"Yes, and I love it." He beamed. The smile that came into her eyes escaped him. If he could have seen it, his bewilderment; would have been sadly increased.

"Say!" whispered the Prince, dropping back as if to impart a grave secret. "See that man over there by the fountain, Mr. King?"

"Bobby!" cried the lady sharply. "Good-bye, Mr. King. Remember me to your sister when you write. She—"

"That's Aunt Loraine's beau," announced the Prince.

"That's Count Eric Vos Engo." Truxton's look turned to one of interest at once. The man designated was a slight, swarthy fellow in the uniform of a colonel. He did not appear to be particularly happy at the moment.

The American observed the lady's dainty ears. They had turned a delicate pink.

"May I ask who—" began Truxton timidly.

"She will know if you merely call me Loraine."

"So long," said the Prince.

They parted company at once, the Prince and the lady in the rajah silk going toward the Castle, King toward the gates, somewhat dazed and by no means sure of his senses. He came down to earth after he had marched along on air for some distance, so to speak, and found himself deciding that she was a duchess here, but Loraine at school. What a wonderful place a girl's school must be! And his sister knew her—knew a lady of high degree!

"Hobbs!" he called, catching sight of a dejected figure in front of the chief steward's door.

"Oh, it's you, is it?" said Mr. Hobbs sullenly.

"It is, Hobbs—very much me. I've been fishing with royalty and chatting with the nobility. Where the devil have *you* been?"

"I've been squaring it with old man Fraasch. I'm through with you, sir. No more for me, not if I know—"

"Come along, Hobbs," said the other blithely, taking Hobbs by the arm. "The Prince sent his love to you."

"Did he mention Cook's?" gasped Hobbs.

"He certainly did," lied Truxton. "He spoke of you most kindly. He wondered if you could find time to come around to-morrow."

CHAPTER V
THE COMMITTEE OF TEN

It has been said before that Truxton King was the unsuspecting object of interest to two sets of watchers. The fact that he was under the surveillance of the government police, is not surprising when we consider the evident thoroughness of that department; but that he should be continually watched by persons of a more sinister cast suggests a mystery which can be cleared up by visiting a certain underground room, scarce two blocks from the Tower of Graustark. It goes without saying that corporeal admittance to this room was not to be obtained easily. In fact, one must belong to a certain band of individuals; and, in order to belong to that band, one must have taken a very solemn pledge of eternal secrecy and a primal oath to devote his life to certain purposes, good or evil, according to his conscience. By means of the friendly Sesame that has opened the way for us to the gentler secrets, we are permitted to enter this forbidding apartment and listen in safety to the ugly business of the Committee of Ten.

There were two ways of reaching this windowless room, with its low ceilings and dank airs. If one had the secret in his possession, he could go down through the mysterious trap door in the workshop of William Spantz, armourer to the Crown; or he might come up through a hidden aperture in the walls of the great government sewer, which ran directly parallel with and far below the walls of the quaint old building. One could take his choice of direction in approaching this hole in the huge sewer: he could come up from the river, half a mile away, or he could come down from the hills above if he had the courage to drop through one of the intakes.

It is of special significance that the trap door in Spantz's workshop was reserved for use by the armourer and his more fastidious comrades—of whom three were women and one an established functionary in the Royal Household. One should not expect ladies to traverse a sewer if oilier ways are open to them. The manner of reaching the workshop was not so simple, however, as you might suppose. The street door was out of the question, with Dangloss on the watch, day and night. As much as can be said for the rear door. It was necessary, therefore, that the favored few should approach the shop by extraordinary paths. For instance, two of the women came through friendly but unknown doors in the basements of adjoining houses, reaching the workshop by the narrow stairs leading up from a cobwebby wine-cellar next door. Spantz and Olga Platanova, of course, were at home in the place. All of which may go to prove that while ten persons comprised the committee, at least as many more of the shopkeepers in that particular neighbourhood were in sympathy with their secret operations.

So cleverly were all these means of approach concealed and so stealthy the movements of the Committee, that the existence of this underground room, far below the street level, was as yet unsuspected by the police. More than that, the existence of the Committee of Ten as an organisation was unknown to the department, notwithstanding the fact that it had been working quietly, seriously for more than a year.

The Committee of Ten represented the brains and the activity of a rabid coterie in Edelweiss, among themselves styled the Party of Equals. In plain language, they were "Reds." Less than fifty persons in Graustark were affiliated with this particular community of anarchists. For more than a year they had been preparing themselves against the all-important hour for public declaration. Their ranks had been augmented by occasional recruits from other lands; their literature was circulated stealthily; their operations were as secret as the grave, so far as the outside world was concerned. And so the poison sprung up and thrived unhindered in the room below the street, growing in virulence and power under the very noses of the vaunted police of Edelweiss, slowly developing into a power that would some day assert itself with diabolical fury.

There were men and women from Axphain and Dawsbergen in this seed circle that made Edelweiss its spreading ground. They were Reds of the most dangerous type—silent, voiceless, crafty men and women who built well without noise, and who gave out nothing to the world from which they expected to take so much.

The nominal leader was William Spantz, he who had a son in the Prince's household, Julius Spantz, the Master-of-arms. Far off in the hills above the Danube there lived the real leader of this deadly group—the Iron Count Marlanx, exile from the land of his birth, hated and execrated by every loyal Graustarkian, hating and execrating in return with a tenfold greater venom. Marlanx, the man who had been driven from wealth and power by the sharp edict of Prince Robin's mother, the lamented Yetive, in the days of her most glorious reign,—this man, deep in his raging heart, was in complete accord with the desperate band of Reds who preached equality and planned disaster.

Olga Platanova was the latest acquisition to this select circle. A word concerning her: she was the daughter of Professor Platanova, one time oculist and sociologist in a large German University. He had been one of the most brilliant men in Europe and a member of a noble family. There was welcome for him in the homes of the nobility; he hobnobbed, so to speak, with the leading men of time Empire. The Platanova home in Warsaw was one of the most inviting and exclusive in that great, city. The professor's enthusiasm finally carried him from the conservative paths in which he had walked; after he had passed his fiftieth year he became an avowed leader among the anarchists and revolutionists in Poland, his native state. Less than a year before the opening of this tale he was executed for treason and conspiracy against the Empire.

His daughter, Olga, was recognised as one of the most beautiful and cultured young women in Warsaw. Her suitors seemed to be without number; nor were they confined to the student and untitled classes with whom she was naturally thrown by force of circumstance. More than one lordly adventurer in the lists of love paid homage to her grace and beauty. Finally there came one who conquered and was beloved. He was the son of a mighty duke, a prince of the blood.

It was true love for both of them. The young prince pledged himself to marry her, despite all opposition; he was ready to give up his noble inheritance for the sake of love. But there were other forces greater than a young man's love at work. The all-powerful ruler of an Empire learned of this proposed mesalliance and was horrified. Two weeks afterward the prince was called. The will of the Crown was made known to him and— he obeyed. Olga Platanova was cast aside but not forgotten. He became the husband of an unloved, scrawny lady of diadems. When the situation became more than he could bear he blew out his brains.

When Olga heard the news of his death she was not stricken by grief. She cried out her joy to a now cloudless sky, for he had justified the great love that had been theirs and would be theirs to the end of time.

From a passive believer in the doctrines of her father and his circle she became at once their most impassioned exponent. Over night she changed from a gentle-hearted girl into a woman whose breast flamed with a lust for vengeance against a class from which death alone could free her lover. She threw herself, heart and soul, into the deliberations and transactions of the great red circle: her father understood and yet was amazed.

Then he was put to death by the class she had come to hate. One more stone in the sepulchre of her tender, girlish ideals. When the time came she travelled to Graustark in response to the call of the Committee of Ten; she came prepared to kill the creature she would be asked to kill. And yet down in her heart she was sore afraid.

She was there, not to kill a man grown old in wrongs to her people, but to destroy the life of a gentle, innocent boy of seven!

There were times when her heart shrank from the unholy deed she had been selected to perform; she even prayed that death might come to her before the hour in which she was to do this execrable thing in behalf of the humanity she served. But there was never a thought of receding from the bloody task set down for her—a task so morbid, so horrid that even the most vicious of men gloated in the satisfaction that they had not been chosen in her place. Weeks before she came to Graustark Olga Platanova had been chosen by lot to be the one to do this diabolical murder. She did not flinch, but came resolute and ready. Even the men in the Committee of Ten looked upon the slender, dark-eyed girl with an awe that could not be conquered. She had not the manner of an assassin, and yet they knew that she would not draw back; she was as soft and as sweet as the Madonnas they secretly worshipped, and yet her heart was steeled to a purpose that appalled the fiercest of them.

On a Saturday night, following the last visit of Truxton King to the armourer, the Committee of Ten met in the underground room to hear the latest word from one who could not be with them in person, but was always there in spirit—if they were to believe his most zealous utterances. The Iron Count Marlanx, professed hater of all that was rich and noble, was the power behind the Committee of Ten. The assassination of the little Prince and the overthrow of the royal family awaited his pleasure: he was the man who would give the word.

Not until he was ready could anything be done, for Marlanx had promised to put the Committee of Ten in control of this pioneer community when it came under the dominion of anarchists.

Alas, for the Committee of Ten! The wiliest fox in the history of the world was never so wily as the Iron Count. Some day they were to find out that he was using them to pull his choicest chestnuts from the fire.

The Committee was seated around the long table in the stifling, breathless room, the armourer at the head. Those who came by way of the sewer had performed ablutions in the queer toilet room that once had been a secret vault for the storing of feudal plunder. What air there was came from the narrow ventilator that burrowed its ways up to the shop of William Spantz, or through the chimney-hole in the ceiling. Olga Platanova sat far down the side, a moody, inscrutable expression in her dark eyes. She sat silent and oppressed through all the acrid, bitter discussions which carried the conclave far past the midnight hour. In her heart she knew that these men and women were already thinking of her as a regicide. It was settled—it was ordained. At Spantz's right lounged Peter Brutus, a lawyer—formerly secretary to the Iron Count and now his sole representative among these people. He was a dark-faced, snaky-eyed young man, with a mop of coarse black hair that hung ominously low over his high, receding forehead. This man was the chosen villain among all the henchmen who came at the beck and call of the Iron Count.

Julius Spantz, the armourer's son, a placid young man of goodly physical proportions, sat next to Brutus, while down the table ranged others deep in the consideration of the world's gravest problems. One of the women was Madame Drovnask, whose husband had been sent to Siberia for life; and the other, Anna Cromer, a rabid Red lecturer, who had been driven from the United States, together with her amiable husband: an assassin of some distinction and many aliases, at present foreman in charge of one of the bridge-building crews on the new railroad.

Every man in the party, and there were eight, for Olga was not a member of the Ten, wore over the lower part of his face a false black beard of huge dimensions. Not that they were averse to recognition among themselves, but in the fear that by some hook or crook Dangloss or his agents might be able to look in upon them—through stone walls, as it were. They were not men to belittle the powers of the wonderful Baron.

As it sat in secret conclave, the Committee of Ten was a sinister-looking group.

Brutus was speaking. "The man is a spy. He has been brought here from America by Tullis. Sooner or later you will find that I am right."

"It is best to keep close watch on him," advised one of the men. "We know that he is in communication with the police and we know that he visits the Castle, despite his declaration that he knows no one there. To-day's experience proves that. I submit that the strictest caution be observed where he is concerned."

"We shall continue to watch his every movement," said William Spantz. "Time will tell. When we are positive that he is a detective and that he is dangerous, there is a way to stop his operations."

His son grinned amiably as he swept his finger across his throat. The old man nodded.

"Dangloss suspects more than one of us" ventured Brutus, his gaze travelling toward Olga. There was lewd admiration in that steady glance. "But we'll fool the old fox. The time will soon be here for the blow that frees

Graustark from the yoke. She will be the pioneer among our estates, we the first of the individuals in equality; here the home seat of perfect rulership. There is nothing that can stop us. Have we not the most powerful of friends? Who is greater and shrewder than Count Marlanx? Who could have planned and perfected an organization so splendid? Will any one dispute this?"

He had the floor, and having the floor means everything to a Red. For half an hour he spoke with impassioned fervour, descanting furiously on the amazing virtues of his wily master and the plans he had arranged. It appeared in the course of his remarks that Marlanx had friends and supporters in all parts of Graustark. Hundreds of men in the hills, including honest shepherds and the dishonest brigands who thrived on them, coal miners and wood stealers, hunters and outlaws were ready to do his bidding when the time was ripe. Moreover, Marlanx had been successful in his design to fill the railway construction crews with the riff-raff of all Europe, all of whom were under the control of leaders who could sway them in any movement, provided it was against law and order. As a matter of fact, according to Brutus, nearly a thousand aliens were at work on the road, all of them ready to revolt the instant the command was given by their advisers.

Something that the Committee of Ten did not know was this: those alien workmen were no less than so many hired mercenaries in the employ of the Iron Count, brought together by that leader and his agents for the sole purpose of overthrowing the Crown in one sudden, unexpected attack, whereupon Count Marlanx would step in and assume control of the government. They had been collected from all parts of the world to do the bidding of this despised nobleman, no matter to what lengths he might choose to lead them. Brutus, of course, knew all this: his companions on the Committee were in complete ignorance of the true motives that brought Marlanx into their operations.

With a cunning that commands admiration, the Iron Count deliberately sanctioned the assassination of the little Prince by the Reds, knowing that the condemnation of the world would fall upon them instead of upon him, and that his own actions following the regicide would at once stamp him as irrevocably opposed to anarchy and all of its practices!

In the course of his remarks, Peter Brutus touched hastily upon the subject of the little Prince.

"He's not very big," said he, with a laugh, "and it won't require a very big bomb to blow him to smithereens. He will—"

"Stop!" cried Olga Platanova, springing to her feet and glaring at him with dilated eyes. "I cannot listen to you! You shall not speak of it in that way! Peter Brutus, you are not to speak of—of what I am to do! Never—never again!"

They looked at her in amazement and no little concern. Madame Drovnask was the first to speak, her glittering eyes fastened upon the drawn, white face of the girl across the table.

"Are you going to fail? Are you weakening?" she demanded.

"No! I am not going to fail! But I will not permit any one to jest about the thing I am to do. It is a sacred duty with me. But, Madame Drovnask—all of you, listen—it is a cruel, diabolical thing, just the same. Were it not in behalf of our great humanity, I, myself, should call it the blackest piece of cruelty the world has ever known. The slaughter of a little boy! A dear, innocent little boy! I can see the horror in all of your faces! You shudder as you sit there, thinking of the thing I am to do. Yes, you are secretly despising me, your instrument of death! I—I, a girl, I am to cast the bomb that blows this dear little body to pieces. I! Do you know what that means? Even though I am sure to be blown to pieces by the same agent, the last thing I shall look upon is his dear, terrified little face as he watches me hurl the bomb. Ah!"

She shuddered violently as she stood there before them, her eyes closed as if to shut out the horrible picture her mind was painting. There were other white faces and ice-cold veins about the table. The sneer on Anna Cromer's face deepened.

"She will bungle it," came in an angry hiss from her lips.

Olga's lids were lifted. Her dark eyes looked straight into those of the older woman.

"No," she said quietly, her body relaxing, "I shall not bungle it."

William Spantz had been watching her narrowly, even suspiciously. Now his face cleared.

"She will not fail," he announced calmly. "Let there be no apprehension. She is the daughter of a martyr. Her blood is his. It will flow in the same cause. Sit down, Olga, my dear. We will not touch upon this subject again—until—"

"I know, uncle," she said quietly, resuming her seat and her attitude of indifference.

The discussion went back to Truxton King. "Isn't it possible that he is merely attracted by the beauty of our charming young friend here?" ventured Madame Drovnask, after many opinions had been advanced respecting his interest in the shop and its contents. "It is a habit with Americans, I am told."

"Miss Platanova is most worthy of the notice of any man," agreed Brutus, with an amiable leer. Olga seemed to shrink within herself. It was plain that she was not a kindred spirit to these vicious natures.

"It is part of his game," said Julius Spantz. "He knows Olga's past; he is waiting for a chance to catch her off her guard. He may even go so far as to make pretty love to you, cousin, in the hope that—no offence, my dear, no offence!" Her look had silenced him.

"Mr. King is not a spy," she said steadily.

"Well," concluded William Spantz, "we are safe if we take no chances with him. He must be watched all the time. If we discover that he is what some of us think he is, there is a way to end his usefulness."

"Let him keep away from the shop downstairs," said Peter Brutus, with a sidelong glance at the delicate profile of the girl down the table.

She smiled suddenly, to the amazement of her sinister companions.

"Have no fear, Brutus. When he hears that you object, he will be very polite and give us a wide berth," she said. Peter flushed angrily.

"He doesn't mean any good by you," he snapped. "He'll fool you and—poof! Away he goes, rejoicing."

She still smiled. "You have a very good opinion of me, Peter Brutus."

"Well," doggedly, "you know what men of his type think of shopgirls. They consider them legitimate prey."

"And what, pray, do men of your type think of us?" she asked quietly.

"Enough of this," interposed William Spantz. "Now, Brutus, what does Count Marlanx say to this day two weeks? Will he be ready? On that day the Prince and the Court are to witness the unveiling of the Yetive memorial statue in the Plaza. It is a full holiday in Graustark. No man will be employed at his usual task and—"

Brutus interrupted him. "That is the very day that the Count has asked me to submit to the Committee. He believes it to be the day of all days. Nothing should go amiss. We conquer with a single blow. By noon of that day, the 26th of July, the Committee of Ten will be in control of the State; the new regime will be at hand. A new world will be begun, with Edelweiss as the centre, about which all the rest shall revolve. We—the Committee of Ten—will be its true founders. We shall be glorified forever—"

"We've heard all this before, Brutus," said Julius Spantz unfeelingly, "a hundred times. It's talk, talk, talk! What we need now is action. Are we sure that the Count will be prepared to do all that he says he will on the 26th of July? Will he have his plans perfected? Are his forces ready for the stroke?"

"Positively. They await the word. That's all I can say," growled Peter. "The death of the Prince is the signal for the overthrow of the present government and the establishment of the new order of equal humanity."

"After all," mused Julius, Master-at-arms in the Castle, "it is more humane to slay the Prince while he is young. It saves him from a long life of trouble and fear and the constant dread of the very thing that is to happen to him now. Yes, it is best that it should come soon." Down in his heart, Julius loved the little Prince.

For an hour longer the Committee discussed plans for the eventful day. Certain details were left for future deliberations; each person had his part to play and each one was settled in his or her determination that nothing should go amiss.

The man they feared was Dangloss. They did not fear God!

When they dispersed for the night, it was to meet again three days hence for the final word from Marlanx, who, it seems, was not so far away that communication with him was likely to be delayed. A sword hung over the head of Truxton King, an innocent outsider, and there was a prospect that it would fall in advance of the blow that was intended to startle the world. Olga Platanova was the only one who did not look upon the sprightly American as a spy in the employ of the government—a dangerously clever spy at that.

Up in the distant hills slept the Iron Count, dreaming of the day when he should rule over the new Graustark—for he would rule!—a smile on his grizzled face in reflection of recent waking thoughts concerning the punishment that should fall swiftly upon the assassins of the beloved Prince Robin.

He would make short shrift of assassins!

CHAPTER VI
INGOMEDE THE BEAUTIFUL

A light, chilling drizzle had been falling all evening, pattering softly upon the roof of leaves that covered the sidewalks along Castle Avenue, glistening on the lamp-lit pavements and blowing ever so gently in the faces of those who walked in the dripping shades. Far back from the shimmering sidewalks, surrounded by the blackest of shadows, and approached by hedge-bordered paths and driveways, stood the mansions occupied by the nobility of this gay little kingdom. A score or more of ancient palaces, in which the spirit, of modern aggression had wrought interior changes but had left the exteriors untouched, formed this aristocratic line of homes. Here were houses that had been built in the fifteenth century,—great, square, solemn-looking structures, grown grey and green with age.

There were lights in a thousand windows along this misty, royal road — lights that reflected the pleasures of the rich and yet caused no envy in time hearts of the loyal poor.

Almost in the centre of the imposing line stood the home of the Duke of Perse, Minister of Finance, flanked on either side by structures as grim and as gay as itself, yet far less significant in their generation. Here dwelt the most important man in the principality, not excepting the devoted prime minister himself. Not that Perse was so well beloved, but that he held the destinies of the land in Midas-like fingers. More than that, he was the father of the far-famed Countess Marlanx, the most glorious beauty at the Austrian and Russian courts. She had gone forth from Graustark as its most notable bride since the wedding day of the Princess Yetive, late in the nineties. Ingomede, the beautiful, had journeyed far to the hymeneal altar; the husband who claimed her was a hated, dishonoured man in his own land. They were married in Buda Pesth. All Europe pitied her at the time; there was but one form of prophecy as to her future. There were those who went so far as to say that her father had delivered her into the hands of a latter-day Bluebeard, who whisked her off into the highlands many leagues from Vienna.

She was seen no more in the gay courts for a year. Then, of a sudden, she appeared before them all, as dazzlingly beautiful as ever, but with a haunting, wistful look in her dark eyes that could not be mistaken. The old Count found an uneasy delight in exhibiting her to the world once more, plainly as a bit of property that all men were expected to look upon with envy in their hearts. She came up out of the sombre hills, freed from what must have been nothing less than captivity in that once feudal castle, to prove to his world that she thrived in spite of prophetic babblers. They danced from court to court, grotesquely mis-mated, deceiving no one as to the true relations that existed between them. She despised him without concealment; he took pride in showing that he could best resent her attitude by the most scrupulous devotion, so marked that its intent could not be mistaken.

Then the Duke of Perse resumed his residence in Edelweiss, opening the old palace once more to the world. His daughter, after the death of the Princess, began her extended visits to the home of her girlhood. So long as the Princess was alive she remained away from Edelweiss, reluctant to meet the friend who had banished her husband long before the wedding day in Buda Pesth. Now she came frequently and stayed for weeks at a time, apparently happy during these escapes from life in the great capitals. Here, at least, she was free from the grim old man whose countess she was; here, all was sweet and warm and friendly, delicious contrast to the cold, bitter life she knew on the Danube.

Without warning she came and without farewells she left Edelweiss on the occasion of these periodical visits. No word was ever spoken concerning her husband, except on the rare occasions when she opened her heart to the father who had bartered her into slavery for the sake of certain social franchises that the Iron Count had at his disposal. The outside world, which loved her, never heard of these bitter passages between father and child. Like Cinderella, she sometimes disappeared from joyous things at midnight; the next heard of her, she was in Vienna, or at Schloss Marlanx.

If the Duke of Perse repented of his bargain in giving his daughter to the Iron Count, he was never known to intimate as much. He loved Ingomede in his own, hard way. No doubt he was sorry for her. It is a fact that she was sorry for him. She could read his bitter thoughts more clearly than he suspected.

Of late she came more frequently to Edelweiss than before. She was seen often at the Castle; no court function was complete without the presence of this lovely noblewoman; no *salon* worth while unless graced by her wit and her beauty.

John Tullis was always to remember the moment when he looked upon this exquisite creature for the first time. That was months ago. After that he never ceased being a secret, silent worshipper at her transient shrine.

Ten o'clock on this rainy night: A carriage has drawn up before the lower gates to the Perse grounds, and a tall, shadowy figure leaves it to hurry through the shrub lined walks to the massive doors. A watchman in the garden salutes him. The tall figure dips his umbrella in response, characteristically laconic. A footman lifts his hand to his forelock at the top of the steps and throws open the doors without question. This visitor is expected, it is plain to be seen; a circumstance which may or may not explain the nervousness that attends him as he crosses the broad hall toward the library.

Tullis had long since ceased to be a welcome visitor in the home of the Duke of Perse. The men were openly unfriendly to each other. The Duke resented the cool interference of the sandy-haired American; on the other hand, Tullis made no effort to conceal his dislike, if not distrust, of the older man. He argued—with unofficial and somewhat personal authority,—that a man who could trade his only child for selfish ends might also be impelled to sacrifice his country's interests without cramping his conscience.

The Countess was alone in the long, warm-tinted library. She stood before the dying embers in the huge old fireplace, her foot upon one of the great iron dogs. Her smiling face was turned toward the door as he entered.

"It is good of you to come," she said, as they shook hands warmly. "Do you know it is almost a year since you last came to this house?"

"It would be a century, Countess, if I were not welcomed in other houses where I am sure of a glimpse of you from time to time and a word now and then. Still, a year's a year. The room hasn't changed so far as I can see. The same old tiger-skin there, the rugs, the books, the pictures—the leopard's skin here and the—yes, the lamp is just where it used to be. 'Pon my soul, I believe you are standing just as you were when I last saw you here. It's uncanny. One might think you had not moved in all these months!"

"Or that it has been a minute instead of a year," she supplemented. His quick, involuntary glance about him did not escape her understanding. "The Duke has gone to Ganlook to play Bridge with friends," she said at once. "He will not return till late. I have just telephoned—to make sure." Her smile did more than to reassure him.

"Of course, you will understand how impossible it is for me to come here, Countess. Your father, the Duke, doesn't mince matters, and I'm not quite a fool." Tullis squinted at the fire.

"Are you quite serious?"

"Quite. I could not have asked you to come to this house for anything trivial. We have become very good friends, you and I. Too good, perhaps, for I've no doubt there are old tabbies in Edelweiss who are provoked to criticism — you know what I mean. Their world is full of imaginary affairs, else what would there be left for old age? But we are good friends and we understand why we are good friends, so there's the end to that. As I say, I could not have asked so true a friend into the house of his enemy for the mere sake of having my vanity pleased by his obedience."

"I am quite sure of that," he said. "Are you in trouble, Countess? Is there anything I can do?"

"It has to do with the Prince, not with me," she said. "And yet I am in trouble — or perhaps I should say, I am troubled."

"The Prince is a sturdy little beggar," he began, but she lifted her hand in protest.

"And he has sturdy, loyal friends. That is agreed. And yet—" she paused, a perplexed line coming between her expressive eyes.

John Tullis opened his own eyes very wide. "You don't mean to say that he is — he is in peril of any sort?"

She looked at him a long time before speaking. He could feel that she was turning something over in her mind before giving utterance to the thought.

At last she leaned nearer to him, dropping the ash from her cigarette into the receiver as she spoke slowly, intensely. "I think he is in peril — in deadly peril."

He stared hard. "What do you mean?" he demanded, with an involuntary glance over his shoulder. She interpreted that glance correctly.

"The peril is not here, Mr. Tullis. I know what you are thinking. My father is a loyal subject. The peril I suggest never comes to Graustark."

She said no more but leaned forward, her face whiter than its wont. He frowned, but it was the effect of temporary perplexity. Gradually the meaning of her simple, though significant remark filtered through his brain.

"Never comes to Graustark?" he almost whispered. "You don't — you can't mean your — your husband?"

"I mean Count Marlanx," she said steadily.

"He means evil to Prince Robin? Good Heavens, Countess, I — I can't believe it. I know he is bitter, revengeful, and all that, but—"

"Do you think ill of me for asking you to come to-night?"

"Not at all," he said cheerfully, "so long as you are quite sure that your father is in Ganlook. He would be perfectly justified in kicking me out if he were to catch me here. And as I'm rather cumbersome and he's somewhat venerable, I don't like to think of the jar it would be to his system. But, so long as he isn't here, and I am, why shouldn't I draw up a chair before the fire for you, and another for myself, with the cigarettes and a world between us, to discuss conditions as they are, not as they might be if we were discovered? Shall I? Good! I defy any one's father to get me out of this chair until I am ready to relinquish it voluntarily."

"I suppose you superintended the 'going-to-bed' of Prince Robin before you left the Castle?" she said, lying back in the comfortable chair and stretching her feet out to the fire. He handed her a match and watched her light the long, ridiculously thin cigarette.

"Yes. I never miss it, Countess. The last thing he does, after saying his prayers, is to recall me from exile. He wouldn't be happy if he couldn't do that. He says amen and hops into bed. Then he grins in a far from imperial way and announces that he's willing to give me another chance, and please won't I tell him the latest news concerning Jack-the-giant-killer. He asked me to-night if I thought you'd mind if he banished your father. They've had a children's quarrel, I believe. If you do mind, I am to let him know: he won't banish him. He's very fond of you, Countess." She laughed gaily.

"He is a dear boy. I adore him. I think I quite understand why you are giving up your life to him. At first I wasn't sure."

"You thought I expected to gain something by it, is not that so? Well, there are a great many people who think so still—your father among them. They'll never understand. I don't blame them, for, I declare to you, I don't fully appreciate it myself. John Tullis playing nurse and story-teller to a seven-year-old boy, to the exclusion of everything else, is more than I can grasp. Somehow, I've come to feel that he's mine. That must be the reason. But you've heard me prate on this subject a hundred times. Don't let me start it again. There's something else you want to talk to me about, so please don't encourage me to tell all the wonderful things he has said and done to-day."

"It is of the Prince that I want to speak, Mr. Tullis," she said, suddenly serious. "I don't care to hear whether he stubbed his toe to-day or just how much he has grown since yesterday, but I do want to talk very seriously with you concerning his future—I might say his immediate future."

He looked at her narrowly.

"He is all that and more," she said. "First, you must let me impress you that I am not a traitor to his cause. I could not be that, for the sufficient reason that I only suspect its existence. I am not in any sense a part of it. I do not *know* anything. I only feel. I dare say you realise that I do not love Count Marlanx—that there is absolutely nothing in common between us except a name. We won't go into that. I—"

"I am overjoyed to hear you say this, Countess," he said very seriously. "I have been so bold on occasion as to assert—for your private ear, of course—that you could not, by any freak of nature, happen to care for Count Marlanx, whom I know only by description. You have laughed at my so-called American wit, and you have been most tolerant. Now, I feel that I am justified. I'm immeasurably glad to hear you confess that you do not love your husband."

"I cannot imagine any one so stupid as to think that I do love Count Marlanx, for that matter, that he loves me. Still, I am relieved to hear you say that you are glad. It simplifies the present for us, and that is what we are to discuss."

"You are very, very beautiful, and young, and unhappy," he said irrelevantly, a darker glow in his cheeks. She smiled serenely, without a trace of diffidence or protest.

"I can almost believe it, you say it so convincingly," she said. For a moment she relaxed luxuriantly into an attitude of physical enjoyment of herself, surveying her toe-tips with a thoughtfulness that comprehended more; and then as abruptly came back to the business of the moment. "You must not spoil it all by saying it too fervently," she went on with a smile of warning. He gave a short laugh of confusion and sank back in the chair.

"You have never tried to make love to me," she went on. "That's what I like about you. I think most men are silly, not because I am so very young, but because my husband is so ridiculously old. Don't you think so? But, never mind! I see you are quite eager to answer—that's enough. Take another cigarette and—listen to what I am going to say." He declined the cigarette with a shake of his head.

After a moment she went on resolutely: "As I said before, I do not know that my suspicions are correct. I have not even breathed them to my father. He would have laughed at me. My husband is a Graustarkian, even as I am, but there is this distinction between us: he despises Graustark, while I love her in every drop of my blood. I know that in his heart he has never ceased to brew evil for the throne that disgraced him. He openly expresses his hatred for the present dynasty, and has more than once said in public gatherings that he could cheerfully assist in its utter destruction. That, of course, is commonly known in Graustark, where he is scorned and derided. But he is not a man to serve his hatred with mere idle words and inaction." She stopped for a moment, and then cried impulsively: "I must first know that you will not consider me base and disloyal in saying these things to you. After all, he is my husband."

He saw the faint curl of her lip. "Before that," he argued simply, "you were a daughter of Graustark. You were not born to serve a cause that means evil to the dear land. Graustark first made you noble; you can't go back on that, you know. Don't let your husband degrade you. I think you can see how I feel about it. Please believe that I know you can do no wrong."

"You are the only man to whom I feel sure that I can reveal myself and be quite understood."

"Thank you," she said, returning the look in his earnest grey eyes with one in which the utmost confidence shone. "You are the only man to whom I feel sure that I can reveal myself and be quite understood. It isn't as if I had positive facts to divulge, for I have not; they are suspicions, fears, that's all, but they are no longer vague shapes to me; they mean something."

"Tell me," he said quietly. He seemed to square his broad shoulders and to set his jaw firmly, as if to resist physical attack. She knew she had come with her fears to a man in whose face it was declared that he could laugh at substance as well as shadow.

"I am seeing you here in this big room, openly, for the simple reason that if I am being watched this manner of meeting may be above suspicion. We may speak freely here, for we cannot be heard unless we raise our voices. Don't betray surprise or consternation. The eyes of the wall may be better than its ears."

"You don't mean to say you are being watched here in your father's house?" he demanded.

"I don't know. This I do know: the Count has many spies in Edelweiss. He is systematically apprised of everything that occurs at court, in the city, or in the council chamber. So you see, he is being well served, whether to an evil purpose or to satisfy his own innate curiosity, I do not know. He has reports almost daily,—voluminous things, partly in cipher, partly free, and he is forever sending men away on secret, mysterious missions. Understand, I do not know that he is actually planning disaster to Graustark. Day before yesterday I saw his secretary in the streets—a man who has been in his employ for five years or more and who now pretends to be a lawyer here. His name is Brutus. I spoke with him. He said that he had left the Count six weeks ago in Vienna, determined to set out for himself in his chosen profession. He knows, of course, that I am not and never have been in the confidences of my husband. I asked him if it was known in Edelweiss that he had served the Count as secretary. He promptly handed me one of his business cards, on which he refers to himself as the former trusted and confidential secretary of Count Marlanx. Now, I happen to know that he is still in my husband's service,—or was no longer ago than last week."

"My dear Countess, he may be serving him legitimately as an attorney. There would be nothing strange in that."

"But he is still serving him as confidential secretary. He is here for a purpose, as my husband's representative. I have not been asleep all these months at Schloss Marlanx. I have seen and heard enough to convince me that some great movement is on foot. My intelligence tells me that it has to do with Graustark. As he wishes the Prince no good, it must be for evil."
"But there is nothing he can do. He has no following here. The Prince is adored by the people. Count Marlanx would not be such a fool as to—"

"He is no fool," she interrupted quickly. "That's why I am afraid. If he is plotting against the Crown, you may depend upon it he is laying his plans well. John Tullis, that man is a devil—a devil incarnate." She turned her face away.

A spasm of utter repugnance crossed her face; she shuddered so violently that his hand went forth to clutch the fingers that trembled on the arm of the chair. He held them in his firm grasp for a moment. They looked into each other's eyes and he saw the flicker of undisguised horror in hers. An instant later she was herself again. Withdrawing her hand, she added, with a short laugh of derision: "Still I did not expect heaven, so why complain."

"But you are an angel," he blurted out.

"I don't believe the Count will agree to that," she said, with a reflective twinkle in her dark eyes. "He has not found me especially angelic. If you imagine that I cannot scratch back, my dear friend, you are very much mistaken. I have had the pleasure of giving him more than one bad half hour. You may be sure he has never called me an angel. Quite the other thing, I assure you. But we are straying from the point."

"Wait a moment, please," he commanded. "I want to say to you here and now: you are the gentlest, loveliest woman I have ever known. I don't say it idly. I mean it. If you gave him half as good as he sent, I rejoice in your spirit. Now, I want to ask if you expect to go back to live with the da—with him."

"That, Mr. Tullis, is hardly a matter I can discuss with you," she said gently, and he was not offended.

"Perhaps not, Countess, but now is the time for you to decide the issue. Why should you return to Castle Marlanx? Why keep up the farce—or I might say, tragedy—any longer? You love Graustark. You love the Prince. You betray them both by consorting with their harshest foe. Oh, I could tell you a thousand reasons why—"

"We haven't time for them," she interrupted, with mock despair in her face. "Besides, I said we cannot discuss it. It requires no learned argument to move me, one way or the other. I can decide for myself."

"You should divorce him," he said harshly.

She laughed easily, softly. "My good friend, if I did that, I'd lose your friendship." He opened his lips to remonstrate, but suddenly caught the undercurrent of the naive remark.

"By Jove," he said, his eyes glowing, "you must not risk finding me too obtuse."

"Bravo!" she cried. "You are improving."

"I could provide a splendid substitute for the friendship you speak of," he said coolly.

"Poof! What is that to me? I could have a hundred lovers—but, ach, friends are the scarcest things in the world. I prefer friendship. It lasts. There! I see disapproval in your face! You Americans are so literal." She gazed into the fireplace for a moment, her lips parted in a whimsical smile. He waited for her to go on; the words were on her tongue's end, he could tell. "A divorce at twenty-five. I believe that is the accepted age, isn't it? If one gets beyond that, she—but, enough of this!" She sprang to her feet and stood before him, the flash dying in her eyes even as it was born that he might see so briefly. "We diverge! You must go soon. It is best not to be seen leaving here at a very late hour—especially as my father is known to be away. I am afraid of Peter Brutus. He is here to watch—*everybody*."

She was leaning against the great carved mantel post, a tall, slender, lissome creature, exquisitely gowned in rarest Irish lace, her bare neck and shoulders gleaming white against the dull timbers beyond, the faint glow from the embers creeping up to her face with the insistence of a maiden's flush. He gazed in rapt admiration, his heart thumping like fury in his great breast. She was little more than a girl, this wife of old Marlanx, and yet how wise, how clever, how brilliant she was!

A face of unusual pallor and extremely patrician in its modelling, surmounted by a coiffure so black that it could be compared only to ebony—black and almost gleaming with the life that was in it. It came low on her forehead, shading the wondrous dark eyes—eyes that were a deep yellowish green in their division between grey and black, eyes that were soft and luminous and unwaveringly steadfast, impelling in their power to fascinate, yet even more dangerously compassionate when put to the test that tries woman's vanity.

There were diamonds on her long, tapering fingers, and a rope of pearls in her hair. A single wide gold band encircled her arm above the elbow, an arm-band as old as the principality itself, for it had been worn by twenty fair ancestors before her. The noblewomen of Graustark never wore bracelets on their wrists; always the wide chased gold band on the upper arm. There was a day, not so far back in history, when they wore bands on their ankles.

She was well named Ingomede, the Beautiful.

A soft, almost imperceptible perfume, languorous in its appeal to the senses, exuded from this perfect creation; added to this, the subtle, unfailing scent of young womanhood; the warm, alive feel of her presence in the atmosphere; a suggestion of something sensuous, clean, pure, delicious. The undescribable.

"Does Baron Dangloss know this man Brutus?" asked Tullis, arising to stand beside her. A sub-conscious, triumphant thrill shot through him as an instantaneous flash of his own physical superiority over this girl's husband came over him. He was young and strong and vital. He could feel the sensation of being strong; he tingled with the glory of it. He was thirty-five, Marlanx seventy. He wondered if Marlanx had ever been as strong as he.

"I don't know," she said thoughtfully. "I have not spoken to him concerning Brutus. Perhaps he knows. The Baron is very wise. Let me tell you how I happen to know that Peter Brutus is still serving Count Marlanx and why I think his presence signifies a crisis of some sort." Tullis stood facing the great fireplace, his back to the hail. He observed that she looked toward the doors quite as often as she looked at him; it struck him that she was extremely cautious despite her apparent ease.

Her voice, always low and even, second lower still. "In the first place, I have a faithful friend in one of the oldest retainers at Schloss Marlanx. His daughter is my maid. She is here with me now. The old man came to see Josepha one day last week. He had accompanied Count Marlanx to the town of Balak, which is in Axphain, a mile beyond the Graustark line. Peter Brutus was with my husband in Balak for two days. They were closeted together from morning till night in the house where Marlanx was stopping. At the end of two days Brutus went away, but he carried with him a vast sum of money provided by my husband. It was given out that he was on his way to Serros in Dawsbergen, where he expected to purchase a business block for his master. Marlanx waited another day in Balak, permitting Josepha's father to come on to Edelweiss with a message for me and to see his daughter. He—"

"And Josepha's father saw Brutus in Edelweiss?"

"No. But he did see him going into Balak as he left for Edelweiss that morning. He wore a disguise, but Jacob says he could not be mistaken. Moreover, he was accompanied by several men whom he recognised as Graustark mountaineers and hunters of rather unsavoury reputation. They left Brutus at the gates of Balak and went off into the hills. All this happened before I knew that Peter was living in Edelweiss. When I saw him here, I knew at once that his presence meant something sinister. I can put many things together that once puzzled me—the comings and goings of months, the secret reports and consultations, the queer looking men who came to the Castle, the long absences of my husband and my—my own virtual imprisonment—yes, imprisonment. I was not permitted to leave the castle for days at a time during his absences."

"Surely you will not go back again"—he began hotly.

"Sh!" She put a finger to her lips. A man-servant was quietly crossing the hall just off the library. "He is a new man. I do not like his appearance."

"Do you think he heard us or observed anything? I can make short work of him if—" He paused significantly. She smiled up into his face.

"He did not hear anything. We've frightened him off, if he intended to play the eavesdropper." The servant had disappeared through a door at the end of the hall.

"Then there were the great sums of money that my husband sent off from time to time, and the strange boxes that came overland to the castle and later went away again as secretly as they came. Mr. Tullis, I am confident in my mind that those boxes contained firearms and ammunition. I have thought it all out. Perhaps I am wrong, but it seems to me that I can almost see those firearms stored away in the caves and cabins outside of Edelweiss, ready for instant use when the signal comes."

"God! An uprising? A plot so huge as that?" he gasped, amazed. It is fortunate that he was not facing the door; the same servant, passing once more, might have seen the tell-tale consternation in his eyes. "It cannot be possible! Why, Dangloss and his men would have scented it long ago."

"I have not said that I am sure of anything, remember that. I leave it to you to analyse. You have the foundation on which to work. I'd advise you to waste no time. Something tells me that the crisis is near at hand."

"Why should Josepha's father tell these things to you?"

"Because, if you will pardon my frankness, I have protected his daughter against Count Marlanx. He understands. And yet he would not betray a trust imposed upon him even by the Count. He has only told me what any one else might have seen with his own eyes. Wait! The new servant is in the hall again." She clapped her hands sharply and called out "Franz!"

The new man appeared in the doorway almost on the instant. "You may replenish the fire, Franz." The man, a sallow, precise fellow, crossed deliberately and poked the half dead fire; with scrupulous care he selected two great chunks of wood from the hopper near by and laid them on the coals, the others watching his movements with curious interest. There was nothing about the fellow to indicate that he was other than what he pretended to be.

"Isn't it strange that we should have fires in July?" she asked casually. "The mountain air and the night fogs make it absolutely necessary in these big old houses."

"We had a jolly fire in the Prince's room when I left the Castle. Our monarch is subject to croup, you see."

"That is all, Franz." The man bowed and left the room. "What do you think of him?" she asked, after a moment.

"He has a very bad liver," was all Tullis deigned to offer in response. The Countess stared for a moment and then laughed understandingly. "I think he needs a change."

"I have a strange feeling that he is but one of a great many men who are in Edelweiss for the purposes I mentioned before. Now I have a favour to ask of you. Will you take this matter up with Baron Dangloss as if on your own initiative? Do not mention me in any way. You can understand why I ask this of you. Let them believe that the suspicions are yours. I trust you to present them without involving me."

"Trust me, my dear Countess. I am a very diplomatic liar. You need have no fear. I shall find a quick way of getting my friend Dangloss on the right track. It may be a wild goose chase, but it is best to be on the safe side. May I now tell you how greatly I appreciate your confidence in—"

She stopped him with a glance. "No, you may not tell me. There is nothing more to be said."

"I think I understand," he said gently.

"Let us change the subject. I have uttered my word to the wise. Eh bien! It may not be so bad as I think. Let us hope so, at least."

"I have a vague notion that you'd rejoice if we should catch your ogre and chop his head off," said he, coolly lighting a fresh cigarette. She liked his assurance. He was not like other men.

Glancing up at his sandy thatch, she said, with a rueful droop at the corners of her mouth, a contradictory smile in her eyes: "I shall rejoice more if you do not lose your head afterwards."

"*Double entendre?*"

"Not at all."

"I thought, perhaps, you referred to an unhappy plight that already casts its shadow before," he said boldly. "I may lose everything else, my dear Countess, but *not* my head."

"I believe you," she said, strangely serious. "I shall remember that."

She knew this man loved her.

"Sit down, now, and let us be comfy. We are quite alone," she added instantly, a sudden confusion coming over her. "First, will you give me that box of candy from the table? Thank you so much for sending it to me. How in the world do you manage to get this wonderful New York candy all the way to Graustark? It is quite fresh and perfectly delicious."

"Oh, Fifth Avenue isn't so far away as you think," he equivocated. "It's just around the corner—of the world. What's eight or nine thousand miles to a district messenger boy? I ring for one and he fetches the candy, before you can wink your eye or say Jack Robinson. It's a marvellous system."

He watched her white teeth set themselves daintily in the rich nougat; then the red lips closed tranquilly only to open again in a smile of rapture. For reasons best known to himself, he chose not to risk losing the thing he had vowed not to lose. He turned his head—and carefully inspected the end of his cigarette. A wholly unnecessary precaution, as any one might have seen that it was behaving beautifully.

Her eyes narrowed ever so slightly as she studied his averted face in that brief instant. When he turned to her again, she was resting her head against the back of the chair, and her eyes were closed as if in exquisite enjoyment of the morsel that lay behind her smiling lips.

"Are you enjoying it?" he asked.

"Tremendously," she replied, opening her eyes slowly.

"'Gad, I believe you are," he exclaimed. She sat up at once, and caught her breath, although he did not know it. His smile distinctly upset her tranquillity.

"By the way," he added, as if dismissing the matter, "have you forgotten that on Tuesday we go to the Witch's hut in the hills? Bobby has dingdonged it into me for days."

"It will be good fun," she said. Then, as a swift afterthought: "Be sure that the bodyguard is strong—and true."

CHAPTER VII
AT THE WITCH'S HUT

The next morning, before setting forth to consult the minister of police at the Tower, he called up the Perse palace on the telephone and asked for the Countess, to tell her in so many words that he had been followed from her door to the very gates of the Castle grounds. Not by one man alone, for that would have excited suspicion, but by half a dozen at least, each one taking up the surveillance in the most casual manner as the watcher before him left off. Tullis was amazed by the cunning which masked these proceedings; there was a wily brain behind it.

The Duke's secretary answered the call. Tullis was completely bowled over by the curt information that the Countess Marlanx had left Edelweiss before six that morning, to join her husband, who was shooting wild boars with a party in Axphain.

"When does she return?" demanded the American, scarcely believing his ears. She had said nothing of this the night before. What could it mean?

"I do not know, sir."

"In a day or two?"

"She took sixteen trunks, sir," was the laconic reply, as if that told the story in full.

"Well, I'm damned!"

"I beg pardon, sir!"

"I beg *your* pardon. Good morning."

In the meantime, our excellent young friend, Truxton King, was having a sorry time of it. It all began when he went to the Cathedral in the hope of seeing the charming aunt of the little Prince once more. Not only did he attend one service, but all of them, having been assured that the royal family worshipped there quite as regularly and as religiously as the lowliest communicant. She did not appear.

More than all this, he met with fresh disappointment when he ambled down to the armourer's shop. The doors were locked and there was no sign of life about the shuttered place. The cafés were closed on this day of rest, so there was nothing left for him to do but to slink off to his room in the Regengetz, there to read or to play solitaire and to curse the progress of civilisation.

Monday was little better than Sunday. Hobbs positively refused to escort him to the Castle grounds again. No amount of bribing or browbeating could move the confounded Englishman from his stand. He was willing to take him anywhere else, but never again would he risk a personally conducted tour into hot waters royal. Mr. King resigned himself to a purely business call at the shop of Mr. Spantz. He looked long, with a somewhat shifty eye, at the cabinet of ancient rings and necklaces, and then departed without having seen the interesting Miss Platanova. If the old man observed a tendency to roam in the young man's eye, he did not betray the fact—at least not so that any one could notice. Truxton departed, but returned immediately after luncheon, vaguely inclined to decide between two desirable rings. After a protracted period of indecision, in which Olga remained stubbornly out of sight, he announced that he could not make up his mind, and would return later for another inspection.

At his room in the hotel, he found a note addressed to himself. It did not have much to say, but it meant a great deal. There was no signature, and the handwriting was that of a woman.

"*Please do not come again.*" That was all.

He laughed with a fine tone of defiance and—went back to the shop at five o'clock, just to prove that nothing so timid as a note could stop him. This, however, was after he had taken a long walk down Castle Avenue, with a supplementary stroll of little incident outside the grim, high walls that enclosed the grounds. If any one had told him that he was secretly hoping to find a crevasse through which he could invade paradise, I make no doubt he would have resented the imputation soundly. On the occasion of this last visit to the shop, he did not stay long, but went away somewhat dazed to find himself the possessor of a ring he did not want and out of pocket just thirty dollars, American. Having come to the conclusion that knight-errantry of that kind was not only profligate but distinctly irritating to his sense of humour, he looked up Mr. Hobbs and arranged for a day's ride in the mountains.

"You'll oblige me, Mr. Hobbs, by removing that band from your cap. I know you're an interpreter. It's an insult to my intelligence to have it flaunted in my face all day long. I'll admit you're what you say you are, so take it off before we start out to-morrow."

And so, minus the beguiling insignia of office, Mr. Hobbs led his hypercritical patron into the mountain roads early the next morning, both well mounted and provided with a luncheon large enough to restore the amiability that was sure to flag at mid-day unless sustained by unæsthetic sandwiches and beer.

The day was bright and clear, warm in the valley where the city lay, cooler to cold as one mounted the winding roads that led past the lofty Monastery of St. Valentine, sombre sentinel among the clouds.

A part of Edelweiss is built along the side of the mountain, its narrow streets winding upward and past countless terraces to the very base of the rocky, jagged eminence at whose top, a full mile above the last sprinkling of houses, stands the isolated, bleak Monastery. The view from these upper streets, before one enters the circuitous and hidden Monastery road that winds afar in its climb, is never to be forgotten by the spectator, no matter how often he traverses the lofty thoroughfares. As far as the eye can reach, lies the green valley, through which winds the silvery river with its evergreen banks and spotless white houses-greens and whites that almost shame the vaunted tints of old Ireland as one views them from the incoming steamers. Immediately below one's feet lies the compact little city, with its red roofs and green chimney pots, its narrow streets and vivid awnings, its wide avenues and the ancient Castle to the north. To the south, the fortress and the bridges; encircling the city a thick, high wall with here and there enormous gates flanked by towers so grim and old that they seem ready to topple over from the sheer fatigue of centuries. A soft, Indian summer haze hangs over the lazy-lit valley; it is always so in the summer time.

Outside the city walls stretch the wheat-fields and the meadows, the vineyards and orchards, all snug in the nest of forest-crowned hills, whose lower slopes are spotted with broken herds of cattle and the more mobile flocks of sheep. An air of tranquillity lies low over the entire vista; one dozes if he looks long into this peaceful bowl of plenty.

From the distant passes in the mountains to the east and north come the dull intonations of dynamite blasts, proving the presence of that disturbing element of progress which is driving the railroad through the unbroken heart of the land.

It is a good three hours' ride to the summit of Monastery Mountain. And, after the height has been attained, one does not care to linger long among the chilly, whistling crags, with their snow-crevasses and bitter winds; the utter loneliness, the aloofness of this frost-crowned crest appals, disheartens one who loves the fair, green things of life. In the shelter of the crags, at the base of the Monastery walls, looking out over the sunlit valley, one has his luncheon and his snack of spirits quite undisturbed, for the monks pay no heed to him. They are not hospitable, neither are they unfriendly. One seldom sees them.

Truxton King and Mr. Hobbs were not long in disposing of their lunch. It was too cold for comfort in their draughty dining-room, and they were not invited to enter the inhospitable gates. In half an hour they were wending their way down the north side of the peak by gradually declining roads, headed for the much-talked-of home of the Witch in Ganlook Gap, some six miles from Edelweiss as the crow flies, but twice that distance over the tortuous bridle paths and post roads.

It was three o'clock when they clattered down the stone road and up to the forbidding vale in which lurked, like an evil, guilty thing, the log-built home of that ancient female who made no secret of her practices in witchcraft. The hut stood back from the mountain road a hundred yards or more, at the head of a small, thicket- grown recess.

A low, thatched roof protruded from the hill against which the hut was built. As a matter of fact, a thin chimney grew out of the earth itself, for all the world like a smoking tree stump. The hovel was a squalid, beggary thing that might have been built over night somewhere back in the dark ages. Its single door was so low that one was obliged to stoop to enter the little room where the dame had been holding forth for three-score years, 'twas said. This was her throne-room, her dining-room, her bed-chamber, her all, it would seem, unless one had been there before and knew that her kitchen was beyond, in the side of the hill. The one window, sans glass, looked narrowly out upon an odd opening in the foliage below, giving the occupant of the hut an unobstructed view of the winding road that led up from Edelweiss. The door faced the Monastery road down which the two men had just ridden. As for the door yard, it was no more than a pebbly, avalanche-swept opening among the trees and rocks, down which in the glacial age perhaps a thousand torrents had leaped, but which was now so dry and white and lifeless that one could only think of bones bleached and polished by a sun that had sickened of the work a thousand years ago.

This brief, inadequate description of the Witch's hut is given in advance of the actual descent of the personally conducted gentleman for the somewhat ambiguous reason that he was to find it not at all as described.

The two horsemen rode into the glen and came plump upon a small detachment of the royal guard, mounted and rather resolute in their lack of amiability.

"Wot's this?" gasped Mr. Hobbs, drawing rein at the edge of the pebbly dooryard.

"Soldiers, I'd say," remarked Mr. King, scowling quite glumly from beneath the rim of his panama. "Hello!" His eyes brightened and his hat came off with a switch. "There's the Prince!"

"My word," ejaculated Mr. Hobbs, and forthwith began to ransack his pockets for the band which said he was from Cook's.

Farther up the glen, in fact at the very door of the Witch's hut, were gathered a small but rather distinguished portion of the royal household. It was not difficult to recognise the little Prince. He was standing beside John Tullis; and it is not with a desire to speak ill of his valour that we add: he was clutching the slackest part of that gentleman's riding breeks with an earnestness that betrayed extreme trepidation. Facing them, on the stone door-step, was the Witch herself, a figure to try the courage of a time-tried hero, let alone the susceptibilities of a small boy in knickers. Behind Tullis and the Prince were several ladies and gentlemen, all in riding garments and all more or less ill at ease.

Truxton King's heart swelled suddenly; all the world grew bright again for him. Next to the tall figure of Colonel Quinnox, of the Royal Guard, was the slim, entrancing lady of his most recent dreams—the Prince's aunt! The lady of the grotto! The lady of the goldfish conspiracy!

The Countess Marlanx, tall and exquisite, was a little apart from the others, with Baron Dangloss and young Count Vos Engo—whom Truxton was ready to hate because he was a recognised suitor for the hand of the slim, young person in grey. He thought he had liked her beyond increase in the rajah silk, but now he confessed to himself that he was mistaken. He liked her better in a grey riding habit. It struck him sharply, as he sat there in the saddle, that she would be absolutely and adorably faultless in point lace or calico, in silk or gingham, low-neck or high. He was for riding boldly up to this little group, but a very objectionable lieutenant barred the way, supported in no small measure by the defection of Mr. Hobbs, who announced in a hoarse, agitated whisper that he's "be 'anged if he'd let any man make a fool of him twice over."

The way was made easy by the intervention of the alert young woman in grey. She caught sight of the restricted adventurers—or one of them, to be quite accurate—and, after speeding a swift smile of astonishment, turned quickly to Prince Bobby.

A moment later, the tall stranger with the sun-browned face was the centre of interest to the small group at the door. He bowed amiably to the smiling young person in grey and received a quick nod in response. As he was adventuring what he considered to be a proper salute for the Prince, he observed that a few words passed between the lad's aunt and John Tullis, who was now surveying him with some interest.

The Prince broke the ice.

"Hello!" he cried shrilly, his little face aglow.

"Hello!" responded the gentleman, readily.

John Tullis found himself being dragged away from the Witch's door toward the newcomer at the bottom of the glen. Mr. Hobbs listened with deepening awe to the friendly conversation which resulted in Truxton King going forward to join the party in front of the hut. He came along in the rear, after having tethered the tired horses, not quite sure that he was awake. The Prince had called him Mr. Cook, had asked him how his Sons were, all of which was highly gratifying when one pauses to consider that he had got his cap band on upside down in his excitement. He always was to wonder how the little monarch succeeded in reading the title without standing on his head to do so.

Truxton was duly presented to the ladies and gentlemen of the party by John Tullis, who gracefully announced that he knew King's parents in New York. Baron Dangloss was quite an old friend, if one were to judge by the manner in which he greeted the young man. The lady in grey smiled so sweetly and nodded so blithely, that Tullis, instead of presenting King to her as he had done to the Countess Marlanx and others, merely said:

"And you know one another, of course." Whereupon she flushed very prettily and felt constrained to avoid Truxton's look of inquiry. He did not lose his wits, but vowed acquiescence and assumed that he knew.

As a result of the combined supplications of the entire party, the old woman grudgingly consented to take them into her hovel, where, in exchange for small pieces of silver, she would undertake certain manifestations in necromancy.

Truxton King, scarcely able to believe his good fortune, crowded into the loathsome, squalid room with his aristocratic companions, managing, with considerable skill, to keep close beside his charming friend. They stood back while the others crowded up to the table where the hag occupied herself with the crystal ball.

Never had Truxton looked upon a creature who so thoroughly vindicated the life-long reliance he had put in the description of witches given by the fairy-tale tellers of his earliest youth. She had the traditional hook-nose and peaked chin, the glittering eyes, the thousand wrinkles and the toothless gums. He looked about for the raven and the cat, but if she had them, they were not in evidence. At a rough guess, he calculated her age at one hundred years. A youth of extreme laziness, who Baron Dangloss said was the old woman's grandson, appeared to be her man-of-all-work. He fetched the old woman's crystal, placed stools for the visitors, lighted the candles on the table, occupying no less than a quarter of an hour in performing these simple acts, so awkward that at least two of his observers giggled openly and whispered their opinions.

"Gruesome lady, isn't she?" whispered King.

"I shall dream of her for months," whispered the lady in grey, shuddering.

"Are you willing to have her read your future in that ball?"

"Do you really think she can tell?"

"I once had a fortune-teller say that I would be married before I was twenty-three," he informed her. She appeared interested.

"And were you?"

"No. But she did her part, you know—the fortune-teller, I mean."

"She warned you. I see. So it really wasn't her fault." She was watching the preparations at the table with eager eyes, her lips parted and her breath coming quick through excitement.

"Would you mind telling me how I am to address you?" whispered King. They were leaning against the mud-plastered wall near the little window, side by side. The whimsical smile that every one loved to see was on his lips, in his eyes. "You see, I'm a stranger in a strange land. That accounts for my ignorance."

"You must not speak while she is gazing into the crystal," she warned, after a quick, searching glance at his face. He could have sworn that he saw a gleam of concern in her eyes, followed instantly by a twinkle that meant mischief.

"Please consider my plight," he implored. "I can't call you Aunt Loraine, you know."

She laughed silently and turned her head to devote her entire attention to the scene at the table. Truxton King was in a sudden state of trepidation. Had he offended her? There was a hot rush of blood to his ears. He missed the sly, wondering glance that she gave him out of the corner of her eye a moment later.

Although it was broad daylight, the low, stuffy room would have been pitch dark had it not been for the flickering candles on the table beside the bent, grey head of the mumbling fortune-teller, whose bony fingers twitched over and about the crystal globe like wiggling serpents' tails. The window gave little or no light and the door was closed, the grinning grandson leaning against it limply. The picture was a weird, uncanny one, despite the gay, lightsome appearance of the visitors. The old woman, in high, shrill tones, had commanded silence. The men obeyed with a grim scepticism, while the women seemed really awed by their surroundings.

The Witch began by reading the fortune of John Tullis, who had been pushed forward by the wide-eyed Prince. In a cackling monotone she rambled through a supposititious history of his past, for the chief part so unintelligible that even he could not gainsay the statements. Later, she bent her piercing eyes upon the Prince and refused to read his future, shrilly asserting that she had not the courage to tell what might befall the little ruler, all the while muttering something about the two little princes who had died in a tower ages and ages ago. Seeing that the boy was frightened, Tullis withdrew him to the background. The Countess Marlanx, who had returned that morning to Edelweiss as mysteriously as she had left, came next. She was smiling derisively.

"You have just returned from a visit to some one whom you hate," began the Witch. "He is your husband. You will marry again. There is a fair-haired man in love with you. You are in love with him. I can see trouble—"

But the Countess deliberately turned away from the table, her cheeks flaming with the consciousness that a smile had swept the circle behind her graceful back.

"Ridiculous," she said, and avoided John Tullis's gaze. "I don't care to hear any more. Come, Baron You are next."

Truxton King, subdued and troubled in his mind, found himself studying his surroundings and the people who went so far to make them interesting. He glanced from time to time at the delicate, eager profile of the girl beside him; at the soft, warm cheek and the caressing brown hair; at the little ear and the white slim neck of her—and realised just what had happened to him. He had fallen in love; that was the plain upshot of it. It had come to pass, just as he had hoped it would in his dearest dreams. He was face to face with the girl of royal blood that the story books had created for him long, long ago, and he was doing just what he had always intended to do: falling heels over head and hopelessly in love with her. Never had he seen hair grow so exquisitely about the temples and neck as this one's hair—but, just to confound his budding singleness of interest, his gaze at that instant wandered off and fell upon something that caused him to stare hard at a certain spot far removed from the coiffure of a fair and dainty lady.

His eye had fallen upon a crack in the door that led to the kitchen, although he had no means of knowing that it was a kitchen. To his amazement, a gleaming eye was looking out upon the room from beyond this narrow crack. He looked long and found that he was not mistaken. There was an eye, glued close to the opposite side of the rickety door, and its gaze was directed to the Countess Marlanx.

The spirit of adventure, recklessness, bravado—whatever you may choose to call it—flared high in the soul of this self-despised outsider. He could feel a strange thrill of exaltation shooting through his veins; he knew as well as he knew anything that he was destined to create commotion in that stately crowd, even against his better judgment. The desire to spring forward and throw open the door, thus exposing a probable con- federate, was stronger than he had the power to resist. Even as he sought vainly to hold himself in check, he became conscious that the staring eye was meeting his own in a glare of realisation.

Without pausing to consider the result of his action, he sprang across the room, shouting as he did so that there was a man behind the door. Grasping the latch, he threw the door wide open, the others in the room looking at him as if he were suddenly crazed.

He had expected to confront the owner of that basilisk eye. There was not a sign of a human being in sight. Beyond was a black little room, at the back of which stood an old cooking stove with a fire going and a kettle singing. He leaped through, prepared to grasp the mysterious watcher, but, to his utter amazement, the kitchen was absolutely empty, save for inanimate things. His surprise was so genuine that it was not to be mistaken by the men who leaped to his side. He had time to note that two of them carried pistols in their hands, and that Tullis and Quinnox had placed themselves between the Prince and possible danger.

There was instant commotion, with cries and exclamations from all. Quick as the others were, the old woman was at his side before them, snarling with rage. Her talon-like fingers sunk into his arm, and her gaze went darting about the room in a most convincing way. Some minutes passed before the old woman could be quieted. Then King explained his action. He swore solemnly, if sheepishly, that he could not have been mistaken, and yet the owner of that eye had vanished as if swallowed up by the mountain.

Baron Dangloss was convinced that the young man had seen the eye. Without compunction he began a search of the room, the old woman looking on with a grin of glee.

"Search! Search!" she croaked. "It was the Spirit Eye! It is looking at you now, my fine baron! It finds you, yet cannot be found. No, no! Oh, you fools!

Get out! Get out! All of you! Prince or no Prince, I fear you not, nor all your armies. This is my home! My castle! Go! Go!"

"There was a man here, old woman," said the Baron coolly. "Where is he? What is your game? I am not to be fooled by these damnable tricks of yours. Where is the man?"

She laughed aloud, a horrid sound. The Prince clutched Tullis by the leg in terror.

"Brace up, Bobby," whispered his big friend, leaning down to comfort him. "Be a man!"

"It—it's mighty hard," chattered Bobby, but he squared his little shoulders.

The ladies of the party had edged forward, peering into the kitchen, alarm having passed, although the exclamation "boo!" would have played havoc with their courage.

"I swear there was some one looking through that crack," protested King, wiping his brow in confusion. "Miss—er—I should say—*you* could have seen it from where you stood," he pleaded, turning to the lady in grey.

"Dear me, I wish I had," she cried. "I've always wanted to see some one snooping."

"There is no window, no trap door, no skylight," remarked the Baron, puzzled. "Nothing but the stovepipe, six inches in diameter. A man couldn't crawl out through that, I'm sure. Mr. King, we've come upon a real mystery. The eye without a visible body."

"I'm sure I saw it," reiterated Truxton. The Prince's aunt was actually laughing at him. But so was the Witch, for that matter. He didn't mind the Witch.

Suddenly the old woman stepped into the middle of the room and began to wave her hands in a mysterious manner over an empty pot that stood on the floor in front of the stove. The others drew back, watching her with the greatest curiosity.

A droning song oozed from the thin lips; the gesticulations grew in weirdness and fervor. Then, before their startled eyes, a thin film of smoke began to rise from the empty pot. It grew in volume until the room was quite dense with it. Even more quickly than it began, it disappeared, drawn apparently by some supernatural agency into the draft of the stove and out through the rickety chimney pipe. Even Dangloss blinked his eyes, and not because they were filled with smoke.

A deafening crash, as of many guns, came to their ears from the outside. With one accord the entire party rushed to the outer door, a wild laugh from the hag pursuing them.

"There!" she screamed. "There goes all there was of him! And so shall we all go some day. Fire and smoke!"

Not one there but thought on the instant of the Arabian nights and the genii who went up in smoke—those never-to-be-forgotten tales of wonder.

Just outside the door stood Lieutenant Saffo of the guard, his hand to his cap. He was scarcely distinguishable, so dark had the day become.

"Good Lord!" shouted Tullis. "What's the matter? What has happened?"

"The storm, sir," said Saffo. "It is coming down the valley like the wind." A great crash of thunder burst overhead and lightning darted through the black, swirling skies.

"Very sudden, sir," added Mr. Hobbs from behind. "Like a puff of wind, sir."

The Witch stood in the door behind them, smiling as amiably as it was possible for her to smile.

"Come in," she said. "There's room for all of you. The spirits have gone. Ha, ha! My merry man! Even the eye is gone. Come in, your Highness. Accept the best I can offer—shelter from the hurricane. I've seen many, but this looks to be the worst. So it came sudden, eh? Ha, ha!"

The roar of wind and rain in the trees above seemed like a howl of confirmation. Into the hovel crowded the dismayed pleasure-seekers, followed by the soldiers, who had made the horses fast at the first sign of the storm.

Down came the rain in torrents, whisked and driven, whirled and shot by the howling winds, split by the lightning and urged to greater glee by the deafening applause of the thunder. Apple carts in the skies!

Out in the dooryard the merry grandson of the Witch was dancing as if possessed by revelling devils.

CHAPTER VIII
LOOKING FOR AN EYE

"Washing the dead men's bones," was the remark King made a few minutes later. The storm was at its height; the sheets of rain that swept down the pebbly glen elicited the gruesome sentence. He stood directly behind the quaking Loraine, quite close to the open door; there is no doubt that the observation was intended for her ears, maliciously or otherwise.

She gave him an awed glance, but no verbal response. It was readily to be seen that she was terrified by the violence of the mountain tornado. As if to shame him for the frivolous remark, she suddenly changed her position, putting herself behind him.

"I like that," he remonstrated, emboldened by the elements. "You leave me in front to be struck by the first bolt of lightning that comes along. And I a stranger, too."

"Isn't it awful?" she murmured, her fingers in her ears, her eyes tightly closed. "Do you think we'll be struck?"

"Certainly not," he assured her. "This is a charmed spot. It's a frolic of her particular devils. She waves her hand: all the goblins and thunder-workers in this neck of the woods hustle up to see what's the matter. Then there's an awful rumpus. In a minute or two she'll wave her hand and—presto! It will stop raining. But," with a distressed look out into the thick of it, "it would be a beastly joke if lightning should happen to strike that nag of mine. I'd not only have to walk to town, but I'd have to pay three prices for the brute."

"I think she's perfectly—ooh!—perfectly wonderful. Goodness, that was a crash! Where do you think it struck?"

"If you'll stand over here a little closer I'll point out the tree. See? Right down the ravine there? See the big limb swaying? That's the place. The old lady is carrying her joke too far. That's pretty close home. Stand right there, please. I won't let it rain in on you."

"You are very good, Mr. King. I—I've always thought I loved a storm. Ooh! But this is too terrible! Aren't you really afraid you'll be struck? Thanks, ever so much." He had squared himself between her and the door, turning his back upon the storm: but not through cowardice, as one might suppose.

"Don't mention it. I won't mind it so much, don't you know, if I get struck in the back. How long ago did you say it was that you went to school with my sister?"

All this time the Witch was haranguing her huddled audience, cursing the soldiers, laughing gleefully in the faces of her stately, scornful guests, greatly to the irritation of Baron Dangloss, toward whom she showed an especial attention.

Tullis was holding the Prince in his arms. Colonel Quinnox stood before them, keeping the babbling, leering beldame from thrusting her face close to that of the terrified boy. Young Vos Engo glowered at Truxton King from the opposite side of the room. Mr. Hobbs had safely ensconced himself in the rear of the six guardsmen, who stood near the door, ready to dash forth if by any chance the terrified horses should succeed in breaking away.

The Countess Marlanx, pale and rigid, her wondrous eyes glowing with excitement, stood behind John Tullis, straight and strong, like a storm spirit glorying in the havoc that raged about her. Time and again she leaned forward to utter words of encouragement in the ear of the little Prince, never without receiving a look of gratitude and surprise from his tall protector.

And all this time the goose-herd grandson of the Witch was dancing his wild, uncanny solo in the thick of the brew, an exalted grin on his face, strange cries of delight breaking from his lips: a horrid spectacle that fascinated the observers.

With incredible swiftness the storm passed. Almost at its height, there came a cessation of the roaring tempest; the downpour was checked, the thunder died away and the lightning trickled off into faint flashes. The sky cleared as if by magic. The exhibition, if you please, was over!

Even the most stoical, unimpressionable men in the party looked at each other in bewilderment and—awe, there was no doubt of it. The glare that Dangloss bent upon the hag proved that he had been rudely shaken from his habitual complacency.

"It is the most amazing thing I've ever seen," he said, over and over again.

The Countess Marlanx was trembling violently. Tullis, observing this, tried to laugh away her nervousness.

"Mere coincidence, that's all," he said. "Surely you are not superstitious. You can't believe she brought about this storm?" "It isn't that," she said in a low voice. "I feel as if a grave personal danger had just passed me by. Not danger for the rest of you, but for me alone. That is the sensation I have: the feeling of one who has stepped back from the brink of an abyss just in time to avoid being pushed over. I can't make you understand. See! I am trembling. I have seen no more than the rest of you, yet am more terrified, more upset than Robin, poor child. Perhaps I am foolish. I *know* that something dreadful has—I might say, touched me. Something that no one else could have seen or felt."

"Nerves, my dear Countess. Shadows! I used to see them and feel them when I was a lad no bigger than Bobby if left alone in the dark. It is a grown-up fear of goblins. You'll be over it as soon as we are outside."

Ten minutes later the cavalcade started down the rain-swept road toward the city, dry blankets having been placed across the saddles occupied by the ladies and the Prince. The Witch stood in her doorway, laughing gleefully, inviting them to come often.

"Come again, your Highness," she croaked sarcastically.

"The next time I come, it will be with a torch to burn you alive!" shouted back Dangloss. To Tullis he added: "'Gad, sir, they did well to burn witches in your town of Salem. You cleared the country of them, the pests."

Darkness was approaching fast among the sombre hills; the great pass was enveloped in the mists and the gloaming of early night. In a compact body the guardsmen rode close about Prince Robin and his friend. Ingomede had urged this upon Tullis, still oppressed by the feeling of disaster that had come over her in the hovel.

"It means something, my friend, it means something," she insisted. "I feel it—I am sure of it." Riding quite close beside him, she added in lower tones: "I was with my husband no longer ago than yesterday. Do you know that I believe it is Count Marlanx that I feel everywhere about me now? *He*— his presence—is in the air! Oh, I wish I could make you feel as I do."

"You haven't told me why you ran away on Sunday," he said, abruptly, dismissing her argument with small ceremony.

"He sent for me. I—I had to go." There was a new, strange expression in her eyes that puzzled him for a long time. Suddenly the solution came: she was completely captive to the will of this hated husband. The realisation brought a distinct, sickening shock with it.

Down through the lowering shades rode the Prince's party, swiftly, even gaily by virtue of relaxation from the strain of a weird half hour. No one revealed the slightest sign of apprehension arising from the mysterious demonstration in which nature had taken a hand.

Truxton King was holding forth, with cynical good humour, for the benefit, if not the edification of Baron Dangloss, with whom he rode—Mr. Hobbs galloping behind not unlike the faithful Sancho of another Quixote's day.

"It's all tommy-rot, Baron," said Truxton. "We've got a dozen stage wizards in New York who can do all she did and then some. That smoke from the kettle is a corking good trick—but that's all it is, take my word for it. The storm? Why, you know as well as I do, Baron, that she can't bring rain like that. If she could, they'd have her over in the United States right now, saving the crops, with or without water. That was chance. Hobbs told me this morning it looked like rain. By the way, I must apologise to him. I said he was a crazy kill-joy. The thing that puzzles me is what became of the owner of that eye. I'll stake my life on it, I saw an eye. 'Gad, it looked right into mine. Queerest feeling it gave me."

"Ah, that's it, my young friend. What became of the eye? Poof! And it is gone. We searched immediately. No sign. It is most extraordinary."

"I'll admit it's rather gruesome, but—I say, do you know I've a mind to look into that matter if you don't object, Baron. It's a game of some sort. She's a wily old dame, but I think if we go about it right we can catch her napping and expose the whole game. I'm going back there in a day or two and try to get at the bottom of it. That confounded eye worries me. She's laughing up her sleeve at us, too, you know."

"I should advise you to keep away from her, my friend. Granted she has tricked us: why not? It is her trade. She does no harm—except that she's most offensively impudent. And I rather imagine she'll resent your investigation, if you attempt it. I can't say that I'd blame her." The Baron laughed.

"Baron, it struck me a bit shivery at the time, but I want to say to you now that the eye that I saw at the crack was not that of an idle peeper, nor was it a mere fakir's substitute. It was as malevolent as the devil and it glared—do you understand? Glared! It didn't *peep!*"

Truxton King, for reasons best known to himself, soon relapsed into a thoughtful, contemplative silence. Between us, he was sorely vexed and disappointed. When the gallant start was made from the glen of "dead men's bones," he found that he was to be cast utterly aside, quite completely ignored by the fair Loraine. She rode off with young Count Vos Engo without so much as a friendly wave of the hand to him. He said it over to himself several times: "not even a friendly wave of her hand." It was as if she had forgotten his existence, or—merciful Powers! What was worse—as if she took this way of showing him his place. Of course, that being her attitude, he glumly found his place—which turned out rather ironically to be under the eye of a police officer—and made up his mind that he would stay there.

Vos Engo, being an officer in the Royal Guard, rode ahead by order of Colonel Quinnox. Truxton, therefore, had her back in view—at rather a vexing distance, too—for mile after mile of the ride to the city. Not so far ahead, however, that he could not observe every movement of her light, graceful figure as she swept down the King's Highway. She was a perfect horsewoman, firm, jaunty, free. Somehow he knew, without seeing, that a stray brown wisp of hair caressed her face with insistent adoration: he could see her hand go up from time to time to brush it back—just as if it were not a happy place for a wisp of hair. Perhaps—he shivered with the thought of it—perhaps it even caressed her lips. Ah, who would not be a wisp of brown hair!

He galloped along beside the Baron, a prey to gloomy considerations. What was the use? He had no chance to win her. That was for story-books and plays. She belonged to another world—far above his. And even beyond that, she was not likely to be attracted by such a rude, ungainly, sunburned lout as he, with such chaps about as Vos Engo, or that what's-his-name fellow, or a dozen others whom he had seen. Confound it all, she was meant for a prince, or an archduke. What chance had he?

But she was the loveliest creature he had ever seen. Yes; she was the golden girl of his dreams. Within his grasp, so to speak, and yet he could not hope to seize her, after all. Was she meant for that popinjay youth with the petulant eye and the sullen jaw? Was he to be the lucky man, this Vos Engo?

The Baron's dry, insinuating voice broke in upon the young man's thoughts. "I think it's pretty well understood that she's going to marry him." The little old minister had been reading King's thoughts; he had the satisfaction of seeing his victim start guiltily. It was on the tip of Truxton's tongue to blurt out: "How the devil did you know what I was thinking about?" But he managed to control himself, asking instead, with bland interest:

"Indeed? Is it a good match, Baron?"

The Baron smiled. "I think so. He has been a trifle wild, but I believe he has settled down. Splendid family. He is desperately in love, as you may have noted."

"I hadn't thought much about it. Is she in love with him?"

"She sees a great deal of him," was the diplomatic answer.

Truxton considered well for a minute or two, and then bluntly asked:

"Would you mind telling me just who she is, Baron? What is her name?"

Dangloss was truly startled. He gave the young man a quick, penetrating glance; then a set, hard expression came into his eyes.

"Do you mean, sir, that you don't know her?" he asked, almost harshly.

"I don't know her name."

"And you had the effrontery to—My excellent friend, you amaze me. I can't believe it of you. Why, sir, how dare you say this to me? I know that Americans are bold, but, by gad, sir, I've always looked upon them as gentlemen. You—"

"Hold on, Baron Dangloss," interrupted Truxton, very red in the face. "Don't say it, please. You'd better hear my side of the story first. She went to school with my sister. She knows me, but, confound it, sir, she refuses to tell me who she is. Do you think that is fair? Now, I'll tell you how it came about." He related the story of the goldfish and the pinhook. The Baron smiled comfortably to himself, a sphinx-like expression coming into his beady eyes as he stared steadily on ahead; her trim grey back seemed to encourage his admiring smile.

"Well, my boy, if she elects to keep you in the dark concerning her name, it is not for me to betray her," he said at the end of the recital. "Ladies in her position, I dare say, enjoy these little mysteries. If she wants you to know, she'll tell you. Perhaps it would be well for you to be properly, officially presented to her hi—to the young lady. Your countryman, Mr. Tullis, will be glad to do so, I fancy. But let me suggest: don't permit your ingenuousness to get the better of you again. She's having sport with you on account of it. We all know her propensities."

It was dusk when they entered the northern gates. Above the Castle, King said good-bye to Tullis and the Countess, gravely saluted the sleepy Prince, and followed Mr. Hobbs off to the heart of the city. He was hot with resentment. Either she had forgotten to say good-bye to him or had wilfully decided to ignore him altogether; at any rate, she entered the gates to the Castle grounds without so much as an indifferent glance in his direction.

Truxton knew in advance that he was to have a sleepless, unhappy night.

In his room at the hotel he found the second anonymous letter, unquestionably from the same source, but this time printed in crude, stilted letters. It had been stuck under the door, together with some letters that had been forwarded from Teheran.

"Leave the city at once. You are in great danger. Save yourself!"

This time he did not laugh. That it was from Olga Platanova he made no doubt. But why she should interest herself so persistently in his welfare was quite beyond him, knowing as he did that in no sense had he appealed to her susceptibility. And what, after all, could she mean by "great danger"? "Save yourself!" He sat for a long time considering the situation. At last he struck the window sill a resounding thwack with his fist and announced his decision to the silent, disinterested wall opposite.

"I'll take her advice. I'll get out. Not because I'm afraid to stay, but because there's no use. She's got no eyes for me. I'm a plain impossibility so far as she's concerned. It's Vos Engo—damn little rat! Old Dangloss came within an ace of speaking of her as 'her Highness.' That's enough for me. That means she's a princess. It's all very nice in novels, but in real life men don't go about picking up any princess they happen to like. No, sir! I might just as well get out while I can. She treated me as if I were a yellow dog to-day—after I'd been damned agreeable to her, too, standing between her and the lightning. I might have been struck. I wonder if she would have been grateful. No; she wouldn't. She'd have smiled her sweetest, and said: "wasn't it lucky?"

He picked up the note once more. "If I were a storybook hero, I'd stick this thing in my pocket and set out by myself to unravel the mystery behind it. But I've chucked the hero job for good and all. I'm going to hand this over to Dangloss. It's the sensible thing to do, even if it isn't what a would-be hero in search of a princess aught to do. What's more, I'll hunt the Baron up this very hour. Hope it doesn't get Olga into trouble."

He indulged in another long spell of thoughtfulness. "No, by George, I'll not turn tail at the first sign of danger. I'll stay here and assist Dangloss in unravelling this matter. And I'll go up to that Witch's hole before I'm a day older to have it out with her. I'll find out where the smoke came from and I'll know where that eye went to." He sighed without knowing it. "By Jove, I'd like to do something to show her I'm not the blooming duffer she thinks I am."

He could not find Baron Dangloss that night, nor early the next day. Hobbs, after being stigmatised as the only British coward in the world, changed his mind and made ready to accompany King to the hovel in Ganlook Gap.

By noon the streets in the vicinity of the Plaza were filled with strange, rough-looking men, undeniably labourers.

"Who are they?" demanded King, as they rode past a particularly sullen, forbidding crowd at the corner below the city hail.

"There's a strike on among the men who are building the railroad," said Hobbs. "Ugly looking crowd, eh?"

"A strike? 'Gad, it's positively homelike."

"I heard a bit ago that the matter has been adjusted. They go back to work to-morrow, slight increase in pay and a big decrease in work. They were to have had their answer to-day. Mr. Tullis, I hear, was instrumental in having the business settled without a row."

"They'd better look out for these fellows," said King, very soberly. "I don't like the appearance of 'em. They look like cut-throats."

"Take my word for it, sir, they are. They're the riff-raff of all Europe. You should have seen them of a Sunday, sir, before the order went out closing the drinking places on that day. My word, they took the town. There was no living here for the decent people. Women couldn't go out of their houses."

"I hope Baron Dangloss knows how to handle them?" in some anxiety. "By the way, remind me to look up the Baron just as soon as we get back to town this evening."

"If we ever get back!" muttered the unhappy Mr. Hobbs. Prophetic lamentation!

In due time they rode into the sombre solitudes of Ganlook Gap and up to the Witch's glen. Here Mr. Hobbs balked. He refused to adventure farther than the mouth of the stony ravine. Truxton approached the hovel alone, without the slightest trepidation. The goose-herd grandson was driving a flock of geese across the green bowl below the cabin. The American called out to him and a moment later the youth, considerably excited, drove his geese up to the door. He could understand no English, nor could Truxton make out what he was saying in the native tongue. While they were vainly haranguing each other the old woman appeared at the edge of the thicket above the hut. Uttering shrill exclamations, she hurried down to confront King with blazing eyes. He fell back, momentarily dismayed. Her horrid grin of derision brought a flush to his cheek; he faced her quite coolly.

"I'll lay you a hundred gavvos that the kettle and smoke experiment is a fake of the worst sort," he announced, after a somewhat lengthy appeal to be allowed to enter the hut as a simple seeker after knowledge.

"Have it your own way! Have it your own way!" she cackled.

"Tell you what I'll do; if I can't expose that trick in ten minutes, I'll make you a present of a hundred gavvos."

She took him up like a flash, a fact which startled and disconcerted him not a little. Her very eagerness augured ill for his proposition. Still, he was in for it; he was determined to get inside the hut and solve the mystery, if it were possible. Exposure of the Witch would at least attract the interest if not the approval of a certain young lady in purple and fine linen. That was surely worth while.

With a low, mocking bow, the shrivelled hag stood aside and motioned for him to precede her into the hovel. He looked back at Mr. Hobbs. That gentleman's eyes seemed to be starting from his head.

"A hundred gavvos is a fortune not easily to be won," said the old dame. "How can I be sure that you will pay me if you lose?"

"It is in my pocket, madam. If I don't pay, you may instruct your excellent grandson to crack me over the head. He looks as though he'd do it for a good deal less money, I'll say that for him."

"He is honest—as honest as his grandmother," cried the old woman. She bestowed a toothless grin upon him. "Now what is it you want to do?"

They were standing in the centre of the wretched living-room. The goose-boy was in the door, looking on with strangely alert, questioning eyes, ever and anon peering over his shoulder toward the spot where Hobbs stood with the horses. He seldom took his gaze from the face of the old woman, a rat-like smile touching the corners of his fuzz-lined lips.

"I want to go through that kitchen, just to satisfy myself of one or two things." King was looking hard at the crack in the kitchen door. Suddenly he started as if shot.

The staring, burning eye was again looking straight at him from the jagged crack in the door!

"I'll get you this time," he shouted, crossing the room in two eager leaps. The door responded instantly to his violent clutch, swung open with a bang, and disclosed the interior of the queer little kitchen.

The owner of that mocking, phantom eye was gone!

Like a frantic dog, Truxton dashed about the little kitchen, looking in every corner, every crack for signs of the thing he chased. At last he paused, baffled, mystified. The old woman was standing in the middle of the outer room, grinning at him with what was meant for complacency, but which struck him at once as genuine malevolence.

"Ha, ha!" she croaked. "You fool! You fool! Search! Smell him out! All the good it will do you! Ha, ha!"

"By gad, I *will* get at the bottom of this!" shouted Truxton, stubborn rage possessing him. "There's some one here, and I know it. I'm not such a fool as to believe—Say! What's that? The ceiling! By the eternal, that scraping noise explains it! There's where the secret trap-door is—in the ceiling! Within arm's reach, at that! Watch me, old woman! I'll have your spry friend out of his nest in the shake of a lamb's tail."

The hag was standing in the kitchen door now, still grinning evilly. She watched the eager young man pound upon the low ceiling with a three-legged stool that he had seized from the floor.

"I don't see how he got up there so quickly, though. He must be like greased lightning."

He was pounding vigorously on the roughly boarded ceiling when the sharp voice of the old woman, raised in command, caused him to lower the stool and turn upon her with gleaming, triumphant eyes. The look he saw in her face was sufficient to check his enterprise for the moment. He dropped the stool and started toward her, his arms extended to catch her swaying form. The look of the dying was in her eyes; she seemed to be crumpling before him.

He reached her in time, his strong arms grasping the frail, bent figure as it sank to the floor. As he lifted her bodily from her feet, intent upon carrying her to the open air, her bony fingers sank into his arm with the grip of death, and—could he believe his ears!—a low, mocking laugh came from her lips.

Down where the pebbly house-yard merged into the mossy banks, Mr. Hobbs sat tight, still staring with gloomy eyes at the dark little hut up the glen. His sturdy knees were pressing the skirts of the saddle with a firmness that left no room for doubt as to the tension his nerves were under. Now and then he murmured "My word!" but in what connection it is doubtful if even he could tell. A quarter of an hour had passed since King disappeared through the doorway: Mr. Hobbs was getting nervous.

The shiftless, lanky goose-herd came forth in time, and lazily drove his scattered flock off into the lower glen.

The horses were becoming impatient. To his extreme discomfort, not to say apprehension, they were constantly pricking their ears forward and snorting in the direction of the hovel; a very puzzling circumstance, thought Mr. Hobbs. At this point he began to say "dammit," and with some sense of appreciation, too.

Presently his eye caught sight of a thin stream of smoke, rather black than blue, arising from the little chimney at the rear of the cabin. His eyes flew very wide open; his heart experienced a sudden throbless moment; his mind leaped backward to the unexplained smoke mystery of the day before. It was on the end of his tongue to cry out to his unseen patron, to urge him to leave the Witch to her deviltry and come along home, when the old woman herself appeared in the doorway—alone.

She sat down upon the doorstep, pulling away at a long pipe, her hooded face almost invisible from the distance which he resolutely held. He felt that she was eyeing him with grim interest. For a few minutes he waited, a sickening doubt growing up in his soul. A single glance showed him that the chimney was no longer emitting smoke. It seemed to him that the old woman was losing all semblance of life. She was no more than a black, inanimate heap of rags piled against the door-jamb.

Hobbs let out a shout. The horses plunged viciously. Slowly the bundle of rags took shape. The old woman arose and hobbled toward him, leaning upon a great cane.

"Whe—where's Mr. King?" called out Hobbs.

She stopped above him and he could see her face. Mr. Hobbs was chilled to the bone. Her arm was raised, a bony finger pointing to the treetops above her hovel.

"He's gone. Didn't you see him? He went off among the treetops. You won't see him again." She waited a moment, and then went on, in most ingratiating tones: "Would you care to come into my house? I can show you the road he took. You—"

But Mr. Hobbs, his hair on end, had dropped the rein of King's horse and was putting boot to his own beast, whirling frantically into the path that led away from the hated, damned spot! Down the road he crashed, pursued by witches whose persistence put to shame the efforts of those famed ladies of Tam O'Shanter in the long ago; if he had looked over his shoulder, he might have discovered that he was followed by a riderless horse, nothing more.

But a riderless horse is a gruesome thing—sometimes.

CHAPTER IX
STRANGE DISAPPEARANCES

The further adventures of Mr. Hobbs on this memorable afternoon are quickly chronicled, notwithstanding the fact that he lived an age while they were transpiring, and experienced sensations that would still be fresh in his memory if he lived to be a hundred.

He was scarcely well out of sight of the cabin when his conscience began to smite him: after all, his patron might be in dire need of his services, and here he was, fleeing from an old woman and a whiff of smoke! Hobbs was not a physical coward, but it took more than a mile of hard-ridden conscience to bring his horse to a standstill. Then, with his heart in his mouth, he slowly began to retrace his steps, walking where he had galloped a moment before. A turn in the road brought him in view of something that caused him to draw rein sharply. A hundred yards ahead, five or six men were struggling with a riderless bay horse.

"My Gawd!" ejaculated Hobbs. "It's *his* horse! I might have known!"

He looked eagerly for his patron. There was no sign of him, so Hobbs rode slowly forward, intent upon asking the woodmen—for such they appeared to be—to accompany him to the glen, now but a short distance ahead.

As he drew nearer, it struck him forcibly that the men were not what he had thought them to be. They were an evil-looking lot, more like the strikers he had seen in the town earlier in the day. Even as he was turning the new thought over in his mind, one of them stepped out of the little knot, and, without a word of warning, lifted his arm and fired point blank at the little Englishman. A pistol ball whizzed close by his head. His horse leaped to the side of the road in terror, almost unseating him.

But Hobbs had fighting blood in his veins. What is more to the point, he had a Mauser revolver in his pocket. He jerked it out, and, despite a second shot from the picket, prepared to ride down upon the party. An instant later half a dozen revolvers were blazing away at him. Hobbs turned at once and rode in the opposite direction, whirling to fire twice at the unfriendly group. Soon he was out of range and at leisure. He saw the futility of any attempt to pass them. The only thing left for him to do was to ride as quickly as possible to the city and give the alarm: at the same time, to acquaint the police with the deliberate assault of the desperadoes.

His mind was so full of the disaster to Truxton King—he did not doubt for an instant that he had been destroyed by the sorceress—that he gave little thought to his own encounter with the rascals in the roadway. He had come to like the impetuous young man with the open purse and the open heart. Despite his waywardness in matters conventional to the last degree he could not but admire him for the smile he had and the courage that never failed him, even when the smile met the frown of rebuke.

Riding swiftly through the narrow, sunless defile he was nearing the point where the road connected with the open Highway; from there on the way was easy and devoid of peril. Suddenly his horse swerved and leaped furiously out of stride, stumbling, but recovering himself almost instantaneously. In the same second he heard the sharp crack of a firearm, far down the unbroken ravine to his left. A second shot came, this time from the right and quite close at hand. His horse was staggering, swaying—then down he crashed, Hobbs swinging clear barely in time to escape being pinioned to the ground. A stream of blood was pouring from the side of the poor beast. Aghast at this unheard of wantonness, the little interpreter knew not which way to turn, but stood there dazed until a third shot brought him to his senses. The bullet kicked up the dust near his feet. He scrambled for the heavy underbrush at the roadside and darted off into the forest, his revolver in his hand, his heart palpitating like mad. Time and again as he fled through the dark thickets, he heard the hoarse shouts of men in the distance. It dawned upon him at last that there had been an uprising of some kind in the city—that there was rioting and murder going on—that these men were not ordinary bandits, but desperate strikers in quest of satisfaction for grievances ignored.

Night came and he dropped to the soft, dank earth, utterly exhausted and absolutely lost for the time being in the pathless hills.

At ten o'clock the next morning Colonel Quinnox and a company of soldiers, riding from the city gates toward the north in response to a call for help from honest herders who reported attacks and robberies of an alarming nature, came upon the stiff, foot-sore, thorn-scratched Mr. Hobbs, not far from the walls of the town. The Colonel was not long in grasping the substance of Hobbs's revelations. He rode off at once for the Witch's hovel, sending Hobbs with a small, instructed escort to the Castle, where Baron Dangloss was in consultation with Mr. Tullis and certain ministers.

The city was peaceful enough, much to the surprise of Hobbs. No disturbance had been reported, said the guardsmen who rode beside him. Up in the hills there had been some depredations, but that was all.

"All?" groaned Mr. Hobbs. "All? Hang it all, man, wot do you call all? You haven't heard 'alf all of it yet. I tell you, there's been the devil to pay. Wait till the Colonel comes back from Ganlook Gap. He'll have news for you; take it from me, he will. That poor chap 'as gone up in smoke, as sure as my name's Hobbs."

They met Baron Dangloss near the barracks, across the park from the Castle. He was in close, earnest conversation with John Tullis and Count Halfont, both of whom seemed to be labouring under intense excitement. Over by the arsenal the little Prince, attended by his Aunt Loraine and Count Vos Engo—with two mechanical guardsmen in the background—was deep in conversation with Julius Spantz, the master-of-arms. If he had been near enough to hear, he might have learned that Prince Robin's air-gun was very much out of order and needed attention at once.

The arrival of Hobbs, a pitiful but heroic object, at once arrested the attention of every one. His story was heard by a most distinguished audience; in fact, Hobbs was near to exploding with his own suddenly acquired importance. Not only were there dark, serious looks from the men in the party, and distressed exclamations from the most beautiful young lady in the world (he had always said that of her), but he had the extreme unction of bringing tears to the eyes of a prince, and of hearing manfully suppressed sobs from the throat of the same august personage.

The looks that went round at the conclusion of his disjointed and oft-interrupted story, expressed something more than consternation.

"There is nothing supernatural about King's disappearance," said Tullis sharply. "That's all nonsense. He had money about him and it perhaps turns out that there really was a man at the crack in the door—a clever brigand who to-day has got the better of our vain-glorious friend. The shooting in the hills is more disturbing than this, to my mind. Gentlemen, you shouldn't lose any time in running these fellows down. It will mean trouble if it gets under way. They're an ugly lot."

"This mystery coming on top of the other is all the more difficult to understand. I mean the disappearance of the Countess Marlanx," said Baron Dangloss, pulling at his imperial in plain perplexity. "But we must not stop here talking. Will you come with me, Mr. Tullis, to the Tower? I shall send out my best man to work on the case of the lady. It is a most amazing thing. I still have hope that she will appear in person to explain the affair."

"I think not," said Tullis gloomily. "This looks like abduction-foul play, or whatever you choose to call it. She has never left her father's house in just this manner before. I believe, Baron, that Marlanx has taken her away by force. She told me yesterday that she would never go back to him if she could help it. I have already given you my suspicions regarding his designs upon the—ahem!" Catching the eager gaze of the Prince, he changed the word "throne" to "treasury." The Baron nodded thoughtfully. "The Countess attended the fête at Baron Pultz's last night, leaving at twelve o'clock. I said good-night to her at the fountain and watched her until she passed through the gate between the Baron's grounds and those of her father adjoining. She would not permit me to accompany her to the doors. Her maid had preceded her and was waiting just beyond the gate—at least, so she says to-day. It is less than two hundred feet from the gate to Perse's doorsteps. Well, she never crossed that space. Her maid waited for an hour near the fernery and then came to the Baron's. The Countess has not been seen since she passed through the gate in the wall. I say that she has been carried away."

"The maid will be at my office at eleven with the Duke of Perse and the house servants. I have detailed a man to look up this fellow Brutus you speak of, and to ascertain his whereabouts last night. Come, we will go to the Tower. The Duke is greatly distressed. He suspects foul play, I am confident, but he will not admit that Marlanx is responsible."

"But what about Mr. King?" piped up a small voice.

"Colonel Quinnox has gone to look for him, Bobby," began Tullis, frowning slightly. He was interested in but one human being at that moment.

"I want the old Witch beheaded," said the Prince. "Why don't you go, Uncle Jack? He's an American. He'd help you, I bet, if you were in danger."

Tullis flushed. Then he patted Prince Robin's shoulder and said, with no little emotion in his voice:

"Perhaps I deserve the rebuke, Bobby, but you must not forget that there is a lady in distress. Which would you have me do—desert the lady whom we all love or the man whom we scarcely know?"

"The lady," said Bobby promptly. "Hasn't she got a husband to look after her? Mr. King has no friends, no relations, nothing. Aunt Loraine likes him and so do I."

"He's a fine chap," asserted Hobbs, and afterward marvelled at his own temerity.

Loraine, her merry eyes now dark with anxiety, her cheeks white with resolution, turned upon John Tullis. "You might leave the rescue of the

Countess to the proper authorities—the police," she said calmly. "I think it is your duty as an American to head the search for Mr. King. If Count Marlanx has spirited his wife away, pray, who has a better right?"

"But we are not sure that he—"

"We are sure that Mr. King is either dead or in dire need of help," she interrupted hotly. He looked at her in surprise, swayed by two impulses.

"Colonel Quinnox is quite competent to conduct the search," he said shortly.

"But Colonel Quinnox has gone forth on another mission. He may be unable to give any of his time to the search for Mr. King. It is outrageous, John Tullis, to refuse help—"

"I don't refuse help," he exclaimed. "They may take the whole army out to look for him, so far as I am concerned. But, I'll tell you this—I consider it my duty as a man to devote what strength I have to the service of a *woman* in trouble. That ends it! Come, Baron; we will go to the Tower."

The amazed young woman looked at him with wide, comprehending eyes. Her lip trembled under the rebuke. Count Halfont intervened, hastily proposing that a second party be sent out at once with instructions to raze the Witch's hut if necessary.

"I shall be happy to lead the expedition," said young Count Vos Engo, bowing deeply to the young lady herself.

"You shall, Vos Engo," said Halfont. "Prepare at once. Take ten men. I shall report to General Braze for you."

Tullis turned suddenly to the resentful girl. "Loraine," he said gently, as the others drew away, "don't be hard with me. You don't understand."

"Yes, I do," she said stubbornly. "You are in love with her."

"Yes; that's quite true."

"A married woman!"

"I can't help it. I must do all I can for her."

She looked into his honest eyes for a moment.

"Forgive me," she murmured, hanging her head. "What is Mr. King to us, after all?"

"He is simply paying for his foolhardiness. Americans do that the world over."

"Be careful that you do not pay for something worse than foolhardiness."

"I think you may trust me."

She smiled brightly up into his face. "Have your way, then. Remember that I am her friend, too." Then she hurried off after the Prince and Vos Engo, who was already giving instructions to an attentive orderly.

"Poor Mr. King!" she said to the Prince, as they stood by watching the preparations. "I am afraid, Bobby, he can't come to your circus this week. I sent the invitation this morning, early. He may never receive it. Isn't it dreadful, Count Vos Engo?"

Count Vos Engo was politely concerned, but it should not be expected that, in his present state of mind regarding her, he could be seriously grieved by anything that might have happened to the rash American.

The guard about the Prince was doubled: orders requiring the strictest care of his person were issued by Count Halfont. By this time, it may be suspected, the suspicions of John Tullis had been communicated to men high in the government; no small amount of credence was attached to them. Baron Dangloss began to see things in a different light; things that had puzzled him before now seemed clear. His office was the busiest place in Edelweiss.

"It is not unreasonable to suspect that Marlanx, or some of his agents, having concluded that the Countess knew too much of their operations, and might not be a safe repository, decided to remove her before it was too late. Understand, gentlemen, I don't believe the Countess is in sympathy with her husband's schemes—"

The Duke of Perse interrupted the doughty baron. "You assume a great deal, Baron, in saying that he has schemes inimical to the best interests of this country."

"I fancy that your Grace will admit that your venerable son-in-law—who, if I mistake not, is some ten years your senior—has no great love for the reigning power in Graustark. We will pass that, however," said the Baron, pointedly. "We should be wise enough to guard against any move he may make; it is imperative that we should not be caught napping."

"I don't believe he has taken my daughter away by force. Why should he do so? She goes to him voluntarily at the end of each visit. There is no coercion." He met John Tullis's stony gaze without flinching. "I insist that she has been stolen by these brigands in the hills, to be held for ransom."

The stories of the maid, the footmen, the groundmen were all to the effect that the Countess had not returned to her father's home after leaving the fête next door. There were no signs of a struggle in the garden, nor had there been the slightest noise to attract the attention of the waiting maid. It was not impossible, after all, that she had slipped away of her own accord, possessed of a sudden whim or impulse.

The new man-servant, suspected by the Countess herself, passed through the examination creditably. Tullis, of course, had not yet told Dangloss of the Countess's own suspicions concerning this man. They were a part of their joint secret. The American felt sure, however, that this man knew more of the night's work than he had told. He conveyed this belief to Dangloss, and a close watch was set upon the fellow. More than once during the long afternoon John Tullis found himself wishing that he had that dare-devil, thoroughbred young countryman of his, Truxton King, beside him; something told him that the young man would prove a treasure in resourcefulness and activity.

Late in the afternoon, a telegram was brought to Tullis which upset all of their calculations and caused the minister of police to swear softly in pure disgust. It was from the Countess Marlanx herself, sent from Porvrak, a station far down the railway, in the direction of Vienna. It was self-explanatory: "I am going to Schloss Marlanx, there to end my days. There is no hope for me. I go voluntarily. Will you not understand why I am leaving Edelweiss? You must know." It was signed "Ingomede."

Tullis was dumbfounded. He caught the penetrating glance of Dangloss and flushed under the sudden knowledge that this shrewd old man also understood why she was leaving Edelweiss. Because of *him!* Because she loved him and would not be near him. His heart swelled exultantly in the next moment; a brave resolve was born within him.

"We don't need a key to that, my boy," said the Baron indulgently. "But I will say that she has damned little consideration for you when she steals away in the dead of night, without a word. In a ball dress, too. Unfeeling, I'd say. Well, we can devote our attention to Mr. King, who *is* lost."

"See here, Baron," said Tullis after a moment, "I want you to give me a couple of good men for a few days. I'm going to Schloss Marlanx. I'll get her away from that place if I have to kill Marlanx and swing for it."

At seven o'clock that night, accompanied by two clever secret service men, Tullis boarded the train for the West. A man who stood in the tobacconist's shop on the station platform smiled quietly to himself as the train pulled out. Then he walked briskly away. It was Peter Brutus, the lawyer.

A most alluring trap had been set for John Tullis!

The party that had gone to Ganlook Gap in charge of Count Vos Engo returned at nightfall, no wiser than when it left the barracks at noon. Riding bravely, but somewhat dejectedly beside the handsome young officer in command was a girl in grey. It was her presence with the troop that had created comment at the gates earlier in the day. No one could understand why she was riding forth upon what looked to be a dangerous mission. Least of all, Count Vos Engo, who had striven vainly to dissuade her from the purpose to accompany the soldiers.

Now she was coming home with them, silent, subdued, dispirited—even more so than she allowed the Count to see.

"I was hateful to him yesterday," she said penitently, as they rode into the city. Vos Engo had been thinking of something else: the remark disturbed him.

"He was very presumptuous-yesterday," he said crossly.

She transfixed him with a look meant to be reproachful.

"That's why I managed the ticket for Bobby's circus," she said, looking ahead with a genuinely mournful droop of her lip. "I was sorry for him. Oh, dear, oh, dear What will his poor mother say—and his sister?"

"We've done all we can, Loraine. Except to cable," he added sourly.

"Yes, I suppose so. Poor fellow!"

Colonel Quinnox and his men had been scouring the hills for bandits. They arrived at the Witch's cabin a few minutes after Vos Engo and his company. Disregarding the curses of the old woman, a thorough search of the place was made. The forest, the ravine, the mountainside for a mile or more in all directions were gone over by the searchers. There was absolutely no sign of the missing man, nor was there the least indication that there had been foul play.

The old woman's story, reflected by the grandson, was convincing so far as it went. She said that the young man remained behind in the kitchen to puzzle himself over the smoke mystery, while she went out to her doorstep. The man with the horses became frightened when she went down to explain the situation to him. He fled. A few minutes later the gentleman emerged, to find his horse gone, himself deserted. Cursing, he struck off down the glen in pursuit of his friend, and that was the last she saw of him. Not long afterward she heard shooting in the Gap and sent her grandson to see if anything could have happened to her late visitor, who, it seems, owed her one hundred gavvos as a forfeit of some sort.

"Bobby! Don't be foolish. How could I be in love with him?"

The further prosecution of the search was left to Colonel Quinnox and his men. Loraine, shuddering, but resolute, had witnessed the ransacking of the hut, had urged the arrest of the hag, and had come away disheartened but satisfied that the woman had told them the truth. Quinnox's theory was accepted by all. He believed that King had fallen into the hands of brigands and that a heavy ransom would be demanded for his release.

In a warm-tinted room at the Castle, later on in the evening, the Prince, in pajamas, was discoursing bravely on the idiosyncrasies of Fate. His only auditor was the mournful Loraine, who sat beside the royal bed in which he wriggled vaguely. The attendants were far down the room.

"Never mind, Aunt Loraine, you can't help it. I'm just as sorry as you are. Say, are you in love with him?"

"In love with whom?"

"Mr. King."

"Of course not, silly. What an absurd question. I do not know him at all."

"That's all right, Aunt Loraine. I believe in love at first sight. He is a—"

"Bobby! Don't be foolish. How could I be in love with *him*?"

"Well, you can't help it sometimes. Even princes fall in love without knowing it."

"I suppose so," dreamily.

"It's mighty hard to make up your mind which one you love best, though. Dr. Barrett's daughter in New York is awful nice, but I think she's—"

"She is twenty years older than you, Bobby, if you mean to say you are in love with her."

"Well, but I'll grow up, auntie. Anyhow, Paula Vedrowski is not so old as I. She is—"

"For heaven's sake, Bobby, do go to sleep!"

"Don't you care to hear about *my* love affairs?"

"You are perfectly ridiculous!"

"All right for you, auntie. I shan't listen when you want to tell me about yours. Gee, Uncle Jack listens, you bet. I wish he was here this minute. Say, is he ever going to get married?" There was no answer. He peered over the top of the pillow. There were tears in his Aunt Loraine's eyes. "Oh, say, auntie, darling, don't cry! I'll—I'll go to sleep, honest!"

She was not in love with Truxton King, but she was a fine, tender-hearted girl, who suffered because of the thing that had happened to him and because she loved his sister.

Over in the Hotel Regengetz, on a little table in the centre of the room, lay a thick envelope with the royal arms emblazoned in the upper corner. It contained an invitation to the private circus that had been arranged for the little Prince, and it bore the name of Truxton King.

Across the foot of the bed hung his evening clothes, laid out by a faithful and well-tipped house valet, snug and ready for instant use.

But where was Truxton King?

CHAPTER X
THE IRON COUNT

When King, in the kindness of his heart, grasped the old woman to keep her from falling to the floor, he played directly into the hands of very material agencies under her control. There was nothing ghostly or even spiritual in the incidents that followed close upon the simulated fainting spell of the fortune-teller. It has been said before that her bony fingers closed upon his arms in a far from feeble manner. He had no time for surprise at this sudden recovery; there was only time to see a fiendish grin flash into her face. The next instant something struck him in the face; then with a fierce jerk this same object tightened about his neck. His attempt to yell out was checked before a sound could issue from his lips.

It all came to him in a flash. A noose had been dropped over his head; as he was pulled backward, his startled, bulging eyes swept the ceiling. The mystery was explained, but in a manner that left him small room for satisfaction. Above him a square opening had appeared in the ceiling; two ugly, bearded faces were leaning over the edge and strong hands were grasping a thick rope. In a frenzy of fear and desperation he cast the old woman from him and tore violently at the rope.

They were drawing hard from above; his toes were barely touching the floor; he was strangling. Frantically he grasped the rope, lifting himself from the floor in the effort to loosen the noose with his free hand. A hoarse laugh broke upon his dinning ears, the leering faces drew nearer; and then, as everything went black, a heavy, yet merciful blow fell upon his head. As consciousness left him, he felt himself rushing dizzily upward, grasped by powerful hands and whisked through the opening into air so hot and stiffling that his last thought was of the fires of Hell.

Not many minutes passed before consciousness, which had been but partially lost, returned to him. The ringing sensation remained in his head, but he was no longer choking. The noose had been removed from his neck; the rope itself was now serving as a bond for his hands and feet, a fact that impressed itself upon him when he tried to rise. For some time he lay perfectly still, urging his senses into play: wondering where he was and what had happened to him.

It was pitch dark and the air was hot and close. Not a sound came to his throbbing ears. With characteristic irrepressibility he began to swear softly, but articulately. Proof that his profanity was mild—one might say genteel—came in an instant. A gruff voice, startlingly near at hand, interrupted him.

"Spit it out, young feller! Swear like a man, not like a damn canary bird."

Truxton tried hard to pierce the darkness, a strange thrill passing through his veins. The hidden speaker was unquestionably an American.

"What the devil does all this mean?" demanded the captive. "Where am I?"

"It means business, and you're here, that's where you are," was the sarcastic answer.

"Are you an American?"

"No. I'm a Chinaman."

"Oh, come off! Answer square."

"Well, I was born in Newport." As an afterthought: "Kentucky."

"You're in a damned nice business, I'll say that for you," growled Truxton. "Who is responsible for this outrage?"

He heard the man yawn prodigiously. "Depends on what you call an outrage."

"This is the damnedest high-handed outrage I've ever—"

"Better save your breath, young feller. You won't have it very long, so save what you can of it."

Truxton was silent for a moment, analysing this unique remark. "You mean I am to stop breathing altogether?"

"Something like that."

"Why?"

"I don't know."

"You don't know? Well, who does?"

"You'll find out when the boss gets good and ready."

"You are a fine American!"

"Look here, young feller, I've been polite to you, so don't get gay. I'll come over there and kick your jaw in."

"Come ahead. Anything to break the monotony."

"Didn't you get enough of the hangman's knot and the sandbag? Want more, eh? Well, if I wasn't so darned comfortable I'd come over there and give it to you. Now don't rile me!"

"I deserve to be kicked for being such a blithering fool as to get into this mess. Come on and kick me."

"You wanted to get a poke at the old man's eye, did ye? By thunder, that's like an American. Never satisfied to let things alone. See what it got you into?"

"The old man's eye? What old man?"

"That's for you to find out, if you can. You've made a hell of a poor start at it."

"You're a good-natured scoundrel"

"Thanks for them kind words."

"Well, what are you going to do with me? I don't like the air in here. It's awful. How long do I stay here?"

"Say, you're a gritty little man. I like your nerve. Too bad we ain't on the same side. I'll tell you this: you won't be here long. How would the old girl down there put it? You're going on a long voyage. That's it. But first we'll get out of this rat hole, just as soon as them other guys come back from the cave. You'll get fresh air purty soon. Now, don't talk any more. I'm through gossipin'!"

"How do you, an American, happen to be mixed up in a deal like this?"

"It's healthier work than makin' barrels at—I was goin' to say Sing Sing, but I hear they've changed the name. I prefer outdoor work."

"Fugitive, eh?"

"You might call it that. I'm wanted in seven States. The demand for me is great."

Truxton saw that he could get nothing out of the satirical rascal, so fell to speculating for himself. That he was still in the loft above the hovel was more or less clear to him. His mind, now active, ran back to the final scene in the kitchen. The trap-door in the ceiling, evidently a sliding arrangement, explained the mysterious disappearance of the owner of the eye; he had been whisked up through the aperture by confederates and the trap-door closed before it could be discovered. The smoking kettle no longer puzzled him, now that he knew of the secret room above the kitchen; a skilfully concealed blow-pipe could have produced the phenomenon. The space in which he was now lying, half suffocated, was doubtless a part of the cleverly designed excavation at the back of the hovel, the lower half being the kitchen, the upper an actual gateway to the open air somewhere in the mountainside.

That he had fallen into the hands of a band of conspirators was also quite clear to him. Whether they were brigands or more important operators against the Crown, he was, of course, in no position to decide. Time would tell.

It was enough that they expected to kill him, sooner or later. This, in itself, was sufficient to convince him that he was not to be held for ransom, but to be disposed of for reasons best known to his captors.

Like a shot the warning of Olga Platanova flashed into his brain. Here, then, was the proof that she actually knew of the peril he was in. But why should he be an object of concern to these men, whoever they were? His guard had mentioned "the old man." Good heavens, could he mean Spantz? The cold perspiration was standing on King's brow. Spantz! He recalled the wickedness in the armourer's face. But why should Spantz wish him evil? Again intuition, encouraged by memory, supplied him with a possible, even plausible explanation.

The Anarchists! The Reds! Olga was an avowed Anarchist; she was almost a prisoner in the house of her uncle. Truxton's guard sat up suddenly and felt for his weapon when the captive let out a bitter oath of understanding and rage.

"By gad, they think I am a detective!" he added, light coming to him with a rush.

"What's that?" snapped the other. Truxton could almost feel the other's body grow tense despite the space between them. "Are you a detective? Are you? By God, if you are, I'll finish you up right here. You—"

"No! They're on the wrong scent. By Jove, the laugh's on old man Spantz."

"Oho! So you *do* know what's up, then? Spantz, eh? Well, what you've guessed at or found out won't make much difference, my fine young fellow. They've got you, and you'll be worse off than Danny Deever in the mornin'! Hello! Here they come. Now we'll get out of this infernal bake-oven. Say, do you know, you've been cuddlin' up against a j'int of warm stove pipe for nearly an hour? Sh!"

The glimmer of a light came bobbing up from somewhere behind Truxton; he could see the flickering shadows on the wall. Two men crept into the room a moment later. One of them carried a lantern; the other turned King's body over with his foot.

"You damned brute," grated the captive.

"Call him what you like, young feller," said his first acquaintance. "He can't understand a word you say. Well, do we pull out?" This to the man with the lantern.

The roof was so low that they were compelled to stoop in moving about. Truxton saw that the three ruffians were great, brutal-faced fellows, with bared arms that denoted toil as well as spoils.

"Immediate!" said the lantern bearer. "Come; we drag him to the cave."

"Drag? Nix; we c'n carry him, pard. I'm not for draggin' him down that passage. Grab hold there,—you! Hey, get his feet, damn you!" The third man was reluctant to understand, but at last grasped the prisoner by the feet, swearing in a language of his own. The Yankee desperado took his shoulders, and together, with earnest grunts, they followed the man with the lantern, Truxton knew not whither except that it was away from the wretched sweat-hole.

He could see that they were crowding through a low, narrow passage, the earthen sides of which reeked with moisture. Twice they paused to rest, resuming the journey after a season of cursing, finally depositing him with scant courtesy upon the rocky floor of what proved to be a rather commodious cave. The breath was almost jarred from his body. He had the satisfaction of driving his two heels viciously against the person of the man who had held them the last ten minutes, receiving a savage kick in return.

Daylight streamed into this convenient "hole in the wall;" lying upon his side, Truxton faced the opening that looked out upon the world. He saw nothing but blue sky. Near the opening, looking down as if into the valley below, stood the tall, gaunt figure of a man, thin-shouldered and stooped. His back was to the captive, but King observed that the three men, with two companions, who sat at the back of the cave, never removed their gaze from the striking figure outlined against the sky.

Many minutes passed before the watcher turned slowly to take in the altered conditions behind him. King saw that he was old; grey-haired and cadaverous, with sharp, hawk-like features. This, then, was the "old man," and he was not William Spantz. Unlike Spantz in every particular was this man who eyed him so darkly, so coldly. Here was a highborn man, a man whose very manners bespoke for him years at court, a life spent in the upper world, not among the common people. Truxton found himself returning the stare with an interest that brought results.

"Your name is King, I believe," came from the thin lips of the old man. The tones were as metallic as the click of steel.

"Yes. May I inquire—"

"No, you may not inquire. Put a gag in his mouth. I don't care to hear anything from him. Gag him and cut the rope from his feet. He may walk from now on."

Three men sprang to do his bidding.

King felt in that instant that he was looking for the first time upon the features of the Iron Count, Marlanx the dishonoured. He lay there helpless, speechless for many minutes, glancing at this cruel tyrant. Into his soul sank the conviction that no mercy would come from this man, this hater of all men; justice would play no part in the final, sickening tragedy. It was enough that Marlanx suspected him of being in the way; to be suspected was to be condemned. The whole, hellish conspiracy flashed through his brain. He closed his eyes with the horror of it all.

Here was Marlanx on Graustark soil, conniving with cutthroats, commanding them without opposition. What could it mean except a swift-growing menace to the Crown—to the little Prince.

Marlanx was speaking. Truxton looked up, as at an executioner. The lean, cruel face of that beautiful girl's husband was not far from his own; the fiery eyes were burning into his. The Iron Count sat upon a boulder near his feet.

"So you are the Quixote who would tilt at invisible windmills, eh? I remember you quite well. We have met before. Perhaps you remember meeting my eye in Dame Babba's cabin—twice, I think. You remember, I see. Ha, ha! You were very slow not to have caught such an old man. You were near to it the first time, but—you missed it, eh? I thought you might have seen my heels as I disappeared. I dare say you are wondering what I intend to do with you, now that I have you. Well, I am not the man to mince words. Mr. King, you are quite young, but the good die young. I am very old, you observe. I will not say that you are to die to-night or to-morrow or any day, for I do not know. I am going to send you to a court. Not an ordinary court, Mr. King, but one of extreme perspicacity. I fancy you will die before long. We can spare you. I do not approve of meddlers. It seems to be quite settled that you are a police agent. Be that as it may, I imagine our little court of last resort will take no chances, one way or the other. A man or two, more or less, will not be counted a year from now."

The steady, cruel eyes fascinated King. He knew that he was in desperate straits, that he had one chance in a million to escape, and yet he found himself held by the spell of those eyes, drinking in certain metallic monotones as if hypnotised.

"I am glad you called again at my temporary abode, Mr. King. Americans are always welcome: the sooner they come, the sooner it's over. It may interest you to know that I am very partial to Americans. Were I a cannibal, I could eat them with relish. If I had my way, all Americans should be in heaven. The earth surely is not good enough nor big enough for them, and hell is already overcrowded. Yes," reflectively pressing his nose with a bony forefinger, "I love the Americans dearly. I should enjoy a similar visit from Mr. John Tullis. Although, I may say, he seems to be choosing another way of testing my hospitality. I expect him to visit me in my humble castle before many days. I should like to have him remain there until his dying day." There was a deep significance in his smile. King shuddered. His gaze followed the gaunt, spidery old man as he returned to the opening for another long survey of the valley below. Night was falling; the sky was growing darker, and the wind was rising. Marlanx's sharp features were not so distinguishable when he returned to the boulder. The men in the cave had not spoken except in whispers. They appeared to be living in abject fear of this grim old nobleman.

"Night is coming. I must say farewell, my bold young friend. My way lies to the north. This is merely a land of promise to me. You go southward, to the city of Edelweiss. But not through the gates; oh, no! There are other ways, as you will find. If you should, by any chance, escape the jurisdiction of the court I am sending you to, I sincerely trust you may honour me with another visit here. I come often to the hovel in the glen. It is the only friendly house I know of in all Graustark. Some day I may be able to recompense its beauteous mistress. My good friends, Dangloss, and Halfont, and Braze—and Tullis, whom I know only by reputation—are, as yet, unaware of my glorious return to Graustark, else they would honour me with their distinguished presence. Some day I may invite them to dine with me. I shall enjoy seeing them eat of the humble pie I can put before them. Good-bye, my brave Sir Galahad; I may never see you again."

With a courtly bow he turned from the tense-muscled captive and directed his final instructions to the men. "Take him at once to the city, but be on your guard. A single false move now means utter ruin for all of us. Our affairs go so well at present that we cannot afford to offend Dame Fortune. She smiles on us, my men. Take this fool to the house on the Monastery road. There you will turn him over to the others. It is for them to drag the truth from his lips. I'd suggest, dear Mr. King, that you tell them all you know before they begin the dragging process. It is a very unpleasant way they have." With a curt nod to the men, he strode out through the mouth of the cave and was gone. Dusk had settled down upon mountain and valley; a thin fog swam high in the air above. One of the men cut the rope that bound Truxton's feet.

"Get up," said the Newport man. "We've got to be movin'. How'd you like the old man? Smart bug, ain't he? Say, he'll throw the hooks into them guys down in Edelweiss so hard one of these days that they won't come out till they rot out."

Still gagged and somewhat dizzy, King was hurried off into the narrow mountain path, closely surrounded by the five men.

"They tell me your friend, the Cook guy, got plugged down in the Gap when he tried to duck this afternoon," volunteered the Yankee unconcernedly.

Hobbs shot? King's eyes suddenly filled with tears, a great wave of pity and shame rushing to his heart. Poor Hobbs! He had led him into this; to gratify a vain-glorious whim, he had done the little Englishman to death.

The silent, cautious march down the valley, through the Gap and along the ridge carried them far into the night. King knew that they were skirting the main roads, keeping to the almost hidden trails of the mountaineers. They carried no light, nor did they speak to each other, except in hoarse whispers. In single file they made their way, the prisoner between them, weary, footsore and now desperate in the full realisation of his position. Being gagged, he could make no appeal to the one man who might befriend him—his villainous countryman. It occurred to him—grim thought—that the astute Marlanx had considered that very probability, and had made it impossible for him to resort to the cupidity of the hireling.

At last, when he could scarcely drag his feet after him, they came to a halt. A consultation followed, but he could not understand a word. This much he knew: they were in the hills directly above the northern gates. Two of the men went forward, moving with extreme caution. In half an hour they returned and the march was resumed.

Their next halt came sooner than he expected. The vague, black shadow of a lightless house loomed up before them. In a twinkling he was hustled across the road and into a door. Then down a flight of stairs, through pitchy darkness, guided by two of the men, a whispered word of advice now and then from the Yankee saving him from perilous stumbles. He was jerked up sharply with a command to stand still. A light flashed suddenly in his face, blinding him for the moment. Voices in eager, quick conversation came to his ears long before his eyes could take in the situation.

Soon he saw that they were in a broad, bare cellar; three men in heavy black beards were in earnest conversation with several of his captors; all were gesticulating fiercely.

His Newport companion enlightened him, between puffs of the pipe he was struggling with. "Here's where we say good-bye, young fellow. We turn you over to these gents, whoever they are. I'm sort of out of it when they get to jabberin' among themselves. I can understand 'em when they talk slow, but, say, did you ever hear a flock of Union Square sparrows chirp faster than them fellers is talkin' now? Nix. You go into the village gay with these Schwabs by the sewer line, I guess." Truxton pricked up his ears. "The old man has had a hole chopped in the sewer here, they tell me, and it's a snap to get into the city. Not very clean or neat, but it gets you there. Well, so long! They're ready, I see. They don't monkey long when they've got a thing to do. I'd advise you not to be too stubborn when they get you to headquarters; it may go easier with you. I'm not so damned bad, young feller. It's just the business I'm in—and the company."

King felt a thrill of real regard for the rascal. He nodded his thanks and tried to smile. The fellow grinned and slapped him on the shoulder, unobserved by the others. In another moment his guardianship was transferred; he was being hurried across the cellar toward an open doorway. Down a few stone steps he was led by the bearded crew, and then pushed through a hole in what appeared to be a heavy brick wall. He realised at once where he was. The gurgle of running water, the odor of foul airs came up to him. It was the great sewer that ran from the hills through the heart of the city, flushed continuously by a diverted mountain stream that swept down from above.

He was wading in cold water over a slippery bottom, tightly held by two men, the third going ahead with the lantern. Always ahead loomed the black, opaque circle which never came nearer, never grew smaller. It was the ever receding wall of darkness.

He did not know how long they traversed the chill sewer in this fashion. In time, however, the water got deeper; rats began to scurry along the sides of the circle or to swim frantically on in front of the disturbers. The smells were sickening, overpowering. Only excitement, curiosity, youth—whatever you may care to term it-kept him up and going. The everlasting glory of youth never ends until old age has provided the surfeit of knowledge; the strife to see ahead, to find out what is to be, to know,—that is youth. Youth dies when curiosity ends. The emotion is even stronger than the dread of what may lie beyond in the pallid sea of uncertainty.

His bones were chilled and creaking with fatigue. He was remorselessly hungry. There was water, but he could not drink it.

At last the strange journey ended. They came to a niche in the slimy wall. Up into this the men climbed, dragging him after them. The man above was cautiously tapping on what appeared to be solid masonry. To King's surprise a section of the wall suddenly opened before them. He was seized from above by strong hands and literally jerked through the hole, his companions following. Up narrow steps, through a sour-smelling passage and—then, into a long, dimly lighted room, in the centre of which stood a long table.

He was not permitted to linger here for long, but passed on into a small room adjoining. Some one, speaking in English, told him to sit down. The gag was removed from his stiff, inflamed mouth.

"Fetch him some water," said a voice that he was sure he recognised—a high, querulous voice.

"Hello, Spantz," articulated Truxton, turning to the black-bearded, bent figure.

There was an instance of silence. Then Spantz spoke, with a soft laugh: "You will not know so much to-morrow, Herr King. Give him the water, man. He has much to say to us, and he cannot talk with a dry throat."

"Nor an empty stomach," added King. He drank long of the pitcher that was held to his lips.

"This is not the Regengetz," growled a surly voice.

"You mean, I don't eat?"

"Not at midnight, my friend."

"It seems to be an all-night joint."

"Enough," cried Spantz. "Bring him out here. The others have come."

King was pushed out into the larger room, where he was confronted by a crowd of bewhiskered men and snaky-eyed women with most intellectual nose-glasses. It required but a glance to convince him that the whiskers were false.

For nearly an hour he was probed with questions concerning his business in Edelweiss. Threats followed close upon his unsatisfactory answers, though they were absolutely truthful. There was no attempt made to disguise the fact that they were conspiring against the government; in fact, they were rather more open than secretive. When he thought of it afterward, a chill crept over him. They would not have spoken so openly before him if they entertained the slightest fear that he would ever be in a position to expose them.

"We'll find a way to make you talk to-morrow, my friend. Starving is not pleasant."

"You would not starve me!" he cried.

"No. You will have the pleasure of starving yourself," said a thin-eyed fellow whom he afterward knew as Peter Brutus.

He was thrown back into the little room. To his surprise and gratification, the bonds on his wrists were removed. Afterward he was to know that there was method in this action of his gaolers: his own utter impotency was to be made more galling to him by the maddening knowledge that he possessed hands and feet and lungs—and could not use them!

He found a match in his box and struck it. There was no article of furniture. The floor was bare, the walls green with age. He had a feeling that there would be rats; perhaps lizards. A search revealed the fact that his purse, his watch and his pocket-knife were missing. Another precious match showed him that there were no windows. A chimney hole in the ceiling was, perhaps, the only means by which fresh air could reach this dreary place.

"Well, I guess I'm here to stay," he said to himself. He sat down with his back to the wall, despair in his soul. A pitiful, weak smile came to him in the darkness, as he thought of the result of his endeavour to "show off" for the benefit of the heartless girl in rajah silk. "What an ass I am," he groaned. "Now she will never know."

Sleep was claiming his senses. He made a pillow of his coat, commended himself to the charity of rats and other horrors, and stretched his weary bones upon the relentless floor.

"No one will ever know," he murmured, his last waking thought being of a dear one at home.

CHAPTER XI
UNDER THE GROUND

Day and night were the same to the occupant of the little room. They passed with equal slowness and impartial darkness. Five days that he could account for crawled by before anything unusual happened to break the strain of his solitary, inexplicable confinement. He could tell when it was morning by the visit of a bewhiskered chambermaid with a deep bass voice, who carried a lighted candle and kicked him into wakefulness. The second day after his incarceration began, he was given food and drink. It was high time, for he was almost famished. Thereafter, twice a day, he was led into the larger room and given a surprisingly hearty meal. Moreover, he was allowed to bathe his face and hands and indulge in half an hour's futile stretching of limbs. After the second day few questions were asked by the men who had originally set themselves up as inquisitors. At first they had treated him with a harshness that promised something worse, but an incident occurred on the evening of the second day that changed the whole course of their intentions.

Peter Brutus had just voiced the pleasure of the majority by urging the necessity for physical torture to wring the government's secrets from the prisoner. King, half famished, half crazed by thirst, had been listening to the fierce argument through the thin door that separated the rooms. He heard the sudden, eager movement toward the door of his cell, and squared himself against the opposite wall, ready to fight to the death. Then there came a voice that he recognised.

A woman was addressing the rabid conspirators in tones of deadly earnestness. His heart gave a bound. It was the first time since his incarceration that he had heard the voice of Olga Platanova, she who had warned him, she who still must be his friend. Once more he threw himself to the floor and glued his ear to the crack; her voice had not the strident qualities of the other women in this lovely company.

"You are not to do this thing," she was saying. King knew that she stood between her companions and the door. "You are not to touch him! Do you hear me, Peter Brutus? All of you?"

There followed the silence of stupefaction, broken at last by a voice which he recognised as that of old man Spantz.

"Olga! Stand aside!"

"No! You shall not torture him. I have said he is no spy. I still say it. He knows nothing of the police and their plans. He has not been spying upon us. I am sure of it."

"How can you be sure of it?" cried a woman's voice, harsh and strident.

"He has played with you," sneered another.

"I will not discuss the point. I know he is not what you say he is. You have no right to torture him. You have no right to hold him prisoner."

"God, girl, we cannot turn him loose now. He must never go free again. He must die." This was from Spantz.

"We cannot release him, I grant you," she said, and Truxton's heart sank. "Not now, but afterward, yes. When it is all over he can do no harm. But, hear me now, all of you. If he is harmed in any way, if he is maltreated, or if you pursue this design to starve him, I shall not perform my part of the work on the 26th. This is final."

For a full minute, it seemed to King, no one spoke.

"You cannot withdraw," exclaimed Peter Brutus. "You are pledged. You are sworn. It is ordained."

"Try me, and see if I will not do as I say. He is to be treated kindly so long as we hold him here and he is to be released when the committee is in power. Then he may tell all that he knows, for it will be of no avail. He cannot escape, that you know. If he were a spy I would offer no objection to your methods. He is an American gentleman, a traveller. I, Olga Platanova, say this to you. It is not a plea, not a petition; it is an ultimatum. Spare him, or the glorious cause must suffer by my defection."

"Sh! Not so loud, girl! He can hear every word you say!"

"Why should it matter, madam? He is where he can do no harm to our cause. Let him hear. Let him understand what it is that we are doing. Are we ashamed of our duty to the world? If so, then we are criminals, not deliverers. I am not ashamed of what God wills me to do. It is horrible, but it is the edict of God. I will obey. But God does not command us to torture an innocent man who happens to fall into our hands. No! Let him hear. Let him know that I, Olga Platanova, am to hurl the thing that is to destroy the life of Prince Robin. I am not afraid to have him know to-day what the world will know next week. Let him hear and revile me now, as the world will do after it is over and I am gone. The glory will be mine when all the people of this great globe are joined to our glorious realm. Then the world will say that Olga Platanova was not a beast, but a deliverer, a creator! Let him hear!"

The listener's blood was running cold. The life of Prince Robin! An assassination! "The thing that will destroy!" A bomb! God!

For half an hour they argued with her, seeking to turn her from the stand she had taken; protesting to the last stage, cursing her for a sentimental fool. Then they came to terms with her. Truxton King owed his life to this strange girl who knew him not at all, but who believed in him. He suffered intensely in the discovery that she was, in the end, to lend herself to the commission of the most heartless and diabolical of crimes—the destruction of that innocent, well-worshipped boy of Graustark.

"You must be in love with this simple-minded American, who comes—" Peter Brutus started to say at one stage of the discussion, when the frail girl was battling almost physically with her tormentors.

"Stop! Peter Brutus, you shall not say that! You know where my love lies! Don't say that to me again, you beast!" she had cried, and Brutus was silenced.

Truxton was brought into the room a few minutes later. He was white with emotion as he faced the Committee of Ten. Before a word could be addressed to him he blurted out:

"You damned cowards! Weak as I am, I would have fought for you, Miss Platanova, if I could have got through that door. Thank you for what you have done to convince these dogs! I would to God I could save you from this thing you are pledged to do. It is frightful! I cannot think it of you! Give it up! All of you, give this thing up! I will promise secrecy—I will never betray what I have heard. Only don't do this awful thing! Think of that dear little boy—"

Olga Platanova cried out and covered her eyes with her hands, murmuring the words "dear little boy" over and over again. She was led from the room by William Spantz. Peter Brutus stood over King, whose arms were held by two stalwart men.

"Enough!" he commanded. "We spare you, not for her sake, but for the sake of the cause we serve. Hear me: you are to be held here a prisoner until our plans are consummated. You will be properly fed and cared for. You have heard Miss Platanova say that she will cook the food for you herself, but you are not to see her. Do not seek to turn her from her purpose. That you cannot do. She is pledged to it; it is irrevocable. We have perhaps made a mistake in bringing you here: it would have been far wiser to kill you in the beginning, but—"

King interrupted him. "I haven't the least doubt that you will kill me in the end. She may not be here to protect me after—after the assassination."

"She is prepared to die by the same bomb that slays the Prince," was all that Brutus would say in response to this, but King observed the sly look that went round amongst them. He knew then that they meant to kill him in the end.

Afterward, in his little room, he writhed in the agony of helplessness. The Prince, his court, the government—all were to be blasted to satisfy the end of this sickening conspiracy. Loraine! She, too, was doomed! He groaned aloud in his misery and awe.

Food and water came after that, but he ate and drank little, so depressed had he become. He sought for every means of escape that suggested itself to him. The walls, the floors, the doors, the stairway to the armourer's shop— all were impassable, so carefully was he guarded. From time to time he heard inklings of the plot which was to culminate on the fatal 26th; he did not get the details in particular, but he knew that the bomb was to be hurled at the Prince near the entrance to the plaza and that Marlanx's men were to sweep over the stricken city almost before the echo died away.

There was a telegraph instrument in the outer room. He could hear it ticking off its messages day and night, and could hear the discussion of reports as they came in or went out. It soon became clear to him that the wire connected the room with Marlanx's headquarters near Balak in Axphain, a branch instrument being stationed in the cave above the Witch's hut. He marvelled at the completeness of the great conspiracy; and marvelled more because it seemed to be absolutely unknown to the omnipresent Dangloss.

On his third night he heard the Committee discussing the failure of one of Marlanx's most cunning schemes. The news had come in over the wire and it created no small amount of chagrin among the Red conspirators. That one detail in their mighty plot should go contrary to expectations seemed to disturb them immeasurably. King was just beginning to realise the stupendous possibilities of the plot; he listened for every detail with a mind so fascinated by horror that it seemed hardly able to grasp the seriousness of his own position.

It seemed that Marlanx deemed it necessary—even imperative—to the welfare of the movement, that John Tullis should be disposed of summarily before the crucial chapter in their operations. Truxton heard the Committee discussing the fiasco that attended his first attempt to draw the brainy, influential American out of the arena. It was clear that Marlanx suspected Tullis of a deep admiration for his wife, the Countess Ingomede; he was prepared to play upon that admiration for the success of his efforts. The Countess disappeared on a recent night, leaving the court in extreme doubt as to her fate. Later a decoy telegram was sent by a Marlanx agent, informing Tullis that she had gone to Schloss Marlanx, never to return, but so shrewdly worded that he would believe that it had been sent by coercion, and that she was actually a prisoner in the hands of her own husband. Tullis was expected to follow her to the Castle, bent on rescue. As a matter of fact, the Countess was a prisoner in the hills near Balak, spirited away from her own garden by audacious agents of the Iron Count. Tullis was swift to fall into the trap, but, to the confusion of the arch-plotter, he was just as swift to avoid the consequences.

He left Edelweiss with two secret service men, bound for Schloss Marlanx. All unknown to him, a selected company of cutthroats were in waiting for him on the hills near the castle. To the amazement of the conspirators, he suddenly retraced his tracks and came back to Edelweiss inside of twenty-four hours, a telegram stopping him at Gushna, a hundred miles down the line. The message was from Dangloss and it was in cipher. A trainman in the service of Marlanx could only say, in explanation, that the American had smiled as he deciphered the dispatch and at once left the carriage with his men to await the up-train at six o'clock.

Peter Brutus repeated a message he had just received from Marlanx at Balak. It was to the effect that he had reason to believe that his wife had managed, through an unknown traitor, to send word to the Tower that she was not at Schloss Marlanx, nor in any immediate danger. He felt himself supported in this belief by the obvious fact that no further efforts had been made by Tullis or the police since that day. The authorities apparently were inactive and Tullis was serenely secure at the Royal Castle. The guard about the Prince, however, had been largely increased.

Tullis was known to be re-organising the Royal Guard, supported by the ministry to a man, it was said; not even the Duke of Perse opposed him.

"The Count is more afraid of this man Tullis than of all the rest," averred Peter Brutus. "He has reasons to hate and fear the Americans. That is why he desires the death of our prisoner. He has said, time and again, over the wire that King will in some way escape and play the deuce with our plans. It does not seem possible, however. We have him absolutely secure, and Olga—well, you know how she feels about it."

"I don't see why he should be so disturbed by Tullis," growled one of the men. "He has no real authority at court and he is but one man against an unseen army that will not strike until everything is ready. There can be no—"

"That is what I have said to my master, Julius, but he will not be convinced. He says that he has had experience with one American, Lorry, and he knows the breed. Tullis has more power at court than the people think. He is shrewd and strong and not to be caught napping. As a matter of fact, the Count says, Tullis has already scented danger in the air and has induced the ministry to prepare for an uprising. Of course, he cannot know of the dynamiting that is to open the way to success, but it is true that if anybody can upset our plans, it is this meddling American. He is a self-appointed guardian of the Prince and he is not to be sneered at. The regents are puppets, nothing more."

Julius Spantz agreed with Brutus. "I know that the guard is being strengthened and that certain precautions are being taken to prevent the abduction of the Prince. It is common rumour among the soldiers that Count Marlanx will some day seek to overthrow the government and take the throne. The air is full of talk concerning this far-distant possibility. Thank God, it is to be sooner than they think. If Tullis and General Braze were given a month or two longer, I doubt if we could succeed. The blow must catch them unprepared."

"This is the 22d, Saturday is the 26th. They can do nothing in four days," said one of the women.

"Count Marlanx will be ready on the 26th. He has said so. A new strike will be declared on the railroad on the 25th and the strikers will be in the city with their grievances. Saturday's celebration will bring men from the mountains and the mines to town. A single blow, and we have won." So spoke Brutus.

"Then why all this fear of Tullis?" demanded Anna Cromer.

"It is not like the Iron Count," added Madame Drovnask with a sneer.

Olga Platanova had not spoken. She was not there to talk. She was only to act on the 26th of July. She was the means to an end.

"Well, fear or no fear, the Count lies awake trying to think of a way to entice him from the city before the 26th. It may be silly, madam, but Count Marlanx is a wiser man than any of us here. He is not afraid of Dangloss or Braze or Quinnox, but he is afraid of what he calls 'American luck!' He is even superstitious about it."

"We must not—we cannot fail," grated William Spantz, and the cry was reiterated by half a dozen voices.

"The world demands success of us!" cried Anna Cromer. "We die for success, we die for failure! It is all one!"

The next morning, after a sleepless night, Truxton King made his first determined attempt to escape. All night long he had lain there thinking of the horrid thing that was to happen on the black 26th. He counted the days, the hours, the minutes. Morning brought the 23d. Only three days more! Oh, if he could but get one word to John Tullis, the man Marlanx feared; if he could only break away from these fiends long enough to utter one cry of warning to the world, even with his dying gasp!

Marlanx feared the Americans! He even feared him, a helpless captive! The thrill of exultation that ran through his veins was but the genesis of an impulse that mastered him later on.

He knew that two armed men stood guard in the outer room day and night. The door to the stairway leading into the armourer's shop was of iron and heavily barred; the door opening into the sewer was even more securely bolted; besides, there was a great stone door at the foot of the passage. The keys to these two doors were never out of the possession of William Spantz; one of his guards held the key to the stairway door. His only chance lay in his ability to suddenly overpower two men and make off by way of the armourer's shop.

When his little door was opened on the morning of the 23d, Truxton King's long, powerful figure shot through as if sped by a catapult. The man with the candle and the knife went down like a beef, floored by a blow on the jaw.

The American, his eyes blazing with hope and desperation, kept onward—to find himself face to face with Olga Platanova!

She was staring at him with frightened eyes, her lips apart, her hands to her breast. The tableau was brief. He could not strike her down. With a curse he was turning to the man on the floor, eager to snatch the keys from his belt. A scream from her drawn lips held him; he whirled and looked into the now haggard face of the girl he had considered beautiful. The penalty for her crime was already written there. She was to die in three days!

"He has not the key!" she cried. "Nor have I. You have no chance to escape. Go back! Go back! They are coming!"

A key rattled in the door. When it swung open, two men stood in the aperture, both with drawn pistols. The girl leaped between them and the helpless, defeated American.

"Remember!" she cried. "You are not to kill him!"

Peter Brutus had risen from the floor, half dazed but furious. He made a vicious leap at King, his knife ready for the lunge.

"I'm glad it's you," roared King, leaping aside. His fist shot out and again Brutus went down. The men in the doorway actually laughed.

"A good blow, even if it avails you nothing," said one of them drily. "He is not an especial favorite with us. Return to your room at once. Miss Platanova, call your uncle. It is now necessary to bind the fellow's hands. They are too dangerous to be allowed to roam at large in this fashion."

All day long Truxton paced his little prison, bitterly lamenting his ill-timed effort. Now he would be even more carefully guarded. His hands were bound behind his back; he was powerless. If he had only waited! Luck had been against him. How was he to know that the guard with the keys had gone upstairs when Olga brought his breakfast down? It was fate.

The 23d dragged itself into the past and the 24th was following in the gloomy wake of its predecessors. Two days more! He began to feel the approach of madness! His own death was not far away. It would follow that of the Prince and of Olga Platanova, his friend. But he was not thinking of his own death; he was thinking of the Prince's life!

The atmosphere of suppressed excitement that characterised the hushed gatherings in the outer room did not fail to leave its impression upon him; he knew there was murder in the hearts of these fanatics; he could feel the strain that held their hitherto vehement lips to tense whisperings and mutterings. He could distinguish the difference between the footsteps of to-day and those of yesterday; the tread was growing lighter, unconsciously more stealthy with each passing hour.

Forty-eight hours! That was all!

Truxton found himself crying bitterly from time to time; not because he was in terror but because he knew of the thing that hourly drew nearer despite the fact that he knew!

Olga Platanova's voice was heard no more before the Committee of Ten. Something told him that she was being groomed and primed in an upstairs room! Primed like a gun of war! He wondered if she could be praying for courage to do the thing that had been set down for her to do. Food now came irregularly to him. She was no longer preparing it.

She was making herself ready!

Early that night, as he lay with his ear to the crack of the door, he heard them discussing his own death. It was to come as soon as Olga had gone to her reward! She was not there to defend him. Spantz had said that she was praying in her room, committing her soul to God! Truxton King suddenly pricked up his ears, attracted by a sentence that fell from the lips of one of the men.

"Tullis is on his way to the hills of Dawsbergen by this time. He will be out of the way on the 26th safe enough."

"Count Marlanx was not to be satisfied until he had found the means to draw him away from Edelweiss," said another. "This time it will work like a charm. Late this afternoon Tullis was making ready to lead a troop of cavalry into the hills to effect a rescue. Sancta Maria! That was a clever stroke! Not only does he go himself, but with him goes a captain with one hundred soldiers from the fort. Ha, ha! Marlanx is a fox! A very exceptional fox!"

Tullis off to the hills? With soldiers, to effect a rescue! Truxton sat up, his brain whirling.

"A wise fox!" agreed Peter Brutus, thickly. His lips were terribly swollen from King's final blow. "Tullis goes off chasing a jack-o'-lantern in the hills; Marlanx sits by and laughs at the joke he's played. It is good! Almost too good to be true. I wonder what our fine prisoner will say to it when the new prisoner comes to keep him company over the 26th."

CHAPTER XII
A NEW PRISONER ARRIVES

It was far past midnight when King was roused from the doze into which he had fallen, exhausted and disconsolate, an hour earlier. Sounds of unusual commotion reached him from the outer room. Instantly he was wide awake, breathing heavily in the sudden overpowering fear that he had slept for many hours and that the time had come for the conspirators to go forth. Was it the 26th?

Loud, quick commands came to his ears; the moving of eager footsteps; the drawing of bolts.

"They are here at last," he heard some one say. "God, this suspense has been horrible. But they are here."

"Stand ready, then, with the guns!" cried Peter Brutus. "It may be a trick, after all. Don't open that door down there, Spantz, until you know who is on the outside."

Then followed a long interval of dead silence.

"It's all right," came at last in the relieved, eager voice of Peter Brutus. "Clear the way, comrades. Give them room! By our Holy Father, this is a brave triumph. Ah!"

Heavy footsteps clogged into the room, accompanied by stertorous breathing and no small amount of grunting from masculine throats. Doors were closed, bolts shot, and then many voices let loose their flow of eager exclamations. Not one, but three or four languages were spoken by the excited, intense occupants of the outer room; King could, make nothing of what they said. Finally the sharp, incisive voice of William Spantz broke through the babble, commanding silence.

"Still unconscious," he said, when some measure of order was secured.

"Yes," grunted one of the men, evidently a newcomer. "Since we left the house above the ramparts. No need for gags or bonds, but we used them, just the same. Now that we are here, what is to be done?"

"We will have our instructions to-morrow. The Count is to inform us before nightfall where she is to be removed to. Next week she is to go to Schloss Marlanx." Brutus inserted a cruel, heartless laugh, and then added: "There she is to remain until he is quite ready to take her to new apartments—in town. Trust the master to dispose of her properly. He knows how to handle women by this time."

A woman, thought Truxton. The Countess! They had brought her here from Balak, after all. What a remorseless brute Marlanx must be to maltreat his beautiful wife as—Truxton did not complete the angry reflection. Words from the other side of the door checked the train of thought.

"To my mind, she is more beautiful than his own wife," observed Anna Cromer. "She will be a fine morsel for the Count, who has even cast longing eyes on so homely a mortal as I."

"All women are alike to him," said Spantz sententiously. "I hope she is not to be left here for long. I don't like women about at a time like this. No offence, Madame Drovnask."

"She'll go to-morrow night, I'm sure," said Peter. "I told the Count we could not keep her here over the—over the 26th. You see, there is a bare possibility that none of us may ever come back after the bomb is hurled. See? We don't want a woman to die of starvation down here, in that event. I don't care what happens to the man in there. But the Count does not want this one to starve. Oh, no; not he."

"We must put her in the room with the American for the present. You are sure he will take her away before Saturday? A woman's cries are most distressing." It was Spantz who spoke.

"I'll stop her crying," volunteered Anna Cromer harshly.

"I fancy you could, my dear," agreed Spantz. They all laughed.

"She's regaining her senses," exclaimed one of the men. "Stand back, every one. Give her air."

"Air?" cried Anna Cromer. "It's at a premium down here, Raoul."

Presently the door to King's room was thrown open. He had got to his feet and was standing in the centre of the room, his eyes blinking in the glare of light.

"Holloh!" cried Peter Brutus, "you up, eh? We've got a fair lady for you, my friend. Get back there, you dog! Keep in your corner."

Truxton faced the ugly crowd beyond the door for a moment and then fell back to the corner to watch the proceedings with wondering, pitying eyes.

"You are a fine bunch of human beings," he blurted out, savage with despair and rage. No one gave heed to the compliment.

A man with a lighted candle entered first, holding the light above his head. He was followed by two others, who supported the drooping, tottering figure of a woman.

"Let her sit there against the wall, Drago. Julius, fetch in more candles. She must not be left in the dark. *He* says she is not to be frightened to death. Women are afraid of the dark—and strange dogs. Let there be light," scoffed Peter Brutus, spitting toward King.

"I'll get you for that some day," grated the American, white with anger. Peter hesitated, then spat again and laughed loudly.

"Enough!" commanded William Spantz. "We are not children." Turning to King he went on, a touch of kindness in his voice: "Cheer her if you can. She is one of your class. Do not let the lights go out."

Raising his hands, he fairly drove the others from the doorway. An instant later, King and his miserable, half-conscious companion were alone, locked in together, the fitful light from the candle on the floor playing hide and seek in shadows he had not seen before during his age of imprisonment.

For a long time he stood in his corner, watching the figure huddled against the opposite wall. Her face was not plainly visible, her head having dropped forward until the chin nestled in the lace jabot at her throat. A mass of tangled hair fell across her eyes; her arms hung limply at her sides; small, modish riding hoots showed beneath the hem of her skin, forlorn in their irresoluteness. Her garments were sadly bedraggled; a pathetic breast rose and fell in choking sobs and gasps.

Suddenly he started forward, his eyes wide and staring. He had seen that grey riding habit before! He had seen the hair!

Two eager steps he took and then halted, half way. She had heard him and was raising her eyes, bewildered and wavering between dreamland and reality.

"Great Jehovah!" he gasped, unbelieving. "You? My God, is it you?"

He dropped to his knees before her, peering into her startled eyes. A look of abject terror crossed the tired, tear-stained face. She shrank away from him, shivering, whimpering like a cowed child.

"What is it? Where am I?" she moaned. "Oh, let me go! What have I done, that you should bring me here? Let me go, Mr. King! You are not so wicked as—"

"I? I bring you here?" he interrupted, aghast. Then he understood. Utter dismay filled his eyes. "You think that I have done this thing to you? God above us! Look! I, too, am a prisoner here. I've been here for days, weeks, years. They are going to kill me after to-morrow. And you think that I have done this to you!"

"I don't know what—Oh, Mr. King, what does it all mean? Forgive me! I see now. You are bound—you are suffering—you are years older. I see now. But why is it? What have you done? What have I done?"

She was growing hysterical with terror.

"Don't shrink from me," he urged. "Try to calm yourself. Try to look upon me as a friend—as a possible saviour. Lie quiet, do, for a little while. Think it all out for yourself."

He knelt there before her while she sobbed out the last agony of alarm. There were no tears in her eyes; racking sobs shook her slender body; every nerve was aquiver, he could see. Patiently he waited, never taking his firm, encouraging gaze from her face. She grew calmer, more rational. Then, with the utmost gentleness, he persuaded her to rise and walk about the little room with him.

"It will give you strength and courage," he urged. "Poor little girl! Poor little girl!"

She looked up into his face, a new light coming into her eyes.

"Don't talk now," he said softly. "Take your time. Hold to my arm, please. There! In a little while you'll be able to tell me all about it—and then we'll set about to find a way to escape these devils. We'll laugh at 'em, after all."

For five or ten minutes he led her back and forth across the room, very tenderly. At first she was faint and uncertain; then, as her strength and wits came back to her, courage took the place of despair. She smiled wanly and asked him to sit down with her.

"A way to escape, you said," she murmured, as he dropped to her side. "Where are we? What is it all about?"

"Not so loud," he cautioned. "I'll be perfectly candid with you. You'll have to be very, very brave. But wait. Perhaps it will be easier for you to tell me what has happened to you, so far as you know. I can throw light on the whole situation, I think. Tell me, please, in your own way and time. We're in a sorry mess, and it looks black, but, this much I can tell you: you are to be set free in a few days, unharmed. You may rest easy. That much is assured."

"And you?" she whispered, clutching his arm tightly, the swift thrill of relief dying almost as it was born. "What of you?"

"Oh, I'll get out all right," he affirmed with a confidence he did not feel. "I'm going to get you out of this or die in the attempt. Sh! Don't oppose me," he went on whimsically. "I've always wanted to be a hero, and here's my chance. Now tell me what happened to you."

Her piquant, ever-sprightly face had lost the arrogance that had troubled all his dreams of conquest. She was pale and shivering and so sorely distressed that he had it in his heart to clasp her in his arms as one might do in trying to soothe a frightened child. Her face grew cloudy with the effort to concentrate her thoughts; a piteous frown settled upon her brow.

"I'm not sure that I can recall everything. It is all so terrible—so unaccountable. It's like a dream that you try to remember and cannot. Finding you here in this place is really the strangest part of it. I cannot believe that I am awake."

She looked long and anxiously into his face, her eyebrows drawn together in an earnest squint of uncertainty. "Oh, Mr. King, I have had such a dreadful—dreadful time. Am I awake?"

"That's what I've been asking of myself," he murmured. "I guess we're both awake all right. Nightmares don't last forever."

Her story came haltingly; he was obliged to supply many of the details by conjecture, she was so hazy and vague in her memory.

At the beginning of the narrative, however, Truxton was raised to unusual heights; he felt such a thrill of exaltation that for the moment he forgot his and her immediate peril. In a perfectly matter-of-fact manner she was informing him that her search for him had not been abandoned until Baron Dangloss received a telegram from Paris, stating that King was in a hospital there, recovering from a wound in the head.

"You can imagine what I thought when I saw you here a little while, ago," she said, again looking hard at his face as if to make sure. "We had looked everywhere for you. You see, I was ashamed. That man from Cook's told us that you were hurt by—by the way I treated you the day before you disappeared, and—well, he said you talked very foolishly about it."

He drew a long breath. Somehow he was happier than he had been before. "Hobbs is a dreadful ass," he managed to say.

It seems that the ministry was curiously disturbed by the events attending the disappearance of the Countess Ingomede. The deception practised upon John Tullis, frustrated only by the receipt of a genuine message from the Countess, was enough to convince the authorities that something serious was afoot. It may have meant no more than the assassination of Tullis at the hands of a jealous husband; or it may have been a part of the vast conspiracy which Dangloss now believed to be in progress of development.

"Development!" Truxton King had exclaimed at this point in her narrative. "Good God, if Dangloss only knew what I know!"

There had been a second brief message from the Countess. She admitted that she was with her husband at the Axphain capital. This message came to Tullis and was to the effect that she and the Count were leaving almost immediately for a stay at Biarritz in France. "Mr. King," said the narrator, "the Countess lied. They did not go to Biarritz. I am convinced now that she is in the plot with that vile old man. She may even expect to reign in Graustark some day if his plans are carried out. I saw Count Marlanx yesterday. He was in Graustark. I knew him by the portrait that hangs in the Duke of Perse's house—the portrait that Ingomede always frowns at when I mention it to her. So, they did not go to France."

She was becoming excited. Her eyes flashed; she spoke rapidly. On the morning of the 23d she had gone for her gallop in the famous Ganlook road, attended by two faithful grooms from the Royal stables.

"I was in for a longer ride than usual," she said, with sudden constraint. She looked away from her eager listener. "I was nervous and had not slept the night before. A girl never does, I suppose."

He looked askance. "Yes?" he queried.

She was blushing, he was sure of it. "I mean a girl is always nervous and distrait after—after she has promised, don't you see."

"No, I don't see."

"I had promised Count Vos Engo the night before that I—Oh, but it really has nothing to do with the story. I—"

Truxton was actually glaring at her. "You mean that you had promised to marry Count Vos Engo!" he stammered.

"We will not discuss—"

"But did you promise to be his wife? Is he the man you love?" he insisted. She stared at him in surprise and no little resentment.

"I beg of you, Mr. King—" she began, but he interrupted her.

"Forgive me. I'm a fool. Don't mind me." He sank back against the wall, the picture of dejection. "It doesn't matter, anyway. I've got to die in a day or two, so what's the odds?"

"How very strangely you talk. Are you sure—I mean, do you think it is fever? One suffers so—"

He sighed deeply. "Well, that's over! Whew! It was a dream, by Jove!"

"I don't understand."

"Please go on."

She waited a moment and then, looking down, said very gently: "I'm so sorry for you." He laughed, for he thought she pitied him because he had awakened from the dream.

Then she resumed her story, not to be interrupted again. He seemed to have lost all interest.

She had gone six or eight miles down the Ganlook road when she came up with five troopers of the Royal Guard. It was a lonely spot at the junction of the King's Highway and the road to the mines. One of the troopers came forward and respectfully requested her to turn off into the mine road until a detachment passed, in charge of a gang of desperadoes taken at the Inn of the Hawk and Raven the night before. Unsuspecting, she rode off into the forest lane for several hundred yards.

It was a trap. The men were not troopers, but brigands gotten up in the uniform of the guard. Once away from the main highway, they made prisoners of her and the two grooms. Then followed a long ride through roads new to her. At noon they came to a halt while the rascals changed their clothing, appearing in their true garb, that of the mountaineer. Half dead with dread, she heard them discussing their plans; they spoke quite freely in the presence of the well-beaten grooms, who were led to expect death before many hours. It was the design of the bandits to make their way to the almost impregnable fastnesses in the hills of Dawsbergen, the wild principality to the south. There they could hold her against all hope of rescue, until an immense sum of money was paid over in ransom by her dispairing friends.

When night came they were high in the mountains back of the Monastery, many hours ahead of any pursuit. They became stupidly careless, and the two grooms made a dash for freedom. One of them was killed, but the other escaped. She was afterward to recall that no effort was made to recapture him; they deliberately allowed him to escape, their cunning purpose becoming only too apparent later on.

Instead of hurrying on to Dawsbergen, they dropped swiftly down into the valley above the city. No secret was made of the ruse they had employed to mislead the prospective pursuers. The rescue party, they swore joyously, would naturally be led by John Tullis; he would go with all haste to the Dawsbergen hills. The word of the trusty groom would be taken as positive proof that the captive was in that country. She shuddered as she listened to their exultant chuckles. It had been a most cunningly conceived plan and it promised to result profitably for them in the end.

Some time during the slow, torturing ride through the forest she swooned. When she came to her senses she was in a dimly lighted room, surrounded by men. The gag had been removed from her mouth. She would have shrieked out in her terror, had not her gaze rested upon the figure of a man who sat opposite, his elbows on the back of the chair which he straddled, his chin on his arms. He was staring at her steadily, his black eyes catching her gaze and holding it as a snake holds the bird it has charmed.

She recognised the hard, hawk-like face. There could be no mistake. She was looking into the face that made the portrait of the Iron Count so abhorrent to her: the leathery head of a cadaver with eyes that lived. A portrait of Voltaire, the likeness of a satyr, a suggestion of Satan—all rushed up from memory's storehouse to hold her attention rapt in contemplation of this sinister figure.

He smiled. It was like the crumpling of soft leather. Then, with a word to one of the men, he abruptly left the room. After that she broke down and cried herself into the sleep of exhaustion.

All the next day she sat limp and helpless in the chair they had brought to her. She could neither eat nor drink. Late in the afternoon Marlanx came again. She knew not from whence he came: he stood before her suddenly, as if produced by the magic of some fabled genie, smiling blandly, his hands clasped behind his back, his attitude one of lecherous calculation.

Truxton King ground his teeth with rage and despair while she was breathlessly repeating the suave compliments that oozed from the lips of the tormentor.

"He laughed when I demanded that he should restore me to my friends. He chided me when I pleaded and begged for mercy. My questions were never answered. He only said that no harm was to come to me; I was merely touching purgatory that I might better appreciate paradise when I came to it. Oh, it was horrible! I thought I would go mad. Finally I called him a beast; I don't know what else I said. He merely smiled. Presently he called one of the men into the room. He said something about a sewer and a hole in the ground. Then the man went out and I heard the clicking of a telegraph instrument. I heard certain instructions. I was to be taken to a certain place in the city at nightfall and kept there until to-morrow night, when I am again to be removed by way of the river. That is all I know. Where am I, Mr. King? Oh, this dreadful place! Why are we here—you and I?"

King's heart throbbed fiercely one more. He was looking straight into the piteous, wondering eyes; his gaze fell to the parted, tremulous lips. A vast hunger possessed his soul. In that moment he could have laid down his life for her, with a smile of rejoicing.

Then he told her why she was there, why he was there—and of the 26th. The dreadful 26th!

Her eyes grew wide with horror and understanding; her bosom rose and fell rapidly with the sobs of suppressed terror. At last he had finished his stupefying tale; they sat side by side staring into each other's eyes, helpless, stricken.

"God in heaven!" she repeated over and over again, in a piteous whisper.

The candle flickered with feeble interest in the shadows that began to grow in the farthest corner. The girl drew closer to the side of the strong yet powerless man. Their gaze went to the sputtering candle. It was going out and they would be in utter darkness. And yet neither thought of the supply of fresh candles in the corner.

King brought himself out of the strange lethargy with a jerk. It was high time, for the light was going.

"Quick!" he cried. "The candle! Light a fresh one. My hands are bound."

She crept to the candles and joined the wicks. A new light grew as the old one died. Then she stood erect, looking down upon him.

"You are bound. I forgot."

She started forward, dropping to her knees beside him, an eager gleam in her eyes. "If I can untie the rope—will that help? Can you do anything? You are strong. There must be a way. There must be one little chance for you—for us. Let me try."

"By Jove," he whispered admiringly, his spirits leaping to meet hers. "You've got pluck. You put new life in me. I—I was almost a—a quitter."

"You have been here so long," she explained quickly. "And tied all these days." She was tugging at the knot.

"Only since I gave that pleasant punch to Peter Brutus."

"That shows what you can do," she whispered warmly. "Oh, I wonder! I wonder if we have a chance! Anyway, your arms will be free. I shall feel safer if your arms are free."

He sat with his back to her while she struggled with the stubborn knots. A delicious thrill of pleasure swept over him. She had said she would feel safer if his arms were free! She was struggling, with many a tense straining of delicate fingers, to undo the bonds which held him helpless. The touch of her eager fingers, the closeness of her body, the warmth of her breathing—he was beginning to hope that the effort might be prolonged interminably.

At last, after many despairing tugs, the knot relaxed. "There!" she cried, sinking back exhausted. "Oh, how it must have hurt you! Your wrists are raw!"

He suppressed the tactless impulse to say that he preferred a rope on the wrists to one about his neck, realising that the jest could only shock and not amuse her under the present conditions.

His arms were stiff and sore and hung like lead at his sides. She watched him, with narrowed eyes, while he stood off and tried to work blood and strength back into his muscles.

"Do you think you can—can do anything now, Mr. King?" she asked, after a long interval.

He would not tell her how helpless he was, even with his hands free. So he smiled bravely and sought to reassure her with the most imposing boasts he could utter. She began to breathe easier; the light in her eyes grew brighter, more hopeful.

"We must escape," she said, as if it were all settled.

"It cannot be to-night," he gently informed her, a sickness attacking her heart. "Don't you think you'd better try to get some sleep?"

He prevailed upon her to lie down, with his coat for a pillow. In two minutes she was asleep.

For an hour or more he sat there, looking sorrowfully at the tired, sweet face, the utmost despair in his soul. At last he stretched himself out on the floor, near the door, and as he went to sleep he prayed that Providence might open a way for him to prove that she was not depending on him in vain.

CHAPTER XIII
A DIVINITY SHAPES

It was pitch dark when he awoke.

"By heaven, it was a dream, after all," he murmured. "Well, thank God for that. She isn't in this damnable hole. And," with a quickening of the blood, "she hasn't said she was going to marry Vos Engo."

The sound of light breathing came to his ears. He sat up. His hands were free. It had not been a dream. She *was* lying over there asleep. The candle had burnt itself out, that was all. He crept softly across the floor; in the darkness he found her, and touched the garments she wore—and drew back enthralled. A strange joy filled him; she was his for the time being. They were equals in this direful, unlovely place; royal prejudice stood for nothing here. The mad desire to pick her up in his arms and hold her close came over him—only to perish as quickly as it flamed. What was he thinking of?

She stirred restlessly as he crept back to the door. The sharp, quick intake of her breath told him that she was awake. He stopped and utter silence fell upon the room.

A little moan escaped her lips: "Who is it? Why is it so dark? What—"

"It is I," he whispered eagerly. "King. Don't be afraid. The candle burnt out while we were asleep. I did not intend to sleep. I'm sorry. We can't have a light now until some one comes in the morning. Don't be afraid."

"I am afraid. Where are you?"

"Here!" He hastened to her side. As he came up she touched his face with her hand timorously. He caught the wayward fingers in his own and held them, drawing quite close to her. "It's all right," he said.

"Will they come soon?"

"I hope not—I mean, yes; it must be morning."

"I loathe the dark," she sighed. Presently her head dropped over against his shoulder and she was asleep again.

"I don't give a damn if they never come," thought Truxton King, intoxicated with bliss.

Afraid to move for fear of disturbing her, he sat there for an hour or more his back twisted and uncomfortable, but never so resolute. He would not have moved for all the world.

All this time his brain was working like mad in the new-found desire to perform miracles for the sake of this lovely, unattainable creature. Was there no way to foil these triumphant conspirators? He was forgetting the Prince, the horrors of the 26th; he was thinking only of saving this girl from the fate that Marlanx had in store for her. Vos Engo may have had the promise, but what could it profit him if Marlanx had the girl?

"I've got about as much chance as a snowball," he reflected, courage and decision growing stronger each moment. "I might just as well die one way as another. If I could only catch 'em napping for a minute, I might turn the trick. God, that would be—" he was lost in ecstatic contemplation of the glory that such an event would bring.

Footsteps in the outer room recalled him to the bitter reality of their position. He awoke her and whispered words of encouragement into her bewildered ears. Then he put on his coat and threw himself on the floor, first wrapping the rope about his wrists to deceive the guard.

A key turned in the padlock and the bolt was raised. Old man Spantz stood in the doorway, peering in at them. In surly tones Truxton replied to his sharp query, saying that the candle had gone out while he slept.

"It is noon," said the old man irascibly. Then he came in and lighted a candle.

"Noon of the 25th," said Truxton bitterly. "In twenty-four hours it will be all over, eh, Spantz?"

"At noon to-morrow," said Spantz grimly.

There were half a dozen men in the outer room, conversing in low, excited tones; the fervent gesticulations which usually marked their discussions were missing, proving the constraint that had descended upon them. One of them—it was Julius Spantz—brought in the food for the prisoners, setting it on the floor between them.

"It is usually the duty of our friend Julius to feed me," observed Truxton to his fellow-prisoner. "I dare say he won't mind if you relieve him of the task."

"She can feed you if she likes," growled Julius.

"Julius?" queried the girl from the Castle, peering at the man. "Not Julius Spantz, of the armoury?"

"The same," said Truxton. Julius laughed awkwardly and withdrew. "Son of our distinguished host here. Permit me to present Herr William—"

"Enough," snarled William Spantz, with a threatening movement toward King. His manner changed completely, however, when he turned to address the young lady. "I beg to inform you, madam, that your stay in this unwholesome place is to be brief. Pray endure it for the remainder of this day. To-night you will be removed to more pleasant quarters, that a friend has prepared for you. I may say to you, however, that it will he necessary to place a gag in your mouth before you depart. This is to be a critical night in our affairs." He lifted an inspired gaze heavenward. "Let me assure you, madam, that the two gentlemen who are to conduct you to the Count's—to your new quarters, are considerate, kindly men; you need feel no further alarm. I am requested to tell you this, so that you may rest easy for the balance of the day. As for you, my friend," turning to Truxton and smiling ironically, "I deeply deplore the fact that you are to remain. You may be lonesome in the dead hours, for, as you may imagine, we, your dearest friends, will be off about a certain business that is known to you, if I mistake not in believing that you have listened at the door these many nights. When we next gather in the room beyond, a new dispensation will have begun. You may be interested then to hear what we have to say—out there."

Truxton was silent for a moment, a sudden, swift thought flooding his brain. Controlling the quiver of anticipation in his voice, he took occasion to say:

"I only hope you'll not forget to come back. I should be lonesome, Spantz."

"Oh, we'll not forget you."

"I suppose not. By the way, would you mind telling me what has become of your niece?"

Spantz glared at him. "She does not meet with us now. My niece is consecrating her every thought to the task that lies before her. You will not see her again."

"It's an infernal shame, that's what it is," exclaimed King, "to put it all upon that poor girl! God, I'd give ten years of my life to lead her out of this devil's mess. She's too good for—for that. It's—"

"She will be out of it, as you say, to-morrow, my excellent Samaritan. She knows." There could be no mistake as to the meaning of the prophetic words.

With a profound bow to the lady and a leer for King, he departed, bolting the door behind him. Instantly King was at her side.

"An idea has come to me," he whispered eagerly. "I think I see a way. By George, if it should only happen as I hope it may!"

"Tell me!" she insisted.

"Not now. I must think it all out carefully. It won't do to get your hopes up and then fail."

Whatever the thought was that had come to him, it certainly had put new life and hope into him. She nibbled at the unwholesome food, never removing her eyes from his tall, restless figure as he paced the floor, his brows knit in thought. Finally he sat down beside her, calmly helping himself to a huge slice of bread and a boiled carrot.

"I've never liked carrots before. I love 'em now. I'm taking them for my complexion."

"Don't jest, Mr. King. What is it you intend to do? Please tell me. I must know. You heard what he said about taking me to the Count's. He meant Marlanx. I will die first."

"No. I will die first. By the way, I may as well tell you that I wasn't thinking altogether of how we are to escape. There was something else on my mind." He stopped and looked at her puzzled face. "Why should I save you from Marlanx just to have you hurry off and get married to Vos Engo? It's a mean thought, I know," hastily, "and unworthy of a typical hero, but, just the same, I hate to think of you marrying some one—else."

"Some one else?" she questioned, a pucker on her forehead.

"Oh, I know I wouldn't have a ghost of a chance, even if there wasn't a Vos Engo. It isn't that," he explained. "I recognise the—er—difference in our stations and—"

"Are you crazy, Mr. King?"

"Not now. I was a bit touched, I think, but I'm over it now. I dare say it was caused by excessive reading of improbable romances. Life rather takes it out of a fellow, don't you know. It's all simple enough in books, but in—"

"What has all this got to do with your plan to escape?"

"Nothing at all. It merely has to do with my ambition to become a true hero. You see, I'm an amateur hero. Of course, this is good practice for me;

in time, I may become an expert and have no difficulty in winning a duchess or even a princess. Don't misunderstand me. I intend to do all I can toward rescuing you to-night. The point I'm trying to get at is this: don't you think it's pretty rough on a hero to save the girl for some other fellow to snap up and marry?"

"I think I begin to see," she said, a touch of pink coming into her cheeks.

"That's encouraging," he said, staring gloomily at the food he had put aside. "You are quite sure you promised Vos Engo that you'd marry him?"

"No. I did not promise him that I'd marry him," she said, leaning back and surveying him between narrowed lids.

"I beg your pardon. You said you had promised—"

"You did not allow me time to finish. I meant to say that I had promised to let him know in a day or two. That is all, Mr. King." There was a suspicious tremor in her voice and her gaze wavered beneath his unbelieving stare.

"What's that?" he demanded. "You—you don't mean to say that—Oh, Lord! I wonder! I wonder if I have a chance—just a ghost of a chance?" He leaned very close, incredulous, fascinated. "What is it that you are going to let him know? Yes or no?"

"That was the question I was considering when the brigands caught me," she answered, meeting his gaze fairly. "I haven't thought of it since."

"Of course, he is in your own class," said Truxton glumly.

She hesitated an instant, her face growing very serious. "Mr. King, has no one told you my name—who I am?" she asked.

"You are the Prince's aunt, that's all I know."

"No more his aunt in reality than Jack Tullis is his uncle. I thought you understood."

"Who are you, then?"

"I am Jack Tullis's sister, a New Yorker bred and born, and I live not more than two blocks from your—"

"For the love of—" he began blankly; then words failed him, which was just as well. He gulped twice, joy or unbelief choking him. The smile that crept into her face dazzled him; he stared at her in speechless amazement. "Then—then, you are not a duchess or a—" he began again.

"Not at all. A very plain New Yorker," she said, laughing aloud in sudden hysteria. For some reason she drew quickly away from him. "You are not disappointed, are you? Does it spoil your romance to—"

"Spoil it? Disappointed? No! By George, I—I can't believe that any such luck—no, no, I don't mean it just that way! Let me think it out. Let me get it through my head." He leaned back against the wall and devoured her with eager, disturbing eyes. "You are Tullis's sister? You live near—Oh, I say, this is glorious!" He arose and took a turn about the room. In some nervousness and uncertainty she also came to her feet, watching him wonderingly. He hurried back to her, a new light in his eyes. She was very desirable, this slender, uncertain person in the crumpled grey.

"Miss Tullis," he said, a thrill in his voice, "you are a princess, just the same. I never was so happy in my life as I am this minute. It isn't so black as it was. I thought I couldn't win you because you—"

"Win me?" she gasped, her lips parted in wonder.

"Precisely. Now I'm looking at it differently. I don't mind telling you that I'm in love with you—desperately in love. It's been so with me ever since that day in the Park. I loved you as a duchess or a princess, and without hope. Now, I—I—well, I'm going to hope. Perhaps Vos Engo has the better of me just now, but I'm in the lists with him—with all of them. If I get you out of this place—and myself as well—I want you to understand that from this very minute I am trying to win you if it lies in the power of any American to win a girl who has suitors among the nobility. Will—will you give me a chance—just a ghost of a chance? I'll try to do the rest."

"Are—are you really in earnest?" she murmured, composure flying to the winds.

"Yes; terribly so," he said gently. "I mean every word of it. I do love you."

"I—I cannot talk about it now, Mr. King," she fluttered, moving away from him in a sudden panic. Presently he went over to her. She was standing near the candle, staring down at the flame with a strangely preoccupied expression in her eyes.

"Forgive me," he said. "I was hasty, inconsiderate. I—"

"You quite took my breath away," she panted, looking up at him with a queer little smile.

"I know," he murmured.

Her troubled gaze resumed its sober contemplation of the flame.

"How was I to tell—" she began, but checked herself. "Please, Mr. King, you won't say anything more to me about—about it,—just now, will you? Shall we talk of our plans for to-night? Tell me about them."

He lowered his eyes, suddenly disheartened. "I only ask you to believe that I am desperately in earnest."

"I cannot comprehend how—I mean, it is so very wonderful. You don't think me unappreciative, or mean, do you?"

"Of course not. You are startled, that's all. I'm a blundering fool. Still, you must agree that I was frightfully bowled over when I found that you were not what I thought. I couldn't hold back, that's all. By Jove, isn't it wonderful? Here I've been looking all over the world for you, only to find that you've been living around the corner from me all these years! It's positively staggering! Why," with a sudden burst of his unquenchable buoyancy, "we might have been married two years ago and saved all this trouble. Just think of it!"

She smiled. "I do like you," she said warmly, giving him her hand. He kissed it gallantly and stepped back—resolutely.

"That's something," he said with his humblest, most conquering smile.

"You won't leave me to my fate because you think I'm going to marry—some one else?"

He grew very sober. "Miss Tullis, you and I have one chance in a thousand. You may as well know the truth."

"Oh, I can't bear the thought of that dreadful old man," she cried, abject distress in her eyes.

He gritted his teeth and turned away. She went back to the corner, dully rearranging the coat he had given her for comfort. She handled it with a tenderness that would have astonished the garment had it been capable of understanding. For a long time she watched him in silence as he paced to and fro like a caged lion. Twice she heard him mutter: "An American girl—good Lord," and she found herself smiling to herself—the strange, vagrant smile that comes of wonder and self-gratification.

Late in the afternoon—long hours in which they had spoken to each other with curious infrequency, each a prey to sombre thoughts—their door was unlocked and Anna Cromer appeared before them, accompanied by two of the men. Crisply she commanded the girl to come forth; she wanted to talk with her.

She was in the outer room for the better part of an hour, listening to Anna Cromer and Madame Drovnask, who dinned the praises of the great Count Marlanx into her ears until she was ready to scream. They bathed the girl's face and brushed her hair and freshened her garments. It occurred to her that she was being prepared for a visit of the redoubtable Marlanx himself, and put the question plainly.

"No," said Anna Cromer. "He's not coming here. You are going to him. He will not be Count Marlanx after to-morrow, but Citizen Marlanx—one of the people, one of us. Ah, he is a big man to do this."

Little did they know Marlanx!

"Julius and Peter will come for you to-night," said Madame Drovnask, with an evil, suggestive smile. "We will not be here to say farewell, but, my dear, you will be one of us before—well, before many days have passed."

Truxton was beginning to tremble with the fear that she would not be returned to their room, when the door was opened and she came in—most gladly, he could see. The two women bade him a cool, unmistakable *Good-bye*, and left him in charge of the men who had just come down from the shop above.

For half an hour Peter Brutus taunted him. It was all he could do to keep his hands wrapped in the rope behind his back; he was thankful when they returned him to his cell. The time was not ripe for the dash he was now determined to make.

"Get a little nap, if you can," he said to Loraine, when the door was locked behind him. "It won't be long before something happens. I've got a plan. You'll have your part to play. God grant that it may work out well for us. You—you might pray if—if—"

"Yes, I *can* pray," she said simply. "I'll do my part, Mr. King."

He waited a moment. "We've been neighbours in New York for years," he said. "Would you mind calling me Truxton,—and for Adele's sake, too?"

"It isn't hard to do, Truxton."

"Good!" he exclaimed.

She rebelled at the mere thought of sleep, but, unfastening her collar and removing the jabot, she made herself a comfortable cushion of his coat and sat back in her corner, strangely confident that this strong, eager American would deliver her from the Philistines—this fighting American with the ten days' growth of beard on his erstwhile merry face.

Sometime in the tense, suffocating hours of the night they heard the sounds of many footsteps shuffling about the outer room; there were hoarse, guttural, subdued good-byes and well-wishes, the creaking of heavy doors and the dropping of bolts. Eventually King, who had been listening alertly, realised that but two of the men remained in the room—Peter Brutus and Julius Spantz.

An hour crept by, and another, seemingly interminable King was fairly groaning under the suspense. The time was slowly, too slowly approaching when he was to attempt the most desperate act in all this sanguinary tragedy—the last act for him, no doubt, but the one in which he was to see himself glorified.

There remained the chance—the slim chance that only Providence considers. He had prayed for strength and cunning; she had prayed for divine intervention. But, after all, Luck was to be the referee.

He had told her of his plan; she knew the part she was to play. And if all went well—ah, then! He took a strange lesson in the language of Graustark: one sentence, that was all. She had whispered the translation to him and he had grimly repeated it, over and over again. "She has fainted, damn her!" It was to be their "Open Sesame"—if all went well!

Suddenly he started to his feet, his jaws set, his eyes gleaming. The telegraph instrument was clicking in the outer room!

He had wrapped his handkerchief about his big right hand, producing a sort of cushion to deaden the sound of a blow with the fist and to protect his knuckles; for all his strength was to go into that one mighty blow. If both men came into the room, his chance was smaller; but, in either event, the first blow was to be a mighty one.

Taking his position near the girl, who was crouching in real dismay, he leaned against the wall, his hands behind him, every muscle strained and taut.

The door opened and Julius Spantz, bewhiskered and awkward, entered. He wore a raincoat and storm hat, and carried a rope in one of his hands. He stopped just inside the door to survey the picture.

"Time you were asleep," he said stupidly, addressing King.

"I'd put you to sleep, Julius, if Miss Tullis could have managed to untie these infernal bonds," said Truxton, with pleasant daring.

"I don't tie lovers' knots," grinned Julius, pleased with his own wit. "Come, madam, I must ask you to stand up. Will you put your own handkerchief in your mouth, or must I use force—ah, that's good! I'm sorry, but I must wrap this cloth about—"

He did not complete the sentence, for he had come within range. The whole weight of Truxton King's body was behind the terrific blow that landed on the man's jaw. Loraine suppressed the scream that rose to her white lips. Julius Spantz's knees crumpled; he lunged against the wall and was sliding down when King caught him in his arms. The man was stunned beyond all power of immediate action. It was the work of an instant to snatch the revolver from his coat pocket.

"Guard the door!" whispered King to the girl, pressing the revolver into her hand. "And shoot if you have to!"

A handkerchief was stuffed into the unconscious man's mouth; the long coat and boots were jerked from his limp body before his hands and feet were bound with the rope he carried; the bushy whiskers and wig were removed from his head and transferred in a flash to that of the American. Then the boots, coat and hat found a new wearer.

Peter Brutus was standing in the stairway, leading to the sewer, listening eagerly for sounds from either side.

"Hurry up, Julius," he called imperatively. "They are below with the boat. They have given the signal."

The new Julius uttered a single sentence; that was all. If Peter heard the noise attending the disposal of his comrade, he was justified in believing that the girl had offered some resistance. When a tall, grunting man emerged from the inner room, bearing the limp figure of a girl in a frayed raincoat, he did not wait to ask questions, but rushed over and locked the cell-door. Then he led the way down the narrow stairway, lighting the passage with a candle. His only reply to King's guttural remark in the Graustark language was:

"Don't speak, you fool! Not a word until we reach the river."

Down the steps they went to the opening in the wall of the sewer. There, before the bolts were drawn by Brutus, a series of raps were exchanged by men outside and the one who held the keys within.

A moment later, the girl was being lowered through the hole into rough, eager arms. Brutus and his companion dropped through, the secret block of masonry was closed, and off through the shallow waters of the sewer glided the party riverward in the noiseless boat that had come up to ferry them.

There were three men in the boat, not counting Truxton King.

CHAPTER XIV
ON THE RIVER

No word was spoken during this cautious, extraordinary voyage underground. The boat drifted slowly through the narrow channel, unlighted and practically unguided. Two of the men sat at the rowlocks, but the oars rested idly in the boat. With their hands they kept the craft from scraping against the walls.

The pseudo-Julius supported his charge in the stern of the boat; Peter Brutus sat in the bow, a revolver in his hand, his gaze bent upon the opaqueness ahead. A whispered word of encouragement now and then passed from the lips of the hopeful American into the ear of the almost pulseless girl, who lay up against his knee.

"We'll do it—sure!" he whispered once, ever so softly.

"Yes," she scarcely, breathed, but he heard and was thrilled. The rope had dropped from her arms; she had taken the handkerchief from her mouth at his whispered command.

At last the boat crept out into the rainy, starless night. He drew the skirts of his own mackintosh over her shoulders and head. A subdued command came from the man in the bow; the oars slipped into the deep, black waters of the river; without a splash or a perceptible sound the little craft scudded toward midstream. The night was so inky black that one could not see his hand before his face.

At least two of the occupants opened up their throats and lungs and gulped in the wet, fresh air. Never had anything been so glorious to Truxton King as these first tremendous inhalations of pure, free air. She felt his muscles expand; his whole body grew stronger and more vital. Her heart was pounding violently against his leg; he could feel its throbs, he could hear the quick, eager panting of her breath.

It was now that he began to wonder, to calculate against the plans of their silent escort. Whither were they bound? When would his chance come to strike the final, surprising blow? Only the greatest effort at self-control kept him from ruining everything by premature action; his exultation was getting the better of him. Coolness and patience were greater assets now than strength and daring.

The boat turned in mid-stream and shot swiftly up the river, past the black fortress with its scattered sentry lights, where slept a garrison in sweet ignorance of the tragedy that was to come upon them when the sun was high. The lights of the city itself soon peeped down into the rain-swept waters; music from the distant cafés came faintly to the ears of the midnight voyagers. A safe haven at their very elbows, and yet unattainable.

The occasional creak of an oar, a whispered oath of dismay, the heavy breathing of toilers, the soft blowing of the mist-that was all; no other sound on the broad, still river. It was, indeed, a night fit for the undertaking at hand.

Truxton began to chafe under the strain. His uneasiness was increased by the certain conviction that before long they would be beyond the city, the walls of which were gradually slipping past He could not even so much as guess at their destination. There was also the likelihood of encountering reinforcements, sent out to meet the boatmen, or for protection at the time of landing. A hundred doubts and misgivings assailed him. To suddenly open fire on the rascals went against the grain. A dashing, running fight on shore was more to his liking. An ill-timed move would foil them even as success was in their grasp.

He considered their chances if he were to overturn the frail boat and strike out for shore in the darkness. This project he gave up at once: he did not know the waters nor the banks between which they glided. They were past the walls now and rowing less stealthily. Before long they would be in a position to speak aloud; it would be awkward for him. The situation was rapidly growing more and more desperate; the time was near at hand when the final effort would have to be exerted. He slipped the revolver from his pocket; somehow he was unable to keep his teeth from chattering; but it was through excitement, not fear.

Suddenly the boat turned to the right and shot toward the unseen bank. They were perhaps half a mile above the city wall. Truxton's mind was working like a trip-hammer. He was recalling a certain nomad settlement north of the city, the quarters of fishermen, poachers and horse-traders: a squalid, unclean community that lay under the walls between the northern gates and the river. These people, he was not slow to surmise, were undoubtedly hand in glove with Marlanx, if not so surely connected with the misguided Committee of Ten. This being the eve of the great uprising, it was not unlikely that a secret host lay here awake and ready for the foul observance of the coming holiday; here, at least, chafed an eager, vicious, law-hating community of mendicants and outcasts.

He had little time to speculate on the attitude of the denizens of this unwholesome place. The prow of the boat grated on the pebbly bank, and Peter Brutus leaped over the edge into the shallow water.

"Come on, Julius—hand her over to me!" he cried, making his way to the stern.

As he leaned over the side to seize the girl in his arms, Truxton King brought the butt of the heavy revolver down upon his skull. Brutus dropped across the gunwale with a groan, dead to all that was to happen in the next half hour or more.

King was anxious to avoid the hullaballoo that shooting was sure to create on shore. Action had been forced upon him rather precipitously, but he was ready. Leaning forward, he had the two amazed oarsmen covered with the weapon.

"Hands up! Quick!" he cried. Two pairs of hands went up, together with strange oaths. Truxton's eyes had grown used to the darkness; he could see the men quite plainly. "What are you doing?" he demanded of Loraine, who, behind him, was fumbling in the garments of the unconscious Brutus.

"Getting his revolver," she replied, with a quaver in her voice.

"Good!" he said exultantly. "Let's think a minute," he went on. "We don't dare turn these fellows loose, even if we disarm them. They'll have a crowd after us in two minutes." Still, keeping the men covered, he cudgelled his brain for the means of disposing of them. "I have it. We must disarm them, tie them up and set 'em adrift. Do you mind getting out into the water? It's ankle deep, that's all. I'll keep them covered while you take their guns."

"Nice way to treat a friend," growled one of the men.

"A friend? By George, it's my Newport acquaintance. Well, this is a pleasure! I suppose you know that I'll shoot if you resist. Better take it quietly."

"Oh, you'll shoot, all right," said the other. "I told them damn fools that a Yankee'd get the better of 'em, even if they ran a steam roller over him two or three times. Say, you're a pippin! I'd like to take off my hat to you."

"Don't bother. I acknowledge the tribute."

Loraine Tullis was in the water by this time. With nervous haste she obeyed King's instructions; the big revolvers were passed back to him.

"I've changed my mind," said Truxton' suddenly. "We'll keep the boat. Get in, Miss Tullis. There! Now, push off, Newport."

"What the devil—" began Newport, but King silenced him. The boat slowly drifted out into the current.

"Now, row!" he commanded. With his free hand he reached back and dragged the limp Brutus into the boat. "'Gad, I believe he's dead," he muttered.

For five minutes the surly oarsmen pulled away, headed in the direction from which they came.

"Can you swim?" demanded King.

"Not a stroke," gasped Newport. "Good Lord, pal, you're not going to dump us overboard. It's ten feet deep along here."

"Pull on your left, hard. That's right. I'm going to land you on the opposite shore-and then bid you a cheerful good-night."

Two minutes later they ran up under the western bank of the stream, which at this point was fully three hundred yards wide. The nearest bridge was a mile and a half away and habitations were scarce, as he well knew. Under cover of the deadly revolver, the two men dropped into the water, which was above their waists; the limp form of Peter Brutus was pulled out and transferred to the shoulders of his companions.

"Good-night," called out Truxton King cheerily. He had grasped the oars; the little boat leaped off into the night, leaving the cursing desperadoes waist-deep in the chilly waters.

"See you later," sang out Newport, with sudden humour.

"We'll go south," said Truxton King to the girl who sat in the stern, clutching the sides of the boat with tense fingers. "I don't know just where we'll land, but it won't be up in Devil's Patch, you may rest assured of that. Pardon me if I do not indulge in small talk and bonmots; I'm going to be otherwise employed for some time, Miss Tullis. Do you know the river very well?"

"Not at all," she replied. "I only know that the barge docks are below here somewhere. I'm sure we can get into the city if we can find the docks. Let me take the oars, too, Mr. King. I can row."

"No. Please sit where you are and keep your eyes ahead. Can you see where we're going?"

"I can see the lights. We're in mid-stream, I think. It's so very dark and the wind is coming up in a gale. It's—it's going to storm. Don't you think we'd better try for a landing along the walls? They say the river is very treacherous." She was trembling like a leaf.

"I'll row over to the east side, but I don't like to get too close to the walls. Some one may have heard the shouts of our friends back there."

Not another word passed between them for ten or twelve minutes. She peered anxiously ahead, looking for signs of the barge dock, which lay somewhere along this section of the city wall. In time, of course, the marooned desperadoes might be expected to find a way to pursue them, or, at least, to alarm watchful confederates on the city side of the river. It was a tense, anxious quarter of an hour for the liberated pair. So near to absolute safety, and yet so utterly in the dark as to what the next moment, might develop—weal or woe.

At least the sound of rapidly working rowlocks came to the girl's ears. They were slipping along in the dense blackness beneath the walls, making as little noise as possible and constantly on the lookout for the long, low dock.

"They're after us," grated Truxton, in desperation. "They've got word to friends one way or another. By Jove! I'm nearly fagged, too. I can't pull much farther. Hello! What's this?"

The side of the boat caromed off' a solid object in the water, almost spilling them into the wind-blown river.

"The docks!" she whispered. "We struck a small scow, I think. Can you find your way in among the coal barges?"

He paddled along slowly, feeling his way, scraping alongside the big barges which delivered coal from the distant mines to the docks along the river front. At last he found an opening and pushed through. A moment later they were riding under the stern of a broad, cargoless barge, plumb up against the water-lapped piles of the dock.

Standing in the bow of the boat he managed to pull himself up over the slippery edge. It was the work of a second to draw her up after him. With an oar which he had thought to remove beforehand, he gave the boat a mighty shove, sending it out into the stream once more.

Then, hand in hand, they edged slowly, carefully along the gravel-strewn dock, between vast piles of lumber and steep walls of coal. It was only necessary to find the railway company's runways leading into the yards above; in time of peace there was little likelihood that the entrances to the dock would be closed, even at night.

Loud curses came up from the river, proclaiming the fact that the pursuers had found the empty boat. Afterwards they were to learn that "Newport's" shouts had brought a boatload of men from the opposite bank, headed by the innkeeper, in whose place Loraine was to have encountered Marlanx later on, if plans had not miscarried. She was to have remained in this outside inn until after the sacking of the city on the following day. The girl translated one remark that came up to them from the boatload of pursuers:

"The old man is waiting back there. He'll kill the lot of us if we don't bring the girl."

By this time King had located the open space which undoubtedly afforded room for the transfer of cargoes from the dock to the company's yards inside the walls. Without hesitation he drew her after him up this wide, sinister roadway. They stumbled on over the rails of the "dummy track," collided with collier trucks, slipped on the soggy chutes, but all the while forged ahead toward the gates that so surely lay above them.

The pursuers were trying for a landing, noisily, even boisterously. It struck Truxton as queer that these men were not afraid of alarming the watchmen on the docks or the man at the gate above. Suddenly it came to him that there would be no one there to oppose the landing of the miscreants. No doubt hundreds of men already had stolen through these gates during the night, secreting themselves in the fastnesses of the city, ready for the morrow's fray. It is no small wonder that he shuddered at the thought of it.

There was no one on the wharf—at least, no one in sight. They rushed up the narrow railway chutes and through one of the numerous gateways that opened out upon the barge docks. No one opposed them; no one was standing guard. From behind came the sound of rushing footsteps. Lightning flashed in the sky and the rumble of thunder broke over the desolate night.

"They'll see us by the lightning," gasped Truxton, almost ready to drop from faintness and exhaustion. He was astounded, even alarmed, to find that his strength had been so gravely depleted by confinement and lack of nourishment.

They were inside the city walls. Ahead of them, in that labyrinth of filthy streets lay the way to the distant square. His arm was now about her waist, for she was half-fainting; he could hear her gasping and moaning softly, inarticulate cries of despair. Switch-lights blinked in the distance. Off to the right of them windows showed lights; the clang of a locomotive bell came to them as from a great distance.

Their progress was abruptly halted by the appearance of a man ahead, standing like a statue in the middle of the network of tracks. They stumbled toward him, not knowing whether he was friend or foe. One look into their faces, aided by the flare of a yardman's lantern, and the fellow turned tail and fled, shouting as he did so.

Following a vivid flash of lightning, two shots were fired by the men who were now plunging up through the gates, a hundred yards or more away. The same flash of lightning showed to King the narrow, muddy street that stretched ahead of them, lined with low, ugly houses of a nondescript character. Instead of doing the obvious thing, he turned sharply to the left, between the lines of freight cars. Their progress was slow; both were ready to drop; the way was dark and unknown to them.

At last they came to the end of their rope: they were literally up against the great city wall! They had reached the limits of the railway yards and were blocked on all sides by they knew not how many rows of cars. Somewhere off to the right there were streets and houses and people, but they did not have the strength to try to reach them.

A car door stood open in front of them. He waited for a second flash of lightning to reveal to him the nature of its interior. It was quite empty. Without hesitation he clambered in and pulled her up after him. They fell over, completely fagged.

A few minutes later the storm broke. He managed to close the door against the driving torrents.

She was sobbing plaintively, poor, wet, bedraggled sweetheart—he called her that, although she did not hear him.

"We've fooled them," he managed to whisper, close to her ear. "They won't look here. You're safe, Loraine. 'Gad, I'd like to see any one get you away from me now."

She pressed his arm, that was all. He found himself wondering what answer she would give to Vos Engo when he took her to him to-morrow. To-morrow! This was the 26th! Would there be a to-morrow for any of them—for Vos Engo, for Tullis, for the Prince? For *her*?

"There will be time to warn them in the morning," he thought, dulled by fatigue. "We can't go on now."

"Truxton," he heard her saying, tremulously, "do you think we can do anything for them—the Prince and those who are with him? How can we lie here when there is so much to be done?"

"When the storm abates—when we are rested—we will try to get away from here. Those devils know that I will give the alarm. They will have hundreds of men watching to head us off. It means everything to them. You see, I know their plans. But, Loraine, dear little girl, brave as you are and willing as I am, we can't go on until we've pulled ourselves together. We're safe here for awhile. Later on, we'll try to steal up to the city. They will be watching every approach to the Castle and to the Tower, hoping to stop me in time. We must out-fox them again. It will be harder, too, little girl. But, if I don't do any more, I pledge you that I'll save you from Marlanx."

"Oh, I know you will. You must, Truxton."

"I'd—I'd like to be sure that I am also saving you from Vos Engo. I hate to think of you throwing yourself away on one of these blithering, fortune-hunting noblemen." She pressed his arm again. "By Jove, it's great fun being a hero, after all—and it isn't so difficult, if the girl helps you as you helped me. It's too bad I couldn't do it all by myself. I have always counted on rescuing you from an Ogre's castle or something of that sort. It's rather commonplace as it is, don't you think?"

"I don't—know what—you're talking about," she murmured. Then she was fast asleep.

The storm raged; savage bursts of wind rocked the little freight car; the rain hissed viciously against their frail hotel; thunder roared and lightning rent sky and earth. The weary night-farers slept with pandemonium dinning in their ears.

He sat with his back against the side of the car, a, pistol in one hand, the other lying tenderly upon the drenched hair of the girl whose head rested upon his leg. She had slipped down from his shoulder; he did not have the desire or the energy to prevent it. At his side lay the discarded whiskers. Manfully as he had fought against the impelling desire to sleep, he could not beat it off. His last waking thought was of the effort he must make to reach Dangloss with the warning.

Then the storm abated; the soft drip of rain from the eaves of the car beat a monotonous tattoo in the pools below; the raw winds from the mountains blew stealthily in the wake of the tornado, picking up the waste that had been left behind only to cast it aside with a moan of derision.

Something stirred in the far end of the car. A still, small noise as of something alive that moved with the utmost wariness. A heavy, breathing body crept stealthily across the intervening space; so quietly that a mouse could have made but little less noise.

Then it stopped; there was not a sound inside the car except the deep, regular breathing of Truxton King. The girl's respiration was so faint that one might have thought she did not breathe at all. Again the sly, cautious movement of a heavy body; the creaking of a joint or two, the sound of a creature rising from a crouching position to the upright; then the gentle rubbing of cloth, the fumbling of fingers in a stubborn pocket.

An instant later the bluish flame of a sulphur match struggled for life, growing stronger and brighter in the hand of a man who stood above the sleepers.

CHAPTER XV
THE GIRL IN THE RED CLOAK

Inside of an hour after the return of the frightened, quivering groom who had escaped from the brigands in the hills, Jack Tullis was granted permission by the war department to take a hundred picked men with him in the effort to overtake and capture the abductors of his sister. The dazed groom's story hardly had been told to the horrified brother before he was engaged in telephoning to General Braze and Baron Dangloss. A hurried consultation followed. Other affairs that had been troubling the authorities for days were forgotten in the face of this distressing catastrophe; there was no time to be lost if the desperadoes were to be headed before they succeeded in reaching the Dawsbergen passes with their lovely captive. Once there, it would be like hunting a needle in a haystack; they could elude pursuit for days among the wild crags of upper Dawsbergen, where none but outlaws lived, and fierce beasts thrived.

Unluckily for the dearest hopes of the rescuing party, the miserable groom did not reach the city until almost noon of the day following the abduction. He had lost his way and had wandered all night in the forests. When Miss Tullis failed to return at nightfall, her brother, having in mind the mysterious disappearance of Truxton King and the flight of Countess Ingomede, was preparing to set forth in search of her. A telephone message from Ganlook, fifteen miles north of the city, came at seven o'clock, just as he was leaving the Castle. The speaker purported to be the Countess Prandeville, a very estimable chatelaine who ruled socially over the grim old village of Ganlook. She informed Tullis that his sister was with her for the night, having arrived in the afternoon with a "frightful headache." She would look after the dear child, of whom she was very fond, and would send her down in the morning, when she would surely be herself again. Greatly relieved, Tullis gave up his plan to ride off in quest of her; he knew the amiable Countess, and felt that his sister was in good hands.

It was not until the return of the groom that he recalled the fact that the voice on the telephone was not quite like that of the Countess. He had been cleverly hoodwinked. Baron Dangloss, obtaining connection with the

Prandeville household in Ganlook, at once discovered that Loraine had not been in the chateau in many days.

The fierce, cock-robin baron was sadly upset. Three prominent persons had been stolen from beneath his nose, so to speak. He was beside himself with rage and dismay. This last outrage was the climax. The old man adored the sister of Jack Tullis; he was heartbroken and crushed by the news of the catastrophe. For a while he worked as if in a daze; only the fierce spurring of Jack Tullis and Vos Engo, who believed himself to be an accepted suitor, awoke him from an unusual state of lethargy. It is even said that the baron shed tears without blowing his nose to discredit the emotion.

The city was soon to know of the fresh outrage at the hands of the bandits in the hills. Great excitement prevailed; there were many sincere lamentations, for the beautiful American girl was a great favourite— especially with those excellent persons who conducted bazaars in the main avenues. Loraine, being an American, did not hesitate to visit the shops in person: something that the native ladies never thought of doing. Hundreds of honest citizens volunteered to join in a search of the hills, but the distinction was denied them.

The war department issued official notice to all merchants that their places of business must be decorated properly against the holiday that would occur on the morrow. Shops were to be closed for two hours at midday, during the ceremonies attending the unveiling of the Yetive monument in the Plaza. The merchants might well give their time to decorating their shops; the soldiers could do all the searching and all the fighting that was necessary. Strict orders, backed by method, were issued to the effect that no one was to pass through the gates during the day, except by special permission from General Braze.

Count Vos Engo was eager to accompany the expedition to Dawsbergen in search of his wayward lady-love. Tullis, who liked the gay young nobleman despite the reputation he had managed to live down, was willing that he should be the one to lead the troops, but Colonel Quinnox flatly refused to consider it.

"To-morrow's celebration in the city will demand the attendance of every noble officer in the guard," he said. "I cannot allow you to go, Count Vos Engo. Your place is here, beside the Prince. Line officers may take charge of this expedition to the hills; they will be amply able to manage the chase. I am sorry that it happens so. The Royal Guard, to a man, must ride with the Prince to-morrow."

Captain Haas, of the dragoons, was put in charge of the relief party, much to the disgust of Vos Engo; and at two o'clock in the afternoon they were ready to ride away. The party was armed and equipped for a bitter chase. Word had been sent to Serros, the capital of Dawsbergen, asking the assistance of Prince Dantan in the effort to overtake the abductors. A detachment, it was announced in reply, was to start from Serros during the afternoon, bound for the eastern passes.

Baron Dangloss rode to the southern gate with the white-faced, suffering Tullis. "We will undoubtedly receive a communication from the rascals this afternoon or to-morrow," he said gloomily. "They will not be slow to make a formal demand for ransom, knowing that you and your sister are possessed of unlimited wealth. When this communication arrives it may give us a clue to their whereabouts; certainly as to their methods. If it should be necessary, Tullis, to apprise you of the nature of this demand, I, myself, will ride post haste to St. Michael's Pass, which you are bound to reach to-morrow after your circuit of the upper gaps. It is possible, you see, that an open attack on these fellows may result in her—er—well, to be frank—her murder. Damn them, they'd do it, you know. My place to-morrow is here in the city. There may be disturbances. Nothing serious, of course, but I am uneasy. There are many strangers in the city and more are coming for the holiday. The presence of the Prince at the unveiling of the statue of his mother—God bless her soul!—is a tremendous magnet. I would that you could be here to-morrow, John Tullis; at Prince Robin's side, so to speak."

"Poor little chap! He was terribly cut up when I told him I was going. He wanted to come. Had his little sword out, and all that. Said the celebration could be postponed or go hang, either one. Look after him closely to-morrow, Dangloss. I'd shoot myself if anything were to happen to him. Marlanx is in the air; I feel him, I give you my word, I do! I've been depressed for days. As sure as there's a sun up yonder, that old scoundrel is planning something desperate. Don't forget that we've already learned a few things regarding his designs." He waited a moment before uttering his gravest fear. "Don't give him a chance to strike at the Prince."

"He wouldn't dare to do that!"

"He'd dare anything, from what I've heard of him."

"You hate him because—"

"Go on! Yes, I hate him because he has made *her* unhappy. Hello, who's this?"

A man who had ridden up to the gates, his horse covered with foam, was demanding admission. The warders halted him unceremoniously as Dangloss rode forward. They found that he was one of the foremen in the employ of the railway construction company. He brought the disquieting news that another strike had been declared, that the men were ugly and determined to tear up the track already laid unless their demands were considered, and, furthermore, that there had been severe fighting between the two factions engaged on the work. He urgently implored Dangloss to send troops out to hold the rioters in check. Many of the men were demanding their pay so that they might give up their jobs and return to their own lands.

"What is your name?" demanded the harassed minister of police.

"Polson," replied the foreman. He lied, for he was no other than John Cromer, the unsavoury husband of Anna Cromer, of the Committee of Ten.

"Come with me," said Dangloss. "We will go to General Braze. Good-bye and good luck, Tullis."

The little baron rode back into the city, accompanied by the shifty-eyed Cromer, while John Tullis sped off to the south, riding swiftly by the side of the stern-faced Captain Haas, an eager company of dragoons behind, a mountain guide in front.

At that very moment, Loraine Tullis was comparing notes with Truxton King in the room beneath the armourer's shop; Count Marlanx was hiding in the trader's inn outside the northern gates; the abductors themselves were scattered about the city, laughing triumphantly over the success of the ruse that had drawn the well-feared American away on a wild-goose chase to the distant passes of Dawsbergen. More than that: at five o'clock in the afternoon a second detachment of soldiers left the city for the scene of the riots in the construction camps, twenty miles away.

Surely the well-laid plans of the Iron Count were being skilfully carried out!

All afternoon and evening men straggled in from the hills and surrounding country, apparently loth to miss the early excitement attending the ceremonies on the following day. Sullen strikers from the camps came down, cursing the company but drinking noisy toasts to the railroad and its future. The city by night swarmed with revelling thousands; the bands were playing, the crowds were singing, and mobs were drinking and carousing in the lower end. The cold, drizzling rain that began to blow across the city at ten o'clock did little toward checking the hilarity of the revellers. Honest citizens went to bed early, leaving the streets to the strangers from the hills and the river-lands. Not one dreamed of the ugly tragedy that was drawing to a climax as he slept the sleep of the just, the secure, the conscience-free.

At three o'clock in the morning word flew from brothel to brothel, from lodging house to lodging house, in all parts of the slumbering city; a thousand men crept out into the streets after the storm, all animated by one impulse, all obeying a single fierce injunction.

They were to find and kill a tall American! They were to keep him or his companion from getting in touch with the police authorities, or with the Royal Castle, no matter what the cost!

The streets were soon alive with these alert, skulking minions. Every approach to the points of danger was guarded by desperate, heavily armed scoundrels who would not have hesitated an instant if it came to their hands to kill Truxton King, the man with all their dearest secrets in his grasp. In dark doorways lounged these apparently couchless strangers; in areaways and alleys, on doorsteps they found shelter; in the main streets and the side streets they roamed. All the time they had an eager, evil eye out for a tall American and a slender girl!

Dangloss's lynx-eyed constabulary kept close watch over these restless, homeless strangers, constantly ordering them to disperse, or to "move on," or to "find a bed, not a doorstep." The commands were always obeyed; churlishly, perhaps, in many instances, but never with physical resistance.

At five o'clock, a stealthy whisper went the rounds, reaching the ear of every vagabond and cutthroat engaged in the untiring vigil. Like smoke they faded away. The silent watch was over.

The word had sped to every corner of the town that it was no longer necessary to maintain the watch for Truxton King. He was no longer in a position to give them trouble or uneasiness!

The twenty-sixth dawned bright and cool after the savage storm from the north. Brisk breezes floated down from the mountain peaks; an unreluctant sun smiled his cheeriest from his seat behind the hills, warmly awaiting the hour when he could peep above them for a look into the gala nest of humanity on the western slope. Everywhere there was activity, life, gladness and good humour.

Gaudy decorations which had been torn away by the storm were cheerfully replaced; workmen refurbished the public stands and the Royal box in the Plaza; bands paraded the avenues or gave concerts in Regengetz Circus; troops of mounted soldiers and constabulary patroled the streets. There was nothing to indicate to the municipality that the vilest conspiracy of the age—of any age—was gripping its tentacles about the city of Edelweiss, the smiling, happy city of mountain and valley. No one could have suspected guile in the laughter and badinage that masked the manner of the men who were there to spread disaster in the bunting-clad thoroughfares.

"I don't like the looks of things," said Baron Dangloss, time and again. His men were never so alert as to-day and never so deceived.

"There can't be trouble of any sort," mused Colonel Quinnox. "These fellows are ugly, 'tis true, but they are not prepared for a demonstration. They are unarmed. What could they do against the troops, even though they are considerably depleted?"

"Colonel, we'll yet see the day when Graustark regrets the economy that has cut our little army to almost nothing. What have we now, all told? Three hundred men in the Royal Guard. Less than six hundred in the fortress. I have a hundred policemen. There you are. To-day there are nearly two hundred soldiers off in the mountains on nasty business of one sort or another. 'Gad, if these ruffians from the railroad possessed no more than pistols they could give us a merry fight. There must be a thousand of them. I don't like it. We'll have trouble before the day's over."

"General Braze says his regulars can put down any sort of an uprising in the city," protested Quinnox. "In case of war, you know we have the twenty thousand reserves, half of whom were regulars until two years ago."

"Perfectly true. Quinnox, it's your duty to take care of the Prince. You've done so in your family for fifteen generations. See to it that Prince Robin is well looked after to-day, that's all."

"Trust me for that, Baron," said Quinnox with his truest smile. Even Marlanx knew that he would have to kill a Quinnox before a Graustark ruler could be reached.

By eleven o'clock the streets in the neighbourhood of the Plaza were packed with people. All along Castle Avenue, up which the Prince was to drive in the coach of State, hung the proud, adoring burghers and their families: like geese to flock, like sheep to scatter. At twelve the Castle gates were to be thrown open for the brilliant cavalcade that was to pass between these cheering rows of people. In less than a quarter of an hour afterward, the Prince and his court, the noble ladies and gentlemen of Graustark, with the distinguished visitors from other lands, would pass into the great square through Regengetz Circus.

At the corner below the crowded Castle Café, in the north side of the square, which was now patroled by brilliant dragoons, two men met and exchanged the compliments of the day. One of them had just come up on horseback. He dismounted, leaving the animal in charge of an urchin who saw a gavvo in sight. This man was young and rather dashing in appearance. The other was older and plainly a citizen of some consequence.

"Well?" said the latter impatiently, after they had passed the time of day for the benefit of the nearest on-lookers. The younger man, slapping his riding boot with his crop, led the way to the steps of a house across the sidewalk. Both had shot a swift, wary glance at one of the upper windows.

"Everything is ready. There will be no hitch," said the horseman in low tones.

"You have seen Spantz?"

"Sh! No names. Yes. The girl is ready."

"And the fortress?"

"Fifty men are in the houses opposite and others will go there—later on."

"We must keep the reserves out of the fortress. It would mean destruction if they got to the gun-rooms and the ammunition houses."

"Is he here?" with a motion toward the upper window.

"Yes. He came disguised as an old market woman, just after daybreak."

"Well, here's his horse," said the other, "but he'll have to change his dress. It isn't a side saddle." The young villain laughed silently.

"Go up now to the square, Peter. Your place is there."

If one had taken the time to observe, he might have seen that the young man wore his hat well forward, and that his face was unnaturally white. We, who suspect him of being Peter Brutus, have reason to believe that there was an ugly cut on the top of his head and that it gave him exceeding pain.

Shortly after half past eleven o'clock certain groups of men usurped the positions in front of certain buildings on the south side of the square. A score here, a half score there, others below them. They favoured the shops operated by the friends of the Committee of Ten; they were the men who were to take possession of the rifles that lay hidden behind counters and walls. Here, there, everywhere, all about the city, other instructed men were waiting for the signal that was to tell them to hustle deadly firearms from the beds of green-laden market wagons. It was all arranged with deadly precision. There could be no blunder. The Iron Count and his deputies had seen to that.

Men were stationed in the proper places to cut all telephone and telegraph wires leading out of the city. Others were designated to hold the gates against fugitives who might seek to reach the troops in the hills.

Marlanx's instructions were plain, unmistakable. Only soldiers and policemen were to be shot; members of the royal household were already doomed, including the ministry and the nobles who rode with the royal carriage.

The Committee of Ten had said that there would not be another ministry, never another Graustark nobility; only the Party of Equals. The Iron Count had smiled to himself and let them believe all that they preached in secret conclave. But he knew that there would be another ministry, a new nobility and a new ruler, and that there would be *no Committee of Ten!*

Two thousand crafty mercenaries, skilled rioters and fighters from all parts of the world stood ready in the glad streets of Edelweiss to leap as one man to the standard of the Iron Count the instant he appeared in the square after the throwing of the bomb. A well-organised, carefully instructed army of no mean dimensions, in the uniform of the lout and vagabond, would rise like a flash of light before the dazzled, panic-stricken populace, and Marlanx would be master. Without the call of drum or bugle his sinister soldiers of fortune would leap into positions assigned them; in orderly, determined company front, led by chosen officers, they would sweep the square, the Circus and the avenues, up-town to the Castle, down-town to the fortress and the railway station, everywhere establishing the pennant of the man who had been banished.

The present dynasty was to end at one o'clock! So said Marlanx! How could Dangloss or Braze or Quinnox say him nay? They would be dead or in irons before the first shock of disaster had ceased to thrill. The others? Pah! They were as chaff to the Iron Count.

The calm that precedes the storm fell upon the waiting throng; an ominous silence spread from one end of the avenue to the other. For a second only it lasted. The hush of death could not have been quieter nor more impressive. Even as people looked at each other in wonder, the tumult came to its own again. Afterward a whole populace was to recall this strange, depressing second of utter stillness; to the end of time that sudden pall was spoken of with bated breath and in awe.

Then, from the distant Castle came the sound of shouts, crawling up the long line of spectators for the full length of the avenue to the eager throng in Regengetz Circus, swelling and growing louder as the news came that the Prince had ridden forth from the gates. Necks were craned, rapt eyes peered down the tree-topped boulevard, glad voices cried out tidings to those in the background. The Prince was coming!

Bonny, adorable Prince Robin!

Down the broad avenue came the Royal Military Band, heading the brilliant procession. Banners were flying; gold and silver standards gleamed in the van of the noble cavalcade; brilliantly uniformed cuirassiers and dragoons on gaily caparisoned horses formed a gilded phalanx that filled the distant end of the street, slowly creeping down upon the waiting thousands, drawing nearer and nearer to the spot of doom.

A stately, noble, inspiring procession it was that swept toward the Plaza. The love of the people for their little Prince welled up and overflowed in great waves of acclamation. Pomp and display, gold and fine raiment were but the creation of man; Prince Robin was, to them, the choicest creation of God. He was their Prince!

On came the splendid phalanx of guardsmen, followed by rigid infantrymen in measured tread; the clattering of horses' hoofs, the beat of drums, the clanking of scabbards and the jangling of royal banners, rising even above the hum of eager voices. The great coach of gold, with its half score of horses, rolled sombrely beneath nature's canopy of green, surrounded on all sides by proud members of the Royal Guard. Word came down the line that the Prince sat alone in the rear seat of the great coach, facing the Prime Minister and Countess Halfont. Two carriages from the royal stables preceded the Prince's coach. In the first was the Duke of Perse and three fellow-members of the Cabinet; the second contained Baron Dangloss and General Braze. After the Prince came a score or more of rich equipages filled with the beauty, the nobility, the splendour of this rich little court.

The curtains in a house at the corner of the square parted gently. A hawk-faced old man peered out upon the joyous crowd. His black eyes swept the scene. A grim smile crept into his face. He dropped the curtains and walked away from the window, tossing a cigarette into a grate on the opposite side of the room. Then he looked at his watch.

All of the bands in the square had ceased playing when the Castle gates were opened for the royal procession: only the distant, rythmic beat of a lively march came up from the avenue to the ears of this baleful old man in the second-story front room of the home of apothecary Boltz.

At the extreme outer side of Regengetz Circus a small group of men and women stood, white-faced and immovable, steadfastly holding a position in the front rank of spectators. Shrinking back among this determined coterie was the slender, shuddering figure of Olga Platanova, haggard-faced, but with the light of desperation in her eyes.

As the procession drew nearer, the companions of this wretched girl slunk away from her side, losing themselves in the crowd, leaving her to do her work while they sought distant spots of safety. Olga Platanova, her arms folded beneath the long red cloak she wore, remained where they had placed her and—waited!

CHAPTER XVI
THE MERRY VAGABOND

The man who stood in the middle of the freight-car, looking down in wonder at the fugitives, was a tall vagabond of the most picturesque type. No ragamuffin was ever so tattered and torn as this rakish individual. His clothes barely hung together on his lank frame; he was barefoot and hatless; a great mop of black hair topped his shrewd, rugged face; coal-black eyes snapped and twinkled beneath shaggy brows and a delighted, knowing grin spread slowly over his rather boyish countenance. He was not a creature to strike terror to the heart of any one; on the contrary, his mischievous, sprightly face produced an impression of genuine good humour and absolute indifference to the harsh things of life.

Long, thin lips curled into a smile of delicious regard; his sides shook with the quiet chuckle of understanding. He did not lose his smile, even when the match burned his finger tips and fell to the floor of the car. Instead, the grin was broader when he struck the second match and resumed his amused scrutiny of his fellow-lodgers. This time he practised thrift: he lighted a cigarette with the match before tossing it aside. Then he softly slid the car door back in its groove and looked out into the moist, impenetrable night. A deep sigh left his smiling lips; a retrospective langour took possession of his long frame; he sighed again, and still he smiled.

Leaning against the side of the door this genial gypsy smoked in blissful silence until the stub grew so short that it burned his already singed fingers. He was thinking of other days and nights, and of many maids in far-off lands, and of countless journeys in which he, too, had had fair and gentle company—short journeys, yes, but not to be forgotten. Ah, to be knight of the road and everlasting squire to the Goddess of Love! He always had been that—ever since he could remember; he had loved a hundred briefly; none over long. It was the only way.

Once more he turned to look upon the sleeping pair. This time he lighted the stub of a tallow candle. The tender, winning smile in his dark eyes grew to positive radiance. Ah, how he envied this great, sleeping wayfarer! How beautiful his mistress! How fortunate the lover! And how they slept—

how tired they were! Whence had they come? From what distant land had they travelled together to reach this holiday-garnished city in the hills? Vagabonds, tramps! They were of his world, a part of his family; he knew and had loved a hundred of her sisters, he was one of a hundred-thousand brothers to this man.

Why should he stay here to spoil their waking hour? The thought came to him suddenly. No; he would surrender his apartment to them. He was free and foot-loose; he could go elsewhere. He *would* go elsewhere.

Softly he tip-toed to his own corner of the car, looking over his shoulder with anxious eyes to see that his movements did not disturb them. He gathered up his belongings: an ancient violin case, a stout walking stick, a goodly sized pack done up in gaudy cloth, a well-worn pair of sandals with long, frayed lacings. As gently he stole back to the door. Here he sat down, with his feet hanging outside the car. Then, with many a sly, wary glance at his good comrades, he put on his sandals and laced them up the leg. He tossed a kiss to the sleeping girl, his dark gypsy face aglow with admiration and mischief, and was about to blow out the light of his candle. Then he changed his mind. He arose and stood over them again, looking long and solemnly at the face of the sleeping girl. Ah, yes, she was the most beautiful he had ever seen—the very fairest. He had known her sisters, but-no, they were not like this one. With a sly grimace of envy he shook his fist at the tall man whose leg served as a pillow for the tired head.

The girl looked wan and tired—and hungry. Poor thing! Never had he seen one so sweet and lovely as she; never had he seen such a shockingly muddy mackintosh, however, as the one she wore, never were hands so dirty as the slender ones which lay limp before her. With a determined shake of his head and a new flash of the eye he calmly seated himself and began to open his ragged pack. Once he paused, a startled look in his face. He caught sight of the revolver at Truxton's side for the first time. The instant of alarm passed and a braver smile than ever came. Ah, here was a knight who would fight for his lady love! Good fellow! Bravo!

At last his small store of food lay exposed. Without hesitation he divided the pieces of smoked venison, giving one part to himself, two to the sleepers; then the miller's bread and the cheese, and the bag of dates he had bought the day before. He tied up his own slender portion and would have whistled for the joy of it all had he not bethought himself in time.

From one of his pockets he drew out tobacco and cigarette papers. With his back planted up against the wall of the car, his legs crossed and his feet wiggling time to the inward tune he sang, he calmly rolled half a dozen cigarettes and placed them, one by one, beside the feast. One match from his thin supply he placed alongside the cigarettes. Then he looked very doubtful. No; one might blow out. He must not be niggardly. So he kept two for himself and gave three to the guest at his banquet.

Again he blew a kiss to the prettiest girl he had ever seen. Snuffing his candle, he dropped to the ground and closed the door against all spying, uncivil eyes.

The first grey of dawn was growing in the sombre east. He looked out over the tops of cars and sniffed the air. The rain was over. He knew. A tinge of red that none but the gypsy could have distinguished betrayed the approach of a sunny day. Jauntily he swung off down the path between the lines of cars, his fickle mind wavering between the joys of the coming day and the memory of the loveliest Romany he had ever encountered.

Daybreak found him at the wharf gates. It was gloomy here and silent; the city above looked asleep and unfruitful. His heart was gay; he longed for company. Whimsical, careless hearted, he always obeyed the impulse that struck him first. As he stood there, surveying the wet, deserted wharf, it came to him suddenly that if he went back and played one soft love-song before the door of the car, they might invite him to join them in the breakfast that the genie had brought.

His long legs were swift. In five minutes he was half way down the line of cars, at the extreme end of which stood the happy lodging place of his heart's desire. Then he paused, a dubious frown between his eyes. No! he said, slapping his own cheek soundly; it would not be fair! He would not disturb them, not he! How could he have thought of such a thing. *Le bon Dieu!* Never! He would breakfast alone!

Coming to an empty flat car, direct from the quarries, he resolutely seated himself upon its edge, and, with amiable resignation, set about devouring his early meal, all the while casting longing, almost appealing glances toward the next car but one. Busy little switch engines began chugging about the yards; the railroad, at least, was exhibiting some signs of life. Here and there the crews were "snaking" out sections and bumping them off to other parts of the gridiron; a car here, a car there—all aflounder, but quite simple to this merry wanderer. He knew all about switching, he did. It did not cause him the least uneasiness when a sudden jar told him that an engine had been attached to the distant end of the string in which he breakfasted. Nor was he disturbed when the cars began to move. What cared he? He would ride in his dining-car to the objective switch, wherever that was, and no doubt would find himself nearer the main freight depot, with little or no walking to do on his journey to the square.

But the "string" was not bound for another track in the yards; it was on its way to the main line, thence off through the winding valley into strange and distant lands.

Sir Vagabond, blissfully swinging his heels and munching his venison, smiled amiably upon the yard men as he passed them by. So genial was the smile, so frank the salutation, that not one scowled back at him or hurled the chunk of coal that bespeaks a surly temper. Down through the maze of sidetracks whisked the little train, out upon the main line with a thin shriek of greeting, past the freight houses—it was then that Sir Vagabond sat up very straight, a look of mild interest in his eyes. Interest gave way to perplexity, perplexity to concern. What's this? Leaving the city? He wasted no time. This would never do! Clutching his belongings to his side, he vaulted from one hand, nimbly and with the gracefulness of wide experience, landing safely on his feet at the roadside.

There he stood with the wry, dazed look of a man who suddenly finds himself guilty of arrant stupidity, watching the cars whiz past on their way to the open country. Just ahead was the breach in the wall through which all trains entered or left the city. Into that breach shot the train, going faster and faster as it saw the straight, clear track beyond. He waited until the tail end whisked itself out of sight in the cut below the city walls, and then trudged slowly, dejectedly in the opposite direction, his heart in his boots. He was thinking of the luckless pair in the empty "box."

Suddenly he stopped, his chin up, his hands to his sides. A hearty peal of laughter soared from his lips. He was regarding the funny side of the situation. The joke was on them! It was rich! The more he thought of their astonishment on awaking, the more he laughed. He leaned against a car.

His immense levity attracted attention. Four or five men approached him from the shadows of the freight houses, ugly, unsmiling fellows. They demanded of him the cause of his unseemly mirth. With tears in his merry black eyes he related the plight of the pretty slumberers, dwelling more or less sentimentally on the tender beauty of the maiden fair. They plied him with questions. He described the couple—even glowingly. Then the sinister fellows smiled; more than that, they clapped each other on the back and swore splendidly. He was amazed and his own good humour gave way to fierce resentment. What right had these ruffians to laugh at the misfortunes of that unhappy maid?

A switchman came up, and one of the men, a lank American whom we should recognise by the sound of his voice (having heard it before), asked whither the train was bound and when it would first stop in its flight.

"At the Poo quarries, seventeen kilometers down the line. They cut out a few empties there. She goes on to the division point after that."

"Any trains up from that direction this morning?" demanded "Newport."

"Not till this afternoon. Most of the crews are in the city for the—" But the switchman had no listeners beyond that statement.

And so it was that the news spread over town at five o'clock that Truxton King was where he could do no harm. It was well known that the train would make forty miles an hour down the steep grade into the lower valley.

Up into the city strolled Sir Vagabond, his fiddle in his hand, his heart again as light as a feather. Some day—ah, some day! he would see her again on the road. It was always the way. Then he would tell her how unhappy he had been—for a minute. She was so pretty, so very pretty! He sighed profoundly. We see no more of him.

When Truxton King first awoke to the fact that they were no longer lying motionless in the dreary yards, he leaped to his feet with a startled shout of alarm. Loraine sat up, blinking her eyes in half-conscious wonder. It was broad daylight, of course; the train was rattling through the long cut just below the city walls. With frantic energy he pulled open the door. For a minute he stared at the scudding walls of stone so close at hand, uncomprehendingly. Then the truth burst upon him with the force of a mighty blow. He staggered back, his jaw dropping, his eyes glaring.

"What the dev—Great God, Loraine! We're going! We're moving!" he cried hoarsely.

"I know it," she gasped, her body rocking violently with the swaying of the wild, top-heavy little car.

"Great Scott! How we're pounding it! Fifty miles an hour. Where are we?" he cried, aghast. He could scarcely keep his feet, so terrific was the speed and so sickening the motion.

She got to her feet and lurched to his side. "Don't fall out!" she almost shrieked. He drew back with her. Together they swayed like reeds in a windstorm, staring dizzily at the wall before them.

Suddenly the train shot out into the open, farm-spattered valley. Truxton fell back dumbfounded.

"The country!" he exclaimed. "We've been carried away. I—I can't believe my senses. Could we have slept—what a fool, what an idiot! God in heaven! The Prince! He is lost!" He was beside himself with anguish and despair, raging like a madman, cursing himself for a fool, a dog, a murderer!

Little less distressed than her companion, Loraine Tullis still had the good sense to keep him from leaping from the car. He had shouted to her that he must get back to the city; she could go on to the next town and find a hiding place. He would come to her as soon as he had given the alarm.

"You would be killed," she cried, clutching his arm fiercely. "You never can jump, Truxton. See how we are running. If you jump, I shall follow. I won't go on alone. I am as much to blame as you."

The big, strong fellow broke down and cried, utterly disheartened.

"Don't cry, Truxton, please don't cry!" she pleaded. "Something will happen. We must stop sometime. Then we can get another train back, or telegraph, or hire a wagon. It must be very early. The sun is scarcely up. Do be brave! Don't give up!"

He squared his shoulders. "You put me to shame!" he cried abjectly. "I'm—I'm unnerved, that's all. It was too much of a blow. After we'd got away from those scoundrels so neatly, too. Oh, it's maddening! I'll be all right in a minute. You plucky, plucky darling!"

The train whirled through a small hamlet without even slackening its speed. Truxton endeavoured to shout a warning to two men who stood by the gates; but they merely laughed, not comprehending. Then he undertook to arrest the attention of the engineer. He leaned from the door and shouted. The effort was futile, almost disastrous. A lurch came near to hurling him to the rocky road bed. Now and then they passed farmers on the high road far above, bound for the city. They called out to them, but the cries were in vain. With every minute they were running farther and farther away from the city of Edelweiss; every mile was adding to the certainty of the doom which hung over the little Prince and his people.

A second small station flew by. "Ronn: seven kilometers to Edelweiss." He looked at her in despair.

"We're going faster and faster," he grated. "This is the fastest train in the world, Loraine, bar none."

Just then his gaze alighted on the pathetic breakfast and the wandering cigarettes. He stared as if hypnotised. Was he going mad? An instant later he was on his hands and knees, examining the mysterious feast. She joined him at once; no two faces ever before were so puzzled and perplexed.

"By heaven!" he exclaimed, drawing her away from the spot in quick alarm, comprehension flooding his brain. "I see it all! We've been deliberately shanghaied! We've been bottled up here, drugged, perhaps, and shipped out of town by fast freight—no destination. Don't touch that stuff! It's probably full of poison. Great Scott! What a clever gang they are! And what a blithering idiot they have in me to deal with. Oh, how easy!"

Whereupon he proceeded to kick the unoffending breakfast, cigarettes and all, out of the car door. To their dying day they were to believe that the food had been put there by agents of the great conspirator. It readily may be surmised that neither of them was given to sensible deductions during their astounding flight. If they had thought twice, they might have seen the folly of their quick conclusions. Marlanx's men would not have sent Loraine off in a manner like this. But the distracted pair were not in an analytical frame of mind just then; that is why the gentle munificence of Sir Vagabond came to a barren waste.

Mile after mile flew by. The unwilling travellers, depressed beyond description, had given up all hope of leaving the car until it reached the point intended by the wily plotters. To their amazement, however, the speed began to slacken perceptibly after they had left the city ten or twelve miles behind. Truxton was leaning against the side of the door, gloomily surveying the bright, green landscape. For some time Loraine had been steadying herself by clinging to his arm. They had cast off the unsightly rain coats and other clumsy articles. Once, through sheer inability to control his impulses, he had placed his arm about her slim waist, but she had gently freed herself. Her look of reproach was sufficient to check all future impulses of a like nature.

"Hello!" said he, coming out of his bitter dream.

"We're slowing up." He looked out and ahead. "No station is in sight. There's a bridge down the road a bit—yes, there's our same old river. By George!" His face was a study.

"What is it?" she cried, struck by his sudden energy of speech.

"They're running slow for the bridge. Afraid of the floods. D'ye see? If they creep up to it as they do in the United States when they're cautious, we'll politely drop off and—'Pon my soul, she's coming down to a snail's pace. We can swing off, Loraine. Now's our chance!"

The train was barely creeping up to the bridge. He clasped her in the strong crook of his left arm, slid down to a sitting position, and boldly pushed himself clear of the car, landing on his feet. Staggering forward with the impetus he had received, he would have fallen except for a mighty effort. A sharp groan escaped his lips as he lowered her to the ground. She looked anxiously into his face and saw nothing there but relief.

The cars rumbled across the bridge, picked up speed beyond, and thundered off in the distance with never so much as a thought of the two who stood beside the track and laughed hysterically.

"Come along," said the man briefly. "We must try to reach that station back there. There I can telegraph in. Oh!" His first attempt to walk brought out a groan of pain.

He had turned his ankle in the leap to the ground. She was deeply concerned, but he sought to laugh it off. Gritting his teeth determinedly, he led the way back along the track.

"Lean on me," she cried despairingly.

"Nonsense," he said with grim stubbornness. "I don't mind the pain. We can't stop for a sprained ankle. It's an old one I got playing football. We may have to go a little slow, but we'll not stop, my dear—not till we get word to Dangloss!"

She found a long, heavy stick for him; thereafter he hobbled with greater speed and less pain. At a wagon-road crossing they paused to rest, having covered two miles. The strain was telling on him; perspiration stood out in great drops upon his brow; he was beginning to despair. Her little cry of joy caused him to look up from the swollen ankle which he was regarding with dubious concern. An oxcart was approaching from the west.

"A ride!" she cried joyously. She had been ready to drop with fatigue; her knees were shaking. His first exclamation of joy died away in a groan of dismay. He laughed bitterly.

"That thing couldn't get us anywhere in a week," he said.

"But it will help," she cried brightly, an optimist by force of necessity.

They stopped the cart and bargained for a ride to Ronn. The man was a farmer, slow and suspicious. He haggled.

"The country's full of evil men and women these days," he demurred. "Besides I have a heavy enough load as it is for my poor beasts."

Miss Tullis conducted the negotiations, making the best of her year's acquaintance with the language of the country.

"Don't tell him why we are in such a hurry," cautioned King. "He may be a Marlanx sympathiser."

"You have nothing in your cart but melons," she said to the farmer, peeping under the corner of the canvas covering.

"I am not going through Ronn, but by the high road to Edelweiss," he protested. "A good ten kilometers."

"But carry us until we come up with some one who can give us horses."

"Horses!" he croaked. "Every horse in the valley is in Edelweiss by this time. This is the great day there. The statue of—"

"Yes, yes, I know. We are bound for Edelweiss. Can you get us there in two hours?"

"With these beasts, poor things? Never!"

"It will be worth your while. A hundred gavvos if you carry us to a place where we can secure quicker transportation."

In time she won him over. He agreed to carry them along the way, at his best speed, until they came up with better beasts or reached the city gates. It was the best he could do. The country was practically deserted on this day. At best there were but few horses in the valley; mostly oxen. They climbed up to the seat and the tortuous journey began. The farmer trotted beside the wheel nearly all of the way, descanting warmly in painful English on the present condition of things in the hills.

"The rascals have made way with the beautiful Miss Tullis. She is the American lady stopping at the Castle. You should see her, sir. Excepting our dear Princess Yetive—God rest her soul—she is the most beautiful creature Graustark has ever seen. I have seen her often. Not quite so grand as the Countess Ingomede, but fairer, believe me. She is beloved by everyone. Many a kind and generous word has she spoken to me. My onion beds are well known to her. She has come to my farm time and again, sir, with the noble personages, while riding, and she has in secret bought my little slips of onions. She has said to me that she adores them, but that she can only eat them in secret. Ah, sir, it is a sad day for Graustark that evil has happened to her. Her brother, they say, is off in the Dawsbergen hills searching for her. He is a grand man."

His passengers were duly interested. She nudged the lugubrious Truxton when the man spoke of the onions. "What a fibber! I hate onions."

"She is to be married to the Count Vos Engo; a fine lad, sir. Now she is gone, I don't know what he will do. Suicide, mayhap. Many is the time I have cautioned her not to ride in the hills without a strong guard. These bandits are getting very bold."

"Do you know the great Count Marlanx?" demanded King, possessed of a sudden thought. The man faced him at the mention of the name, a suspicious gleam in his eyes.

"Count Marlanx!" he snorted. Without another word, he drew the beasts to a standstill. There was no mistaking the angry scowl. "Are you friends of that snake? If you are, get out of my cart."

"He's all right," cried Truxton. "Tell him who we are, Loraine, and why we *must* get to the city."

Five minutes later, the farmer, overcome by the stupendous news, was lashing his oxen with might and main; the astonished beasts tore down the road to Ronn so bravely that there seemed some prospect of getting a telegram through in time. All the way the excited countryman groaned and swore and sputtered his prayers. At Ronn they learned that the operator had been unable to call Edelweiss since seven o'clock. The wires were down or had been cut. Truxton left a message to be sent to Dangloss in case he could get the wire, and off they started again for the city gates, having lost considerable time by the diverted mile or two.

Not man, woman or child did they encounter as the miles crept by. The country was barren of humanity. Ahead of them was the ascent to be conquered by oxen so old and feeble that the prospect was more than dubious.

"If it should be that my team gives out, I will run on myself to give the alarm," cried the worthy, perspiring charioteer. "It shall not be! God preserve us!"

Three times the oxen broke down, panting and stubborn; as many times he thwacked them and kicked them and cursed them into action again. They stumbled pitifully, but they *did* manage to go forward.

In time the city gates came in sight—far up the straight, narrow road. "Pray God we may not be too late," groaned the farmer. "Damn the swine who took their horses to town before the sun was up. Curse them for fools and imbeciles. Fools never get into heaven. Thank the good Lord for that."

It seemed to the quivering Americans that the gates were mocking them by drawing farther away instead of coming nearer.

"Are we going backward?" groaned Truxton, his hands gripping the side of the bounding seat.

Near the gates, which were still open, it occurred to him in a single flash of dismay that he and Loraine would be recognised and intercepted by Marlanx watchers. Between the fierce jolts of the great cart he managed to convey his fears to her.

It was she who had the solution. They might succeed in passing the gates if they hid themselves in the bed of the cart, underneath the thick canvas covering. The farmer lifted the cloth and they crawled down among the melons. In this fashion they not only covered the remainder of the distance, half stifled by the heat and half murdered by the uncomfortable position, but passed through the gates and were taken clattering down the streets toward the centre of town.

"To the Tower!" cried the anxious Truxton.

"Impossible!" shouted the farmer. "The streets are roped off and the crowds are too great."

"Then let us out as near to the Tower as possible, cried the other.

"Here we are," cried the driver, a few minutes later, pulling up his half dead oxen and leaping to the ground. He threw off the covering and they lost no time in tumbling from their bed of melons to the cobble-stone pavement of a narrow alley into which he had turned for safety. "Through this passage!" he gasped, hoarse with excitement. "The Tower is below. Follow me! My oxen will stand. I am going with you!" His rugged face was aglow.

Off through the alley they hurried, King disdaining the pain his ankle was giving him. They came to the crowded square a few minutes later. The clock in the Cathedral pointed to twelve o'clock and after! The catastrophe had not yet taken place; the people were laughing and singing and shouting. They were in time. Everywhere they heard glad voices crying out that the Prince was coming! It was the Royal band that they heard through dinning ears!

"Great God!" cried Truxton, stopping suddenly and pointing with trembling hand to a spot across the street and a little below where they had pushed through the resentful, staring throng on the sidewalk. "There she is! At the corner! Stop her!"

He had caught sight of Olga Platanova.

The first row of dragoons was already passing in front of her. Less than two hundred feet away rolled the royal coach of gold! All this flashed before the eyes of the distracted pair, who were now dashing frantically into the open street, disregarding the shouts of the police and the howls of the crowd.

"An anarchist!" shouted King hoarsely. He looked like one himself. "The bomb! The bomb! Stop the Prince!"

Colonel Quinnox recognised this bearded, uncouth figure, and the flying, terrified girl at his heels. King was dragging her along by the hand.

There was an instant of confusion on the part of the vanguard, a drawing of sabres, a movement toward the coach in which the Prince rode.

Quinnox alone prevented the dragoons from cutting down the pallid madman who stumbled blindly toward the coaches beyond. He whirled his steed after an astonished glance in all directions, shouting eager commands all the while. When he reached the side of the gasping American, that person had stopped and was pointing toward the trembling Olga, who had seen and recognised him.

"Stop the coach!" cried King. Loraine was running frantically through the ranks of horsemen, screaming her words of alarm.

The Duke of Perse leaped from his carriage and ran forward, shouting to the soldiers to seize the disturbers. Panic seized the crowd. There was a mad rush for the corner above. Olga Platanova stood alone, her eyes wide and glassy, staring as if petrified at the face of Truxton King.

He saw the object in her wavering hand. With a yell he dashed for safety down the seething avenue. The Duke of Perse struck at him as he passed, ignoring the frantic cry of warning that he uttered. A plain, white-faced farmer in a smock of blue was crossing the street with mighty bounds, his eyes glued upon the arm of the frail, terrified anarchist. If he could only arrest that palsied, uncertain arm!

But she hurled the bomb, her hands going to her eyes as she fell upon her knees.

CHAPTER XVII
THE THROWING OF THE BOMB

The scene that followed beggars all powers of description.

A score of men and horses lay writhing in the street; others crept away screaming with pain; human flesh and that of animals lay in the path of the frenzied, panic-stricken holiday crowd; blood mingled with the soft mud of Regengetz Circus, slimy, slippery, ugly!

Rent bodies of men in once gaudy uniforms, now flattened and bruised in warm, oozy death, were piled in a mass where but a moment before the wondering vanguard of troopers had clustered. For many rods in all directions stunned creatures were struggling to their feet after the stupendous shock that had felled them. The clattering of frightened horses, the shouts and screams of men and women, the gruesome rush of ten thousand people in stampede—all in twenty seconds after the engine of death left the hand of Olga Platanova.

Olga Platanova! There was nothing left of her! She had failed to do the deed expected of her, but she would not hear the execrations of those who had depended upon her to kill the Prince. We draw a veil across the picture of Olga Platanova after the bomb left her hand; no one may look upon the quivering, shattered thing that once was a living, beautiful woman. The glimpse she had of Truxton King's haggard face unnerved her. She faltered, her strength of will collapsed; she hurled the bomb in a panic of indecision. Massacre but not conquest!

Down in an alley below the Tower, a trembling, worn team of oxen stood for a day and night, awaiting the return of a master who was never to come back to them. God rest his simple soul!

Truxton King picked himself up from the street, dazed, bewildered but unhurt. Everywhere about him mad people were rushing and screeching. Scarcely knowing what he did, he fled with the crowd. From behind him came the banging of guns, followed by new shouts of terror. He knew what it meant! The revolutionists had begun the assault on the paralysed minions of the government.

Scores of Royal Guardsmen swept past him, rushing to the support of the coach of gold. The sharp, shrill scream of a single name rose above the tumult. Some one had seen the Iron Count!

"Marlanx!"

He looked back toward the gory entrance to the Circus. There was Marlanx, mounted and swinging a sabre on high. Ahead was the mass of carriages, filled with the white-faced, palsied prey from the Court of Graustark. Somewhere in that huddled, glittering crowd were two beings he willingly would give his own life to save.

Foot soldiers, policemen and mounted guardsmen began firing into the crowd at the square, without sense or discretion, falling back, nevertheless, before the well-timed, deliberate advance of the mercenaries. From somewhere near the spot where Olga Platanova fell came a harsh, penetrating command:

"Cut them off! Cut them off from the Castle!"

It was his cue. He dashed into the street and ran toward the carriages, shouting with all his strength:

"Turn back! It is Marlanx! To the Castle!"

Then it was that he saw the Prince. The boy was standing on a seat on the royal coach of state, holding out his eager little hands to some one in the thick of the crowd that surged about him. He was calling some one's name, but no one could have heard him.

Truxton's straining eyes caught sight of the figure in grey that struggled forward in response to the cries and the extended hands. He pushed his way savagely through the crowd; he came up with her as she reached the side of the coach, and with a shout of encouragement grasped her in his arms.

"Aunt Loraine! Aunt Loraine!" He now heard the name the boy cried with all his little heart.

Two officers struck at the uncouth, desperate American as he lifted the girl from the ground and deliberately tossed her into the coach.

"Turn back!" he shouted. A horseman rode him down. He looked up as the plunging animal's hoofs clattered about his head. Vos Engo, with drawn sword, was crowding up to the carriage door, shouting words of rejoicing at sight of the girl he loved.

Somehow he managed to crawl from under the hoofs and wheels, not without thumps and bruises, and made his way to the sidewalk. The coach had swung around and the horses were being lashed into a gallop for the Castle gates.

He caught a glimpse of her, holding the Prince in her arms, her white, agonised face turned toward the mob. Distinctly he heard her cry:

"Save him! Save Truxton King!"

From the sidewalks swarmed well-armed hordes of desperadoes, firing wildly into the ranks of devoted guardsmen grouped in the avenue to cover the flight of their royal charge. Truxton fled from the danger zone as fast as his legs would carry him. Bullets were striking all about him. Later on he was to remember his swollen, bitterly painful ankle; but there was no thought of it now. He had played football with this same ankle in worse condition than it was now—and he had played for the fun of it, too.

He realised that his life was worth absolutely nothing if he fell into the hands of the enemy. His only chance lay in falling in with some sane, loyal citizen who could be prevailed upon to hide him until the worst was over. There seemed no possibility of getting inside the Castle grounds. He had done his duty and—he laughed bitterly as he thought of it—he had been ridden down by the men he came to save.

Some one was shouting his name behind in the scurrying crowd. He turned for a single glance backward. Little Mr. Hobbs, pale as a ghost, his cap gone, his clothing torn, was panting at his elbow.

"God save us!" gasped Hobbs. "Are you alive or am I seeing all the bloody ghosts in the world?"

"I'm alive all right," cried King. "Where can we go? Be quick, Hobbs! Think! Don't sputter like that. I want to be personally conducted, and damned quick at that."

"Before God, sir, I 'aven't the idea where to go," groaned Hobbs. "It's dreadful! Did you see what the woman did back there—"

"Don't stop to tell me about it, Hobbs. Keep on running. Go ahead of me. I'm used to following the man from Cook's."

"Right you are, sir. I say, by Jove, I'm glad to see you—I am. You came right up out of the ground as if—"

"Is there no way to get off this beastly avenue?" panted King. "They're shooting back there like a pack of wild men. I hate to think of what's going on."

"Dangloss will 'ave them all in the jug inside of ten minutes, take my word—"

"They'll have Dangloss hanging from a telephone; pole, Hobbs! Don't talk! Run!"

Soldiers came riding up from behind, turning to fire from their saddles into the throng of cutthroats, led by the grim old man with the bloody sabre. In the centre of the troop there was a flying carriage. The Duke of Perse was lying back in the seat, his face like that of a dead man. Far ahead rattled the royal coach and the wildly flying carriages of state.

"The Prince is safe!" shouted King joyously. "They'll make it! Thank God!"

Colonel Quinnox turned in his saddle and searched out the owner of that stirring voice.

"Come!" he called, drawing rein as soon as he caught sight of him.

Even as King rushed out into the roadway a horseman galloped up from the direction of the Castle. He pulled his horse to his haunches almost as he was riding over the dodging American.

"Here!" shouted the newcomer, scowling down upon the young man. "Swing up here! Quick, you fool!"

It was Vos Engo, his face black with fury. Quinnox had seized the hand of Mr. Hobbs on seeing help for King and was pulling him up before him. There was nothing for Truxton to do but to accept the timely help of his rival. An instant later he was up behind him and they were off after the last of the dragoons.

"If you don't mind, Count, I'll try my luck," grated the American. Holding on with one arm, he turned and fired repeatedly in the direction of the howling crowd of rascals.

"Ride to the barracks gates, Vos Engo!" commanded Colonel Quinnox. "Be prepared to admit none but the Royal Reserves, who are under standing orders to report there in time of need."

"God grant that they may be able to come," responded the Count. Over his shoulder he hissed to his companion. "It was not idle heroics, my friend, nor philanthropy on my part. I was commanded to come and fetch you. She would never have spoken to me again if I had refused."

"She? Ah, yes; I see. Good! She did not forget me!" cried Truxton, his heart bounding.

"My own happiness depends on my luck in getting you to safety," rasped the Count. "My life's happiness. Understand, damn you, it is not for you that I risk my life."

"I understand," murmured Truxton, a wry smile on his pale lips. "You mean, she is going to pay you in some way for picking me up, eh? Well, I'll put an end to that. I'll drop off again. Then you can ride on and tell her—I wouldn't be a party to the game. Do you catch my meaning?"

"You would, eh?" said the Count angrily. "I'd like to see you drop off while we're going at this—"

"I've got my pistol in the middle of your back," grated Truxton. "Slow up a bit or I'll scatter your vertebræ all over your system. Pull up!"

"As you like," cried Vos Engo. "I've done my part. Colonel Quinnox will bear witness." He began pulling his horse down. "Now, you are quite free to drop off."

Without a word the American swung his leg over and slid to the ground. "Thanks for the lift you've given me," he called up to the astonished officer.

"Don't thank me," sang out his would-be saviour as he put spur to his horse.

It is a lamentable thing to say, but Truxton King's extraordinary sacrifice was not altogether the outgrowth of heroism. We have not been called upon at any time to question his courage; we have, on the other hand, seen times when he displayed the most arrant foolhardiness. I defy any one to prove, however, that he ever neglected an opportunity to better himself by strategy at the expense of fortitude. Therefore, it is not surprising that even at such a time as this we may be called upon to record an example of his spectacular cunning.

Be sure of it, he did not decide to slide from Vos Engo's horse until he saw a way clear to better his position, and at the same time to lessen the glory of his unpleasant rescuer.

Less than a hundred yards behind loped a riderless horse; the dragoon who had sat the saddle was lying far back in the avenue, a bullet in his head. Hobbling to the middle of the road, the American threw up his hands and shouted briskly to the bewildered animal. Throwing his ears forward in considerable doubt, the horse came to a standstill close at hand. Five seconds later King was in the saddle and tearing along in the wake of the retreating guard, his hair blowing from his forehead, his blood leaping with the joy of achievement.

Mr. Hobbs afterward informed him that Count Vos Engo's oaths were worth going miles to avoid.

"We need such men as King!" cried Colonel Quinnox as he waited inside the gates for the wild rider. A moment later King dashed through and the massive bolts were shot.

As he pulled up in front of the steward's lodge to await the orders of the Colonel, the exultant American completed the soliloquy that began with the mad impulse to ride into port under his own sails.

"I'll have to tell her that he did a fine thing in coming back for me, much as he hated to do it. What's more, I shan't say a word about his beastly temper. We'll let it pass. He deserves a whole lot for the part he played. I'll not forget it. Too bad he had to spoil it all by talking as he did. But, hang me, if he shall exact anything from her because he did a thing he didn't want to do. I took a darned sight bigger chance than he did, after all. Good Lord, what a mess I would have been in if the nag hadn't stopped! Whew! Well, old boy, you did stop, God bless you. Colonel," he spoke, as Quinnox came up, "do you think I can buy this horse? He's got more sense than I have."

Small bodies of foot soldiers and policemen fighting valiantly against great odds were admitted to the grounds during the next half hour. Scores had been killed by the fierce, irregular attack of the revolutionists; others had become separated from their comrades and were even now being hunted down and destroyed by the infuriated followers of Marlanx. A hundred or more of the reserves reached the upper gates before it occurred to the enemy to blockade the streets in that neighbourhood. General Braze, with a few of his men, bloody and heartsick, was the last of the little army to reach safety in the Castle grounds, coming up by way of the lower gates from the fortress, which they had tried to reach after the first outbreak, but had found themselves forestalled.

The fortress, with all guns, stores and ammunition, was in the hands of the Iron Count and his cohorts.

Baron Dangloss had been taken prisoner with a whole platoon of fighting constables. This was the last appalling bit of news to reach the horrified, disorganised forces in the Castle grounds.

Citizens had fled to their homes, unmolested. The streets were empty, save for the armed minions of the Iron Count. They rushed hither and thither in violent detachments, seeking out the men in uniform, yelling and shooting like unmanageable savages.

Before two o'clock the city itself was in the hands of the hated enemy of the Crown. He and his aliens, malefactors and all, were in complete control of the fortress, the gates and approaches, the Tower and the bloody streets. A thousand of them,—eager, yelling ruffians,—marched to within firing distance of the Castle walls and held every approach against reinforcements. Except for the failure to destroy the Prince and his counsellors, the daring, unspeakable plans of Count Marlanx had been attended by the most horrifying results. He was master. There was no question as to that. The few hundred souls in the Castle grounds were like rats in a trap.

A wise as well as a cruel man was Marlanx. He lost no time in issuing a manifesto to the stunned, demoralised citizens of Edelweiss. Scores of criers went through the streets during the long, wretched afternoon, announcing to the populace that Count Marlanx had established himself as dictator and military governor of the principality—pending the abdication of the Prince and the beginning of a new and substantial regime. All citizens were commanded to recognise the authority of the dictator; none except those who disobeyed or resented this authority would be molested. Traffic would be resumed on the following Monday. Tradespeople and artisans were commanded to resume their occupations under penalty of extreme punishment in case of refusal. These and many other edicts were issued from Marlanx's temporary headquarters in the Plaza—almost at the foot of the still veiled monument of the beloved Princess Yetive.

Toward evening, after many consultations and countless reports, Marlanx removed his headquarters to the Tower. He had fondly hoped to be in the Castle long before this. His rage and disappointment over the stupid miscarriage of plans left no room for conjecture as to the actual state of his feelings. For hours he had raved like a madman. Every soldier who fell into his hands was shot down like a dog.

The cells and dungeons in the great old tower were now occupied by bruised, defeated officers of the law. Baron Jasto Dangloss, crushed in spirit and broken of body, paced the blackest and narrowest cell of them all. The gall and wormwood that filled his soul was not to be measured by words. He blamed himself for the catastrophe; it was he who had permitted this appalling thing to grow and burst with such sickening results. In his mind there was no doubt that Marlanx had completely overthrown the dynasty and was in full possession of the government. He did not know that the Prince and his court had succeeded in reaching the Castle, whose walls and gates were well-nigh impregnable to assault, even by a great army. If he had known this he might have rejoiced!

Late in the evening he received a visit from Marlanx, the new master.

The Iron Count, lighted by a ghostly lantern in the hands of a man who, ten hours before, had been a prisoner within these very walls, came up to the narrow grating that served as a door and gazed complacently upon the once great minister of police.

"Well," said Dangloss, his eyes snapping, "what is it, damn you?"

Marlanx stroked his chin and smiled. "I believe this is my old confrère, Baron Dangloss," he remarked. "Dear me, I took you, sir, to be quite impeccable. Here you are, behind the bars. Will wonders never cease?"

Dangloss merely glared at him.

The Iron Count went on suavely: "You heard me, Baron. Still, I do not require an answer. How do you like your new quarters? It may please you to know that I am occupying your office, and also that noble suite overlooking the Plaza. I find myself most agreeably situated. By the way, Baron, I seem to recall something to mind as I look at you. You were the kindly disposed gentleman who escorted me to the city gates a few years ago and there turned me over to a detachment of soldiers, who, in turn, conveyed me to the border. If I recall the occasion rightly, you virtually kicked me out of the city. Am I right?"

"You are!" was all that the bitter Dangloss said, without taking his fierce gaze from the sallow face beyond the bars.

"I am happy to find that my memory is so good," said Marlanx.

"I expect to be able to repeat the operation," said Dangloss.

"How interesting! You forget that history never repeats itself."

"See here, Marlanx, what is your game? Speak up; I'm not afraid of you. Do you intend to take me out and shoot me at sunrise?"

"Oh, dear me, no! That would be a silly proceeding. You own vast estates in Graustark, if I mistake not, just as I did eight or nine years ago. Well, I have come into my own again. The Crown relieved me of my estates, my citizenship, my honour. I have waited long to regain them. Understand me, Dangloss; I am in control now; my word is law. I do not intend to kill you. It is my intention to escort you to the border and kick you out of Graustark. See for yourself how it feels. Everything you possess is to be taken away from you. You will be a wanderer on the face of the earth—a pauper. All you have is here. Therein lies the distinction: I had large possessions in other lands. I had friends and a following, as you see. You will have none of these, Baron."

"A splendid triumph, you beast!"

"Of course, you'd much prefer being shot."

"Not at all. Banish me, if you please; strip me of all I possess. But I'll come back another day, Count Marlanx."

"Ah, yes; that reminds me. I had quite forgotten to say that the first ten years of your exile are to be spent in the dungeons at Schloss Marlanx. How careless of me to have neglected to state that in the beginning. In ten years you will be seventy-five, Baron. An excellent time of life for one to begin his wanderings over the world which will not care to remember him."

"Do you expect me to get down on my knees and plead for mercy, you scoundrel?"

"I know you too well for that, my dear Baron."

"Get out of my sight!"

"Pray do not forget that I am governor of the Tower at present. I go and come as I choose."

"God will punish you for what you have done. There's solace in that."

"As you like, Baron. If it makes it easier for you to feel that God will take a hand in my humble affairs, all well and good. I grant you that delectable privilege."

Baron Dangloss turned his back upon his smiling enemy, his body quivering with passion.

"By the way, Baron, would you care to hear all the latest news from the seat of war? It may interest you to know that the Castle is besieged in most proper fashion. No one—"

"The Castle besieged? Then, by the Eternal, you did not take the Prince!"

"Not at all! He is in the Castle for a few hours of imaginary safety. To-night my men will be admitted to the grounds by friends who have served two masters for a twelve-month or longer."

"Traitors in the Castle?" cried Dangloss in horror. He was now facing the Count.

"Hardly that, my dear sir. Agents, I should call them. Isn't it splendid?"

"You are a—"

"Don't say it, Baron. Save your breath. I know what you would call me, and can save you the trouble of shouting it, as you seem inclined to do."

"Thank God, your assassins not only failed to dynamite the boy, but your dogs failed to capture him. By heaven, God *is* with Prince Robin, after all!"

"How exalted you seem, Baron! It is a treat to look at you. Oh, another thing: the Platanova girl was not *my* assassin."

"That's a lie!"

"You shall not chide me in that fashion, Baron. You are very rude. No; the girl was operating for what I have since discovered to be the Committee of Ten, leading the Party of Equals in Graustark. To-morrow morning I shall have the Committee of Ten seized and shot in the public square. We cannot harbour dynamiters and assassins of that type. There are two-score or more of anarchist sympathisers here. We will cheerfully shoot all of them—an act that you should have performed many days ago, my astute friend. It might have saved trouble. They are a dangerous element in any town. Those whom I do not kill I shall transport to the United States in exchange for the Americans who have managed to lose themselves over here. A fair exchange, you see. Moreover, I hear that the United States Government welcomes the Reds if they are white instead of yellow. Clever, but involved, eh? Well, good night, Baron. Sleep well. I expect to see you again after the rush of business attending the adjustment of my own particular affairs. In a day or two I shall move into the Castle. You may be relieved to know that I do not expect to find the time to kick you out of Graustark under a week or ten days."

"My men: what of them? The brave fellows who were taken with me? You will not deprive—"

"In time they will be given the choice of serving me as policemen or serving the world as examples of folly. Rest easy concerning them. Ah, yes, again I have stupidly forgotten something. Your excellent friend, Tullis, will not re-enter Edelweiss alive. That is quite assured, sir. So you see, he will, after all, be better off than you. I don't blame him for loving my wife. It was my desire to amicably trade my wife off to him for his charming sister, but the deal hangs fire. What a scowl! I dare say you contemplate saying something bitter, so I'll retire. A little later on I shall be chatting with the Prince at the Castle. I'll give him your gentlest felicitations."

But Marlanx was doomed to another disappointment before the night was over. The Castle gates were not opened to his forces. Colonel Quinnox apprehended the traitors in time to prevent the calamity. Ten hostlers in the Royal stables were taken redhanded in the attempt to overpower the small guard at the western gates. Their object was made plain by the subsequent futile movement of a large force of men at that particular point.

Prince Robin was safe for the night.

CHAPTER XVIII
TRUXTON ON PARADE

Count Marlanx was a soldier. He knew how to take defeat and to bide his time; he knew how to behave in the hour of victory and in the moment of rout. The miscarriage of a detail here and there in this vast, comprehensive plan of action did not in the least sense discourage him. It was no light blow to his calculations, of course, when the designs of an organisation separate and distinct from his own failed in their purpose. It was part of his plan to hold the misguided Reds responsible for the lamentable death of Prince Robin. The people were to be given swift, uncontrovertible proof that he had no hand in the unforeseen transactions of the anarchists, who, he would make it appear, had by curious coincidence elected to kill the Prince almost at the very hour when he planned to seize the city as a conqueror.

His own connection with the operations of the mysterious Committee of Ten was never to be known to the world. He would see to that.

At nine o'clock on Sunday morning a small group of people gathered in the square: a meeting was soon in progress. A goods-box stood over against the very spot on which Olga Platanova died. An old man began haranguing the constantly growing crowd, made up largely of those whose curiosity surpassed discreetness. In the group might have been seen every member of the Committee of Ten, besides a full representation of those who up to now had secretly affiliated with the Party of Equals. A red flag waved above the little, excited group of fanatics, close to the goods-box rostrum. One member of the Committee was absent from this, their first public espousal of the cause. Later on we are to discover who this man was. Two women in bright red waists were crying encouragement to the old man on the box, whose opening sentences were no less than an unchanted requiem for the dead martyr, Olga Platanova.

In the midst of his harangue, the hand of William Spantz was arrested in one of its most emphatic gestures. A look of wonder and uncertainty came into his face as he gazed, transfixed, over the heads of his hearers in the direction of the Tower.

Peter Brutus was approaching, at the head of a group of aliens, all armed and marching in ominously good order. Something in the face of Peter Brutus sent a chill of apprehension into the very soul of the old armourer.

And well it may have done so.

"One moment!" called out Peter Brutus, lifting his hand imperatively. The speaker ceased his mouthings. "Count Marlanx desires the immediate presence of the following citizens at his office in the Tower. I shall call off the names." He began with William Spantz. The name of each of his associates in the Committee of Ten followed. After them came a score of names, all of them known to be supporters of the anarchist cause.

"What is the business, Peter?" demanded William Spantz.

"Does it mean we are to begin so soon the establishing of the new order—" began Anna Cromer, her face aglow. Peter smiled wanly.

"Do not ask me," he said, emphasising the pronoun. "I am only commanded to bring the faithful few before him."

"But why the armed escort?" growled Julius Spantz, who had spent an unhappy twenty-four hours in bondage.

"To separate the wheat from the chaff," said Peter. "Move on, good people, all you whose names were not called." The order was to the few timid strangers who were there because they had nowhere else to go. They scattered like chaff.

Ten minutes later every member of the Committee of Ten, except Peter Brutus, was behind lock and bar, together with their shivering associates, all of them dumbly muttering to themselves the awful sentence that Marlanx had passed upon them.

"You are to die at sunset. Graustark still knows how to punish assassins. She will make an example of you to-day that all creatures of your kind, the world over, will not be likely to forget in a century to come. There is no room in Graustark for anarchy. I shall wipe it out to-day."

"Sir, your promise!" gasped William Spantz. "We are your friends—the true Party of—"

"Enough! Do not speak again! Captain Brutus, you will send criers abroad to notify the citizens that I, Count Marlanx, have ordered the execution of the ringleaders in the plot to dynamite the Prince. At sunset, in the square. Away with the carrion!"

Then it was, and not till then, that the Committee of Ten found him out! Then it was that they came to know Peter Brutus! What were their thoughts, we dare not tell: their shrieks and curses were spent against inpenetrable floors and walls. Baron Dangloss heard, and, in time, understood. Even he shrank back and shuddered.

It has been said that Marlanx was a soldier. There is one duty that the soldier in command never neglects: the duty to those who fell while fighting bravely for or against him. Sunday afternoon a force of men was set to work burying the dead and clearing the pavements. Those of his own nondescript army who gave up their lives on the 26th were buried in the public cemeteries. The soldiers of the Crown, as well as the military police, were laid to rest in the national cemetery, with honours befitting their rank. Each grave was carefully marked and a record preserved. In this way Marlanx hoped to obtain his first footing in the confidence and esteem of the citizens. The unrecognisable corpse of Olga Platanova was buried in quicklime outside the city walls. There was something distinctly gruesome in the fact that half a dozen deep graves were dug alongside hers, hours before death came to the wretches who were to occupy them.

At three o'clock the Iron Count coolly sent messengers to the homes of the leading merchants and bankers of the city. They, with the priests, the doctors, the municipal officers and the manufacturers were commanded to appear before him at five o'clock for the purpose of discussing the welfare of the city and its people. Hating, yet fearing him, they came; not one but felt in his heart that the old man was undisputed ruler of their destinies. Hours of horror and despair, a night and a day of bitter reflection, had brought the trembling populace to the point of seeing clearly the whole miserable situation. The reserves were powerless; the Royal Guard was besieged and greatly outnumbered; the fortress was lost. There was nothing for them to do but temporise. Time alone could open the way to salvation.

Marlanx stated his position clearly. He left no room for doubt in their minds. The strings were in his hands: he had but to pull them. The desire of his life was about to be attained. Without hesitation he informed the leading men of the city that he was to be the Prince of Graustark.

"I have the city," he said calmly. "The farms and villages will fall in line. I do not worry over them. In a very short time I shall have the Castle. The question for you to decide for yourselves is this: will you be content to remain here as thrifty, peaceable citizens, protecting your fortunes and being protected by a man and not by a child. If not, please say so. The alternative is in the hands of the Crown. I am the Crown. The Crown may at any time confiscate property and banish malcontents and disturbers. A word to the wise, gentlemen. Inside of a week we will have a new government. You will not suffer under its administration. I should be indeed a fool to destroy the credit or injure the integrity of my own dominion. But, let me say this, gentlemen," he went on after a pause, in which his suavity gave way to harshness; "you may as well understand at the outset that I expect to rule here. I will rule Graustark or destroy her."

The more courageous in his audience began to protest against the high-handed manner in which he proposed to treat them. Not a few declared that they would never recognise him as a prince of the realm. He waited, as a spider waits, until he thought they had gone far enough. Then he held up his hand and commanded silence.

"Those of you who do not expect or desire to live under my rule—which, I promise you, shall be a wise one,—may leave the city for other lands just as soon as my deputies have completed the formal transfer of all your belongings to the Crown treasury—all, I say, even to the minutest trifle. Permit me to add, in that connection, gentlemen: the transfer will not be a prolonged affair."

They glared back at him and subsided into bitter silence.

"I am well aware that you love little Prince Robin. Ha! You may not cheer here, gentlemen, under penalty of my displeasure. It is quite right that you should, as loyal subjects, love your Prince, whoever he may be. I shall certainly expect it. Now, respecting young master Robin: I have no great desire to kill him."

He waited to see the effect of this brutal announcement. His hearers stiffened and—yes, they held their breath.

"He has one alternative—he and his lords. I trust that you, as sensible gentlemen, will find the means to convey to him your advice that he seize the opportunity I shall offer him to escape with his life. No one really wants to see the little chap die. Let me interrupt myself to call to your attention the fact that I am punishing the anarchists at sunset. This to convince you that assassination will not be tolerated in Graustark. To resume: the boy may return to America, where he belongs. He is more of an American than one of us. I will give him free and safe escort to the United States. Certain of his friends may accompany him; others whom I shall designate will be required to remain here until I have disposed of their cases as I see fit. These conditions I shall set forth in my manifesto to the present occupant of the Castle. If he chooses to accept my kindly terms, all well and good. If not, gentlemen, I shall starve him out or blow the Castle down about his smart little ears. You shudder! Well, I can't blame you. I shudder myself sometimes when I think of it. There will be a great deal of royal blood, you know. Ah, that reminds me: It may interest you to hear that I expect to establish a new nobility in Graustark. The present house of lords is objectionable to me. I trust I may now be addressing at least a few of the future noble lords of Graustark. Good day, gentlemen. That is all for the present. Kindly inform me if any of my soldiers or followers overstep the bounds of prudence. Rapine and ribaldry will not be tolerated."

The dignitaries and great men of the city went away, dazed and depressed, looking at each other from bloodshot eyes. Not one friend had Marlanx in that group, and he knew it well. He did not expect them to submit at once or even remotely. They might have smiled, whereas they frowned, if they could have seen him pacing the floor of his office, the moment the doors closed behind their backs, clenching his hands and cursing furiously.

At the Castle the deepest gloom prevailed. It was like a nightmare to the beleaguered household, a dream from which there seemed to be no awakening. Colonel Quinnox's first act after posting his forces in position to repel attacks from the now well-recognised enemy, was to make sure of the safety of his royal master. Inside the walls of the Castle grounds he, as commander of the Royal Guard, ruled supreme. General Braze tore off his own epaulets and presented himself to Quinnox as a soldier of the file; lords and dukes, pages and ministers, followed the example of the head of the War Department. No one stood on the dignity of his position; no one does, as a rule, with the executioner staring him in the face. Every man took up arms for the defence of the Castle, its Prince and its lovely women.

Prince Robin, quite recovered from his fright, donned the uniform of a Colonel of the Royal Dragoons, buckled on his jewelled sword, and, with boyish zeal, demanded Colonel Quinnox's reasons for not going forth to slay the rioters.

"What is the army for, Colonel Quinnox?" he asked with impatient wonder.

It was late in the afternoon and the Prince was seated in the chair of state, presiding over the hurriedly called Council meeting. Notably absent were Baron Dangloss and the Duke of Perse. Chief officers of the Guard and the commissioned men of the army were present—that is, all of them who had not gone down under the treacherous fire.

"Your Highness," said the Colonel bitterly, "the real army is outside the walls, not inside. We are a pitiful handful-less than three hundred men, all told, counting the wounded. Count Marlanx heads an army of several thousand. He—"

"He wants to get in here so's he can kill me? Is that so, Colonel Quinnox?" The Prince was very pale, but quite calm.

"Oh, I wouldn't put it just that way, your—"

"Oh, I know. You can't fool me. I've always known that he wants to kill me. But how can he? That's the question; how can he when I've got the Royal Guard to keep him from doing it? He can't whip the Royal Guard. Nobody can. He ought to know that. He must be awful stupid."

His perfect, unwavering faith in the Guard was the same that had grown up with every prince of Graustark and would not be gainsaid. A score of hearts swelled with righteous pride and as many scabbards rattled as heels clicked and hands went up in salute.

"Your Highness," said Quinnox, with a glance at his fellow-officers, "you may rely upon it, Count Marlanx will never reach you until he has slain every man in the Royal Guard."

"And in the army—our poor little army," added General Braze.

"Thank you," said the Prince. "You needn't have told me. I knew it." He leaned back in the big chair, almost slipping from the record books on which he sat, a brave scowl on his face. "Gee, I wish he'd attack us right now," he said, with ingenuous bravado.

The council of war was not a lengthy one. The storm that had arisen out of a perfectly clear sky was briefly discussed in all its phases. No man there but realised the seriousness of the situation. Count Halfont, who seemed ten years older than when we last saw him, addressed the Cabinet.

"John Tullis is still outside the city walls. If he does not fall into a trap through ignorance of the city's plight, I firmly believe he will be able to organise an army of relief among the peasants and villagers. They are loyal. The mountaineers and shepherds, wild fellows all, and the ones who have fallen into the spider's net. Count Marlanx has an army of aliens; they are not even revolutionists. John Tullis, if given the opportunity, can sweep the city clear of them. My only fear is that he may be tricked into ambush before we can reach him. No doubt Marlanx, in devising a way to get him out of the city, also thought of the means to keep him out."

"We must get word to Tullis," cried several in a breath. A dozen men volunteered to risk their lives in the attempt to find the American in the hills. Two men were chosen—by lot. They were to venture forth that very night.

"My lords," said the Prince, as the Council was on the point of dissolving, "is it all right for me to ask a question now?"

"Certainly, Robin," said the Prime Minister.

"Well, I'd like to know where Mr. King is."

"He's safe, your Highness," said Quinnox.

"Aunt Loraine is worried, that's all. She's sick, you see—awful sick. Do you think Mr. King would be good enough to walk by her window, so's she can see for herself? She's in the royal bedchamber."

"The royal bedchamber?" gasped the high chamberlain.

"I gave up my bed right off, but she won't stay in it. She sits in the window most of the time. It's all right about the bed. I spoke to nurse about it. Besides, I don't want to go to bed while there's any fighting going on. So, you see, it's all right. Say, Uncle Caspar, may I take a crack at old Marlanx with my new rifle if I get a chance? I've been practising on the target range, and Uncle Jack says I'm a reg'lar Buffalo Bill."

Count Halfont unceremoniously hugged his wriggling grand-nephew. A cheer went up from the others.

"Long live Prince Robin!" shouted Count Vos Engo.

Prince Robin looked abashed. "I don't think I could hit him," he said with becoming modesty. They laughed aloud. "But, say, don't forget about Mr. King. Tell him I want him to parade most of the time in front of my windows."

"He has a weak ankle," began Colonel Quinnox lamely.

"Very difficult for him to walk," said Vos Engo, biting his lips.

The Prince looked from face to face, suspicion in his eyes. It dawned on him that they were evading the point. A stubborn line appeared between his brows.

"Then I command you, Colonel Quinnox, to give him the best horse in the stables. I want him to ride."

"It shall be as you command, your Highness."

A few minutes later, his grand-uncle, the Prime Minister, was carrying him down the corridor; Prince Robin was perched upon the old man's shoulder, and was a thoughtful mood.

"Say, Uncle Caspar, Mr. King's all right, isn't he?"

"He is a very brave and noble gentleman, Bobby. We owe to his valour the life of the best boy in all the world."

"Yes, and Aunt Loraine owes him a lot, too. She says so. She's been crying, Uncle Caspar. Say, has she just got to marry Count Vos Engo?"

"My boy, what put that question into your mind?"

"She says she has to. I thought only princes and princesses had to marry people they don't want to."

"You should not believe all that you hear."

Bobby was silent for twenty steps. Then he said: "Well, I think she'll make an awful mistake if she lets Mr. King get away."

"My boy, we have other affairs to trouble us at present without taking up the affairs of Miss Tullis."

"Well, he saved her life, just like they do in story books," protested the Prince.

"Well, you run in and tell her this minute that Mr. King sends his love to her and begs her to rest easy. See if it doesn't cheer her up a bit."

"Maybe she's worried about Uncle Jack. I never thought about that," he faltered.

"Uncle Jack will come out on top, never fear," cried the old man.

Half an hour later, Truxton King, shaven and shorn, outfitted and polished, received orders to ride for twenty minutes back and forth across the Plaza. He came down from Colonel Quinnox's rooms in the officer's row, considerably mystified, and mounted the handsome bay that he had brought through the gates. Haddan, of the Guard, rode with him to the Plaza, but could offer no explanation for the curious command.

Five times the now resentful American walked his horse across the Plaza, directly in front of the terrace and the great balconies. About him paced guardsmen, armed and alert; on the outer edge of the parade ground a company of soldiers were hurrying through the act of changing the Guard; in the lower balcony excited men and women were walking back and forth, paying not the least attention to him. Above him frowned the grey, lofty walls of the Castle. No one was in view on the upper balcony, beyond which he had no doubt lay the royal chambers. He had the mean, uncomfortable feeling that people were peering at him from remote windows.

Suddenly a small figure in bright red and gold and waving a tiny sword appeared at the rail of the broad upper gallery. Truxton blinked his eyes once or, twice and then doffed his hat. The Prince was smiling eagerly.

"Hello!" he called. Truxton drew rein directly below him.

"I trust your Highness has recovered from the shock of to-day," he responded. "I have been terribly anxious. Are you quite well?"

"Quite well, thank you." He hesitated for a moment, as if in doubt. Then: "Say, Mr. King, how's your leg?"

Truxton looked around in sudden embarrassment. A number of distressed, white-faced ladies had paused in the lower gallery and were staring at him in mingled curiosity and alarm. He instantly wondered if Colonel Quinnox's riding clothes were as good a fit as he had been led to believe through Hobbs and others.

"It's—it's fine, thank you," he called up, trying to subdue his voice as much as possible.

Bobby looked a trifle uncertain. His glance wavered and a queer little wrinkle appeared between his eyes. He lowered his voice when he next spoke.

"Say, would you mind shouting that a little louder," he called down, leaning well over the rail.

Truxton flushed. He was pretty sure that the Prince was not deaf. There was no way out of it, however, so he repeated his communication.

"It's all right, your Highness."

Bobby gave a quick glance over his shoulder at one of the broad windows. Truxton distinctly saw the blinds close with a convulsive jerk.

"Thanks! Much obliged! Good-bye!" sang out the Prince, gleefully. He waved his hand and then hopped off the chair on which he was standing. Truxton heard his little heels clatter across the stone balcony. For a moment he was nonplused.

"Well, I'm—By Jove! I understand!" He rode off toward the barracks, his head swimming with joy, his heart jumping like mad. At the edge of the parade ground he turned in his saddle and audaciously lifted his hat to the girl who, to his certain knowledge, was standing behind the tell-tale blind.

"Cheer up, Hobbs!" he sang out in his new-found exuberance as he rode up to the dismal Englishman, who moped in the shade of the stable walls. "Don't be down-hearted. Look at me! Never say die, that's my motto."

"That's all very well, sir," said Hobbs, removing the unlighted pipe from his lips, "but you 'aven't got a dog and a parrot locked up in your rooms with no one to feed them. It makes me sick, 'pon my soul, sir, to think of them dying of thirst and all that, and me here safe and sound, so to speak."

That night Haddan and a fellow-subaltern attempted to leave the Castle grounds by way of the private gate in the western wall, only to be driven back by careful watchers on the outside. A second attempt was made at two o'clock. This time they went through the crypt into the secret underground passage. As they crawled forth into the blackest of nights, clear of the walls, they were met by a perfect fusillade of rifle shots. Haddan's companion was shot through the leg and arm and it was with extreme difficulty that the pair succeeded in regaining the passage and closing the door. No other attempt was made that night. Sunday night a quick sortie was made, it being the hope of the besieged that two selected men might elude Marlanx's watchdogs during the melee that followed. Curiously enough, the only men killed were the two who had been chosen to run the gauntlet in the gallant, but ill-timed attempt to reach John Tullis.

On Monday morning the first direct word from Count Marlanx came to the Castle. Under a flag of truce, two of his men were admitted to the grounds. They presented the infamous ultimatum of the Iron Count. In brief, it announced the establishment of a dictatorship pending the formal assumption of the crown by the conqueror. With scant courtesy the Iron Count begged to inform Prince Robin that his rule was at an end. Surrender would result in his safe conduct to America, the home of his father; defiance would just so surely end in death for him and all of his friends. The Prince was given twenty-four hours in which to surrender his person to the new governor of the city. With the expiration of the time limit mentioned, the Castle would be shelled from the fortress, greatly as the dictator might regret the destruction of the historic and well-beloved structure. No one would be spared if it became necessary to bombard; the rejection of his offer of mercy would be taken as a sign that the defenders were ready to die for a lost cause. He would cheerfully see to it that they died as quickly as possible, in order that the course of government might not be obstructed any longer than necessary.

The defenders of the Castle tore his message in two and sent it back to him without disfiguring it by a single word in reply. The scornful laughter which greeted the reading of the document by Count Halfont did not lose any of its force in the report that the truce-bearers carried, with considerable uneasiness, to the Iron Count later on.

No one in the Castle was deceived by Marlanx's promise to provide safe conduct for the Prince. They knew that the boy was doomed if he fell into the hands of this iniquitous old schemer. More than that, there was not a heart among them so faint that it was not confident of eventual victory over the usurper. They could hold out for weeks against starvation. Hope is an able provider.

A single, distant volley at sunset had puzzled the men on guard at the Castle. They had no means of knowing that the Committee of Ten and its wretched friends had been shot down like dogs in the Public Square. Peter Brutus was in charge of the squad of executioners.

Soon after the return of Marlanx's messengers to the Tower, a number of carriages were observed approaching in Castle Avenue. They were halted a couple of hundred yards from the gates and once more a flag of truce was presented. There was a single line from Marlanx:

"I am sending indisputable witnesses to bear testimony to the thoroughness of my conquest.

"MARLANX."

Investigation convinced the captain of the Guard that the motley caravan in the avenue was made up of loyal, representative citizens from the important villages of the realm. They were admitted to the grounds without question.

The Countess Prandeville of Ganlook, terribly agitated, was one of the first to enter the haven of safety, such as it was. After her came the mayors and the magistrates of a dozen villages. Count Marlanx's reason for delivering these people over to their friends in the Castle was at once manifest.

By the words of their mouths his almost complete mastery of the situation was conveyed to the Prince's defenders. In every instance the representative from a village sorrowfully admitted that Marlanx's men were in control. Ganlook, an ancient stronghold, had been taken without a struggle by a handful of men. The Countess's husband was even now confined in his own castle under guard.

The news was staggering. Count Halfont had based his strongest hopes on the assistance that would naturally come from the villages. Moreover, the strangely commissioned emissaries cast additional gloom over the situation by the report that mountaineers, herdsmen and woodchoppers in the north were flocking to the assistance of the Iron Count, followed by hordes of outlaws from the Axphain hills. They were swarming into the city. These men had always been thorns in the sides of the Crown's peace-makers.

"It is worse than I thought," said Count Halfont, after listening to the words of the excited magistrates. "Are there no loyal men outside these walls?"

"Thousands, sir, but they are not organised. They have no leader, and but little with which to fight against such a force."

"It is hard to realise that a force of three or four thousand desperadoes has the power to defy an entire kingdom. A city of 75,000 people in the hands of hirelings! The shame of it!"

Truxton King was leaning against a column not far from the little group, nervously pulling away at the pipe Quinnox had given him. As if impelled by a common thought, a half dozen pairs of eyes were turned in his direction. Their owners looked as quickly away, again moved by a common thought.

The Minister of Mines gave utterance to a single sentence that might well have been called the epitome of that shrewd, concentrated thought:

"There must be some one who can get to John Tullis before it is too late."

They looked at one another and then once more at the American who had come among them, avowedly in quest of adventure.

CHAPTER XIX
TRUXTON EXACTS A PROMISE

Truxton King had been in a resentful frame of mind for nearly forty-eight hours. In the first place, he had not had so much as a single glimpse of the girl he now worshipped with all his heart. In the second place, he had learned, with unpleasant promptness, that Count Vos Engo was the officer in command of the House Guard, a position as gravely responsible as it was honourable. The cordon about the Castle was so tightly drawn in these perilous hours that even members of the household were subjected to examination on leaving or entering.

Truxton naturally did not expect to invade the Castle in search of the crumb of comfort he so ardently desired; he did not, however, dream that Vos Engo would deny him the privilege of staring at a certain window from a rather prim retreat in a far corner of the Plaza.

He had, of course, proffered his services to Colonel Quinnox. The Colonel, who admired the Americans, gravely informed him that there was no regular duty to which he could be assigned, but that he would expect him to hold himself ready for any emergency. In case of an assault, he was to report to Count Vos Engo.

"We will need our bravest men at the Castle," he had said. Truxton glowed under the compliment. "In the meantime, Mr. King, regain your strength in the park. You show the effect of imprisonment. Your adventures have been most interesting, but I fancy they invite rest for the present."

It was natural that this new American should become an object of tremendous interest to every one in and about the Castle. The story of his mishaps and his prowess was on every lip; his timely appearance in Regengetz Circus was regarded in the light of divine intervention, although no one questioned the perfectly human pluck that brought it about. Noble ladies smiled upon him in the park, to which they now repaired with timorous hearts; counts and barons slapped him on the back and doughty guardsmen actually saluted him with admiration in their eyes.

But he was not satisfied. Loraine had not come forward with a word of greeting or relief; in fact, she had not appeared outside the Castle doors.

Strangely enough, with the entire park at his disposal, he chose to frequent those avenues nearest the great balconies. More than once he visited the grotto where he had first seen her; but it was not the same. The occasional crack of a rifle on the walls no longer fired him with the interest he had felt in the beginning. Forty-eight hours had passed and she still held aloof. What could it mean? Was she ill? Had she collapsed after the frightful strain?

Worse than anything else: was she devoting all of her time to Count Vos Engo?

Toward dusk on Monday, long after the arrival of the refugees, he sat in gloomy contemplation of his own unhappiness, darkly glowering upon the unfriendly portals from a distant stone bench.

A brisk guardsman separated himself from the knot of men at the Castle doors and crossed the Plaza toward him.

"Aha," thought Truxton warmly, "at last she is sending a message to me. Perhaps she's—no, she couldn't be sending for me to come to her."

Judge his dismay and anger when the soldier, a bit shamefaced himself, briefly announced that Count Vos Engo had issued an order against loitering in close proximity to the Castle. Mr. King was inside the limit described in the order. Would he kindly retire to a more distant spot, etc.

Truxton's cheek burned. He saw in an instant that the order was meant for him and for no one else—he being the only outsider likely to come under the head of "loiterer." A sharp glance revealed the fact that not only were the officers watching the little scene, but others in the balcony were looking on.

Resisting the impulse to argue the point, he hastily lifted his hat to the spectators and turned into the avenue without a word.

"I am sorry, sir," mentioned the guardsman earnestly.

Truxton turned to him with a frank smile, meant for the group at the steps. "Please tell Count Vos Engo that I am the last person in the world to disregard discipline at a time like this."

His glance again swept the balcony, suddenly becoming fixed on a couple near the third column. Count Vos Engo and Loraine Tullis were standing there together, unmistakably watching his humiliating departure. To say that Truxton swore softly as he hurried off through the trees would be unnecessarily charitable.

The next morning he encountered Vos Engo near the grotto. Two unsuccessful attempts to leave the Castle grounds had been made during the night. Truxton had aired his opinion to Mr. Hobbs after breakfast.

"I'll bet my head I could get away with it," he had said, doubly scornful because of a sleepless night. "They go about it like a lot of chumps. No wonder they are chased back."

Catching sight of Vos Engo, he hastened across the avenue and caught up to him. The Count was apparently deep in thought.

"Good morning," said Truxton from behind. The other whirled quickly. He did not smile as he eyed the tall American. "I haven't had a chance to thank you for coming back for me last Saturday. Allow me to say that it was a very brave thing to do. If I appeared ungrateful at the time, I'm sure you understood my motives."

"The whole matter is of no consequence, Mr. King," said the other quietly.

"Nevertheless, I consider it my duty to thank you. I want to get it out of my system. Having purged myself of all that, I now want to tell you of a discovery that I made last evening."

"I am not at all interested."

"You will be when I have told you, however, because it concerns you."

"I do not like your words, Mr. King, nor the way in which you glare at me."

"I'm making it easier to tell you the agreeable news, Count Vos Engo; that's all. You'll be delighted to hear that I thought of you nearly all night and still feel that I have not been able to do you full justice."

"Indeed?" with a distinct uplifting of the eyebrows.

"Take your hand off your sword, please. Some other time, perhaps, but not in these days when we need men, not cripples. I'll tell you what I have discovered and then we'll drop the matter until some other time. We can afford a physical delay, but it would be heartless to keep you in mental suspense. Frankly, Count, I have made the gratifying discovery that you are a damned cur."

Count Vos Engo went very white. He drew his dapper figure up to its full height, swelled his Robin Redbreast coat to the bursting point, and allowed his right hand to fly to his sword. Then, as suddenly, he folded his arms and glared at Truxton.

"As you say, there is another and a better time. We need dogs as well as men in these days."

"I hope you won't forget that I thanked you for coming back last Saturday."

The Count turned and walked rapidly away.

Truxton leaned against the low wall alongside the Allée. "I don't know that I've helped matters any," he said to himself ruefully. "He'll not let me get within half a mile of the Castle after this. If she doesn't come out for a stroll in the park, I fancy I'll never see her—Heigho! I wish something would happen! Why doesn't Marlanx begin bombarding? It's getting devilish monotonous here."

He strolled off to the stables, picking up Mr. Hobbs on the way.

"Hobbs," he said, "we've got to find John Tullis, that's all there is to it." He was scowling fiercely at a most inoffensive lawn-mower in the grass at the left.

"I daresay, sir," said Mr. Hobbs with sprightly decisiveness. "He's very much needed."

"I'm going to need him before long as my second."

"Your second, sir? Are you going to fight a duel?"

"I suppose so," lugubriously. "It's too much to expect him to meet me with bare fists. Oh, Hobbs, I wish we could arrange it for bare knucks!" He delivered a mighty swing at an invisible adversary. Hobbs's hat fell off with the backward jerk of surprise.

"Oh, my word!" he exclaimed admiringly, "wot a punch you've got!"

Later on, much of his good humour was restored and his vanity pleased by a polite request from Count Halfont to attend an important council in the "Room of Wrangles" that evening at nine.

Very boldly he advanced upon the Castle a few minutes before the appointed hour. He went alone, that he might show a certain contempt for Count Vos Engo. Notwithstanding the fact that he started early enough for the Chamber, he was distressingly late for the meeting.

He came upon Loraine Tullis at the edge of the Terrace. She was walking slowly in the soft shadows beyond the row of lights on the lower gallery. King would have passed her without recognition, so dim was the light in this enchanted spot, had not his ear caught the sound of a whispered exclamation. At the same time the girl stopped abruptly in the darkest shadow. He knew her at a glance, this slim girl in spotless white.

"Loraine!" he whispered, reaching her side in two bounds. She put out her hands and he clasped them. A quick, hysterical little laugh came from her lips. Plainly, she was confused. "I've been dying for a glimpse of you. Do you think you've treated me—"

"Don't, Truxton," she pleaded, suddenly serious. She sent a swift glance toward the balconies. "You must not come here. I saw—well, you know. I was so ashamed. I was so sorry."

He still held her hands. His heart was throbbing furiously.

"Yes, they ordered me to move on, as if I were a common loafer," he said, with a soft chuckle. "I'm used to it, however. They ran me out of Meshed for taking snapshots; they banished me from Damascus, and they all but kicked me out of Jerusalem—I won't say why. But where have you kept yourself? Why have you avoided me? After getting the Prince to parade me in front of your windows, too. It's dirt mean, Loraine."

"I have been ill, Truxton—truly, I have," she said quickly, uneasily.

"See here, what's wrong? You are in trouble. I can tell by your manner. Tell me—trust me."

"I am worried so dreadfully about John," she faltered.

"That isn't all," he declared. "There's something else. What promise did you make to Vos Engo last Saturday after—well, if you choose to recall it—after I brought you back to him—what did you promise him?"

"Don't be cruel, Truxton," she pleaded. "I cannot forget all you have done for me."

"You told Vos Engo to ride back and pick me up," he persisted. "He told me in so many words. Now, I want a plain answer, Loraine. Did you promise to reward him if he—well, if he saved me from the mob?"

She was breathlessly silent for a moment. "No," she said, in a low voice.

"What was it, then? I must know, Loraine." He was bending over her, imperiously.

"I am very—oh, so very unhappy, Truxton," she murmured. He was on the point of clasping her in his arms and kissing her. But he thought better of it.

"I came near spoiling everything just now," he whispered hoarsely.

"What?"

"I almost kissed you, Loraine,—I swear it was hard to keep from it. That would have spoiled everything."

"Yes, it would," she agreed quickly.

"I'm not going to kiss you until you have told me you love Vos Engo."

"I—I don't understand," she cried, drawing back and looking up into his face with bewildered eyes.

"Because then I'll be sure that you love me."

"Be sensible, Truxton."

"I'll know that you promised to love him if he'd save me. It's as clear as day to me. You *did* tell him you'd marry him if he got me to a place of safety."

"No. I *refused* to marry him if he did not save you. Oh, Truxton, I am so miserable. What is to become of all of us? What is to become of John, and Bobby—and you?"

"I—I think I'll kiss you now, Loraine," he whispered almost tremulously. "God, how I love you, little darling!"

"Don't!" she whispered, resolutely pushing him away after a sweet second of indecision. "I cannot—I cannot, Truxton dear. Don't ask me to—to do that. Not now, please—not now!"

He stiffened; his hands dropped to his sides, but there was joy in his voice.

"I can wait," he said gently. "It's only a matter of a few days; and I—I won't make it any harder for you just now. I think I understand. You've—you've sort of pledged yourself to that—to him, and you don't think it fair to—well, to any of us. I'm including you, you see. I know you don't love him, and I know that you're going to love me, even if you don't at this very instant. I'm not a very stupid person, after all. I can see through things. I saw through it all when he came back for me. That's why I jumped from his horse and took my chances elsewhere. He did a plucky thing, Loraine, but I—I couldn't let it go as he intended it to be. Confound him, I would have died a thousand times over rather than have you sacrifice yourself in that way. It was splendid of you, darling, but—but very foolish. You've got yourself into a dreadful mess over it. I've got to rescue you all over again. This time, thank the Lord, from a Castle."

She could not help smiling. His joyousness would not be denied.

"How splendid you are!" she said, her voice thrilling with a tone that could not be mistaken.

He put his hands upon her shoulders and looked down into the beautiful, upturned face, a genuinely serious note creeping into his voice when he spoke again.

"Don't misconstrue my light-heartedness, dearest. It's a habit with me, not a fault. I see the serious side to your affair—as you view it. You have promised to marry Vos Engo. You'll have to break that promise. He didn't save me. Colonel Quinnox would have accomplished it, in any event. He can't hold you to such a silly pledge. You—you haven't by any chance told him that you love him?" He asked this in sudden anxiety.

"Really, Truxton, I cannot discuss—"

"No, I'm quite sure you haven't," he announced contentedly. "You couldn't have done that, I know. Now, I want you to make me a promise that you'll keep."

"Oh, Truxton—don't ask me to say that I'll be your—" She stopped, painfully embarrassed.

"That will come later," he said consolingly. "I want you to promise, on your sacred word of honour, that you'll kiss no man until you've kissed me."

"Oh!" she murmured, utterly speechless.

"Promise!"

"I—I cannot promise that," she said in tones almost inaudible. "I am not sure that I'll ever—ever kiss anybody. How silly you are!"

"I'll make exception in the case of your brother—and, yes, the Prince."

"I'll not make such a promise," she cried.

"Then, I'll be hanged if I'll save you from the ridiculous mess you've gotten yourself into," he announced with finality. "Moreover, you're not yet safe from old Marlanx. Think it over, my—"

"Oh, he cannot seize the Castle—it is impossible!" she cried in sudden terror.

"I'm not so sure about that," he said laconically.

"What is it you really want me to say?" she asked, looking up with sudden shyness in her starry eyes.

"That you love me—and me only, Loraine," he whispered.

"I will not say it," she cried, breaking away from him. "But," as she ran to the steps, a delicious tremor in her voice—"I *will* consider the other thing you ask."

"Darling—don't go," he cried, in eager, subdued tones, but she already was half way across the balcony. In a moment she was gone. "Poor, harassed little sweetheart!" he murmured, with infinite tenderness. For a long time he stood there, looking at the window through which she had disappeared, his heart full of song.

Then, all at once, he remembered the meeting. "Great Scott!" in dismay. "I'm late for the pow-wow." A twisted smile stole over his face. "I wonder how they've managed to get along without me." Then he presented himself, somewhat out of breath, to the attendants at the south doors, where he had been directed to report. A moment later he was in the Castle of Graustark, following a stiff-backed soldier through mediæval halls of marble, past the historic staircase, down to the door of the council chamber. He was filled with the most delicious sensation of awe and reverence. Only in his dearest dreams had he fancied himself in these cherished halls. And now he was there—actually treading the same mosaic floors that had known the footsteps of countless princes and princesses, his nostrils tingling with the rare incense of five centuries, his blood leaping to the call of a thousand romances. The all but mythical halls of Graustark—the sombre, vaulted, time-defying corridors of his fancy. Somewhere in this vast pile of stone was the girl he loved. Each shadowy nook, each velvety recess, seemed to glow with the wizardry of love-lamps that had been lighted with the building of the Castle. How many hearts had learned the wistful lesson in these aged halls? How many loves had been sheltered here?

He walked on air. He pinched himself—and even then was not certain that he was awake. It was too good to be true.

He was ushered into a large, sedately furnished room. A score of men were there before him—sitting or standing in attitudes of attention, listening to the words of General Braze. King's entrance was the signal for an immediate transfer of interest. The General bowed most politely and at once turned to Count Halfont with the remark that he had quite finished his suggestions. The Prime Minister came forward to greet the momentarily shy American. King had time to note that the only man who denied him a smile of welcome was Count Vos Engo. He promptly included his rival in his own sweeping, self-conscious smile.

"The Council has been extolling you, Mr. King," said the Prime Minister, leading him to a seat near his own. Truxton sat down, bewildered. "We may some day grow large enough to adequately appreciate the invaluable, service you have performed in behalf of Graustark."

Truxton blushed. He could think of nothing to say, except: "I'm sorry to have been so late. I was detained."

Involuntarily he glanced at Vos Engo. That gentleman started, a curious light leaping into his eyes.

"Mr. King, we have asked you here for the purpose of hearing the full story of your experiences during the past two weeks, if you will be so good as to relate them. We have had them piecemeal. I need not tell you that Graustark is in the deepest peril. If there is a single suggestion that you can make that will help her to-night, I assure you that it will be given the most grateful consideration. Graustark has come to know and respect the resourcefulness and courage of the American gentleman. We have seen him at his best."

"I have really done no more than to—er—save my own neck," said Truxton simply. "Any one might be excused for doing the same. Graustark owes a great deal more to Miss Tullis than it does to me, believe me, my lords. She had the courage, I the strength."

"Be assured of our attitude toward Miss Tullis," said Halfont in reply. "Graustark loves her. It can do no more than that. It is from Miss Tullis that we have learned the extent of your valorous achievements. Ah, my dear young friend, she has given you a fair name. She tells us of a miracle and we are convinced."

Truxton stammered his remonstrances, but glowed with joy and pride.

"Here is the situation in a nutshell," went on the Prime Minister. "We are doomed unless succor reaches us from the outside. We have discussed a hundred projects. While we are inactive, Count Marlanx is gaining more power and a greater hold over the people of the city. We have no means of communication with Prince Dantan of Dawsbergen, who is our friend. We seem unable to get warning to John Tullis, who, if given time, might succeed in collecting a sufficient force of loyal countrymen to harass and eventually overthrow the Dictator. Unless he is reached before long, John Tullis and his combined force of soldiers will be ambushed and destroyed. I am loth to speak of another alternative that has been discussed at length by the ministers and their friends. The Duke of Perse, from a bed of pain and anguish, has counselled us to take steps in the direction I am about to speak of. You see, we are taking you into our confidence, Mr. King.

"We can appeal to Russia in this hour of stress. Moreover, we may expect that help will be forthcoming. But we will have to make an unpleasant sacrifice. Russia is eager to take over our new issue of railway bonds. Hitherto, we have voted against disposing of the bonds in that country, the reason being obvious. St. Petersburg wants a new connecting line with her possessions in Afghanistan. Our line will provide a most direct route—a cut-off, I believe they call it. Last year the Grand Duke Paulus volunteered to provide the money for the construction of the line from Edelweiss north to Balak on condition that Russia be given the right to use the line in connection with her own roads to the Orient. You may see the advantage in this to Russia. Mr. King, if I send word to the Grand Duke Paulus, agreeing to his terms, which still remain open to us, signing away a most valuable right in what we had hoped would be our own individual property, we have every reason to believe that he will send armed forces to our relief, on the pretext that Russia is defending properties of her own. That is one way in which we may oust Count Marlanx. The other lies in the ability of John Tullis to give battle to him with our own people carrying the guns. I am confident that Count Marlanx will not bombard the Castle except as a last resort. He will attempt to starve us into submission first; but he will not destroy property if he can help it. I have been as brief as possible. Lieutenant Haddan has told us quite lately of a remark you made which he happened to overhear. If I quote him correctly, you said to the Englishman Hobbs that you could get away with it, meaning, as I take it, that you could succeed in reaching John Tullis. The remark interested me, coming as it did from one so resourceful. May I not implore you to tell us how you would go about it?"

Truxton had turned a brick red. Shame and mortification surged within him. He was cruelly conscious of an undercurrent of irony in the Premier's courteous request. For an instant he was sorely crushed. A low laugh from the opposite side of the room sent a shaft to his soul. He looked up. Vos Engo was still smiling. In an instant the American's blood boiled; his manner changed like a flash; blind, unreasoning bravado succeeded embarrassment.

He faced Count Halfont coolly, almost impudently.

"I think I was unfortunate enough to add that your men were going about it—well, like amateurs," he said, with a frank smile. "I meant no offense." Then he arose suddenly, adjusted his necktie with the utmost *sang froid*, and announced:

"I did say I could get to John Tullis. If you like, I'll start to-night."

His words created a profound impression, they came so abruptly. The men stared at him, then at each other. It was as if he had read their thoughts and had jumped at once to the conclusion that they were baiting him. Every one began talking at once. Soon some one began to shake his hand. Then there were cheers and a dozen handshakings. Truxton grimly realised that he had done just what they had expected him to do. He tried to look unconcerned.

"You will require a guide," said Colonel Quinnox, who had been studying the *degage* American in the most earnest manner.

"Send for Mr. Hobbs, please," said Truxton.

A messenger was sent post haste to the barracks. The news already was spreading throughout the Castle. The chamber door was wide open and men were coming and going. Eager women were peering through the doorway for a glimpse of the American.

"There should be three of us," said King, addressing the men about him. "One of us is sure to get away."

"There is not a man here—or in the service—who will not gladly accompany you, Mr. King," cried General Braze quickly.

"Count Vos Engo is the man I would choose, if I may be permitted the honour of naming my companion," said Truxton, grinning inwardly with a malicious joy.

Vos Engo turned a yellowish green. His eyes bulged.

"I—I am in command of the person of his Royal Highness," he stammered, suddenly going very red.

"I had forgotten your present occupation," said Truxton quietly. "Pray pardon the embarrassment I may have caused you. After all, I think Hobbs will do. He knows the country like a book. Besides, his business in the city must be very dull just now. He'll be glad to have the chance to personally conduct me for a few days. As an American tourist, I must insist, gentlemen, on being personally conducted by a man from Cook's."

They did not know whether to laugh or to treat it as a serious announcement.

Mr. Hobbs came. That is to say, he was produced. It is doubtful if Mr. Hobbs ever fully recovered from the malady commonly known as stage fright. He had never been called Mr. Hobbs by a Prime Minister before, nor had he ever been asked in person by a Minister of War if he had a family at home. Moreover, no assemblage of noblemen had ever condescended to unite in three cheers for him. Afterward Truxton King was obliged to tell him that he had unwaveringly volunteered to accompany him on the perilous trip to the hills. Be sure of it, Mr. Hobbs was not in a mental condition for many hours to even remotely comprehend what had taken place. He only knew that he had been invited, as an English *gentleman*, to participate in a council of war.

But Mr. Hobbs was not the kind to falter, once he had given his word; however hazy he may have been at the moment, he knew that he had volunteered to do something. Nor did it seem to surprise him when he finally found out what it was.

"We'll be off at midnight, Hobbs," said Truxton, feeling in his pocket for the missing watch.

"As you say, Mr. King, just as you say," said Hobbs with fine indifference.

As Truxton was leaving the Castle ten minutes later, Hobbs having gone before to see to the packing of food-bags and the filling of flasks, a brisk, eager-faced young attendant hurried up to him.

"I bear a message from his Royal Highness," said the attendant, detaining him.

"He should be sound asleep at this time," said Truxton, surprised.

"His Royal Highness insists on staying awake as long as possible, sir. It is far past his bedtime, but these are troublesome times, he says. Every man should do his part. Prince Robin has asked for you, sir."

"How's that?"

"He desires you to appear before him at once, sir."

"In—in the audience chamber?"

"In his bedchamber, sir. He is very sleepy, but says that you are to come to him before starting away on your mission of danger."

"Plucky little beggar!" cried Truxton, his heart swelling with love for the royal youngster.

"Sir!" exclaimed the attendant, his eyes wide with amazement and reproof.

"I'll see him," said the other promptly, as if he were granting the audience.

He followed the perplexed attendant up the grand staircase, across thickly carpeted halls in which posed statuesque soldiers of the Royal Guard, to the door of the Prince's bedchamber. Here he was confronted by Count Vos Engo.

"Enter," said Vos Engo, with very poor grace, standing aside. The sentinels grounded their arms and Truxton King passed into the royal chamber, alone.

CHAPTER XX
BY THE WATER-GATE

It was a vast, lofty apartment, regal in its subdued lights. An enormous, golden bed with gorgeous hangings stood far down the room. So huge was this royal couch that Truxton at first overlooked the figure sitting bolt upright in the middle of it. The tiny occupant called out in a very sleepy voice:

"Here I am, Mr. King. Gee, I hate a bed as big as this. They just make me sleep in it."

An old woman advanced from the head of the couch and motioned Truxton to approach.

"I am deeply honoured, your Highness," said the visitor, bowing very low. Through the windows he could see motionless soldiers standing guard in the balcony.

"Come over here, Mr. King. Nurse won't let me get up. Excuse my nighty, will you, please? I'm to have pajamas next winter."

Truxton advanced to the side of the bed. His eyes had swept the room in search of the one person he wanted most to see of all in the world. An old male servitor was drawing the curtains at the lower end of the room. There was no one else there, except the nurse. They seemed as much a part of the furnishings of this room as if they had been fixtures from the beginning.

"I am sure you will like them," said Truxton, wondering whether she were divinely secreted in one of the great, heavily draped window recesses. She had been in this room but recently. A subtle, delicate, enchanting perfume that he had noticed earlier in the evening—ah, he would never forget it.

The Prince's legs were now hanging over the edge of the bed. His eyes were dancing with excitement; sleep was momentarily routed.

"Say, Mr. King, I wish I was going with you to find Uncle Jack. You will find him, won't you? I'm going to say it in my prayers to-night and every night. They won't hardly let me leave this room. It's rotten luck. I want to fight, too."

"We are all fighting for you, Prince Robin."

"I want you to find Uncle Jack, Mr. King," went on Bobby eagerly. "And tell him I didn't mean it when I banished him the other day. I really and truly didn't." He was having difficulty in keeping back the tears.

"I shall deliver the message, your Highness," said Truxton, his heart going out to the unhappy youngster. "Rest assured of that, please. Go to sleep and dream that I have found him and am bringing him back to you. The dream will come true."

"Are you sure?" brightening perceptibly.

"Positively."

"Americans always do what they say they will," said the boy, his eyes snapping. "Here's something for you to take with you, Mr. King. It's my lucky stone. It always gives good luck. Of course, you must promise to bring it back to me. It's an omen."

He unclasped his small fingers; in the damp palm lay one of those peculiarly milky, half-transparent pebbles, common the world over and of value only to small, impressionable boys. Truxton accepted it with profound gravity.

"I found it last 4th of July, when we were celebrating out there in the park. I'm always going to have a 4th of July here. Don't you lose it, Mr. King, and you'll have good luck. Baron Dangloss says it's the luckiest kind of a stone. And when you come back, Mr. King, I'm going to knight you. I'd do it now, only Aunt Loraine says you'd be worrying about your title all the time and might be 'stracted from your mission. I'm going to make a baron of you. That's higher than a count in Graustark. Vos Engo is only a count."

Truxton started. He looked narrowly into the frank, engaging eyes of the boy in the nighty.

"I shall be overwhelmed," he said. Then his hand went to his mouth in the vain effort to cover the smile that played there.

"My mother used to say that American girls liked titles," said the Prince with ingenuous candor.

"Yes?" He hoped that she was eavesdropping.

"Nurse said that I was not to keep you long, Mr. King," said the Prince ruefully. "I suppose you are very busy getting ready. I just wanted to give you my lucky stone and tell you about being a baron. I won't have any luck till you come back. Tell Mr. Hobbs I'm thinking of making him a count. You're awful brave, Mr. King."

"Thank you, Prince Robin. May I—" he glanced uneasily at the distant nurse—"may I ask how your Aunt Loraine is feeling?"

"She acted very funny when I sent for you. I'm worried about her."

"What did she do, your Highness?"

"She rushed off to her room. I think, Mr. King, she was getting ready to cry or something. You see, she's in trouble."

"In trouble?"

"Yes. I can't tell you about it."

"She's worried about her brother, of course—and you."

"I just wish I could tell you—no, I won't. It wouldn't be fair," Bobby said, checking himself resolutely. "She's awful proud of you. I'm sure she likes you, Mr. King."

"I'm very, very glad to hear that."

Bobby had great difficulty in keeping his most secret impressions to himself. In fact, he floundered painfully in an attack on diplomacy.

"You should have seen her when Uncle Caspar came in to say you were going off to find her brother. She cried. Yes, sir, she did. She kissed me and—but you don't like to hear silly things about girls, do you? Great big men never do."

"I've heard enough to make me want to do something very silly myself," said Truxton, radiant. "I I don't suppose I could—er—see your Aunt Loraine for a few minutes?"

"I think not. She said she just—now, you mustn't mind her, Mr. King—she just couldn't bear it, that's all. She told me to say she'd pray for you and—Oh, Mr. King, I do hope she won't marry that other man!"

Truxton bent his knee. "Your Highness, as it seems I am not to see her, and as you seem to be the very best friend I have, I should very much like to ask a great favour of you. Will you take this old ring of mine and wish it on her finger just as soon as I have left your presence?"

"How did you know she was coming in again?" in wide-eyed wonder. "Excuse me. I shouldn't ask questions. What shall I wish?" It was the old ring that had come from Spantz's shop. The Prince promptly hid it beneath the pillow.

"I'll leave that to you, my best of friends."

"I bet it'll be a good wish, all right. I know what to wish."

"I believe you do. Would you mind giving her something else from me?" He hesitated before venturing the second request. Then, overswept by a warm, sweet impulse, he stepped forward, took the boy's face between his eager hands, and pressed a kiss upon his forehead. "Give her that for me, will you, Prince Robin Goodfellow."

Bobby beamed. "But I never kiss her *there!*"

"I shall be ten thousand times obliged, your Highness, if you will deliver it in the usual place."

"I'll do it!" almost shouted the Prince. Then he clapped his hand over his mouth and looked, pop-eyed with apprehension, toward the nurse.

"Then, good-bye and God bless you," said Truxton. "I must be off. Your Uncle Jack is waiting for me, up there in the hills."

Bobby's eyes filled with tears. "Oh, Mr. King, please give him my love and make him hurry back. I—I need him awful!"

Truxton found Mr. Hobbs in a state bordering on collapse.

"I say, Mr. King, it's all right to say we'll go, but how the deuce are we to do it? My word, there's no more chance of getting out of the—"

"Listen, Hobbs: we're going to swim out," said Truxton. He was engaged in stuffing food into a knapsack. Colonel Quinnox and Haddan had been listening to Hobbs's lamentations for half an hour, in King's room.

"Swim? Oh, I say! By hokey, he's gone clean daffy!" Hobbs was eyeing him with alarm. The others looked hard at the speaker, scenting a joke.

"Not yet, Hobbs. Later on, perhaps. I had occasion to make a short tour of investigation this afternoon. Doubtless, gentlemen, you know where the water-gate is, back of the Castle. Well, I've looked it over—and under, I might say. Hobbs, you and I will sneak under those slippery old gates like a couple of eels. I forgot to ask if you can swim."

"To be sure I can. *Under* the gates? My word!"

"Simple as rolling off a log," said Truxton carelessly. "The Cascades and Basin of Venus run out through the gate. There is a space of at least a foot below the bottom of the gate, which hasn't been opened in fifty years, I'm told. A good swimmer can wriggle through, d'ye see? That lets him out into the little canal that connects with the river. Then—"

"I see!" cried Quinnox. "It can be done! No one will be watching at that point."

The sky was overcast, the night as black as ebony. The four men left the officers' quarters at one o'clock, making their way to the historic old gate in the glen below the Castle. Arriving at the wall, Truxton briefly whispered his plans.

"You remember, Colonel Quinnox, that the stream is four or five feet deep here at the gate. The current has washed a deeper channel under the iron-bound timbers. The gates are perhaps two feet thick. For something like seven or eight feet from the bottom they are so constructed that the water runs through an open network of great iron bars. Now, Hobbs and I will go under the gates in the old-clothes you have given us. When we are on the opposite side we'll stick close by the gate, and you may pass our dry clothes out between the bars above the surface of the water. Our guns, the map and the food, as well. It's very simple. Then we'll drop down the canal a short distance and change our clothes in the underbrush. Hobbs knows where we can procure horses and he knows a trusty guide on the other side of the city. So long, Colonel. I'll see you later."

"God be with you," said Quinnox fervently. The four men shook hands and King slipped into the water without a moment's hesitation.

"Right after me, Hobbs," he said, and then his head went under.

A minute later he and Hobbs were on the outside of the gate, gasping for breath. Standing in water to their necks, Quinnox and Haddan passed the equipment through the barred openings. There were whispered good-byes and then two invisible heads bobbed off in the night, wading in the swift-flowing canal, up to their chins. Swimming would have been dangerous, on account of the noise.

Holding their belongings high above their heads, with their hearts in their mouths, King and the Englishman felt their way carefully along the bed of the stream. Not a sound was to be heard, except the barking of dogs in the distance. The stillness of death hung over the land. So still, that the almost imperceptible sounds they made in breathing and moving seemed like great volumes of noise in their tense ears.

A hundred yards from the gate they crawled ashore and made their way up over the steep bank into the thick, wild underbrush. Not a word had been spoken up to this time.

"Quietly now, Hobbs. Let us get out of these duds. 'Gad, they're like ice. From now on, Hobbs, you lead the way. I'll do my customary act of following."

Hobbs was shivering from the cold. "I say, Mr. King, you're a wonder, that's wot you are. Think of going under those bally gates!"

"That's right, Hobbs, think of it, but don't talk."

They stealthily stripped themselves of the wet garments, and, after no end of trouble, succeeded in getting into the dry substitutes. Then they lowered the wet bundles into the water and quietly stole off through the brush, Hobbs in the lead, intent upon striking the King's Highway, a mile or two above town. It was slow, arduous going, because of the extreme caution required. A wide detour was made by the canny Hobbs—wider, in fact, than the impatient American thought wholly necessary. In time, however, they came to the Highway.

"Well, we've got a start, Hobbs. We'll win out, just as I said we would. Easy as falling off a log."

"I'm not so blooming sure of that," said Hobbs. He was recalling a recent flight along this very road. "We're a long way from being out of the woods."

"Don't be a kill-joy, Hobbs. Look at the bright side of things."

"I'll do that in the morning, when the sun's up," said Hobbs, with a sigh. "Come along, sir. We take this path here for the upper road. It's a good two hours' walk up the mountain to Rabot's, where we get the horses."

All the way up the black, narrow mountain path Hobbs kept the lead. King followed, his thoughts divided between the blackness ahead and the single, steady light in a certain window now far behind. He had seen the lighted window in the upper balcony as he passed the Castle on the way to the gate. Somehow he knew she was there saying good-bye and Godspeed to him.

At four o'clock, as the sun reached up with his long, red fingers from behind the Monastery mountain, Truxton King and Hobbs rode away from Rabot's cottage high in the hills, refreshed and sound of heart. Rabot's son rode with them, a sturdy, loyal lad, who had leaped joyously at the chance to serve his Prince. Undisturbed, they rode straight for the passes below St. Valentine's. Behind and below them lay the sleeping, restless, unhappy city of Edelweiss, with closed gates and unfriendly, sullen walls. There reigned the darkest fiend that Graustark, in all her history, had ever come to know.

Truxton King had slipped through his fingers with almost ridiculous ease. So simple had it been, that the two messengers, gloating in the prospect ahead, now spoke of the experience as if it were the most trivial thing in their lives. They mentioned it casually; that was all.

Now, let us turn to John Tullis and his quest in the hills. It goes without saying that he found no trace of his sister or her abductors. For five days he scoured the lonely, mysterious mountains, dragging the tired but loyal hundred about at his heels, distracted by fear and anguish over the possible fate of the adored one. On the fifth day, a large force of Dawsbergen soldiers, led by Prince Dantan himself, found the fagged, dispirited American and his half-starved men encamped in a rocky defile in the heart of the wilderness.

That same night a Graustark mountaineer passed the sentinels and brought news of the disturbance in Edelweiss. He could give no details. He only knew that there had been serious rioting in the streets and that the gates were closed against all comers. He could not tell whether the rioters—most of whom he took to be strikers, had been subdued or whether mob-law prevailed. He had been asked to cast his lot with the strikers, but had refused. For this he was driven away from his home, which was burned. His wife and child were now at the Monastery, where many persons had taken refuge.

In a flash it occurred to John Tullis that Marlanx was at the bottom of this deviltry. The abduction of Loraine was a part of his plan! Prince Dantan advised a speedy return to the city. His men were at the command of the American. Moreover, the Prince himself decided to accompany the troops.

Before sunrise, the command, now five or six hundred strong, was picking its way down the dangerous mountain roads toward the main highway. Fifteen miles below Edelweiss they came upon the company of soldiers sent out to preserve order in the railroad camps.

The officer in charge exhibited a document, given under the hand and seal of Baron Dangloss, directing him to remain in command of the camps until the strikers, who were unruly, could be induced to resume work once more. This order, of course, was a forgery, designed to mislead the little force until Marlanx saw fit to expose his hand to the world. It had come by messenger on the very day of the rioting. The messenger brought the casual word that the government was arresting and punishing the lawless, and that complete order would hardly be established for several days at the outside. He went so far as to admit that an attempt on the life of the Prince had failed. Other reports had come to the camps, and all had been to the effect that the rioting was over. The strikers, it seemed, were coming to terms with their employers and would soon take up the work of construction once more. All this sufficed to keep the real situation from reaching the notice of the young captain; he was obeying orders and awaiting the return of the workmen.

The relief that swept into the souls of the newly arrived company was short-lived. They had gone into camp, tired, sore and hungry, and were preparing to take a long needed rest before taking up the last stage of their march toward the city. John Tullis was now in feverish haste to reach the city, where at least he might find a communication from the miscreants, demanding ransom. He had made up his mind to pay whatever they asked. Down in his heart, however, there was a restless fear that she had not fallen into the hands of ordinary bandits. He could not banish the sickening dread that she was in the power of Marlanx, to whom she alone could pay the ransom exacted.

Hardly had the men thrown themselves from their horses when the sound of shooting in the distance struck their ears. Instantly the entire force was alert. A dozen shots were fired in rapid succession; then single reports far apart. The steady beat of horses' feet was now plain to the attentive company. There was a quick, incisive call to arms; a squad stood ready for action. The clatter of hoofs drew nearer; a small group of horsemen came thundering down the defile. Three minutes after the firing was first heard, sentries threw their rifles to their shoulders and blocked the approach of the riders.

A wild, glad shout went up from the foremost horseman. He had pulled his beast to its haunches almost at the muzzles of the guns.

"Tullis!" he shouted, waving his hat.

John Tullis ran toward the excited group in the road. He saw three men, one of whom was shouting his name with all the power in his lungs.

"Thank God, we've found you!" cried the horseman, swinging to the ground despite the proximity of strange rifles. "Put up your guns! We're friends!"

"King!" exclaimed Tullis, suddenly recognising him. A moment later they were clasping hands.

"This is luck! We find you almost as soon as we set out to do so. Glory be! You've got a fair-sized army, too. We'll need 'em—and more."

"What has happened, King? Where have you been? We looked for you after your disap—"

"That's ancient history," interrupted the other. "How soon can you get these troops on the march? There's not a moment to be lost."

"Good God, man, tell me what it is—what has happened? The Prince? What of him?" cried Tullis, grasping King's arm in the clutch of a vise.

"He sends his love and rescinds the order of exile," said King, smiling. Then seriously: "Marlanx has taken the city. It was all a game, this getting rid of you. He's superstitious about Americans. There was bomb-throwing in the square and a massacre afterward. The Prince and all the others are besieged in the Castle. I'll tell you all about it. Hobbs and I are the only men who have got away from the Castle alive. We left last night. Our object was to warn you in time to prevent an ambush. You've got to save the throne for Prince Robin. I'll explain as we go along. I may as well inform you right now that there's a big force of men waiting for you in the ravine this side of the Monastery. We saw them. Thank God, we got to you in time. You can now take 'em by surprise and—whiff! They'll run like dogs. Back here a couple of miles we came upon a small gang of real robbers. We had a bit of shooting and—I regret to say—no one was bagged. I'd advise you to have this force pushed along as rapidly as possible. I have a message from your sister, sir."

"Loraine? Where is she, King?"

"Don't tremble like that, old man. She's safe enough—in the Castle. Oh, it was a fine game Marlanx had in his mind."

While the troopers were making ready for the march, Truxton King and Hobbs related their story to eager, horrified groups of officers. It may be well to say that neither said more of his own exploits than was absolutely necessary to connect the series of incidents. Prince Dantan marvelled anew at this fresh demonstration of Yankee courage and ingenuity. King graphically narrated the tale from beginning to end. The full force of the amazing tragedy was brought home to the pale, half-dazed listeners. There were groans and curses and bitter cries of vengeance. John Tullis was crushed; despair was written in his face, anguish in his eyes.

What was to become of the Prince?

"First of all, Tullis, we must destroy these scoundrels who are lying in wait for you in the ravine," said Prince Dantan. "After that you can be in a position to breathe easily while collecting the army of fighters that Mr. King suggests. Surely, you will be able to raise a large and determined force. My men are at Prince Robin's disposal. Captain Haas may command them as his own. I deplore the fact that I may not call upon the entire Dawsbergen army. Marlanx evidently knows our laws. Our army cannot go to the aid of a neighbor. We have done so twice in half a century and our people have been obliged to pay enormous indemnity. But there are men here. I am here. We will not turn back, Mr. Tullis. My people will not hold me at fault for taking a hand in this. I shall send messengers to the Princess; she, of course, must know."

The battalion, augmented by the misguided company from the deserted railroad camps, moved swiftly into the defile, led by young Rabot. Truxton King rode beside the brother of the girl he loved, uttering words of cheer and encouragement.

"King, you *do* put new courage into me. You are surcharged with hope and confidence. By heaven, I believe we can drive out that damned beast and his dogs. We *will* do it!"

"There's a chap named Brutus. I ask special permission to kill him. That's the only request I have to make."

"I very strongly oppose the appeal to Grand Duke Paulus. We must act decisively before that alternative is forced upon the unhappy Halfont. It was Perse's scheme, months ago. Perse! Confound him, I believe he has worked all along to aid—"

"Hold on, Tullis," interrupted King soberly. "I wouldn't say that if I were you. The Duke was wounded by the dynamiters and I understand he lies on his bed and curses Marlanx from morning till night. He prays constantly that his daughter may be freed from the old scoundrel."

"The Countess Ingomede—has anything been heard from her?" asked Tullis. He had been thinking of her for days—and nights.

"Well, nothing definite," said King evasively. He was reminded at this moment of his own love affair. Seized by the boldest impulse that had ever come to him, he suddenly blurted out: "Tullis, I love your sister. I have loved her from the beginning. All that has happened in the last week has strengthened my adoration. I think she cares for me, but,—but—"

"My dear Mr. King, I'm sorry—" began Tullis, genuinely surprised.

"But it seems that she's promised to marry Vos Engo. I'll tell you how it happened." Then he related the episode of the rout in Castle Avenue. "It's all wrong for her to marry that chap. If she hasn't been bullied into it before we get back to her, I'd like to know if you won't put a stop to his damned impudence. What right has such a fellow as Vos Engo to a good American girl like Loraine? None whatever. Besides, I'm going to fight him when we're through fighting Marlanx. I want you as my second. Can't say whether it will be swords, pistols or knuckles. I hope you'll oblige me. As a matter of fact, I had two primary objects in looking you up out here in the hills. First, to ask you for Loraine; second, to engage you as my second."

Tullis was silent for a while. Then he said, quite seriously: "King, I have looked with some favour upon Vos Engo. I thought she liked him. He isn't a bad fellow, believe me. I want Loraine to be happy. As for this promise to him, I'll talk that over with her—if God permits me to see her again I shall allow her to choose, King. You or Vos Engo—the one she loves, that's all. As for seconding you, I am at your service."

King beamed. "That means, I take it, that you want me to win at least one of the contests. Well," with his whimsical, irresistible smile, "it won't be necessary to try for the other if Vos Engo shoots me in this one."

"You will never know the extent of my gratitude, King. You have saved her from a hellish fate. I shall be disappointed in her if she does not choose you. I owe you a debt of gratitude almost as great for saving that dear little boy of—ours. I shall not forget what you have done—never!"

Early in the afternoon the force under Captain Haas was divided into three companies, for strategic purposes. The plan to surprise and defeat the skulkers in the ravine had been carefully thought out. Two strong companies struck off into the hills; the third and weakest of the trio kept the road, apparently marching straight into the trap. Signals had been arranged. At a given sign the three parties were to swoop down upon the position held by the enemy.

Several hours passed. The troop in the highroad prepared to camp just below the treacherous pass in which the ambush was known to be laid. Scouts had located the confident rascals in the ravines above the highway. With the news that their prey was approaching, they were being rapidly rushed into position at the head of the pass.

Shortly before sunset the troop in the road began to advance, riding resolutely into the ravine. Even as the gloating, excited desperadoes prepared to open fire from their hidden position at the head of the pass, their pickets came running in with the word that two large forces were drawing in on them from the north and east.

The trappers were trapped. They realised that they had been outgeneralled, and they understood their deficiencies. Not a man among them knew the finer points of warfare. They were thugs and roustabouts and illomened fellows who could stab in the back; they were craven in the face of an open peril.

There were few shots fired. The men in ambuscade tried to escape to the fastnesses of the hills. Some of them stood ground and fought, only to be mown down by the enemy; others were surrounded and made captive; but few actually succeeded in evading the troopers. All were ready to sue for mercy and to proclaim their willingness to divert allegiance from dictator to Crown. Herded like so many cattle, guarded like wolves, they were driven city-ward, few if any of them exhibiting the slightest symptom of regret or discomfiture. In fact, they seemed more than philosophic: they were most jovial. These were soldiers of fortune, in the plainest sense. It mattered little with whom they were allied or against whom they fought, so long as the pay was adequate and prompt.

Indeed, the leaders of the party—officers by grace of lucky tosses—benignly proffered the services of themselves and men in the movement to displace Count Marlanx!

"He cannot hold out," said the evil-faced captain in cool derision. "He cannot keep his promises to us. So why should we cut our own throats? All we ask is transportation to Austria after the job's over. That's where most of us came from, your Excellencies. Count on us, if you need us. Down with Marlanx!"

"Long live Prince—" Three-fourths of them stopped there because they did not even know the name of the little ruler.

CHAPTER XXI
THE RETURN

From the highlands below the Monastery, Captain Haas and his men were able to study the situation in the city. The impracticability of an assault on any one of the stubborn, well-guarded gates was at once recognised. A force of seven hundred men, no matter how well trained or determined, could not be expected to surmount walls that had often withstood the attack of as many thousands. The wisdom of delaying until a few thousand loyal, though poorly armed countrymen could be brought into play against the city appealed at once to Prince Dantan and John Tullis.

Withdrawing to an unexposed cut in the hills, safe from the shells that might be thrown up from the fortress, they established their camps, strongly entrenched and practically invulnerable against any attack from below. Squads of men were sent without delay into the hills and valleys to call the panic-stricken, wavering farmers into the fold. John Tullis headed the company that struck off into the well-populated Ganlook district.

Marlanx, as if realising the nature of the movement in the hills, began a furious assault on the gates leading to the Castle. The watchers in the hills could see as well as hear the conflict that raged almost at their feet, so to speak. They cheered like mad when the motley army of the usurper was frustrated in the attempt to take the main gates. From the walls about the park, Quinnox's men, few as they were, sent such deadly volleys into the streets below that the hordes fell back and found shelter behind the homes of the rich. With half an eye, one could see that the rascals were looting the palaces, secure from any opposition on the part of the government forces; through the glasses, scattered crowds of men could be seen carrying articles from the houses; more than one of the mansions went up in flames as the day grew old and the lust of the pillagers increased.

The next morning, Captain Haas announced to his followers that Marlanx had begun to shell the Castle. Big guns in the fortress were hurling great shells over the city, dropping them in the park. On the other hand, Colonel Quinnox during the night had swung three Gatling guns to the top of the wall; they were stationed at intervals along the wall, commanding every point from which an assault might be expected. It was a well-known fact that there was no heavy ordnance at the Castle. All day long, Marlanx's men, stationed in the upper stories of houses close to the walls, kept up a constant rifle fire, their bullets being directed against the distant windows of the Castle. That this desultory fusillade met with scant response at the hands of Quinnox, was quite apparent to the uneasy, champing watchers near the Monastery.

"Marlanx will not begin the actual bombardment until he knows that Tullis is drawing together a formidable force," prophesied Prince Dantan.

"But when he does begin the real shelling," mourned Truxton King, chafing like a lion under the deadly inaction. "I can't bear the thought of what it means to those inside the Castle. He can blow it to pieces over their heads. Then, from the house tops, he can pick them off like blackbirds. It's awful! Is there nothing that we can do, Prince? Damn it all, I know we can force a gate. And if we once get in where those cowardly dogs are lording it, you'll see 'em take the walls like steeple-chasers."

"My dear Mr. King," said Prince Dantan calmly, "you don't know Colonel Quinnox and the House Guard. The Quinnoxs have guarded Graustark's rulers for I don't know how many generations. History does not go back so far, I fear. You may depend on it, there will be no living guardsmen inside those walls when Marlanx lays his hands on the Prince."

That night recruits from the farms and villages began to straggle into the camp. They were armed with rifles, ordinary shotguns and antique "blunderbusses;" swords, staves and aged lances. All were willing to die in the service of the little Prince; all they needed was a determined, capable leader to rally them from the state of utter panic. They reported that the Crown foragers might expect cheerful and plenteous tribute from the farmers and stock growers. Only the mountaineers were hostile.

The army now grew with astonishing rapidity. The recruits were not fighting men in a military sense, but their hearts were true and they hungered for the chance to stamp out the evil that lay at their feet. By the close of the second day nearly three thousand men were encamped above the city. Late that night John Tullis rode into camp at the head of a great company from the Ganlook province. He had retaken the town of Ganlook, seized the fortress, and recruited the entire fighting strength of the neighbourhood. More than that, he had unlimbered and conveyed to the provisional camp two of the big guns that stood above the gates at the fortress. There had been a dozen skirmishes between the regulars and roving bands of desperadoes. A savage fight took place at Ganlook and another in the gap below the witch's hut. In both of these sanguinary affrays the government forces had come off victorious, splendid omens that did not fail to put confidence into the hearts of the men.

Marlanx trained two of his big guns on the camp in the hills. From the fortress he threw many futile shells toward their place of shelter. They did no damage; instead of death, they brought only laughter to the scornful camp. Under cover of night, the two Ganlook cannons were planted in a position commanding the southeastern city gate. It was the plan of the new besiegers to bombard this gate, tearing it to pieces with shot. When their force was strong enough offensively, an assault would be flung against this opening. Drill and discipline were necessary, however, before the attempt could be made. In the present chaotic, untrained condition of their forces, an assault would prove not only ineffectual, but disastrous. Day after day the recruits were put through hard drill under the direction of the regular officers. Every day saw the force increased. This made hard work for the drill-masters. The willingness of the recruits, however, lessened the task considerably.

The knowledge that Marlanx had no big guns except those stationed in the fortress was most consoling to Tullis and his friends. He could not destroy the Castle gates with shells, except by purest chance. He could drop shells into the Castle, but to hit a gate twenty feet wide? Never! Field ordnance was unknown to this country of mountains.

The Iron Count's inability to destroy the Castle gates made it feasible for the men in the hills to devote considerable more time to drill and preparation than they might have sacrificed if the conditions were the reverse. They were confident that Quinnox could hold the Castle for many days. With all this in mind, Captain Haas and Prince Dantan beat down the objections of the impatient Americans; the work of preparation against ignominious failure went on as rapidly as possible. Haas would not attack until he was ready, or it became absolutely certain that the men at the Castle were in dire need.

Signalling between the Castle and the hills had been going on for days. The absence of the "wigwag" system made it impossible to convey intelligible messages.

Truxton King was growing haggard from worry and loss of sleep. He could not understand the abominable, criminal procrastination. He was of a race that did things with a dash and on the spur of the moment. His soul sickened day by day. John Tullis, equally unhappy, but more philosophical, often found him seated upon a rock at the top of the ravine, an unlighted pipe in his fingers, his eyes intent upon the hazy Castle.

"Cheer up, King. Our time will come," he was wont to say.

"I've just got to do something, Tullis. This standing around is killing me." Again he would respond: "Don't forget that I love some one down there, old man. Maybe she's worrying about me, as well as about you." Once he gave poor Mr. Hobbs a frightful tongue-lashing and was afterward most contrite and apologetic. Poor Hobbs had been guilty of asking if he had a headache.

Truxton was assigned to several scouting expeditions, simply to provide him with action and diverting excitement. One of these expeditions determined the impossibility of entering the city through the railroad yards because of the trestle-work and the barricade of freight cars at the gap in the wall.

They had been in camp for a week. The stategists had practically decided that the assault could be made within a day or two. All was in readiness—or as near as it could be—and all was enthusiasm and excitement.

"If Haas puts it off another day I'm going to start a round robin, whatever that is," said Truxton. As he said it to a Dawsbergen officer who could not understand English, it is doubtful if that gentleman's polite nod of acquiescence meant unqualified approval of the project.

At first they had built no fires at night. Now the force was so formidable that this precaution was unnecessary. The air was chill and there were tents for but a few of the troopers. The fires in the ravine always were surrounded by great circles of men, eagerly discussing the coming battle. At the upper end of the ravine were the tents of the officers, Prince Dantan and John Tullis. The latter shared his with King and Mr. Hobbs. Up here, the circle about the kindly pile of burning logs was small, select and less demonstrative. Here they smoked in silence most of the time, each man's thoughts delivered to himself.

Above, on the jutting rock, sat the disconsolate, lovesick Truxton. It was the night before the proposed assault on the gates. The guns were in position and the cannonading was to begin at daybreak. He was full of the bitterness of doubt and misgiving. Was she in love with Vos Engo? Was the Count's suit progressing favourably under the fire of the enemy? Was his undoubted bravery having its effect upon the wavering susceptibilities of the distressed Loraine?

Here was he, Truxton King, idle and useless for more than a week, beyond range of the guns of the foe, while down there was Vos Engo in the thick of it, at the side of the girl he loved in those long hours of peril, able to comfort her, to cheer her, to fight for her. It was maddening. He was sick with uncertainty, consumed by jealousy. His pipe was not out now: he was smoking furiously.

The sound of a voice in sharp command attracted his attention. One of the sentries in the road below the elbow of the ridge had stopped some one who was approaching the camp. There was a bright moon, and Truxton could see other pickets hurrying to join the first. A few moments later the trespassers were escorted through the lines and taken directly to headquarters. A man and two women, King observed. Somewhat interested, he sauntered down from his lonely boulder and joined the group of officers.

John Tullis was staring hard at the group approaching from the roadway. They were still outside the circle of light, but it was plain to all that the newcomers were peasants. The women wore the short red skirts and the pointed bonnets of the lower classes. Gaudy shawls covered their shoulders. One was tall and slender, with a bearing that was not peasant-like. It was she who held Tullis's intense, unbelieving gaze until they were well inside the fire-light. She walked ahead of her companions. Suddenly he sprang forward with a cry of amazement.

It was the Countess Ingomede.

Her arrival created a sensation. In a moment she was in the centre of an amazed circle of men. Tullis, after his first low, eager greeting at the edge of the fire circle, drew her near to the warmth-giving flames. Prince Dantan and Captain Haas threw rugs and blankets in a great heap for her to sit upon. Every one was talking at once. The Countess was smiling through her tears.

"Make room for my maid and her father. They are colder and more fatigued than I," she said, lifting her tired, glorious eyes to John Tullis, who stood beside her. "We have come from Balak. They suffered much, that I might enjoy the slender comforts I was so ready to share with them."

"Thank God, you are here," he said in low, intense tones. She could not mistake the fervour in his voice nor the glow in his eyes. Her wondrous, yellowish orbs looked steadily into his, and he was satisfied. They paid tribute to the emotion that moved him to the depths of his being. Love leaped up to him from those sweet, tired eyes; leaped with the unerring force of an electric current that finds its lodestone in spite of mortal will.

"I knew you were here, John. I am not going back to Count Marlanx. It is ended."

"I knew it would come, Ingomede. You will let me tell you how glad I am—some day?"

"Some day, when I am truly, wholly free from him, John. I know what you will say, and I think you know what I shall say in reply." Both understood and were exalted. No other word passed between them touching upon the thing that was uppermost in their minds.

Food was provided for the wayfarers, and Tullis's tent was made ready for the Countess and her maid.

"Truxton," said he, "we will have to find other quarters for the night. I've let my apartment—furnished."

"She's gloriously beautiful, John," was all that Truxton said, puffing moodily at his pipe. He was thinking of one more beautiful, however. "I suppose you'd think it a favour if I'd pot Marlanx for you to-morrow."

"It doesn't matter whether he's potted or not, my friend. She will not go back to him. He will have to find another prisoner for his household."

Truxton's thoughts went with a shudder to the underground room and the fair prisoner who had shared it with him. The dread of what might have been the fate of Loraine Tullis—or what might still be in store for her—brought cold chills over him. He abruptly turned away and sat down at the outer edge of the group.

The Countess's story was soon told. Sitting before the great fire, surrounded by eager listeners, she related her experiences. Prince Dantan was her most attentive listener.

She had been seized on the night of the ball as she started across her father's garden. Before sunrise she was well on her way to Balak, in charge of three of the Count's most faithful henchmen. As for the messages that were sent to Edelweiss, she knew nothing of them, except the last, which she had managed to get through with the assistance of Josepha's father. She was kept a close prisoner in a house just outside of Balak, and came to learn all of the infamous projects of her husband. At the end of ten days her maid was sent to her from Edelweiss. She brought the news of the calamity that had befallen the city. It was then that she determined to break away from her captors and try to reach the Monastery of St. Valentine, where protection would be afforded her for the time being. After several days of ardent persuasion, she and Josepha prevailed upon the latter's father to assist them in their flight. Not only was he persuaded, but in the end he journeyed with them through the wildest country north of Ganlook. They were four days in covering the distance, partly on foot, partly by horse. Near the city they heard of the presence of troops near the Monastery. Farmers' wives told them of the newly formed army and of its leaders. She determined to make her way to the camp of those who would destroy her husband, eager to give them any assistance that her own knowledge of Marlanx's plans might provide.

Many details are omitted in this brief recital of her story. Perhaps it is well to leave something to the imagination.

One bit of information she gave created no end of consternation among the would-be deliverers of the city. It had the effect of making them all the more resolute; the absolute necessity for immediately regaining control in the city was forced upon them. She told them that Count Marlanx had lately received word that the Grand Duke Paulus was likely to intervene before many days, acting on his own initiative, in the belief that he could force the government of Graustark to grant the railway privileges so much desired by his country. Marlanx realised that he would have to forestall the wily Grand Duke. If he were in absolute control of the Graustark government when the Russian appeared, he and he alone would be in a position to deal with the situation. Unless the Castle fell into his hands beforehand, insuring the fall of the royal house and the ministry, the Grand Duke's natural inclination would be to first befriend the hapless Prince and then to demand recompense in whatsoever form he saw fit.

"The Grand Duke may send a large force of men across the border at any time," said the Countess in conclusion. "Count Marlanx is sure to make a decisive assault as soon as he hears that the movement has begun. He had hopes of starving them out, thus saving the Castle from destruction, but as that seems unlikely, his shells will soon begin to rain in earnest upon the dear old pile."

Truxton King was listening with wide open ears. As she finished this dreary prediction he silently arose to his feet and, without a word to any one, stalked off in the darkness. Tullis looked after him and shook his head sadly.

"I'll be happy on that fellow's account when daybreak comes and we are really at it," he said to Prince Dantan, who knew something of King's affliction.

But Truxton King was not there at daybreak. When he strode out of the camp that night, he left it behind forever.

The unfortunate lack of means to communicate with the occupants of the Castle had been the source of great distress to Captain Haas. If the defenders could be informed as to the exact hour of the assault from the outside, they could do much toward its speedy success by making a fierce sortie from behind their own walls. A quick dash from the Castle grounds would serve to draw Marlanx's attention in that direction, diminishing the force that he would send to check the onslaught at the gates. But there was no means of getting word to Colonel Quinnox. His two or three hundred men would be practically useless at the most critical period of the demonstration.

Truxton King had all this in mind as he swung off down the mountain road, having stolen past the sentries with comparative ease. He was smiling to himself. If all went well with him, Colonel Quinnox would be able to rise to the occasion. If he failed in the daring mission he had elected to perform, the only resulting harm would be to himself; the plans of the besiegers would not suffer.

He knew his ground well by this time. He had studied it thoroughly from the forlorn boulder at the top of the ravine. By skirting the upper walls, on the mountain side, he might, in a reasonably short space of time, reach the low woodlands north of the Castle walls. The danger from Marlanx's scouts outside the city was not great; they had been scattered and beaten by Haas's recruiting parties. He stood in more danger from the men he would help, they who were the watchful defenders of the Castle.

It must have been two o'clock when he crossed the King's Highway, a mile or more above the northern gates, and struck down into the same thick undergrowth that had protected him and Hobbs on a memorable night not long before.

At three o'clock, a dripping figure threw up his hands obligingly and laughed with exultation when confronted by a startled guardsman *inside* the Castle walls and not more than fifty yards from the water gates!

He had timed his entrance by the sound of the guardsman's footstep on the stone protecting wall that lined the little stream. When he came to the surface inside the water gate, the sentry was at the extreme end of his beat. He shouted a friendly cry as he advanced toward the man, calling out his own name.

Ten minutes later he was standing in the presence of the haggard, nerve-racked Quinnox, pouring into his astonished ears the news of the coming attack. While he was discarding his wet clothing for others, preparations for the sortie were getting under way. The Colonel lost no time in routing out the sleeping guardsmen and reserves, and in sending commands to those already on duty at the gates. The quick rattle of arms, the rush of feet, the low cries of relief, the rousing of horses, soon usurped the place of dreary, deadly calm.

When the sun peeped over the lofty hills, he saw inside the gates a restless, waiting company of dragoons, ready for the command to ride forth. Worn, haggard fellows, who had slept but little and who had eaten scarcely anything for three days; men who would have starved to death. Now they were forgetting their hunger and fatigue in the wild, exultant joy of the prospect ahead.

Meantime, King had crossed the grounds with Colonel Quinnox, on the way to the Castle. He was amazed, almost stupefied by the devastation that already had been wrought. Trees were down; great, gaping holes in the ground marked the spots where shells had fallen; the plaza was an almost impassable heap of masonry and soil, torn and rent by huge projectiles. But it was his first clear view of the Castle itself that appalled the American.

A dozen or more balls had crashed into the façade. Yawning fissures, gigantic holes, marked the path of the ugly messengers from Marlanx. Nearly all of the windows had been wrecked by riflemen who shot from the roofs of palaces in and about the avenue. Two of the smaller minarets were in ruins; a huge pillar in the lower balcony was gone; the terrace had been ploughed up by a single ricochetting shell.

"Great God!" gasped King. "It is frightful!"

"They began bombarding yesterday afternoon. We were asked to surrender at three o'clock. Our reply brought the shells, Mr. King. It was terrible."

"And the loss of life, Colonel?" demanded the other breathlessly.

"After the first two or three shells we found places of shelter for the Prince and his friends. They are in the stone tower beyond the Castle, overlooking what still remains of the ancient moat. Ah, there are no faltering hearts here, Mr. King. The most glorious courage instead. Count Vos Engo guards the Prince and the ladies of the household. Alas! it was hunger that we feared the most. To-day we should have resorted to horse's flesh. There was no other way. We knew that relief would come some day. John Tullis was there. We had faith in him and in you. And now it is to-day! This shall be our day, thank God! Nothing can stand before us!"

"Tullis is very anxious about his sister," ventured Truxton. Quinnox looked straight ahead, but smiled.

"She is the pluckiest of them all."

"Is she well?"

"Perhaps a trifle thin, sir, that is all. I dare say that is due to scarcity of nourishment, although the Prince and his closest associates were the last to feel deprivation."

"How does the Prince take all this, Colonel?"

"As any Prince of Graustark would, sir. There is no other way. It is in the blood."

"Poor little chap!"

"He will rejoice to know that you have found his lucky stone so effective. The Prince has never wavered in his loyalty to that pebble, sir."

Together they entered the Castle. Inside there were horrid signs of destruction, particularly off the balconies.

"No one occupies the upper part of the Castle now, sir."

Attendants sped to the tower, shouting the battle tidings. No compunction was felt in arousing the sleeping household. As a matter of fact, there was no protest from the eager ladies and gentlemen who hurried forth to hear the news.

The Prince came tumbling down the narrow iron stairs from his room above, shouting joyously to Truxton King. No man was ever so welcome. He was besieged with questions, handshakings and praises. Even the Duke of Perse, hobbling on crutches, had a kindly greeting for him. Tears streamed down the old man's cheeks when King told him of his daughter's safe arrival in the friendly camp.

Truxton picked the Prince up in his arms and held him close to his breast, patting his back all the while, his heart so full that he could not speak.

"I knowed you'd come back," Bobby kept crying in his ear. "Aunt Loraine said you wouldn't, but I said you would. I knowed it—I knowed it! And now you're going to be a baron, sure enough. Isn't he, Uncle Caspar?"

But Truxton was not listening to the eager prattle. He remembered afterward that Bobby's hands and face were hot with fever. Just now he was staring at the narrow staircase. Vos Engo and Loraine were descending slowly. The former was white and evidently very weak. He leaned on the girl for support.

Count Halfont offered the explanation. "Vos Engo was shot last week, through the shoulder. He is too brave to give up, as you may see. It happened on the terrace. There was an unexpected fusilade from the housetops. Eric placed himself between the marksmen and Miss Tullis. A bullet that might have killed her instantly, struck him in the shoulder. They were fleeing to the balcony. He fell and she dragged him to a place of safety. The wound is not so serious as it might have been, but he should be in bed. He, like most of us, has not removed his clothing in five days and nights."

King never forgot the look in Loraine's eyes as she came down the steps. Joy and anguish seemed to combine themselves in that long, intense look. He saw her hand go to her heart. Her lips were parted. He knew she was breathing quickly, tremulously.

The Prince was whispering in his ear: "Keep the lucky stone, Mr. King. Please keep it. It will surely help you. I gave her your kiss. She was happy—awful happy for awhile. 'Nen the Count he saved her from the bullet. But you just keep the lucky stone." King put him down and walked directly across to meet her at the foot of the steps.

She gave him her hands. The look in her tired eyes went straight to his heart. Vos Engo drew back, his face set in a frown of displeasure.

"My brother?" she asked, without taking her gaze from his eyes.

"He is well. He will see you to-day."

"And you, Truxton?" was her next question, low and quavering.

"Unharmed and unchanged, Loraine," he said softly. "Tell me, did Vos Engo stand between you and the fire from the—"

"Yes, Truxton," she said, dropping her eyes as if in deep pain.

"And you have not—broken your promise to him?"

"No. Nor have I broken my promise to you."

"He is a brave man. I can't help saying it," said the American, deep lines suddenly appearing in his face. Swiftly he turned to Vos Engo, extending his hand. "My hand, sir, to a brave man!"

Vos Engo stared at him for a moment and then turned away, ignoring the friendly hand. A hot flush mounted to Loraine's brow.

"This is a brave man, too, Eric," she said very quietly.

Vos Engo's response was a short, bitter laugh.

CHAPTER XXII
THE LAST STAND

Soon after five o'clock, a man in the topmost window of the tower called down that the forces in the hills were moving in a compact body toward the ridges below the southern gates.

"Give them half an hour to locate themselves," advised Truxton King. "They will move rapidly and strike as soon as the shells have levelled the gates. The proper time for your sortie, Colonel, would be some time in advance of their final movement. You will in that way draw at least a portion of Marlanx's men away from the heart of the city. They will come to the assistance of the gang bivouacked beyond the Duke of Perse's palace."

One hundred picked men were to be left inside the Castle gates with Vos Engo, prepared to meet any flank movement that might be attempted. Three hundred mounted men were selected to make the dash down Castle Avenue, straight into the camp of the sharpshooters. It was the purpose of the house guard to wage a fierce and noisy conflict off the Avenue and then retire to the Castle as abruptly as they left it, to be ready for Marlanx, should he decide to make a final desperate effort to seize their stronghold.

King, fired by a rebellious zeal, elected to ride with the attacking party. His heart was cold with the fear that he was to lose Loraine, after all. The fairy princess of his dreams seemed farther away from him than ever. "I'll do what I can for the Prince," he said to himself. "He's a perfect little brick. Damn Vos Engo! I'll make him repent that insult. Every one noticed it, too. She tried to smooth it over, but—oh, well, what's the use!"

The dash of the three hundred through the gates and down the avenue was the most spectacular experience in Truxton's life. He was up with Quinnox and General Braze, galloping well in front of the yelling troop. These mounted carbineers, riding as Bedouins, swept like thunder down the street, whirled into the broad, open arena beyond the Duke's palace, and were upon the surprised ruffians before they were fully awake to the situation.

They came tumbling out of barns and sheds, clutching their rifles in nerveless hands, aghast in the face of absolute destruction. It was all over with the first dash of the dragoons. The enemy, craven at the outset, threw down their guns and tried to escape through the alleys and side streets at the end of the common. Firing all the time, the attacking force rode them down as if they were so many dogs. The few who stood their ground and fought valiantly were overpowered and made captive by Quinnox. Less than a hundred men were found in the camp. Instead of retreating immediately to the Castle, Quinnox, acting on the suggestion of the exhilarated King, kept up a fierce, deceptive fire for the benefit of the distant Marlanx.

After ten or fifteen minutes of this desultory carnage, it was reported that a large force of men were entering the avenue from Regengetz Circus. Quinnox sent his chargers toward this great horde of foot-soldiers, but they did not falter as he had expected. On they swept, two or three thousand of them. At their head rode five or six officers. The foremost was Count Marlanx.

The cannons were booming now in the foothills. Marlanx, if he heard them and realised what the bombardment meant, did not swerve from the purpose at present in his mind.

Quinnox saw now that the Iron Count was determined to storm the gates, and gave the command to retreat. Waving their rifles and shouting defiance over their shoulders, the dragoons drew up, wheeled and galloped toward the gates.

Truxton King afterward recalled to mind certain huge piles of fresh earth in a corner of the common. He did not know what they meant at the time of observation, but he was wiser inside of three minutes after the whirlwind brigade dashed through the gates.

Scarcely were the massive portals closed and the great steel bars dropped into place by the men who attended them, when a low, dull explosion shook the earth as if by volcanic force. Then came the crashing of timbers, the cracking of masonry, the whirring of a thousand missiles through the air. Before the very eyes of the stunned, bewildered defenders, dismounting near the parade ground, the huge gates and pillars fell to the ground.

The gates have been dynamited!

Then it was that Truxton King remembered. Marlanx's sappers had been quietly at work for days, drilling from the common to the gates. It was a strange coincidence that Marlanx should have chosen this day for his culminating assault on the Castle. The skirmish at daybreak had hurried his arrangements, no doubt, but none the less were his plans complete. The explosives had been laid during the night; the fuses reached to the mouth of the tunnel, across the common. As he swept up the avenue at the head of his command, hawk-faced and with glittering eyes, he snarled the command that put fire to the fuses. He was still a quarter of a mile away when the gates crumbled. With short, shrill cries, scarcely human in their viciousness, he urged his men forward. He and Brutus were the first to ride up to the great hole that yawned where the gates had stood. Beyond they could see the distracted soldiers of the Prince forming in line to resist attack.

A moment later his vanguard streamed through the aperture and faced the deadly fire from the driveway.

Like a stone wall the men under Quinnox stood their ground; a solid, defiant line that fired with telling accuracy into the struggling horde. On the walls two Gatling guns began to cackle their laugh of death. And still the mercenaries poured through the gap, forming in haphazard lines under the direction of the maddened Iron Count.

At last they began to advance across the grassy meadow. When one man fell under the fire of the Guardsmen, another rushed into his place. Three times the indomitable Graustarkians drove them back, and as often did Marlanx drag them up again, exalted by the example he set.

"'Gad, he *is* a soldier," cried Truxton, who had wasted a half dozen shots in the effort to bring him down. "Hello! There's my friend Brutus. He's no coward, either. Here's a try for you, Brutus."

He dropped to his knee and took deliberate aim at the frenzied henchman. The discovery that there were three bullets in Brutus's breast when he was picked up long afterward did not affect the young man's contention that his was the one that had found the heart.

The fall of Brutus urged the Iron Count to greater fury. His horse had been shot from under him. He was on his feet, a gaunt demon, his back to the enemy, calling to his men to follow him as he moved toward the stubborn row of green and red. Bullets hissed about his ears, but he gave no heed to them. More than one man in the opposing force watched him as if fascinated. He seemed to be absolutely bullet-proof. There were times when he stumbled and almost fell over the bodies of his own men lying in the path.

By this time his entire force was inside the grounds. Colonel Quinnox was quick to see the spreading movement on the extreme right and left.

Marlanx's captains were trained warriors. They were bent on flanking the enemy. The commander of the Guard gave the command to fall back slowly toward the Castle.

Firing at every step, they crossed the parade ground and then made a quick dash for the shelter of the long balconies. They held this position for nearly an hour, resisting each succeeding charge of the now devilish foe. Time and again the foremost of the attacking party reached the terrace, only to wither under the deadly fire from behind the balustrades. Marlanx, down in the parade ground, was fairly pushing his men into the jaws of death. There was no question as to the courage of the men he commanded. These were not the ruffians from all over the world. They were the reckless, devil-may-care mountaineers and robbers from the hills of Graustark itself.

Truxton King's chance to pay his debt to Vos Engo came after one of the fiercest, most determined charges. The young Count, who had transferred his charges from the old tower to the strong north wing of the Castle, had been fighting desperately in the front rank for some time. His weakness seemed to have disappeared entirely. As the foe fell back in the face of the desperate resistance, Vos Engo sprang down the steps and rushed after them, calling others to join him in the attempt to complete the rout. Near the edge of the terrace he stopped. His leg gave way under him and he fell to the ground. Truxton saw him fall.

He leaped over the low balustrade, dropping his hot rifle, and dashed across the terrace to his rival's assistance. A hundred men shot at him. Vos Engo was trying to get to his feet, his hand upon his thigh; he was groaning with pain.

"It's my turn," shouted the American. "I'll square it up if I can. Then we're even!"

He seized the wounded man in his strong arms, threw him over his shoulder and staggered toward the steps.

"Release me, damn you!" shrieked Vos Engo, striking his rescuer in the face with his fist.

"I'm saving you for another day," said King as he dropped behind the balustrade, with his burden safe. A wild cheer went up from the lips of the defenders, scornful howls from the enemy.

"I pray God it may be deferred until I am capable of defending myself," groaned Vos Engo, glaring at the other with implacable hatred in his eyes.

"You might pray for my preservation, too, while you're at it," said Truxton, as he crept away to regain his rifle.

There were other witnesses to Truxton's rash act. In a lofty window of the north wing crouched a white-faced girl and a grim old man. The latter held a rifle in his tense though feeble hands. They had been there for ten minutes or longer, watching the battle from their eerie place of security. Now and then the old man would sight his rifle and fire. A groan of anger and dismay escaped his lips after each attempt to send his bullet to the spot intended. The girl who crouched beside him was there to designate a certain figure in the ever-changing mass of humanity on the bloody parade ground. Her clear eyes sought for and found Marlanx; her unwavering finger pointed him out to the old marksman.

She saw Vos Engo fall. Then a tall, well-known figure sprang into view, dashing toward her wounded lover. Her heart stopped beating. The blood rushed to her eyes. Everything before her turned red—a horrid, blurring red. With her hands to her temples, she leaned far over the window ledge and screamed—screamed words that would have filled Truxton King with an endless joy could he have heard them above the rattle of the rifles.

"A brave act!" exclaimed the old man at her side. "Who is he?"

But she did not hear him. She had fallen back and was gasping supplication, her eyes set upon the old man's face with a stare that meant nothing.

The corner of the building had shut out the picture; it was impossible for her to know that the man and his burden had reached the balcony in safety. Even now, they might be lying on the terrace, riddled by bullets. The concentrated aim of the enemy had not escaped her horrified gaze. The cheering did not reach her ears.

The old man roused her from the stupor of dread. He called her name several times in high, strident tones. Dully she responded. Standing bolt upright in the window she sought out the figure of Marlanx, and pointed rigidly.

"Ah," groaned the old man, "they will not be driven back this time! They will not be denied. It is the last charge! God, how they come! Our men will be annihilated in—Where is he? Now! Ah, I see! Yes, that is he! He is near enough now. I cannot miss him!"

Marlanx was leading his men up to the terrace. A howling avalanche of humanity, half obscured by smoke, streamed up the slope.

At the top of the terrace, the Iron Count suddenly stopped. His long body stiffened and then crumpled like a reed. A score of heavy feet trampled on the fallen leader, but he did not feel the impact.

A bullet from the north wing had crashed into his brain.

"At last!" shrieked the old man at the window. "Come, Miss Tullis; my work is done."

"He is dead, your Grace?" in low, awed tones.

"Yes, my dear," said the Duke of Perse, a smile of relief on his face. "Come, let me escort you to the Prince. You have been most courageous. Graustark shall not forget it. Nor shall I ever cease thanking you for the service you have rendered to me. I have succeeded in freeing my unhappy daughter from the vile beast to whom I sold her youth and beauty and purity. Come! You must not look upon that carnage!"

Together they left the little room. As they stepped into the narrow hall beyond they realised that the defenders had been driven inside the walls of the Castle. The crash of firearms filled the halls far below; a deafening, steady roar came up to them.

"It is all over," said the Duke of Perse, hobbling across the hall and throwing open the door to a room opposite.

A group of terrified women were huddled in the far corner of the spacious room. In front of them was the little Prince, a look of terror in his eyes, but with the tiny sword clutched in his hand—a pathetic figure of courage and dread combined. The Duke of Perse held open the door for Loraine Tullis, but she did not enter. When he turned to call, she was half way down the top flight of stairs, racing through the powder smoke toward the landing below.

At every step she was screaming in the very agony of gladness:

"Stand firm! Hold them! Help is coming! Help is coming!"

A last look through the window at the end of the hail had revealed to her the most glorious of visions.

Red and green troops were pouring through the dismantled gateway, their horses surging over the ugly ground-rifts and debris as if possessed of the fabled wings.

She had seen the rear line in the storming forces hesitate and then turn to meet the whirlwind charge of the cavalrymen. Her brother was out there and all was well. She was crying the joyous news from the head of the grand stairway when Truxton King caught sight of her.

Smoke writhed about her slim, inspiriting figure. Her face shone through the drab fog like an undimmed star of purest light. He bounded up the steps toward her, drawn as by magnet against which there was no such thing as resistance.

He was powder-stained and grimy; there was blood on his face and shirt front.

"You are shot," she cried, clutching the post at the bend in the stairs. "Truxton! Truxton!"

"Not even scratched," he shouted, as he reached her side. "It's not my—" He stopped short, even as he held out his arms to clasp her to his breast. "It's some one else's blood," he finished resolutely. She swayed toward him and he caught her in his arms.

"I love you—oh, I love you, Truxton!" she cried over and over again. He was faint with joy. His kisses spoke the adoration he would have cried out to her if emotion had not clogged his throat.

"Eric?" she whispered at last, drawing back in his arms and looking up into his eyes with a great pity in her own. "Is he—is he dead, Truxton?"

"No," he said gently. "Badly hurt, but—"

"He will not die? Thank God, Truxton. He is a brave—oh, a very brave man." Then she remembered her mission into this whirlpool of danger. "Go! Don't lose a moment, darling! Tell Colonel Quinnox that Jack has come! The dragoons are—"

He did not hear the end of her cry. A quick, fierce kiss and he was gone, bounding down the stairs with great shouts of encouragement.

Leaderless, between the deadly fires, the mercenaries gave up the fight after a brief stand at the terrace. Six hundred horsemen ploughed through them, driving them to the very walls of the Castle. Here they broke and scattered, throwing down their arms and shouting for mercy. It was all over inside of twenty minutes.

The Prince reigned again.

Nightfall brought complete restoration of order, peace and security in the city of Edelweiss. Hundreds of lives had been lost in the terrific conflict of the early morning hours; hundreds of men lay on beds of suffering, crushed and bleeding from the wounds they had courted and received.

"I knowed we'd whip them," shouted the Prince, wriggling gleefully in John Tullis's straining embrace half an hour after the latter had ridden through the gate. Tears streamed down the big man's face. One arm held the boy, the other encircled the sister he had all but lost. In the Monastery of St. Valentine there was another woman, waiting for him to come to her with the news of a glorious victory. Perhaps she was hoping and praying for the other news that he would bring her, who knows? If he came to her with kisses, she would know without being told in so many words.

Truxton did not again see Loraine until late in the afternoon. He had offered his services to Colonel Quinnox and had worked manfully in the effort to provide comfort for the wounded of both sides. General Braze was at work with his men in the open city, clearing away the ugly signs of battle. The fortress and Tower were full of the prisoners of war. Baron Dangloss, pale, emaciated, sick but resolute, was free once more and, with indomitable zeal, had thrown himself and his liberated men at once into the work of rehabilitation.

It was on the occasion of the Baron's first visit to the Prince, late in the day, that Truxton saw the girl he worshipped.

Prince Robin had sent for him to appear in the devastated state chamber. Publicly, in the presence of the Court and Ministry, the little ruler proclaimed him a baron and presented to him a great seal ring from among the ancient crown jewels.

"Say, Mr. King," said Bobby, after he had called the American quite close to him by means of a stealthy crooking of his finger, "would you mind giving me my lucky stone? I don't think you'll need it any longer. I will, I'm sure. You see a prince has such a lot of things to trouble him. Wars and murders and everything."

"Thank you, Prince Robin," said King, placing the stone in the little hand. "I couldn't have got on without it. May it always serve you as well."

"Noblesse oblige, Baron," said Prince Robin gravely.

"Hello!" in an excited whisper. "Here's Baron Dangloss. He's been in his own gaol!"

Truxton withdrew. Near the door he met Loraine. She had just entered the room. There was a bright look of relief in her eyes.

"Count Vos Engo has asked for you, Truxton," she said in a low voice. A delicate flush crept into her cheeks; a sudden shyness leaped into her eyes, and she looked away.

"Loraine, have you told him?"

"Yes. I am so sorry for him. He is one of the bravest men I have ever known, Truxton dear. And, as it is with all men of his race, love knew no reason, no compromise. But I have made him see that I—that I cannot be his wife. He knows that I love you."

"Somehow, darling, I'm sorry for him."

"He will not pretend friendship for you, dear," she went on painfully. "He only wants to thank you and to apologise, as you did, not so long ago. And he wants to ask you to release him from a certain obligation."

"You mean our—our fight?"

"Yes. He is to lose his right arm, Truxton. You understand how it is with him now."

CHAPTER XXIII
"YOU WILL BE MRS. KING"

Late that night it was reported at the Castle that a large force of men were encamped on the opposite side of the river. A hundred camp-fires were gleaming against the distant uplands.

"The Grand Duke Paulus!" exclaimed Count Halfont. "Thank God, he did not come a day earlier. We owe him nothing to-day—but yesterday! Ah, he could have demanded much of us. Send his messengers to me, Colonel Quinnox, as soon as they arrive in the morning. I will arise early. There is much to do in Graustark. Let there be no sluggards."

A mellow, smiling moon crept up over the hills, flooding the laud with a serene radiance. Once more the windows in the Castle gleamed brightly; low-voiced people strolled through the shattered balconies; others wandered about the vast halls, possessed by uncertain emotions, torn by the conflicting hands of joy and gloom. In a score of rooms wounded men were lying; in others there were dead heroes. At the barracks, standing dully against the distant shadows, there were many cots of suffering. And yet there was rejoicing, even among those who writhed in pain or bowed their heads in grief. Victory's wings were fanning the gloom away; conquest was painting an ever-widening streak of brightness across the dark, drear canvas of despair.

In one of the wrecked approaches to the terrace, surrounded by fragments of stone and confronted by ugly destruction, sat a young man and a slender girl. There were no lights near them; the shadows were black and forbidding. This particular end of the terrace had suffered most in the fierce rain of cannon-balls. So great was the devastation here that one attained the position held by the couple only by means of no little daring and at the risk of unkind falls. From where they sat they could see the long vista of lighted windows and yet could not themselves be seen.

His arm was about her; her head nestled securely against his shoulder and her slim hands were willing prisoners in one of his.

She was saying "Truxton, dear, I did *not* love Eric Vos Engo. I just thought it was love. I never really knew what love is until you came into my life. Then I knew the difference. That's what made it so hard. I had let him believe that I might care for him some day. And I *did* like him. So I—"

"You are sure—terribly sure—that I am the only man you ever really loved?" he interrupted.

She snuggled closer. "Haven't I just told you that I didn't know what it was until—well, until now?"

"You will never, never know how happy I am, Loraine!" he breathed into her ear.

"I hope I shall always bring happiness to you, Truxton," she murmured, faint with the joy of loving.

"You will make me very unhappy if you don't marry me to-morrow."

"I couldn't think of it!"

"I don't ask you to think. If you do, you may change your mind completely. Just marry me without thinking, dearest."

"I will marry you, Truxton, when we get to New York," she said, but not very firmly. He saw his advantage.

"But, my dear, I'm tired of travelling."

It was rather enigmatic. "What has that to do with it?" she asked.

"Well, it's this way: if we get married in New York we'll have to consider an extended and wholly obligatory wedding journey. If we get married here, we can save all that bother by bridal-tripping to New York, instead of away from it. And, what's more, we'll escape the rice-throwing and the old shoes and the hand-painted trunk labels. Greater still: we will avoid a long and lonely trip across the ocean on separate steamers. That's something, you know."

"We *could* go on the same steamer."

"Quite so, my dear. But don't you think it would be nicer if we went as one instead of two?"

"I suppose it would be cheaper."

"They say a fellow saves money by getting married."

"I hate a man who is always trying to save money."

"Well, if you put it that way, I'll promise never to save a cent. I'm a horrible spendthrift."

"Oh, you'll have to save, Truxton!"

"How silly we are!" he cried in utter joyousness. He held her close for a long time, his face buried in her hair. "Listen, darling: won't you say you'll be my wife before I leave Graustark? I want you so much. I can't go away without you."

She hesitated. "When are you going, Truxton? You—you haven't told me."

It was what he wanted. "I am going next Monday," he said promptly. As a matter of fact, he had forgotten the day of the week they were now living in.

"Monday? Oh, dear!"

"Will you?"

"I—I must cable home first," she faltered.

"That's a mere detail, darling. Cable afterward. It will beat us home by three weeks. They'll know we're coming."

"I must ask John, really I must, Truxton," she protested faintly.

"Hurray!" he shouted—in a whisper. "He is so desperately in love, he won't think of refusing anything we ask. Shall we set it for Saturday?"

They set it for Saturday without consulting John Tullis, and then fell to discussing him. "He is very much in love with her," she said wistfully.

"And she loves him, Loraine. They will be very happy. She's wonderful."

"Well, so is John. He's the most wonderful man in all this world."

"I am sure of it," he agreed magnanimously. "I saw him talking with her and the Duke of Perse as I came out awhile ago. They were going to the Duke's rooms up there. The Duke will offer no objections. I think he'll permit his daughter to select his next son-in-law."

"How could he have given her to that terrible, terrible old man?" she cried, with a shudder.

"She won't be in mourning for him long, I fancy. Nobody will talk of appearances, either. She could marry Jack to-morrow and no one would criticise her."

"Oh, that would be disgusting, Truxton!"

"But, my dear, he isn't to have a funeral, so why not? They buried his body in quicklime this afternoon. No mourners, no friends, no tears! Hang it all, she's foolish if she puts on anything but red."

"They can't be married for—oh, ever so long," she said very primly.

"No, indeed," he said with alacrity. But he did not believe what he said. If he knew anything about John Tullis, it would not be "ever so long" before Prince Robin's friend turned Benedict and husband to the most noted beauty in all Graustark.

"I shall be sorry to leave Graustark," she said dreamily, after a long period of silent retrospection. "I've had the happiest year of my life here."

"I've had the busiest month of my life here. I'll never again say that the world is a dull place. And I'll never advise any man to go out of his own home city in search of the most adorable woman in the world. She's always there, bless her heart, if he'll only look around a bit for her."

"But you wouldn't have found me if you hadn't come to Graustark."

"I shudder when I think of what might have happened to you, my Princess Sweetheart, if I hadn't come to Edelweiss. No; I would not have found you." Feeling her tremble in his arms, he went on with whimsical good humour: "You would have been eaten up by the ogre long before this. Or, perhaps, you would have succeeded in becoming a countess."

"As it is, I shall be a baroness."

"In Graustark, but not in New York. That reminds me. You'll be more than a baroness—more than a princess. You will be a queen. Don't you catch the point? You will be Mrs. King."

The Grand Duke Paulus was distinctly annoyed. He had travelled many miles, endured quite a number of hardships, and all to no purpose. When dawn came, his emissaries returned from the city with the lamentable information that the government had righted itself, that Marlanx's sensational revolution was at an end, and that the regents would be highly honoured if his Excellency could overlook the distressingly chaotic conditions at court and condescend to pay the Castle a visit. The regents, the Prince and the citizens of Graustark desired the opportunity to express their gratitude for the manner in which he had voluntarily (and unexpectedly) come to their assistance in time of trouble. The fact that he had come too late to render the invaluable aid he so nobly intended did not in the least minimise the volume of gratefulness they felt.

The Grand Duke admitted that he was at sea, diplomatically. He was a fifth wheel, so to speak, now that the revolution was over. Not so much as the tip of his finger had he been able to get into the coveted pie. There was nothing for him to do but to turn round with his five thousand Cossacks and march disconsolately across the steppes to an Imperial railroad, where he could embark for home. However, he would visit the Castle in a very informal way, extend his congratulations, offer his services—which he knew would be declined with thanks—and profess his unbounded joy in the discovery that Graustark happily was so able to take care of herself. Incidentally, he would mention the bond issue; also, he would find the opportunity to suggest to the ministry that his government still was willing to make large grants and stupendous promises if any sort of an arrangement could be made by which the system might be operated in conjunction with branch lines of the Imperial roads.

And so it was that at noon he rode in pomp and splendour through the city gates, attended by his staff and a rather overpowering body-guard. His excuse for the early call was delicately worded. He said in his reply to the message from the Count that it would give him great pleasure to remain for some time at the Castle, were it not for the fact that he had left his own province in a serious state of unrest; it was imperative that he should return in advance of the ever-possible and always popular uprising. Therefore he would pay his respects to his serene Highness, renew his protestations of friendship, extend his felicitations, and beg leave to depart for his own land without delay.

As he rode from Regengetz Circus into Castle Avenue, a small knot of American tourists crowded to the curb and bent eager, attentive ears to the words of a stubby little person whom we should recognise by his accent; but, for fear that there may be some who have forgotten him in the rush of events, we will point to his cap and read aloud: "Cook's Interpreter."

Mr. Hobbs was saying: "The gentleman on the gray horse, ladies and gentlemen, is his *Highness*, the Grand Duke Paulus. He has come to pay his respects to his Serene Highness. Now, if you will kindly step this way, I will show you the spot where the bomb was thrown. 'Aving been an eye-witness to the shocking occurrence, I respectfully submit that I," etc. With a pride and dignity that surpassed all moderate sense of appreciation, he delivered newly made history unto his charges, modestly winding up his discourse with the casual remark that the Prince had but recently appointed him twelfth assistant steward at the Castle, and that he expected to assume the duties of this honorary position just as soon as Cook & Sons could find a capable man to send up in his place.

The American tourists, it may be well to observe, arrived by the first train that entered the city from the outside world.

The audience was at two o'clock. Prince Robin was in a state of tremendous excitement. Never before had he been called upon to receive a grand duke. He quite forgot yesterday's battle in the face of this most imposing calamity. More than that, he was in no frame of mind to enjoy the excitement attending the rehabilitation of the Castle; oppressed by the approaching shadow of the great man, he lost all interest in what was going on in the Castle, about the grounds and among his courtiers.

"What'll I do, Uncle Jack, if he asks any questions?" he mourned. They were dressing him in the robes of state.

"Answer 'em," said his best friend.

"But supposin' I can't? Then what?"

"He won't ask questions, Bobby. People never do when a potentate is on his throne. It's shockingly bad form."

"I hope he won't stay long," prayed Bobby, a grave pucker between his brows. He was a very tired little boy. His eyes were heavy with sleep and his lips were not very firm.

"Count Halfont will look after him, Bobby; so don't worry. Just sit up there on the throne and look wise. The regents will do the rest. Watch your Uncle Caspar. When he gives the signal, you arise. That ends the audience. You walk out—"

"I know all about that, Uncle Jack. But I bet I do something wrong. This thing of receiving grand dukes is no joke. 'Specially when we're so terribly upset. Really, I ought to be looking after the men who are wounded, attending to the funerals of—"

"Now, Bobby, don't flunk like that! Be a man!"

Bobby promptly squared his little shoulders and set his jaw. "Oh, I'm not scared!" He was thoughtful for a moment. "But, I'll tell you, it's awful lonesome up in that big chair, so far away from all your friends. I wish Uncle Caspar would let me sit down with the crowd."

The Grand Duke, with all the arrogance of a real personage, was late. It was not for him to consider the conditions that distressed the Court of Graustark. Not at all. He was a grand duke and he would take his own time in paying his respects. What cared he that every one in the Castle was tired and unstrung and sad and—sleepy? Any one but a grand duke would have waited a day or two before requiring a royal audience. When he finally presented himself at the Castle doors, a sleepy group of attendants actually yawned in his presence.

A somnolent atmosphere, still touched by the smell of gunpowder, greeted him as he strode majestically down the halls. Somehow each person who bowed to him seemed to do it with the melancholy precision of one who has been up for six nights in succession and doesn't care who knows it.

No one had slept during the night just passed. Excitement and the suffering of others had denied slumber to one and all—even to those who had not slept for many days and nights. Now the reaction was upon them. Relaxation had succeeded tenseness.

When the Grand Duke entered the great, sombre throne room, he was confronted by a punctiliously polite assemblage, but every eyelid was as heavy as lead and as prone to sink.

The Prince sat far back in the great chair of his ancestors, his sturdy legs sticking straight out in front of him, utterly lost in the depths of gold and royal velvet. Two-score or more of his courtiers and as many noble ladies of the realm stood soberly in the places assigned them by the laws of precedence. The Grand Duke advanced between the respectful lines and knelt at the foot of the throne.

"Arise, your Highness," piped Bobby, with a quick glance at Count Halfont. It was a very faint, faraway voice that uttered the gracious command. "Graustark welcomes the Grand Duke Paulus. It is my pleasure to—to—to—" a helpless look came into his eyes. He looked everywhere for support. The Grand Duke saw that he had forgotten the rehearsed speech, and smiled benignly as he stepped forward and kissed the hand that had been extended somewhat uncertainly.

"My most respectful homage to your Majesty. The felicitations of my emperor and the warmest protestations of friendship from his people."

With this as a prologue, he engaged himself in the ever-pleasurable task of delivering a long, congratulatory address. If there was one thing above another that the Grand Duke enjoyed, it was the making of a speech. He prided himself on his prowess as an orator and as an after-dinner speaker; but, more than either of these, he gloried in his ability to soar extemporaneously.

For ten minutes he addressed himself to the throne, benignly, comfortably. Then he condescended to devote a share of his precious store to the courtiers behind him. If he caught more than one of them yawning when he turned in their direction, he did not permit it to disturb him in the least. His eyes may have narrowed a bit, but that was all.

After five minutes of high-sounding platitudes, he again turned to the Prince. It was then that he received his first shock.

"His Majesty appears to have—ahem—gone to sleep," remarked the Grand Duke tartly "

Prince Robin was sound asleep. His head was slipping side-wise along the satiny back of the big chair, and his chin was very low in the laces at his neck. The Grand Duke coughed emphatically, cleared his throat, and grew very red in the face.

The Court of Graustark was distinctly dismayed. Here was shocking state of affairs. The prince going to sleep while a grand duke talked!

"His Majesty appears to have—ahem—gone to sleep," remarked the Grand Duke tartly, interrupting himself to address the Prime Minister.

"He is very tired, your Excellency," said Count Halfont, very much distressed. "Pray consider what he has been through during the—"

"Ah, my dear Count, do not apologise for him. I quite understand. Ahem! Ahem!" Still he was very red in the face. Some one had laughed softly behind his back.

"I will awaken him, your Excellency," said the Prime Minister, edging toward the throne.

"Not at all, sir!" protested the visitor. "Permit him to have his sleep out, sir. I will not have him disturbed. Who am I that I should defeat the claims of nature? It is my pleasure to wait until his Majesty's nap is over. Then he may dismiss us, but not until we have cried: 'Long live the Prince!'"

For awhile they stood in awkward silence, this notable gathering of men and women. Then the Prime Minister, in hushed tones, suggested that it would be eminently proper, under the circumstances, for all present to be seated. He was under the impression that His Serene Highness would sleep long and soundly.

Stiff-backed and uncomfortable, the Court sat and waited. No one pretended to conceal the blissful yawns that would not be denied. A drowsy, ineffably languid feeling took possession of the entire assemblage. Here and there a noble head nodded slightly; eyelids fell in the silent war against the god of slumber, only to revive again with painful energy and ever-weakening courage.

The Prime Minister sat at the foot of the throne and nodded in spite of himself. The Minister of the Treasury was breathing so heavily that his neighbor nudged him just in time to prevent something even more humiliating. John Tullis, far back near the wall, had his head on his hand, bravely fighting off the persistent demon. Prince Dantan of Dawsbergen was sound asleep.

The Grand Duke was wide awake. He saw it all and was equal to the occasion. After all, he was a kindly old gentleman, and, once his moment of mortification was over, he was not above charity.

Bobby's poor little head had slipped over to a most uncomfortable position against the arm of the chair. Putting his finger to his lips, the Grand Duke tip-toed carefully up to the throne. With very gentle hands he lifted Bobby's head, and, infinitely tender, stuffed a throne cushion behind the curly head. Still with his finger to his lips, a splendid smile in his eyes, he tip-toed back to his chair.

As he passed Count Halfont, who had risen, he whispered:

"Dear little man! I do not forget, my lord, that I was once a boy. God bless him!"

Then he sat down, conscious of a fine feeling of goodness, folded his arms across his expansive chest, and allowed his beaming eyes to rest upon the sleeping boy far back in the chair of state. Incidentally, he decided to delay a few days before taking up the bond question with the ministry. The Grand Duke was not an ordinary diplomat.

In one of the curtained windows, far removed from the throne, sat Truxton King and Loraine Tullis.

All about them people were watching the delicate little scene, smiling drowsily at the Grand Duke's tender comedy. No one was looking at the two in the curtained recess. Her hand was in his, her head sank slowly toward his inviting shoulder; her heavy lids drooped lower and lower, refusing to obey the slender will that argued against complete surrender. At last her soft, regular breathing told him that she was asleep. Awaiting his opportunity, he tenderly kissed the soft, brown hair, murmured a gentle word of love, and settled his own head against the thick cushions.

Everywhere they dozed and nodded. The Grand Duke smiled and blinked his little eyes. He was very wide awake.

That is how he happened to see the Prince move restlessly and half open his sleep-bound eyes. The Grand Duke leaned forward with his hand to his ear, and listened. He had seen the boy's lips move. From dreamland came Bobby's belated:

"Good-ni—ight."